Suzanne Wright lives in England with her husband and two children. When she's not spending time with her family, she's writing, reading or doing her version of housework – sweeping the house with a look.

She's worked in a pharmaceutical company, at a Disney Store, at a primary school as a voluntary teaching assistant, at the RSCPA and has a First Class Honours degree in Psychology and Identity Studies.

As to her interests, she enjoys reading, writing, reading, writing (sort of eat, sleep, write, repeat), spending time with her family, movie nights with her sisters and playing with her two Bengal kittens.

To connect with Suzanne online:

Website: http://www.suzannewright.co.uk
Facebook: https://www.facebook.com/
suzannewrightfanpage
Instagram: Instagram.com/Suzanne_wright_author

SUZANNE WRIGHT

HUNTED

A *Dark in You* novel

PIATKUS

PIATKUS

First published in Great Britain in 2023 by Piatkus

1 3 5 7 9 10 8 6 4 2

A CIP catalogue record for this book
is available from the British Library.

ISBN: 978-0-349-42849-9

Typeset in Goudy by M Rules

Printed and bound in Great Britain by
Clays Ltd, Elcograf S.p.A.

Papers used by Piatkus are from well-managed forests
and other responsible sources.

MIX
Supporting
responsible forestry
FSC® C104740

Piatkus
An imprint of
Little, Brown Book Group
Carmelite House
50 Victoria Embankment
London EC4Y 0DZ

An Hachette UK Company
www.hachette.co.uk

www.littlebrown.co.uk

For my niece, Becky C.

CHAPTER ONE

From her seat on the balcony, Larkin Yates heard a voice inside the VIP box screaming in delight, "It won! It won!"

Well, of course the hellhorse won. It always did.

Teague Sullivan's steed was not only undefeated but considered to be the fastest of its kind. At the moment, it was also proudly holding its head high, exposing its elegantly arched neck. One of the racing stadium's high-powered floodlights beamed down directly on the stallion, showing the steam wafting from its coat. A metallic black, the aforementioned coat was positively stunning and currently gleamed with a fine sheen of sweat.

Cheers rang out from the many spectators, particularly those that filled the tiered grandstand and stood behind the track's perimeter fence. Few demons bet against Teague's hellhorse, so there were rarely many boos.

Despite her foul mood, which was thanks to the annoying machinations of her friends and honorary brothers, Larkin found herself smiling when the stallion arrogantly tossed its long, lush, dark mane as it trotted off the track, swishing its high-carried tail.

There was something so very regal about hellhorses. They moved with grace and poise on those long, powerful legs, their sleek muscles rippling and flexing. They could honestly steal a person's breath with how beautiful they were.

They could also scare the living shit out of a person. And not simply due to their all-black, wide-set eyes. Hellhorses were as predatory, conscienceless, and unforgiving as all demonic entities. Psychotic, too—as evidenced by their willingness to partake in this sadistic sport.

Hellhorse race tracks were full of nasty surprises, such as pits of bubbling lava or sharp spikes. The hurdles were high, wide, and dangerous to any who didn't jump them *just right*. As such, a lot of pain was involved, and injuries were often severe.

So. Yeah. These entities were crazy.

Not that Larkin could judge. Her issue-riddled inner demon was all-out nuts.

Though hellhorses tended to suffer many wounds during races, few died. That was the thing about this most resilient breed of demon. They were quick to heal and hard to kill. Like *really* hard. She was quite sure they'd survive an apocalypse easily while every other living creature perished.

Breathing in the scents of dirt, horses, and concession food, she watched as the stadium's staff members walked around the track, putting obstacles to rights and kicking clumps of fake grass back into place. All the while, she ignored the thread of delicious anticipation worming its way through her blood; she point-blank refused to acknowledge its source.

Gambling on hellhorse racing was just one of the many ways that demons could spend their time here in the Underground—a subterranean demonic playground located beneath Las Vegas.

You could shop. Eat. Drink. Dance. Hit casinos. Watch shows. Partake in competitions. Stay at fancy hotels. Enjoy the fairground. The list went on and on.

And on.

As one of her lair's four sentinels, she didn't have as much spare time as the average demon. But she spent much of it in the Underground these days. Mostly to escape the irritating crap going on that was centered on her.

Hearing the glass door behind her slide open, Larkin felt her muscles tense. She had hoped to be left alone, and the people within the VIP box knew that well.

Glancing over her shoulder, she saw Piper striding toward her. Immediately, Larkin relaxed. The pretty dark-haired nightmare was one of only two people who weren't on her shit list.

Piper gave her a soft smile, took the seat beside her, and held out a can of soda. "Here."

Larkin tried returning the smile, but it was more like a grimace. "Thanks." She took the can and flicked open the ring tab, hearing the liquid inside fizz slightly.

"I know they're getting on your last nerve," began Piper, "but they mean well."

Larkin looked at her askance. "Did they push you to come out here and convince me to go talk to them?"

"No one pushes me to do anything." Piper's nose wrinkled. "Actually, correction: Levi tries it. I'm waiting for him to realize that it doesn't actually work and never will. But we've been mates for nine months now and he hasn't yet caught on."

Larkin felt the side of her mouth kick up. Levi was one of her four honorary brothers. Like Tanner and Keenan, he was also a fellow sentinel while Knox was Prime of their lair. Each of the four males were *all* alpha ... which had to suck for their mates at times, in Larkin's opinion.

Take Levi, for example. He was not only Piper's mate but her predestined anchor. Being extremely dominant and overprotective, the reaper did his best to maneuver the female tattooist and cover her in bubble wrap. Luckily for him, Piper found it cute rather than frustrating.

Every demon had an anchor—or psi-mate if you wanted to be more specific. It wasn't an emotional pairing, merely a psychic one, though some demons did enter into relationships with their anchors. Whatever the case, they were extremely loyal to and protective of each other; deeply enmeshed themselves in one another's lives.

The purpose of a psi-mate was to strengthen a demon and prevent their inner entities from taking over. Sharing your soul with a psychopathic entity had its trials, since they often pushed for supremacy, so turning rogue was always a possibility unless a demon bonded with their anchor.

Not all found their psi-mate, though. Larkin had, but she would have considered herself one of the lucky ones if things had played out differently. She wished she hadn't found him at all, if she was honest. Because then she wouldn't know what it was like to feel the mental tug of an anchor bond. She wouldn't know what it was like to live without it; to forever feel its call. She wouldn't know how it felt to be abandoned by this person who should have been one of the people closest to her.

Tanner had stumbled upon his own anchor long ago, but they hadn't claimed each other either. It had been just as hard for him, but the bond's call had thankfully weakened with each decade that passed. The call had vanished altogether when his psi-mate died.

Admittedly, both Larkin and her inner demon had moments where they wished their own anchor met a sticky end. Cruel, perhaps, but neither she nor the entity were forgiving creatures.

For now, she was merely grateful that time and distance had dimmed the bond's call.

"I've asked them to stop playing cupid. So has Khloë," Piper added, referring to a crazy imp who'd mated Keenan. "But Harper, Devon, and Raini are convinced you're unhappy. They figure that having a dude in your life—or, more precisely, an abundance of orgasms on a regular basis—will lift your mood."

"I have a vibrator; it does the job just fine."

Piper tipped back her head and barked a quick laugh.

"As for my mood, it will improve once the matchmaking stops." It had begun shortly after Levi took Piper as his mate . . . leaving Larkin the last single person in their circle.

The instigator seemed to be Knox's mate and anchor, Harper. But the sphinx had roped two of her best friends into her plan easily enough. Both Raini and Devon were massive contributors.

They'd signed Larkin up on demon dating apps, paraded single males in front of her, and practically *shoved* her onto the laps of men at clubs. They'd even given her cell numbers of 'decent guys' and pressured her into calling them.

Then, just last night, they'd asked her to meet them at a bar . . . only to not turn up but instead send a dude from their old lair in their place. Once Larkin had realized they'd set her up on a blind date with a perfect stranger—one who was clearly only looking for a booty call—she'd been furious. And she hadn't been shy about telepathically expressing it to them.

Honestly, the way they all invested so much time into meddling in her affairs, you'd think they didn't have busy lives of their own.

Larkin sipped some of her soda. "I resent that they seem to feel I can't possibly be happy merely because I don't have a man by my side."

"They don't think you need a guy to complete you or

anything. Their feeling that you'd be happier if you met someone is really more of a reflection on how much happier they are for being mated."

"I guess." Larkin's hand flexed on her can. "I can't believe the guys are actually supportive of the cupid games, though. It's not their style."

Piper sighed. "No, it's not. But when they look at you, they see what I see."

"Which is what?"

"That you seem lonely."

Lonely? *Pfft*. Larkin wasn't ... All right, fine, she felt a little lonely now and then. But demons weren't built to be alone. Hence why they came in predestined pairs.

"The guys don't like it," Piper continued. "They want to fix it. So Harper managed to convince them that it would be good for you to have someone in your life. The guys are pretty picky about 'who', though. If they hear Harper talking about introducing you to someone they don't approve of, they veto him right away. Or if they haven't heard of him, they'll make her wait until Tanner has looked into him."

Larkin frowned. "What, like I'm a teenager whose potential boyfriends need to be vetted? If I'd ever tried doing that when it came to *their* sex lives, they wouldn't have stood for it. Hell, I couldn't even advise them on relationships or ask minor questions without them expressly telling me that it wasn't my business." Not a fan of double standards, she gave an annoyed shake of the head while her equally irritated demon hissed out a breath.

"I did point that out but, in their view, they're simply looking out for you like all good brothers should. As I said before, they—"

"Mean well," Larkin finished. "I get that. But this whole thing is embarrassing on so many levels." She drank more of her soda.

"Thank you for not jumping on the 'let's find the harpy a boyfriend' bandwagon."

"Hey, don't get me wrong, I'd like for you to meet someone. But the bottom line is that you don't like what they're doing and you want it to stop. So it should stop."

Larkin really did adore Piper. The newest member of their group had seamlessly slotted into it, even making a solid place for herself at Harper and Raini's tattoo studio.

"Khloë has the same opinion and refuses to be swayed by Harper or the others," Piper added.

"It surprises me that Khloë isn't involving herself. I mean, she can quite clearly see that the whole thing is driving me nuts—she normally lives for that shit."

"But taking part would annoy only *you*. Refusing to partake in it enables her to irritate *several* people. So she chose to go down the latter route."

"Ah, I see." Hearing the glass door again glide open, Larkin felt her muscles bunch once more. She looked over her shoulder. *Speak of the she-devil.* It was Khloë.

Although—like Piper—the imp wasn't on her shit list, Larkin didn't immediately relax this time. In fact, her pulse skittered. Because the petite, olive-skinned female wasn't alone. Just behind Khloë stood the source of the anticipation that had been beating at Larkin. A source that was tall, inked, powerfully built, and possessed an air as untamed as the hellbeast with whom he shared his soul.

Teague.

Larkin had known in advance that he'd head up to the VIP box after his race. He always came to say hello to Khloë, who happened to be his anchor. They were so close that Larkin felt a pinch of envy at times. In truth, she secretly had a little thing for this male.

As his vivid, all-knowing hazel eyes locked on her, Larkin's belly fluttered. Explicitly sexy and unquestionably alpha-male, Teague could walk into a room and instantly snare the attention of everyone in it. Add in his slow smiles, dominant posture, confident walk, and rich smoky voice, and he possessed an unchecked sex appeal that packed a real punch.

His short hair was the same onyx black as his steed's coat. Dark stubble dusted his strong jawline and upper lip. Intriguing tattoos peeked out of the collar of his tee and crawled up the left side of his neck. More tats covered his chest and toned, ropey arms.

Usually, Larkin had no issue with making her interest in a male clear—she was no shy flower. But she hadn't done so with Teague. It would have been pointless for two reasons.

One, Khloë had forbidden him from crossing platonic lines with her friends.

Two, he was anti-relationship. At this point in her life, Larkin was done with 'casual'. She wanted what her friends and brothers had.

Still, trying to switch off her attraction to him wasn't proving easy—and not merely due to the effect he had on her body. See, although he was a skilled seducer who came with a no-strings-attached mantra, he wasn't a shallow sex toy.

Teague was genuine. Loyal. Made time for people. Never stood around complaining, criticizing others, or spouting negativity. He was quick to smile, and quicker to laugh.

Not that he was sweet. Nah, his moral code was somewhat skewed. He was as cunning as they came and completely unpredictable. Unstable, even.

Nonetheless, pretty much everyone enjoyed his company. Including Larkin. He was so desired that if he ever took someone as his mate, they'd be the envy of many. Including Larkin. It annoyed the holy hell out of her.

He annoyed the holy hell out of her. On purpose. And he thought it made them friends, the weirdo. Yet, she couldn't help but like him.

Her inner demon found him something of a delight to be around—particularly since they both had that whole 'crazy' thing in common.

Right then, Teague gave her a slow, lazy smile that made her hormones a little dizzy. "Hey, pretty harpy. Have you missed me?"

"Every minute without you felt like a year," she deadpanned.

He chuckled and, God, the sound was all smoke and gravel. More addictive than any drug.

"Congratulations on your win," Piper told him.

Inclining his head in thanks, he prowled further onto the balcony with that steady, long-legged stride. It was the prowl of a hunter.

That was the other thing about Teague, his relaxed manner put people at ease. He was always so mellow and chronically unfazed by life. But underneath all that, there was an intense edge of *something* about him. Something raw and almost bestial.

It was like being around a caged zoo predator. They looked calm as they lazed in the grass or stalked the width of their enclosure. And yet, there was still an intense undercurrent of wildness about them. You never once forgot you were in the presence of something dangerous.

Larkin forced herself not to tense as Teague leaned back against the balcony rail directly in front of her, his gaze wholly fixed on hers. He did that a lot. Stared at her. She wished she could say she hated it, but there was a little thrill that came with being the center of his hyper-focus.

Her demon liked that he so boldly looked his fill—not a lot of people were bold around the entity. And for good reason.

Plucking at the dark hair she'd tied up in a messy swirl, Khloë let her gaze flit from Larkin to Piper. "What were you two talking about? Are you plotting something? Because if so, I want in on it. I don't even care what it is."

"We weren't plotting," said Larkin. "We were talking about you, actually."

The imp grinned. "Best topic ever. Expand."

It was Piper who elaborated. "I was explaining to Larkin why you're not helping the others with the matchmaking extravaganza."

"Matchmaking?" echoed Teague.

Khloë turned to him. "Yeah, the others are intent on pairing our poor harpy up with someone. Moreso the girls than the guys, but they're all doing their part."

Teague shrugged at Larkin. "If you want them to stop, just tell them you've met someone."

She felt her eyelid twitch as annoyance surged through her. "What, like *you* do?"

A line dented his brow. "What's that supposed to mean?"

"Twice now you've claimed to women that you and I are dating just to get them off your back."

He braced his hands on the rail behind him. "Okay, first of all, I can't believe you're still holding that against me—it happened months ago. And second of all ..." He trailed off, his brows knitting. "I can't remember what I was going to say."

She had no way of guessing what it might have been, because his thought patterns baffled her. He didn't seem to think or reason like normal people. There was one thing she was sure of, though. "You don't think you did anything wrong, do you?"

"If the situation was reversed, *I* wouldn't have been mad. I'd have been happy to help you get people to stop trying to push you into parenting agreements."

Larkin knew he constantly had female hellhorses pestering

him in such a way. Like with hellhounds, the males of Teague's breed rarely took a mate; they instead tended to father children to different mothers while forever remaining single. It was just their nature.

Hellhorses weren't designed to be partners and full-time parents; their innate reason for being was simple—to be part of the Dark Host, hell's army. Their loyalty was intended to primarily be to the realm itself, no one else.

"Look, in my defense, I didn't think the women would tell anyone," he added.

"Well, they told a whole lot of people."

"And you got me back for that, remember? The jar of hell-ice chips in my apartment is evidence of it. They made my face ache and burn like a mother."

He'd plucked the chips out and kept them as 'mementos'. See, total weirdo. The fact that her demon found the memento thing cute irritated her even more.

Khloë lifted a hand. "Wait, *that's* how the rumors of you two dating started?" Her gray eyes slid to Larkin. "That's why you blasted him with hell-ice?"

"Yes." It had been a cathartic moment.

"What about the time you blasted his ass with it?"

Feeling her lips tighten, Larkin crossed one leg over the other. "Oh. Well. Seabiscuit here told one of the women who wouldn't leave him alone that I was pregnant with his baby."

He raised his broad shoulders. "It just popped out."

Larkin gaped. "How can such a lie merely *pop out*?"

"I don't know, it just did. But people obviously know now that it isn't true, considering that was, like, nine or ten months ago and you have no kid."

"Yeah, I've had several people comment on my 'pregnancy scare'."

He sighed. "Come on, Lark, I apologized, remember?"

"No, you didn't."

His forehead creased. "I didn't?"

"No."

"Huh." He shrugged, his frown smoothing out. "Then I'm sorry."

"You're not at all."

"True," he admitted with not one trace of sheepishness.

It was an honest to God's struggle not to throw her soda at him.

"But don't take it personally," he continued. "I don't think I've ever actually regretted anything in my life. Not sure it's an emotion that's on my spectrum."

Looking from him to Khloë, Larkin shook her head. "And some people wonder why fate paired up you two . . ." *She* didn't wonder. The imp was as unstable and shameless as he was.

Piper hummed, thoughtful. "Well, Teague, I'd say you owe Larkin."

His brows dipped. "Owe her?"

The nightmare gave an emphatic nod. "Yep."

"I agree," said Larkin with a smile, thinking of the fun she could have with this. "He absolutely does."

"Also," began Piper, pointing at him, "what you said before about her putting an end to the matchmaking by telling people she's met someone? That idea was a good one."

He flashed her a little grin. "Thank you."

Larkin frowned. "It won't be that simple, Piper. They'll all want details, and I'd have to come up with some big story and invent a guy from scratch. No, thanks."

"You don't have to invent one," Piper told her. "You can have a guy pretend to be your boyfriend. And this one here, well, he has a debt to pay."

Larkin stared at her for a long moment. "Wait, what?"

"No, I wouldn't make a good pretend boyfriend," said Teague, scratching the un-inked side of his neck. "Trust me on that."

Piper leaned toward him. "But just—"

"No." Larkin slashed an arm through the air. "Not happening. No way am I spending more time around him than I absolutely have to."

He gave a mock frown of offense. "That's not nice."

"You telling lies about me isn't nice," Larkin shot back.

"I apologized for that."

"But, as you admitted, you didn't mean it."

He sighed again. "How about this? I regret that I'm incapable of regretting it."

"If you don't experience regret, you *can't* possibly regret that you're unable to feel regret."

"Only if you want to get technical about it."

Yep, she was totally gonna throw her soda at him. Which Piper must have sensed, because she laid a restraining hand on Larkin's arm.

"Putting all that aside for a second," Khloë cut in, turning to Teague, "you *would* make a terrible fake boyfriend—that much is true. But Piper's right, you do owe Larkin. This would get the others off her back."

Larkin shook her head. "I'm not even going to pretend to date a well-known hit-and-run."

He cast her a distinct look of affront. "I'm not a hit-and-run."

"Now you're just lying. Again."

"It's a habit."

"*Break it.*"

Khloë pursed her lips. "Granted, Teague is in fact a fan of hook-ups—"

"Which is a good reason for Larkin not to use me as her fake boyfriend," he said. "Knox and the other guys in your circle wouldn't want her dating me. They'd get all het up about it."

Larkin paused with her soda halfway to her mouth. "Yeah, they really would." And the thought of them het up about anything made her feel all warm inside. A little payback would be nice. Her demon smirked at the idea.

Piper looked at her, her pale-green eyes dancing with mischief. "They'd likely freak, though not outwardly. And yes, I can see that that thought fills you with joy. Personally, I think it makes sense to hop on this plan. It would be easier to pretend that *he's* your boyfriend than any other guy, what with all the rumors that you two are involved. And who else is crazy enough to risk the wrath of Knox and the sentinels by playing this game?"

"It would work," Khloë chipped in. She turned to Teague when he went to object. "It would also make female hellhorses stop hounding you to father their children."

He stared at his anchor, his lips parted. "Yeah, it really would." His brows dipped low. "But I thought you don't want me sexing-up your friends. You made me take a blood oath not to date them without asking you first. *Then*, when I once joked that I was gonna find a nice girl and settle down, you made me take an oath not to seek anything serious from your friends."

Khloë waved that away. "This wouldn't be real. It would be an act. You could pull it off."

"Yeah, I could." He gestured at Larkin, adding, "But *she* couldn't."

Larkin's back snapped straight. "Excuse me?"

He slid his gaze back to her. "You have those things. You know. Morals. You'll feel bad lying to people you care about, and it will show. People will see right through your act."

Both Larkin and her inner demon bristled at his dismissive tone. "If anyone will struggle to keep up the pretense, it's *you*.

Purely because you'll get bored fast, and you won't want to remain celibate—which you'd have to do, because I'm not dating someone who's 'cheating' on me. As such, you'll throw in the towel, leaving me hanging."

"Wrong. I could pull it off. I could even do temporary celibacy. And I could keep both up for however long I needed to."

"It would need to be for at least four months," Piper interjected. "Five would be better."

"Five?" echoed Larkin while Teague asked, "That long?"

"Yes." Piper looked at her. "You want to make it seem like it's serious, because then our cupids in there won't go back to matchmaking when you two 'break up'. They'll feel that you need time alone."

Khloë pointed her finger at the nightmare. "Good point."

"Also," began Piper, "maybe five months of celibacy will discourage him from ever again involving you in his lies, Larkin. If nothing else, it'll make an excellent punishment."

Hmmm, another good point. One that made Larkin want to smile.

"Five months it is, then." Khloë looked at Teague. "Yes, you'll miss sex, but you owe Larkin. You could stick it out that long, right?"

He exhaled heavily in resignation. "Right."

"So could I," said Larkin.

He arched a challenging brow at her and pushed off the rail. "Yeah?" Crossing to her, he leaned over and gripped the back of her seat, practically curling his body over hers. His eyes held hers as his psyche bumped her own, and then his voice flowed into her mind. *You'd let me kiss you, touch you? Because that's what I'd do.*

Larkin forced a blasé shrug. *It would look weird to people if you didn't.*

She just hoped he never sensed that her act wasn't really an act; that she wanted him more than she'd wanted anyone in a very long time; that her demon would quite simply like to ravish him.

A dare glittered in those hazel eyes. "I say we make this more interesting."

"Interesting?"

"If either of us calls it quits before the five months are up, they have to sing on the karaoke at one of the Underground bars, and they have to do it naked."

Larkin felt her face scrunch up. "What? Why does there have to be a wager? And why did your mind even leap to 'naked singing'?"

"Hey, if you're not confident that you can win, that's fine, we could skip the wager," he offered, all innocence.

"I don't worry that I'll lose—"

"Then it's all good." He held out a hand. "We on?" It was clear that he expected her to balk at that and back out . . . which was the point of the wager, she realized. He was trying to pressure her into scrapping the whole thing.

As if Larkin would be so easily manipulated.

She shook his hand. "We're on."

The glass door once more slid open.

"What the hell's going on out here?" demanded Tanner.

Larkin slid her gaze the hellhound's way, finding him eyeing her and Teague with suspicion. The male who was curled over her didn't straighten or release her hand. In fact, he gave her hand a little squeeze. She returned her focus to Teague only to see that he was staring down at her with a serious look on his face.

"Do you want to tell everyone, or should I?" he asked. "I've told you, Lark, I'm tired of being a secret."

Oh, hell.

"What does he mean, Larkin?" Tanner asked, wary.

A pinch of humor briefly flashed in Teague's gaze as he continued to stare down at her. *Well, are we gonna do this or not? It's okay if you'd rather back out while you still can.*

She squinted slightly. He clearly thought she wouldn't be able to pull this off; thought she'd stammer and blush and be so unconvincing that the others wouldn't buy it.

He really should have given her more credit.

Teague almost chuckled at the brief glimmer of anger he saw in the depths of her eyes. Poking at a harpy wasn't much different from taunting a rabid dog. Most people would likely swerve it, but he liked flirting with danger. Always had.

And this particular harpy was very dangerous. She had a reputation for being as pitiless and unforgiving as she was fearless. He could believe it.

Larkin was as cuddly as shattered glass. She could be rude and bitchy and standoffish. As if she saw no point in making a real effort with those outside her circle because she felt no need or desire to expand it. So, of course, he had fun trying to push his way into that circle. It was healthy to have hobbies.

He watched as a mask slipped over her stunning face. Her eyes warmed. The set of her jaw softened. Her mouth was no longer a flat line of annoyance—it smoothed out, regaining its usual lush shape.

She let out a long sigh and then nodded. "You're right. It's time we stopped hiding this; let's tell them."

Teague's brows almost flicked up in surprise at how convincing that looked and sounded. It would be interesting to see if she could keep it up when she had to stare directly into the eyes of those she cared for and lie her phenomenal ass off.

He straightened and tugged gently on her hand. "Then let's do this."

She stood, squared her shoulders, and turned to Tanner. "We'll talk inside."

The sentinel's wolfish gaze darted from her to Teague. "I'm not going to like this. I just know I'm not." He retreated back into the VIP box, followed closely by Piper and Khloë.

Teague didn't release Larkin's hand. He kept possession of it as they trailed behind the others. *This* element of their deal—that he could touch her, hold her, kiss her—he'd for sure enjoy. Any male would.

She was built like an Amazon. Tall, strong, toned, round hips. Her maple-brown braid was long and sleek and intricately woven. He wanted to see all that hair free of ties and raining down her back. Her mouth ... he'd had all sorts of fantasies about just what he could do with it.

In truth, Larkin was his own personal catnip, because she was a warrior through and through. One that was lethal and powerful and downright captivating. He had the distinct feeling that one taste of her would intoxicate him quicker than any liquor.

Her wide eyes missed nothing. At times, they were a striking gray-green, but there were some occasions when they became an equally striking gray-blue. It happened sometimes with harpies—the shade of their irises varied slightly whenever their inner demons were close to the surface. Like a warning system to those nearby. So whenever her eyes were gray-green as they were now, he knew her entity was close.

His own demon was often near the surface when she was around. It liked her. Liked how prickly and no-nonsense she was. At that moment, it was sending Teague mental images of the many indecent things it wanted to do to her.

Things that Teague would sure be happy to do to her.

But he hadn't acted on his attraction to her for very good reasons, and it wasn't solely about the oaths he'd made to Khloë.

Inside the spacious VIP box, he swiftly took in the position of every individual. Larkin's Primes stood near the mini bar, talking among themselves. Their young son, Asher, sat on a seat beside Raini, swinging his little legs. Levi was eyeing the selection of finger foods on the buffet table while munching on a carrot stick. Devon was rolling her eyes at Keenan, who held her infant daughter away from his body as though she was a ticking bomb. The little girl was reaching for his face, wearing the cutest dimply smile.

Anaïs was approximately nine months old but, since demonic babies were more advanced than human infants, she looked more like a one-year-old. A hellhound like her father, Tanner, she had his liquid-gold eyes. Her hair was a short mop of ringlets that were the same ultraviolet color as her mother's longer locks.

Devon sighed at Keenan. "Stop being a drama queen."

The incubus frowned in affront. "There's nothing dramatic about wanting to live."

"Anaïs isn't trying to kill you," Devon insisted.

"She tries to kill *everyone*." Keenan's head jerked when the hellpup snapped her teeth at him. Anaïs then chuckled like a loon.

"She only placed her hand over your mouth to stop you from talking. It wasn't an attempt to suffocate you."

"Are you forgetting the part where she held my nose with her other hand so I couldn't breathe?"

"That was a coincidence," Devon upheld, but Teague noticed a few others furtively cast her skeptical looks.

"All six times she's done it, it was a coincidence? Really?" Keenan's voice dripped with disbelief. "And how about when she unsheathed her claws and went right for Levi's eyes? Are you going to tell me that's—dammit, Devon, get this kid's teeth out of my arm."

With another eyeroll, the hellcat crossed to him. She dislodged her daughter's jaw from Keenan's skin—and no, it wasn't an easy feat—and then took Anaïs into her arms.

Rubbing at the little bite mark, Keenan looked at Tanner. "You need to do something about . . ." He trailed off as he drank in the sentinel's expression. "What's going on?"

Tanner cleared his throat, earning everyone's attention. "Apparently, Larkin has something she needs to tell us."

All eyes turned her way. Eyes that were quick to drop down to where her hand was joined with Teague's. The other adult males in the room predictably tensed.

She didn't shy away from the scrutiny. She lifted her chin, set her soda can on the high table beside her, and then spoke. "Those rumors you heard that Teague and I are dating? They aren't actually untrue."

A stunned silence descended on the room. People glanced from him to her or exchanged looks. A short crackle came through the intercom followed quickly by an announcement, which seemed to snap everyone out of their shocked states.

"I'm confused," said Knox, his tone as carefully neutral as his expression. "If the rumors hold truth, why were you so angry about them?" he asked her.

"Because I'd wanted to keep our relationship on the downlow for a while. You guys make it impossible for me to officially date people," she added, sweeping her gaze over Knox and the sentinels. "You start sticking your noses in where they don't belong and I didn't want that to happen this time. I wanted to see if it could go somewhere without you interfering, so I kept it quiet."

Hmm, she was much better at deception than Teague had expected. He kind of liked it.

She let out a sigh. "But Teague's right, it's unfair of me to keep him a secret. And I don't want to hide it anymore anyway."

Levi gave his head a little shake. "You two are together? Like a couple?"

She did a slow blink. "That is what it means to be in a relationship."

Teague almost laughed at her wry tone.

"Relationship?" Tanner set his hands on his hips, his jaw clenched as if to bite back a curse—they made an effort not to swear in front of the kids. "You've got to be kidding me." He cut his gaze to Teague. "Hey, look, I like you. I've got no issues with you as a person. But you're not a guy who sticks around."

"It's different with Larkin." Teague gently drew her closer to his side. "She's important to me."

Keenan looked at his mate, frowning. "Wait a minute, what about the oaths you made him take?"

"I was *not* happy that he broke them," Khloë told the incubus, standing off to the side with Piper. "I just gave him a ration of crap about it out on the balcony. But he broke his word because he cares for her. I can't be mad at him for that."

Knox squinted at Teague, visibly suspicious. "You care for Larkin?" Again, his tone was even.

Teague raised his shoulders. "What guy wouldn't?"

The Prime closed his mouth. Well, there wasn't much he could say to that without seeming as though he didn't agree, was there?

"Personally, I think this is all fabulous," declared Devon.

Tanner glared down at the hellcat who was also his mate. "Fabulous?"

"Something's been brewing between them for ages. I was beginning to think they'd never act on it." Devon's cat-green eyes flicked from Larkin to Teague. "I'm so glad you did."

Raini nodded, smiling. "You make a cute couple. I always figured you would."

Harper looked at Larkin, her mouth curved. "If anyone can handle Teague, it's you. Sort of. Okay, I'll rephrase . . . if anyone can handle the fact that he's unmanageable, it's you."

"Hold the hell on here," Tanner burst out. "There's nothing good about this."

"Agreed," said Levi, his eyes hard. "I like you, Teague, I just don't like you for Larkin. She needs a guy with staying power. When it comes to women, you don't have it."

Teague understood why they were so protective of her. Larkin might be fierce, but she had a softer side—a kind, compassionate, caring side that she exposed to very few people. He'd caught glimpses of it at times. "As I told Tanner, it's different with her."

Keenan arched a doubtful brow. "We're supposed to believe that? Really?"

Larkin bristled. "Actually, you can believe whatever you like. He doesn't need to stand here and convince you of his feelings or intentions. Don't for a second think differently. If I'd have asked it of Khloë, you'd have freaked."

The incubus offered her an appeasing look. "Lark—"

"I didn't make this announcement with the intention of explaining or justifying it," she stated. "I simply wanted to share it with you. And I've done that. Now I'm going to go."

Harper took a fast step toward her. "No, wait, you don't need to leave."

"Actually, I do. Teague and I have plans." Larkin skimmed her gaze over the other males and gave a prim little sniff. "We'll talk more tomorrow at the office, I'm sure." She cast Teague a quick look that was somewhat softer. "Come on, let's get out of here."

CHAPTER TWO

Still holding her hand, Teague escorted Larkin out of the VIP box and down the long corridor. She was a way smoother liar than he'd have ever given her credit for.

He telepathically reached out to her. *What a performance. Bravo, harpy.* If his beast could have given her a clap of appreciation, it would have.

Her mind clipped his, buzzing with irritation. *Fuck off, Seabiscuit.*

He felt his mouth hitch up. *We have such a beautiful friendship, don't we?*

She fired him a look of exasperation and swiped her hand from his. "You're an idiot."

"I can live with that."

Outside the stadium, he fell into step beside her as she joined the throngs of pedestrians walking along the Underground's 'strip'. They made a beeline for the exit, passing numerous venues such as bars and eateries and casinos.

"So where are we going?" he asked her. "Or did you just say we had plans because you wanted to get that scene over with?"

"The latter," she said. "The guys reacted on emotion just now. But when they put those emotions away and really think about it, it's going to occur to them that I could be lying to put an end to the matchmaking. In their shoes, *I* would have suspected it. If I'd stuck around while they acted like you were on trial, it would have cast doubt on my claims—I'm too protective of the people who matter to me to allow something like that."

Huh. "They took it better than I expected." Which was certainly a disappointment—Teague had been looking forward to seeing them all worked up. Small pleasures and all that.

She snorted. "They were only reasonably calm because Asher and Anaïs were there. Trust me, if I can make them believe it's true, they're gonna be all in a tizzy over it."

"Which you like," he accused.

"I do, yeah."

"Riling people *is* entertaining—that can't be denied."

Her brow furrowed. "Actually, it can. I'm only finding some satisfaction in their annoyance because of the way they've been acting lately. I wouldn't otherwise do it."

He shrugged. "It's not for everyone, I suppose."

"But you really do love it, don't you?" She shook her head in wonder. "I've only witnessed this kind of behavior in two types of people. Imps—because, well, they're imps. And demons who've lived *far* too long—their mental patterns get all muddled, and they're so desensitized to standard forms of amusement that they'll slip into finding joy in the strangest shit."

It took everything in Teague not to tense or let his expression change.

"But you're only, what, fifty? Sixty?" Most demons tended to age at an excruciatingly slow pace once they reached adulthood. "You can't be much older than that, if at all. You've only been racing for the past, like, thirty years."

He flashed her a smile. "Been looking into me, have you?"

"Of course. You're in close contact with people who matter to me." She paused. "There wasn't much info to dig up, though. You strays never leave many traces of yourselves. But, obviously, Khloë vouched for you. So did Jolene," she added, referring to a woman who was not only a Prime but the grandmother of both Harper and Khloë.

He gently patted her head. "Don't worry, little harpy. I'm not a threat to the people you care about. I'd never hurt my girlfriend's loved ones."

She squinted. "You said the latter with a little too much seriousness. You know we're not actually dating, right?"

"Of course." As they finally reached the elevator that would take them up to the club that was built above the Underground to conceal its entrance, Teague pushed the 'up' button on the panel. "On another note, I've got to admit, you're a better actress than I thought you'd be. You still won't hold out for the whole five months, though."

She made a dismissive sound. "Think what you want. I couldn't give a ferret's last shit."

"Are you ever going to drop the 'I hate you' act?"

Her brow creased. "I don't hate you. I couldn't muster up that level of emotion for you."

His low chuckle was overridden by the *ping* that filled the air. Then the elevator doors glided open.

"Disclaimer: whenever you get all snarky with me," he began as he splayed a hand on her back and urged her forward, "it makes my demon want to bite you."

Larkin's step faltered—something that, as a rule, did not

happen. But this male had a talent for poking at her emotional balance.

"In a good way," he assured her, jabbing the button on the panel.

"A good way?"

"Yeah."

She set her hands on her hips as the metal doors closed, asking, "How can there possibly be a good way for it to bite me? All hellbeasts are venomous." Surely he hadn't forgotten that.

"And?"

"And only other hellbeasts are immune to your venom. I'm not a hellbeast. Which means I'd end up writhing in agony or getting struck by paralysis."

"And?"

She was pretty sure a muscle in her cheek ticked. Because he wasn't being deliberately obtuse; no, he genuinely didn't see her point. "*And* there's therefore not a good way for you or your demon to bite me."

He shrugged. "The effects would be temporary."

What worried Larkin was that he clearly wasn't joking. He'd see no harm in biting her because, in his book, the important part was that she'd be fine in the long run. She pointed hard at him. "You *will* keep your teeth out of my skin."

"Will I?"

"Yes, you goddamn will."

"I love it when you snarl at me. There's something mesmerizing about the way your face morphs into a glower. The transformation is beautiful."

Muttering beneath her breath, she pressed her fingers down on her closed eyelids. "Why are you trying to drive me to the brink of insanity, Teague? Because it honestly feels like that's what you're aiming to do."

"Why would I only drive you to the brink? I don't half-ass shit, gorgeous." He paused. "I have to ask, though ... What makes you so sure you're sane?"

She lowered her hands to her sides and opened her eyes. "What?"

"How can you be sure?"

"I would know if I was crazy."

"Crazy people don't know they're bonkers. Mostly. There are some exceptions. For all you know, you could be mad as a barrel of monkeys."

She flapped her arms. "Why do I always have the most sense-less conversations with you?"

"Why would you want to have typical conversations?"

"Normal people do that."

"Where's the fun in being normal?"

The elevator slowed to a halt. When the doors again glided open with yet another *ping*, they stepped out of the elevator. Now in the basement of the club, they briefly greeted the demons who stood guard there to ensure that no humans or other preternatural species found their way to a place they had no business being.

Outside the venue, Teague glanced around the parking lot. He quickly spotted Larkin's car and walked her straight to it. Boyfriends did that sort of stuff, right?

"Where are you parked?" she asked him, using her key fob to unlock her vehicle.

He pointed at his beloved bike. "There."

She spared it a quick, covetous glance that wasn't as subtle as she clearly hoped it would be. He'd noticed her eye it apprecia-tively on a number of occasions.

He would have offered to take her for a ride if his demon wouldn't balk at it. Just as the beast would never tolerate anyone it didn't wholeheartedly trust mounting it, it wouldn't allow someone it didn't wholeheartedly trust to ride on the back of the bike either—the two acts felt too much like one and the same to the entity.

It was a hellhorse thing. They basically had a *no passengers* rule that they only broke for very few people. Teague's demon wouldn't break it for Larkin. It liked her a whole lot, but it didn't trust her. It didn't know her well enough to trust her.

Teague watched her slide into her car. "By the way . . ." He trailed off, letting a taunting smile curve his mouth. "I'm looking forward to watching you sing while naked. It'll be a fuck of a sight."

Her eyes flashed with challenge. "That ain't how it's gonna go down, Sullivan. The one who'll be on stage is you."

Teague felt his smile widen. "We'll see." He let her door swing shut and then stood back so that she couldn't run over his toes. He really wouldn't put it past her.

Once she'd driven off, he crossed to his bike and opened up the saddlebag. It was bespelled, allowing him to store an endless number of items inside. First, he took out his leather jacket and slipped it on. Then he pulled on his helmet, despite not really needing it—he only wore it to deter cops from pulling him over.

He grabbed one handle, shifted his weight onto his left leg, and then smoothly tossed his other leg over the bike—mounting it in one quick, practiced movement. He'd been riding for longer than he could remember. Five of the other six stray hellhorses in his unofficial lair—one they referred to as a clan—also rode motorcycles, but Saxon preferred his truck.

Teague switched on the engine, making his bike roar to life. Speeding down the road en route to his home, he thought of how his clan would react to hearing that he was now the pretend boyfriend of Knox Thorne's female sentinel.

Probably not well.

Not that any of them had anything against her or Knox. It was simply that there were things they'd rather neither demon discovered. And Larkin, well, she was sharp as a tack, not to mention suspicious by nature. Having her around him on a frequent basis was risky.

If she uncovered anything she shouldn't, she'd for sure share it with her Prime. Knox wouldn't exactly have warm, fuzzy feelings about the secrets the clan kept. Hence why Teague had resisted acting on his attraction to her—the oaths he'd made to Khloë wouldn't have been enough to ensure it.

So long as he was careful, he figured he could play the part of Larkin's boyfriend without her learning things about him that she shouldn't. It wouldn't be long before she called it quits anyway. And then he could watch her sing naked. He looked forward to it.

Soon, Teague turned onto the unmarked stretch of land that his clan had claimed, feeling his skin prickle as he bypassed the repellent spell that made humans go no further. Driving deep into the forested area, he wondered what Larkin would say if she knew that—despite having walked the Earth for centuries—she was a baby compared to him.

She wasn't wrong that a demon who'd lived a too-long lifespan would mentally suffer for it. It had impacted his beast in much the same way. He didn't see how any person, no matter their species, could exist for such a lengthy period of time and remain sane in the accepted sense of the word.

The sound of dogs barking split the air before he finally reached the clearing where he and his clan lived. Seven traditional horse-drawn wagons were scattered around—minus any steeds, obviously. The exterior of each large, live-in wagon was similar in many ways. All were gilded, lavishly decorated, boasted intricate carvings, and were masterfully crafted. They

were used by Romanichal Travelers—also known as gypsies—
once upon a time.

A laundry line hung between two of the tall trees that ringed
the clearing; the hanging clothes flapped with the breeze.
Hammocks also hung here and there, along with nesting boxes.

Near the shed at the rear of the clearing, there was a huge-ass
dog house the size of a small barn for the bloodhound-pack to
use. But some of the dogs chose to sleep under wagons or out
in the open.

A picnic table was situated near the large grill that was currently covered with protective tarp. A few folded lawn chairs
leaned against Saxon's wagon beside his ax and a pile of wood
that was intended for the firepit.

Often, Teague would find his clan gathered around the pit,
but not this evening. Going by the music coming from Gideon's
wagon, he suspected they might be gathered inside. They weren't
really people who sought 'alone time'.

Teague parked outside his own wagon and unmounted his
bike. The dogs danced around his legs—well, all except for the
eldest bloodhound, Hugo. That lazy fucker remained sprawled
on the ground near one of the logs surrounding the pit. The
canine lifted his head, spared Teague a brief look, and then
settled again.

The other dogs were bundles of energy at all times. Moreso,
Baxter and Reggie, who still acted like pups. Temperament
wise, Dutch was more of a troublesome juvenile. Barron,
the calmly assertive Alpha, somehow managed to keep the
others in line.

Teague gave their heads quick pats, removed his protective
gear, and then stowed said gear in his saddlebag. He looked up as
a whistling Leo exited the neighboring wagon, his arm wrapped
around several bottles of liquor.

Teague frowned. Leo liked a drink, especially whiskey. But he didn't overindulge—they left that sort of thing to Gideon and Tucker. "Are we supposed to be celebrating something?"

His deep-brown gaze sliding to Teague, the lean male adjusted the position of the glasses he didn't actually need to wear, since his vision was perfect. Leo believed that they made him look 'distinguished'.

Why he *wanted* to look distinguished no one was actually sure. Just as they weren't sure why he persisted in always dressing like a golfer—collared polo shirt, flat-front chinos, white socks, golf shoes, and a baseball cap to cover his short dark hair. Sometimes, he went the extra mile and wore one white glove as well.

"Gideon wants us all to have a few birthday drinks in his wagon," said Leo, descending the wooden steps attached to his tiny porch.

Teague felt his frown deepen. "It's not his birthday."

"We're gonna overlook that." Leo ducked as a squawking raven swooped down low, aiming for his head. The bird sailed through the air and settled on a nearby tree branch beside one of its small flock. "Fucker," he spat at it.

"You've been throwing wood chips at him again, haven't you?"

"He keeps biting Dutch."

"Who keeps pissing on his favorite tree. The three of you are caught up in some kind of revenge cycle, and I don't know why you won't admit that you like it."

Leo smiled. "There are moments when it's fun." He tipped his chin toward Gideon's wagon. "You coming?"

Why not? He had some news to share with the clan anyway. Teague nodded, turning toward his home. "Just give me a sec."

The wooden steps creaked beneath Teague's feet as he climbed them to reach his porch deck. It was small, but there was enough room that he'd been able to add a rocking chair.

A chair he'd painted to match the deep burgundy color of the wagon's exterior.

Gold carvings of birds, scrolls, leaves, horses, and wolves decorated the entire front of the wagon, including the glass-paned door and the arched crown boards above it. Similar carvings could be found on the sides and rear of the wagon.

He pulled open the door and then stepped inside. The gold carvings and burgundy paint continued here, running along the walls and curved ceiling. Moonlight beamed through the stained-glass window on his left, which sat above the kitchenette that was equipped with a small cast-iron cooking stove resting on a wooden fireplace.

Built-in cushioned seats ran along the opposite side of the wagon. Another bench had once been situated beside the fireplace, but he'd replaced it years ago with a small table and two dining chairs. Opposite those stood a tall, vintage, glass-fronted china cabinet.

The wagon might not be very spacious, but he had more storage than he knew what to do with. Small intricately carved cubby holes, lockers, and cupboards were built into several places—including high up on the walls, within the bench seat, and even between the wooden frames on the ceiling.

Teague stalked through the arched opening that led to the rear of the wagon. In the small bedroom there, he pulled out the thick wad of cash he'd won from a few well-placed bets at the stadium. The money he'd won from participating in the race would be wired directly into his bank account.

He stuffed the cash in the hidden compartment in his chest of drawers. The piece of furniture was made of the same mahogany wood as not only the slim wardrobe beside it but the frame of the double bed that sat beneath the rear stained-glass window.

Needing to answer a call of nature before heading out, he

went into the small en suite bathroom. Once he'd done his business and washed his hands, he walked back into the—

He stilled as the heavy smell of smoke and brimstone wafted toward him.

A dark blur leaped out of the shadows, one leg extended. A heavy foot slammed into his solar plexus, sending him crashing to the hard floor even though he'd braced himself for impact.

Tensing, he watched as an all-black humanoid figure squatted between his legs. At a distance, it could easily be mistaken for a shadowy spectre, even with those white eyes. But Teague had come across this species before; he knew what he was dealing with.

And he knew it shouldn't be in this realm.

Distantly aware of the dogs barking outside, he conjured an orb of hellfire wickedly fast and hurled it at the humanoid. As the orb hit home, the demon flew backward, crashing into the chest of drawers. These particular demons might *look* as if they were made of shadow energy, but that was only a defensive trick.

Still, being corporeal didn't make them easy to harm. They were built differently. They weren't made of flesh, blood, and bones. So they couldn't be sliced, bruised, or broken.

But they could be burned. Punctured. Even crushed. However, only hell-based weapons could kill them.

Jumping to his feet, Teague tossed another flaming ball at the intruder. Again, the orb met its target. But not before a thick tentacle shot out of the demon's side so preternaturally fast that there was no way for him to avoid it.

That tentacle curled tight around Teague's throat, red-hot and thick as a snake, and lifted him off the floor. Shit, he'd forgotten how strong and fast the fuckers were.

Unable to breathe, he wheezed as he snapped a flaming fist around the tentacle, scorching it with hellfire just as an identical tentacle slinked out of its other side. *Shit.* Teague knew how this breed killed; knew what it would do next.

He tossed orb after orb in such rapid succession that the demon couldn't dodge them. It flinched and jerked backwards, the tentacle's grip on Teague's throat loosening enough for him to suck in a breath.

As he curled another flaming fist around the tentacle, he heard the door burst open. Heard barks and the scrabble of claws. Heard footsteps thundering along the wooden floor. Heard those footsteps screech to a stunned halt. Heard a string of curses and the crackling of hellfire orbs.

The tentacle disappeared from Teague's throat in a flash and he was abruptly dropped. The bloodhounds lunged for the humanoid but, supernaturally fast, it vanished into a shadow, returning to the realm from where it had come. The dogs growled and padded around the now empty space, finding nothing, as the scent of smoke and brimstone quickly faded.

Motherfucker.

Coughing and heaving air into his lungs, Teague sat up. The dogs surrounded him, whimpering and licking at him—even the lazy-ass Hugo. The bloodhound could move quickly when it suited him.

Grinding his teeth against the pain of the blistering flesh on his throat, Teague slid his gaze to his clan, who all looked varied degrees of shocked.

Archer pointed to the spot where the intruder had vanished. "Did anyone else just see one of the shadowkin in the bedroom, or have I eaten too many mushrooms tonight?"

"No, we all saw it," a grim-looking Saxon told him.

"Okay," said Archer. "I just needed to hear that."

Teague pushed to his feet with another cough. "It was here to kill me."

Leo scratched at his stubbly cheek. "Yeah, I got that impression."

"It makes no sense, though," said Gideon. "Shadowkin don't target people of their own accord. They're mere minions."

Tucker nodded, confusion all but whirling in his brown eyes—the shade so deep that they were almost black. "They don't even leave hell unless ordered to."

"A few figures of authority can pull their strings, though," Slade pointed out, his green gaze on Teague. "One of them obviously sent it here. And they clearly want you dead."

CHAPTER THREE

A short time later, Teague and his clan were sprawled around the living space of his wagon, their minds still blown. The skin of his throat felt unbearably hot and tight, but the blisters were beginning to fade. His breed healed quickly, but injuries delivered by hell-born species tended to take longer to heal, for some reason.

Tucker rubbed a dark-skinned hand over his buzzcut. "I think I speak for all of us here when I say that—"

"Don't," said Saxon, petting the Alpha bloodhound who sat between his spread thighs. "Don't bother. Because most of the time, no one else here is thinking what you're thinking."

"So it's not just plain *wrong* for any demon to be able to grow tentacles on a whim?" Tucker challenged.

Leo twisted his mouth, sliding his gaze to Saxon. "That wasn't what I was thinking, but he does have a point."

"*Thank* you." Tucker leaned forward in his seat, sending the scent of marijuana wafting toward Teague, and then braced his elbows on the dining table. "It's been a long time since we last saw any shadowkin, huh?"

Leaning against the side of the china cabinet from his spot on the cushioned bench, Archer dug a hand into his paper bag, plucked out a mushroom, and tossed it into his mouth. "Not long enough."

"I'd forgotten just how damn speedy they were," said Teague, stroking Reggie's head. The dog hadn't moved far from his side since rushing into the wagon and now sat beside his chair like a sentry. "I'm pissed that it got away. They're slippery little fuckers."

Shadowkin might be powerful and difficult to kill, but that didn't mean they wouldn't flee from a losing battle. They were predators who thought in a more animalistic sense than the humans they vaguely resembled in shape. Even a lion would turn away if outnumbered.

"The question is," began Gideon, sitting on the floor with his liquor bottle between his legs, ignoring that Baxter kept sniffing at it, "who sent the shadowkin after you, will it come back, and *why* were you targeted?"

"That was three questions," Archer pointed out.

Gideon's forehead creased, his expression pensive. After a few moments, he shook his head in annoyance, making his wavy shoulder-length red hair flutter. "You've got nothing better to do than count?"

"You've got nothing better to do than pour brandy down your throat?" Archer shot back with enough piousness to rival that of any priest.

"It helps me think," Gideon insisted, inching up his bearded chin. "And where do you get off on being so judgmental about big drinkers? You practically live on weed and magic mushrooms."

"That's different. They were put here by nature. Alcohol wasn't."

On the opposite end of the cushioned bench from Archer,

Saxon let out a heavy sigh. "Can we focus on what's important here?" He cut his blue gaze to Teague. "Did the shadowkin tell you anything?"

"No. I didn't get a chance to communicate with it." The only way it could converse was through telepathic images. "There wasn't much of a showdown. The demon appeared out of nowhere, attacked hard and fast, and left just as quickly when you all turned up."

Rasping a hand over the blond scruff on his jaw, Slade said, "Shadowkin can only be called on by three people." He absently plucked at his collar, which sported an old bloodstain—most of his clothes did, but he didn't bother replacing many. "I don't think Vine would have sent it. He wished us well when we went our own way, and he has no personal beef with you. I can't think of a reason he'd want you dead."

"Same goes with Zagan," said Leo, sitting on the floor with his back propped up against the doorjamb between the living space and bedroom. "You two butted heads occasionally, Teague, but he always respected you, just as you respected him."

"Which leaves one person." Slade shifted in his seat, almost knocking the bag of mushrooms out of Archer's hands and into the jaws of Dutch, who'd been eyeing the bag while licking his muzzle. "Only one other figure of authority can pull shadowkin-strings. But we don't know who exactly holds that position of power nowadays."

His gaze on Teague, Saxon swiped a hand over his clean-shaven head. "There's a way to find out. But to go down that metaphorical path would be to walk right into the hands of whoever wants you dead. Once they learn that the shadowkin failed, they'll be ready for you to retaliate. They'll be waiting."

Teague stroked the underside of Reggie's tan-furred jaw. "Then they should know better. I would never make it easy for anyone to kill me. If they want me dead, they'll have to come for me themselves. Because I will kill every other minion they send until they have no option but to back down or face me in person."

Not that taking out each of the aforementioned minions would be easy. Shadowkin were never easy to take down.

"Let's look on the bright side," said Gideon with a smile. "We'll now have a little action coming our way." He took a quick gulp of brandy. "It's been a while since we got any. I miss it."

Saxon shot him a quelling look. "Then maybe get a job more exciting than producing counterfeit paintings and selling them via our imp-contacts."

Gideon arched an imperious brow. "What, like contract killing? Not all of us feel comfortable with assassinating people for money."

Saxon shrugged his wide shoulders. "It's a more honest profession than how you, Tucker, and Leo make a living."

Tucker bristled, his elbows slipping off the table as he straightened in his seat. "Now hold on—"

"He's right, you know," Leo told Tucker matter-of-factly. The two hustlers could give a masterclass on thievery. They often went on 'jobs' with imps. There wasn't a vault in the world that Leo couldn't crack open.

Tucker let out a defensive huff. "We do what we must during difficult times."

Gideon gave a hard nod and then took another long swig of his drink. "So, Teague, our plan is to basically toy with whoever is on your ass by killing their henchmen over and over in whatever creative ways we have in mind?"

Teague pursed his lips. "Yeah. And let's not make it easy for them. It'll add to their puppeteer's frustration and prod them to show here. I don't suppose anyone has any black salt lying around?"

"You're thinking we should surround our land with it," guessed Archer.

Teague nodded. Shadowkin were unable to cross black salt. A circle of it—large or small—would form a barrier so potent it would even act as one between realms, preventing shadowkin from entering the camp either by foot or by a shadow they'd hitched on from hell itself.

"I can buy some from—*don't you dare, Dutch.*" Archer protectively hugged his bag of mushrooms against his chest. "The little shit just lurched forward to steal my goods. Go lie with Hugo or something," he told the dog, tipping his chin toward where the old bloodhound was sprawled in front of the fireplace, but Dutch didn't move.

Teague cleared his throat. "There's something else we need to discuss. Something you're not going to like." He paused. "As of today, I'm playing the part of someone's boyfriend to keep matchmakers off her back."

Everyone exchanged looks.

Gideon snickered in amusement. "*You?* Do you even know how to act like a boyfriend? I mean, do you know what it entails to be one?"

Teague lifted his shoulders. "Not really. I'll make it up as I go along. It can't be too hard."

"You said we wouldn't like it," Saxon noted, his eyes narrowing. "Why?"

Teague sat up a little straighter. "Because the woman in question is Knox Thorne's sentinel."

A grim silence met his statement.

Finally, Gideon broke it. "This is a joke, right? Of course it is." He grimaced. "I don't get it."

"No joke," Teague told him.

Slade shook his head fast. "Why would you do this? There's a lot we need to keep hidden. If she gets even a *whiff* of any of it, she'll relay it to her Prime."

"Larkin's not gonna find out anything," Teague stated, confident. "It would require her to get close to me, and she'll never do that. She's a person who holds back from everyone outside her circle. I'm not part of it."

Tucker folded his arms. "She's hired you to be her fake boyfriend. Doesn't sound like she considers you an outsider."

"Firstly, she didn't hire me—"

"Wait, you're not even getting paid for this gig?" Tucker's face scrunched up. "Then why do it?"

"Two reasons. One, it will keep the female hellhorses with baby-fever off my case for a while—I need the break."

"They *are* frustrating as all hell," muttered Slade, who was often pestered by them—they were drawn to the strength he displayed when taking part in the Underground's pit fights. There, opponents were not allowed to use their preternatural abilities but could otherwise fight as dirty as they liked.

"Two," Teague went on, "I owe her a debt."

Tucker shrugged. "So?"

"*So* I don't like being indebted to people. Makes me antsy. And Khloë wants me to repay Larkin by doing this for her."

"Khloë had a hand in this?" Tucker's lips thinned. "See, this is why I don't want an anchor. They complicate things. I like shit to be simple." He looked at Leo. "Would you want to find yours?"

Fiddling with his cap, Leo frowned. "I don't know. Would she iron my clothes? I hate ironing. If she'd be up for that, maybe."

"I'm not looking to find mine," declared Slade, scratching at his short blond hair. "She'd want to know my business. It would be hard to keep any secrets from her."

"But you'd be able to trust her to keep them," said Archer,

chewing on another mushroom. "Khloë's never shared Teague's secrets with anyone. Not even her own mate."

Gideon let out a sigh of longing. "I miss her. You should bring her to see us again sometime, Teague. She's *the best* drinking partner."

"All right, we've wandered off topic," Saxon interjected before pinning Teague with a skeptical look. "I'm not buying that you agreed to play the part of Leanne's—"

"Larkin's," Teague corrected.

"Yeah, her," said Saxon, waving off his error. "I'm not buying that you agreed to act as her boyfriend just to put off female hellhorses and wriggle out of being indebted to her. There's more to this. What?"

Archer lifted a hand like a kid in the classroom. "I'll bet I know." He pointed at Teague. "You're hot for the harpy. You want an excuse to get your hands on her."

Teague dug his teeth into his lower lip. "Basically, yeah." And if this was the most he'd ever get to enjoy with Larkin, he was going to let himself have it.

"How long is the gig gonna last?" asked Tucker.

"At the longest, it'll be five months."

"Five?" Leo echoed, frowning.

"She'll bow out way before then," said Teague, scratching Reggie behind his ear. "She doesn't like being around me. And she'll soon feel bad lying to the people she cares for."

"Why?" asked Archer, his brow knitting.

"Some people don't like to lie," explained Leo.

Archer tilted his head, making his short dark ponytail tip to the side. "But why?"

Leo shrugged. "I don't know. They just don't."

Teague leaned back in his chair. "Look, you don't need to worry. It's a *fake* relationship, so our personal lives will remain separate to the same extent they do now. I'll never bring her here. I'll never introduce her to any of you. I'll never let anything slip that could tip her off. Knox Thorne will therefore remain in the dark."

Gideon sighed. "I hope you're right. Because he'll want us dead for sure. I'd rather we didn't have to go head-to-head with him."

"It won't come to that." Teague lightly stroked his throat, which was no longer burning, and found that the blisters were gone. "Now, unless anyone has any other questions, I say we get on with our evening."

When no one threw out any queries, Gideon perked up a little and asked, "Does this mean we can get back to celebrating my birthday?"

Teague felt compelled to point out ... "It isn't actually your birthday for another seven months."

"I want to celebrate it early this year." Gideon stood. "So, you up for it?"

Teague gave a slight shrug. "Yeah, sure, why not?"

Hearing the door to Knox's main office in the Underground creak open the next morning, Larkin glanced away from her laptop. He, Tanner, Levi, and Keenan all breezed inside, all slow and casual. They offered her their usual soft smiles or tips of the chin, acting no different than they normally did.

All right.

"Morning," she briefly bid before returning her attention to her laptop screen. She had a designated desk, but she much preferred doing as she'd done this morning and curling up on one of the two cozy armchairs. They were upholstered with black, butter-soft Italian leather, just like the sofa and desk chairs.

Larkin always chose this particular seat because it was positioned near the large window that overlooked the combat circle, where Levi often fought. Observing bloodthirsty duels was something that both she and her inner demon found somewhat relaxing.

The sleek, modern office was spacious enough to provide workspace for each of the sentinels as well as Knox, though no one's desk was quite as big as his. The surface of the swanky, executive monstrosity was neat as a pin despite being crowded. The hi-tech, three-screened computer sat on its center, flanked by stationery and papers and other office devices.

Skimming through yet another report from a member of their Force, Larkin didn't look up when she sensed her fellow sentinels crowd her chair.

Keenan cleared his throat and then placed something on the armrest.

Recognizing the logo on the box, Larkin didn't need to open it to know that a cupcake would be inside. He'd apparently ventured to her favorite Underground bakery.

"Peace offering," he told her.

Larkin swept her gaze over the three faces staring down at her, taking in their soft expressions that held a hint of sheepishness. No, she realized, this wasn't really a peace offering. Just as their sheepishness wasn't truly genuine. They merely wanted her to relax and lower her guard so that she'd more easily answer their questions.

She'd seen them use this trick before on others, particularly during interrogations. She was offended that they evidently thought she wouldn't notice they were now attempting to use it on her.

Idiots.

Tanner slipped his hands into the pockets of his jeans. "We shouldn't have reacted the way we did yesterday. We were out of line."

Levi nodded. "Your news took us by surprise, and we handled it wrong."

"If Teague is who you really want, we'll support you," said Keenan.

It took everything Larkin had not to snort. They would never behave so reasonably at the idea of her being with someone who had Teague's reputation. So their current behavior meant one thing only—they very strongly suspected that her claim was pure bullshit.

She cut her gaze to Knox. He was leaning back in his desk chair, speaking quietly into his phone, but his eyes were on her. And those dark orbs held a smidgeon of skepticism. He didn't believe her either, but he'd apparently decided not to question her.

She wasn't worried that she wouldn't be able to convince them they were wrong. Larkin had been deceiving them for years, and they hadn't noticed. She'd lied every time she told them that she was 'over' what her anchor had done; that she didn't feel the call of the bond anymore; that she didn't worry her unstable demon would one day gain supremacy.

As things currently stood, the entity was too protective of Larkin to want to take total control of her. But if that changed, if the demon ever decided to *really* fight for dominance, it might well get what it wanted.

Larkin had a will as strong as iron.

Her demon's will was stronger.

"So," began Keenan, flicking her laptop a quick look, "did anything go down last night that we need to know about?"

"No," she replied. "Nothing major happened. There was a minor argument between two neighbors, but that was quickly resolved. A drunk couple had a somewhat loud dispute in their friend's front yard, but they were quick to simmer down when members of the Force showed up. Personally, I'd say that our lair will continue to be on their best behavior until they've emotionally recovered from the video that Levi leaked of our newest prisoners being tortured in Knox's Chamber."

The reaper shrugged his broad shoulders. "I thought it would be good for the lair to have a reminder of how bad it would be for them if they betrayed their Primes."

Larkin let out a soft snort. "You thought it would be good for them all to have a reminder of how terribly they'd suffer if they caused any harm to your mate the way those other two bastards did," she corrected.

Levi inclined his head. "That, too."

Minutes went by as the guys engaged in more chit-chat. They asked her general, easy, mundane questions, clearly attempting to lull her into a false sense of security. And she knew that, at any moment, they'd slip in a more serious question.

But she didn't call them on it. Didn't reveal that she'd sensed what they were doing. No, she waited patiently for them to get to the point.

Tanner scratched at his jaw, his blunt nails scraping the five o'clock shadow that was slightly darker than his short hair. "So, how long exactly have you and Teague been dating?"

And there it was.

"Long enough for me to know that it's going somewhere," she replied simply.

His gold eyes narrowed slightly. "Huh." Doubt rang through the word. "I never got the impression that you two were seeing each other."

"Yeah, you really did fly under the radar," said Levi ever so casually.

"That was the plan," Larkin reminded him.

"Why change it?" asked Keenan, a small note of challenge in his voice.

She closed the lid of her laptop. "As I said yesterday, I don't want to hide the relationship anymore."

Levi observed her closely, his steel-gray gaze unflinching. "You're truly serious about Teague?"

She let her brow furrow, as though she were confused by the question. "I don't know why you feel the need to ask that. You know I don't enter relationships lightly."

Folding his arms, Keenan cocked his head. "I wouldn't have thought he was your type."

"I wouldn't have thought that Khloë was yours." She shrugged, adding, "Life is just full of surprises."

The incubus snapped his mouth shut, his neutral expression cracking briefly. His frustration was perfectly evident to see. For all of two seconds. Then his 'I'm simply curious' mask slammed back up.

Tanner licked the front of his teeth. "I didn't even think that you and Teague got along. You always seemed to be sniping at each other."

Larkin lifted a brow. "A little like you and Devon used to, huh?" She almost smiled when his mouth flattened. "That kind of stuff seems to be foreplay for hellbeasts."

Widening his stance, Levi carved his fingers through his rich brown hair. "What I don't get is why you gave him a chance in the first place. I mean, you usually avoid hit-and-runs. That's what he is. Until now, obviously," he hurried to add.

If she hadn't known him so well, she might not have picked up the trace of disbelief in his tone. She also might not have sensed that it was *killing* them all to feign cool and casual when they most wanted to accuse her of blowing smoke up their asses. Which they likely would have done if they hadn't been perfectly aware that it would only make her clam up and flip them the finger—that wouldn't gain them the answers they wanted.

She had to admit, it was fun to know that they were internally antsy and annoyed. *Welcome to my world, boys*, she thought to herself.

Levi flicked up a brow. "Well?"

She tipped her head to the side. "Well, what?"

"You're ignoring my question."

"You didn't *ask* me a question."

His lips thinned. "What makes him so special that you'd go against your personal rule and take him for a one-night spin that, evidently, turned into more?"

She skimmed her gaze over the three males in front of her. "What makes you all so special that I should tell you every little detail about my relationship when you're closemouthed about your own?" she calmly shot back. "I can't count the number of times I've been told that something isn't my business."

His mouth bopping open and closed, Keenan thumbed his earlobe. "We're just curious, that's all."

"So was I when I had questions," she said. "I was also concerned and feeling a mite protective. You all still told me to butt out. Well, now I'm telling you the same thing."

The three men exchanged looks.

Blowing out a long breath, Keenan carved a hand through his blond hair. "Fine."

"Fine," Tanner chimed in, clearly unhappy.

Levi sighed, scratching at his nape. After a few moments, he dropped his arm and shrugged in defeat. "All right, Lark, if Teague means something to you and makes you happy . . . well, that's what's important. We'll make an effort to get to know him better."

A pinch of cunning flickered in Keenan's hooded blue eyes. "Yeah. I suppose you're coming with him tonight."

"Tonight?" she echoed.

Keenan dipped his chin. "For a family dinner at Jolene's house. Me, Khloë, Harper, and Knox will be there, among others. Teague's always invited. He surely asked you to be his plus-one now that you two are out of the closet."

God, she was gonna punch the incubus right in the dick if he didn't just back off sometime soon. "I told him I'd skip it," lied Larkin. "It's a family thing. I'm not family."

"Neither is Teague, technically. As Khloë's anchor, he's an honorary member—she always took him as her plus-one before we became mates. Now she takes me. But Jolene didn't stop inviting him; she likes having him at her table. Which, of course, I'm sure you know. She'd love it if he brought you along."

"It's too short notice for her—"

"Seriously, she'd be fine with it. She's added extra people at the last minute before." Keenan smiled, and there was a shrewd edge to it. "If you and Teague are serious, it's only right that you're there with him."

Tanner nodded, a smirk playing around the corners of his mouth. "Absolutely."

"I'll let Jolene know you'll be there," Levi told her, fishing out his phone.

The three then dispersed, looking very pleased with themselves.

God, there were such twats.

They'd backed her into a corner. She could get out of it, of course. But the more excuses she made for why she shouldn't be there, the more suspicious they would become.

While she'd have no problem eating at Jolene's table—the woman was a great cook—Larkin wasn't keen on being present. Why? Because there was *no way* that Teague wouldn't push her by touching her in very non-platonic ways, hoping to make her crack so he'd win their wager.

The thought of him touching her caused mixed emotions to whirl in her stomach. Anticipation, because she'd enjoy it for certain. Unease, because she'd be mortified if he sensed how much she liked it.

Silently cursing her fellow sentinels, she telepathically reached out to Teague. *The guys aren't buying that we're together, though they're pretending that they are. They're pushing for me to go with you to Jolene's house tonight for dinner. Keenan basically wants to watch us together, and Knox will no doubt join him in that.*

More, they figured she wouldn't be able to keep up the act if it meant kissing and touching Teague . . . much as the hellhorse himself figured she wouldn't.

Moments later, his familiar psyche touched hers. *Then it's best you come along. What time do you want me to pick you up?*

Pick me up?

Boyfriends do that, don't they?

Well, yeah, but . . . *Your demon wouldn't be down with me hopping on the back of your bike.* She knew enough about hellhorses to know that that sort of thing would be a hot button for his entity.

I'll borrow my friend's truck.

All right. Pick me up at six. I'll be ready.

And naked, microphone in hand, to practice your upcoming bar performance?

She felt her eyes narrow. *Won't happen, Seabiscuit. Now go chew some grass or something.*

His low chuckle echoed around her head, and then his mind withdrew.

Opening the lid of her laptop, she got back to work. The other sentinels didn't quiz her further throughout the day. But they occasionally made dumb little comments while smiling . . .

I'm looking forward to getting to know Teague better.

*It's so great that you've finally met someone you really like, Lark.
We'll have to take him on a guys' night out. Don't worry, we'll
bring him back. He'll even be in one piece. Probably.*

Knox didn't contribute. Mr. Tall, Dark, and Far Too Perceptive
continued to watch her with those penetrating eyes. He didn't
hide that he doubted her claims, but he also didn't comment on
it—just silently conveyed that he wasn't yet convinced.

Whatever.

She was glad when her shift was over. She needed a break
from the assholes. Especially when she'd be having a not-so-
relaxing dinner with two of them later.

The drive to her complex was relatively short. Knox owned
it, along with many other properties, and he only rented the
apartments to demons from their lair. He, Harper, and their
little boy lived in a huge-ass mansion. All three male sentinels
used to reside in this very complex, but Keenan moved in with
Khloë shortly after they mated.

After pulling into the building's private parking lot, Larkin
whipped her car into her designated spot. Contemplating what
to wear for the meal, she hopped out of the vehicle and locked
it with the key—

She wasn't alone.

Larkin whirled on the spot, her muscles bunching.

Slow, easy footsteps sounded from within the shadowed area
in front of her, becoming louder with each stride. Then a long,
lean male, dressed in what was likely a tailored suit, stepped out
of the shadows and came to a smooth halt. He fixed his cool blue
eyes on hers. "Hello, Larkin."

She froze. Froze from head to fucking toe. The sight of him
was a nauseating punch to her gut. Her demon stirred with a
furious hiss.

This was no stranger. This was someone she hadn't seen or

heard from in over thirty years. Someone she hadn't expected to ever come in contact with again.

As her pulse lost its steady rhythm, her psyche violently lunged for his, instinctively attempting to connect with it. Larkin acted fast, slamming up a barrier that would prevent the anchor bond from forming.

Yeah, he was her goddamn anchor.

Technically, anyway. In practice? Oh, he couldn't be further from it.

Psi-mates were everything you needed—a friend, a close confidant, a rock, a protector, someone who you could trust to never betray you. But Holt had been none of those things to Larkin. Never would be.

Taking a subtle, steadying breath, she mentally fortified her psychic defenses, bolstering the chokehold she'd put on the mental magnetic *pull* she felt around him.

Anger surged through her. Anger that he'd hurt her. Anger that he hadn't stayed away. Anger that fate had unfairly lumbered her with an anchor who felt no loyalty toward her.

"It's been a long time." His gaze swept over her, intent and glinting with a possessiveness that made her demon emit another outraged hiss. "You look good."

She hated that there was such a soothing quality to his low, rich voice. Nothing about the big blond bastard should be soothing. Holt might come across as calm, cultured, and elegant, but a civilized aggression lurked beneath the surface.

He was dangerous. Ruthless. Devious. Powerful for his kind. Cambions—being a hybrid of human and demon—tended to sit low on the power spectrum, and their inner entities could lie dormant. In most cases, they were more human than demon. Holt was an exception to that.

He briefly glanced at her building. "Can we go inside and talk?"

"No," she said, her voice dead.

He didn't seem surprised by her response. "Ten minutes. Just give me ten minutes to say what I came to say. Then I'll go."

If he truly thought she'd let him into her home, he was high. But she would hear him out, because she knew Holt; knew he'd only come back if she refused. She wanted him gone from here and from her life.

Larkin folded her arms and planted her feet. "You have five minutes. Make them count."

A slight sigh escaped him. "I don't blame you if you hate me."

There had been a time when she'd hated him with a darkly pathological passion. But she had refused to hold onto that black emotion, because clinging to it hadn't harmed anyone but herself. Nowadays, what she felt toward him was what she considered a healthy anger. It was bright and hot, but not toxic or edged with bitterness.

"*I'd* hate me in your position," he went on. "I let you down."

That was putting it lightly.

"Not a day goes by when I don't wish I could rewind time and do something different. But I don't suppose you believe the latter."

"No, I don't," she readily admitted. "Nothing stopped you from trying to fix things. You could have come back at any point."

He took a slow step toward her. "I'm here now."

"Why?"

"To do what I should have done years ago. To claim you as my anchor. I want us to form the bond."

Larkin barked an incredulous laugh. "You're out of your mind if you think I'd be up for that." Her demon didn't laugh. It snarled and flipped him the finger, imagining stabbing that finger right into his eye.

His blue gaze went icy. "Don't tell me that you can't feel the bond's call. It's like a pull in the back of my head day and night. It never goes away. I know it's the same for you."

For a long time, the call had been a low pulse that existed in a deep recess of her mind. A pulse she'd gotten so accustomed to that it no longer caused her the same level of discomfort that it once had. But now that he was here, the call was stronger. More intense. Worse, it was front and center in her mind all over again.

"That doesn't mean I want to do anything about it," she said.

A muscle in his cheek ticked. "We're psi-mates, Larkin. We're linked by fate itself."

"That hasn't been much of a factor for you until now." It had long ago ceased meaning anything to her and her demon. "I won't ask what's changed for you, because I simply don't care."

"I don't believe that. I won't believe for a moment that you don't wish things could be different. They *can* be different, Larkin."

"No, they can't. I don't want them to be. I'm perfectly fine without you." She was *better off* without him—Levi had been right on that score.

Holt's nostrils flared. "I fucked up. I know that. But people change, people—"

"You expect me to believe you've changed? Really?" He couldn't be serious.

"It's the truth. That's why things can be different now. I know it won't be easy for me to gain your trust. I'm not expecting it to be."

"It wouldn't be tricky, Holt. It would be impossible. My demon isn't even inclined to attempt to trust you—it wants not one thing to do with you. And neither do I." Shaking her head, she took a step back. "You shouldn't have come here."

His eyes narrowed. "Larkin—"

"Your time is up. Go. And *stay* gone."

She spun on her heel and made a fast, graceful beeline for her building without once looking back. Inside the complex, she went straight to her apartment, shut the door, and leaned back against it.

Then she promptly started to shake.

Fuck.

CHAPTER FOUR

No sooner had Teague pulled up outside Larkin's building than she came striding out of it, moving with the same purpose and confidence as always. Damn, she looked good. Her everyday outfits tended to be casual, such as tee-and-jeans combos. But she generally took things up a notch for occasions such as dinners or events. Tonight, she was wearing a pretty lavender blouse and black, skintight pants that highlighted the curves of her toned, shapely legs. Oh, and also fuck-me heels.

His demon sent him an image of her wearing those heels and nothing else while he was buried deep in her body.

Feeling his cock stir, Teague figured it was best not to think about that.

He exited Saxon's truck, skirted the hood, and opened the front passenger door for her.

She gave him a questioning look.

"I'm being, you know, well-mannered and courtly. Guys do that for their girlfriends." Or so Gideon said.

She sighed, shaking her head.

He didn't miss how her gaze swept the lot almost … suspiciously. Huh. Once she'd hopped into the truck, he let the door swing closed, rounded the hood once more, and then slid back into the driver's seat.

"For future reference," she began, jamming on her seatbelt, "you don't need to open doors for me or stuff like that."

His skin prickled, because something about her tone was off. It was too smooth, too level, too mellow.

Larkin could be cool and calm. But mellow? No. Her default setting was 'tetchy as fuck'. Her voice—the perfect blend of honey and smoke—was typically full of thorns and spines and barbs.

"I like doing those things for myself," she added, her tone again uncharacteristically even. It made his demon's hackles lift.

Knowing better than to question her about it straight off the bat, he casually clicked on his belt and then started the engine. "But a boyfriend would insist on doing it for you." Driving forward, he cast her a sideways look. "You *have* had one, right?"

She shrugged, looking out of the window, the image of laidback. "I've had a few. They respected that I don't want my chair pulled out, my coat held up, my doors opened, and all that jazz."

"Respected it, or were easy to push around?"

She slid him a brief look but didn't respond.

"My guess is that it was the latter." He pulled out onto the main road. "Is 'spineless' really your type?" It was more of a taunt than a question. Normally, she'd narrow her eyes and toss a smart remark at him. This time, she only gave him a look of mild exasperation.

Yeah, mild.

Something was wrong. So wrong she'd slipped on an 'I'm

totally at ease and relaxed' suit to hide it from everyone. Those closest to her weren't going to buy it, though.

"They weren't spineless; they were simply easygoing," she said.

Doubtful. "It doesn't weaken you or make you any less self-reliant to have others do such things for you, you know." That earned him no response. "Were you serious about any of the guys you were with? As in, like, you-almost-took-one-as-your-mate serious?" His demon pricked up its ears, interested in her response.

She cast him another quick look. "Why do you want to know?"

He gave a slight shrug. "Just making conversation. We can instead talk about what's bothering you, if you want."

Oh, her look wasn't brief this time. No, she practically pinned him to the seat with her gaze.

"Why would you think that something's bothering me?" she asked, airy and aloof.

"Because you're completely relaxed."

She blinked. "That makes no sense."

"Sure it does. In general, you've got this restless energy about you. Like a bird braced to take flight and pounce at its prey. Right now, you seem *way* too chilled out. That's not you. Something is obviously wrong, and you don't want to broadcast it." He paused as he made a sharp turn. "Want to tell me about it?"

She faced forward. "No. It's nothing I can't handle."

Not entirely surprised that she'd brushed him off, he pursed his lips. "Okay." And then he once more found himself the sole focus of her intent gaze.

"You never push," she mused.

"Hmm?"

"It's something I've noticed about you. If a person says that they don't want to talk about something or can't share it with you, you don't push for answers. You let it go, and you don't bristle about it. It's unusual for someone with an alpha personality."

He shrugged again. "If someone doesn't want to share something then they shouldn't have to."

"Spoken like a person who has their own secrets."

"Everyone has secrets." Before she could press for his, he added, "I bet I can guess what you're so desperately trying to hide from me."

She sighed. "This ought to be good."

"You're acting overly casual because you don't want me to sense that you've fallen hard for me." He gave her a sympathetic smile. "It's okay. I expected it to happen."

Her lips twitched in amusement. "Expected it?"

"I'm easy to fall for," he said with a *'what can you do?'* shrug, pleased when her mouth quirked again. "And I have a big cock—women tend to get attached to it."

She started to laugh, her shoulders shaking.

"It's true. They write it love letters and everything."

"Oh, I'm sure they do."

"I tell ya, being well-endowed isn't all it's cracked up to be. Especially when, like me, you're a grower *and* a shower."

"Poor you."

"I know, right?"

Larkin could only shake her head. The dude might be nuts, but he knew how to pull a girl out of her funk. There was simply no way to *not* smile or laugh when he was around.

Having Knox and the sentinels as brothers, she'd become accustomed to people pressuring her to talk, shoving themselves into her business, giving her no room to *think*, and insisting on dealing with her problems for her. Teague was different. The opposite, even.

It wasn't that he didn't care. No, if Teague thought that

someone needed help, he wouldn't ignore it. For him to back off so easily when she'd turned down his offer to be an ear for her problem showed that he respected her wish to process her issue alone. More, him not trying to worm his way into her business meant that he trusted she could take care of the matter herself. And Larkin had had no real idea how attractive she'd find that until she found herself in a situation where it was what she so needed.

Not that she would keep Holt's visit completely to herself. She'd share it with her brothers so that they'd know he was in Vegas. But not tonight. Her demon was too tightly wound—it needed time to calm its tits, or it might surface and go hunting. That would not be good.

Since hopping into the truck with Teague, the sharp, spiky edges to her entity's foul mood had little by little smoothed out. Everything about him was a distraction for her demon—his strength, his power, his confidence, his devastating good looks, even his strange idea of humor.

On the one hand, it was a good thing that he'd diverted some of her entity's attention. On the other hand, it wasn't so great. Because her demon had decided that they should spend the night in his bed, using him to distract themselves further.

The idea was seriously cold. And, if she was honest, somewhat appealing. She wasn't going to act on it, though. She wouldn't use him that way. But she could throw herself into their little 'act', could use *that* to distract her.

It would be hard not to think about Holt at all when she couldn't shift the sinking sensation in her gut. But she was up for the challenge. The cambion didn't deserve to take up any of her mental space.

Soon, Teague parked outside Jolene's house and then turned to her. "Now, if you want to fool those people in there into thinking you're fine, you need to go back to being your usual prickly self."

She felt her brow crease. "I'm prickly?"

"As a goddamn porcupine. I like porcupines. They're fun to play catch with, though it hurts like a mother."

Larkin studied him carefully. "I can't tell if you're being serious or not. You know what, it doesn't matter. Right now, our act matters. I'll work on not looking overly casual. You don't overdo the PDA, it'll look suspicious."

"And you don't want to end up all wet and needy at a dinner table," he said with a nod of understanding. "I get it."

She gave him a flat look. "I'm quite sure my hormones can handle it." Her demon snorted, knowing that was a total lie.

His eyes lit up. "Oh, you're throwing down a gauntlet? Excellent."

An arrow of panic zipped through her. "No. I was simply stating a fact."

"That was a challenge if ever I've heard one."

"No, it wasn't. Now focus. We have a show to put on. I need you to concentrate on that."

He saluted her. "I'm focused, I swear."

Hearing the easy rumble of an engine behind them, she glanced back to see a familiar car. "That's Keenan and Khloë pulling up." She slid her gaze back to Teague. "You ready for this? Because both he and Knox are gonna watch us like a hawk."

"And what they'll see is how hard you're falling for me and my cock."

She crossed her eyes. "I don't know how to talk to you sometimes."

"I hear that a lot. Now stay here." Then he was gone from the truck.

Wait, what? She opened the door and slid out.

Skirting the hood, he shot her a look. "I asked you to wait."

Conscious of Keenan watching them, she sighed at Teague and responded *exactly* how she'd have responded if they truly were dating. "Didn't I tell you that I don't need you to be all chivalrous?"

He hummed, closing in on her. "You *did* mention it. Several times. But all I ever hear is 'Blah, blah, blah, I'm a tough independent badass who doesn't know how to handle courteousness. Blah'."

She rolled her eyes, ignoring how her body perked up at having him so close. "I don't want a Prince Charming. They're all dull and one-dimensional." Her demon would likely skin such a person alive for being so boring—it really hated to be bored.

Teague took her hand in his and began pulling her toward the house. "I am many things, but I am never dull."

No truer statement had ever been spoken.

He smiled at a beaming Khloë. "Hey, gorgeous."

Jealousy nipped at Larkin, even as she knew that he had nothing but platonic feelings for the imp. Her inner entity drummed its fingers on its thigh, no less irritated.

Keenan glared at him. "Should you be calling another woman 'gorgeous' now that you have a girlfriend?"

Khloë frowned at her mate. "Why wouldn't he? His relationship status doesn't change that I'm gorgeous. You come out with the weirdest stuff."

The incubus's eyes widened. "Pot, kettle, black." He glanced at the truck and then at Teague. "You didn't give Larkin a ride on the back of your bike," he noted, a trace of suspicion in his voice.

Teague shrugged. "She doesn't like being so close behind me unless she's wearing a jockstrap."

Larkin closed her eyes. "This is where you stop talking."

"I don't know if I can," said Teague.

Opening her eyes, Larkin caught Khloë's subtle, conspiratorial wink just before the imp and her mate strode up Jolene's gravelly path. Their hands still joined, Larkin and Teague followed, careful not to brush against the Mustang parked in the driveway.

Stepping onto the porch, Khloë pressed the doorbell. Five times. Not out of impatience, but simply because she felt like it.

The door soon opened, and there stood Khloë's younger sister. Heidi was ten, maybe eleven—Larkin wasn't sure. The little girl dived at Khloë with a beaming smile, who then hugged her tight while the kid nattered a mile a minute.

The sisters didn't share much of a resemblance, though they had similar mannerisms and the same petite build. Heidi had the look of an angel—vivid aquamarine eyes, adorable dimples, rosy cheeks, and long ringlets that were a stunning white-blonde. She'd also rob you blind if you didn't watch those sticky fingers of hers. In that sense, she was an imp through and through, not to mention a manipulative plotter like Jolene.

Finally, Heidi stepped back and waved them all inside, *still* chatting away to Khloë.

So many smells washed over Larkin as she entered the house. The overpowering and delicious scents of grilled meat and hot spices overlaid the softer smells of lavender, cookies, and coffee.

Shutting the door, she gave Heidi a smile. "Hey, kiddo."

Teague ruffled the imp's hair and said, "Well, if it isn't my favorite thief."

Heidi giggled. "My favorite thief is Leo. Want to see what he taught me last week?"

"Sure," he replied.

She crooked a finger at Larkin. "You're tall, so I'm gonna need you to bend over."

Sighing, Larkin obliged her. "All right, but I'll want back whatever you steal."

Heidi fingered the necklace that dangled from Larkin's neck. "I can undo the clasp on the chain without you even feeling it."

Teague folded his arms. "Hmm, prove it."

The kid tiptoed two of her fingers along the side of Larkin's neck and around to her nape.

Larkin felt a whisper of a touch on the clasp, but the necklace stayed on. Heidi's face scrunched up in concentration, and there was *another* slight 'flick' to the clasp. Again, though, the necklace didn't fall off.

Her shoulders slumping, Heidi scowled and lowered her arm to her side. "I need to practice more."

Larkin straightened. "I'm sure you'll get it eventually, and I don't know how I should feel about that."

Teague chuckled, unfolding his arms.

Heidi lifted her hand . . . and then smiled. "Oh, would ya look at this." She was holding one end of a bracelet, letting the piece of jewelry swing gently in the air. *Larkin's* bracelet.

Her lips parting, Larkin stared at it. "You made me focus on the necklace so I wouldn't sense you were stealing my bracelet."

"Uh-huh." Heidi returned it to her, and then held up her other hand. "And this, too."

Larkin took the ring, gaping. "How the hell did you get that off my finger without me feeling it?"

Grinning, the kid swung her arms forwards and backwards. "Pure skill."

Amusement trickling through him, Teague flashed Heidi a smile. "I bow down to your brilliance." Leo would be proud.

"Brilliance," muttered Larkin. "Yeah, that's one word for it."

Probably not a word many would use in this instance. Other breeds of demon tended to sit in judgement over imps. Teague personally thought it unfair.

Imps might be as crazy as they were unethical and have no issue committing all manner of crimes from embezzling to identity theft, but they never pretended to be anything else. You knew where you stood with them. You didn't have to worry that they'd stab you in the back or screw you over—unless, of course, you wronged them.

In that sense, they were honestly dishonest. It was why Teague and his clan got along with them so well. They were on the same wavelength in this respect.

"Now, how about we go see if dinner's ready?" Larkin proposed.

"I'm up for that." Heidi wrinkled her little nose. "I should probably give you this back first." She held out a small, compact mirror.

Her lips once more parting, Larkin took it. "Okay, I don't know what disturbs me more: that you stole *three things* pretty much at once without me knowing it; or that it's like you afterwards produced your ill-gotten goods out of thin air. Seriously, where do you put this stuff when you swipe it?"

Heidi tapped the side of her nose. "An imp never tells." With that, she skipped away.

Dropping her mirror back in her purse, Larkin looked at him. "Who is this Leo person that taught her that trick?"

Claiming her hand again, Teague slid her a sideways smile as they slowly walked along the hardwood floor of the hallway, following the sounds of laughter and chatter. "Like you don't already know he's one of my clan." She would have discovered that much when she did her homework on Teague.

"Okay, fine, I know their first names and some other basic details. But that was all I could dig up. You guys erased your trails so successfully that even *I* can't unearth anything about your pasts."

Pausing a few feet away from the noisy kitchen, Teague used

his grip on her hand to pull her closer, liking how her pupils dilated. "What can I say? We prefer to be men of mystery."

"Bullshit," she said, her voice low. "You"—she gently poked his chest—"are just a cagey motherfucker, plain and simple. People don't notice, because you're so damn chatty and social. They don't seem to pick up that you don't talk about the things that matter, or that you very expertly redirect a conversation if it's going down a path you don't like."

Teague couldn't quite fight the smile that tugged at his lips. "Full of astute observations, aren't you, harpy? And it makes me wonder . . ."

Her brow dented. "What?"

He dipped his head, leaving inches between their mouths. "If you've sensed just what filthy things I've imagined doing to you."

She swallowed, heat flickering in her eyes. Then she gave her head a quick shake and poked his chest once more. "Now, see, you're doing it again. Tossing something into the conversation that will distract and divert."

He shrugged. "It has a high success rate."

Just then, Keenan popped his head out of the kitchen, his eyes narrowed. "What are you two whispering about?"

"Whips and floggers," Teague said, straight-faced.

The incubus opened and closed his mouth a few times. With a sigh, he flapped an arm. "I have nothing." He retreated into the kitchen.

Teague led Larkin into the space. By the looks of things, dinner wasn't quite ready. Jolene was still pottering around, much like her two usual helpers. One was her anchor, Beck. The other was her only daughter, Martina.

"Evening all," Teague greeted, earning himself a nod from Beck and a wave from Martina.

Jolene smiled as she said, "Larkin, Teague. Always a pleasure."

She gave off her usual veneer of elegance with her smart blouse, pencil skirt, and sophisticated hairdo. Beneath that surface lay a shrewd, daring, manipulative woman who would protect and avenge her loved ones at any cost—even if said costs involved leaving behind scenes of utter carnage.

Teague liked the female Prime a lot.

Still smiling, she looked from him to Larkin, noting their joined hands. "I did hear about this new development. I approve."

Keenan grumbled something unintelligible, making Khloë roll her eyes.

"The food will be ready in ten minutes or so," said Jolene. "You four might as well go wait in the dining room. Harper and Knox are already seated."

Larkin gave her a polite smile. "Thank you for finding room for me at the table."

"There's always room for you here. And since Richie and Robbie couldn't make it this evening," Jolene began, referring to Khloë's father and brother, "you won't be uncomfortably squeezed between two people or stuck sitting on Teague's lap."

His brows lifted. "Shame. That would have been interesting."

Larkin snorted. "Only you would think that." She led the way as the four of them strolled into the dining room. With its earthy colors, soft lighting, and the many wall-mounted framed photos, the space had a very warm vibe. The little knick-knacks and keepsakes that could be found on the windowsill, shelves, and surface of the antique cabinet added to the homey feel.

Jolene kept photos and mementos in almost every room. The batshit badass had a sentimental streak a mile wide, and she made no attempt to hide it; not worried it would be perceived as a weakness.

In the center of the dining room was a long table with lots of chairs and stools of various types, styles, and sizes gathered around it. Only Larkin's Primes were currently seated.

Harper gave them all a bright smile. "Well, hey."

Greetings were quickly exchanged as Larkin and the other newcomers made a move to claim a seat. She felt her lips thin when Teague pulled out a chair for her, his eyes dancing. "You're gonna keep doing this gallant shit, aren't you?" It wasn't a question, it was an observation. "Can you not cease trying to annoy me for *just* a little while?"

Opposite her, Khloë chuckled. "He likes hearing you growl at him. That's all."

Larkin took her seat and scooted forward before he could push her chair closer to the table. "I don't growl."

"Oh, you do," said Teague with a smile, claiming the chair beside hers. "It's a low, sexy sound that me and my demon *love*."

Not sure if he was messing with her or not, Larkin waved a hand his way. "Whatever."

She almost tensed when he hooked his arm over the back of her chair. She couldn't help it. She was just so *aware* of him; so conscious of his proximity. It left her feeling strung tight.

She glanced around. "Where's Asher?"

"Playing in the backyard with Heidi. Ciaran is supervising," Harper added, referring to Khloë's twin.

Larkin went to speak again, but then the sphinx raised her hand.

"I just want to say something before we get on with our evening." Harper took a long breath. "I have an apology to make. I'm sorry about all the matchmaking attempts, Lark. I can understand now why they drove you insane. You were already involved with someone, and you were serious about him. Which I'm glad of, because you two suit so well."

Khloë grinned. "My thoughts exactly."

"Yes, because they have so much in common," Keenan said, his voice bone dry.

Harper cast him a frown. "Opposites attract. Take you and Khloë, for example."

The incubus only grunted.

It was no easy thing for Larkin to bite back a smile. For him to be so surly meant he wasn't quite as skeptical about her and Teague as he'd been earlier. She wondered if Khloë had been filling his head with shit in an effort to convince him.

Larkin's inner smile faltered as Teague danced his fingertips over her nape. The sensitive skin there prickled as little bumps rose. His touch was so light, so gentle, yet she'd *swear* it seared her just beneath her skin. Like a brand.

Harper leaned forward in her seat. "Now, tell me how you two ended up doing the horizontal rodeo."

"Oh no," said Larkin. "I don't kiss and tell."

The sphinx let out a put-upon sigh. "I had a feeling you'd say that."

A round of small talk began. And, of course, Larkin's chatty fake boyfriend was fully engaged in it. All the while, he alternated between doodling light circles on her nape and playing with the thin, curly whisps of hair there that were too short to add to her braid.

They were such simple things, so she had no logical answer for why they fired up her libido. Or for why excitement pounded through her so vehemently that her nerve-endings soon felt raw and tingly. Her demon, equally affected, didn't care to reason it out. The entity merely wanted more.

It got what it wanted.

He loosely clasped her nape, skating his thumb up and down one side of her neck while fluttering his fingertips along the other side. Easy though his hold was, there was a heavy dose of possessiveness there. One she begrudgingly liked.

Soon, her skin was so hypersensitized it left her feeling jumpy. And horny. Only her awareness that she was being very closely watched by Keenan and Knox stopped her from shying away from Teague's touch out of self-preservation.

There was *one* benefit to him persisting in so boldly touching her. Keenan looked like he wanted to explode. Yeah, well, she'd felt the same way when he wouldn't stop playing cupid with the others.

The small talk came to an abrupt end when, finally, Jolene entered the room with plates of food. In no time at all, everyone was gathered around the table, eating and talking and drinking. And Larkin thankfully got a breather from Teague's touchy-feely ways.

"How is your clan doing?" Jolene asked him at one point.

Once he'd finished chomping down a mouthful of steak, he replied, "They're good."

"I'll box up some leftovers for you to take home for them. They're growing boys after all." Jolene sniffed. "And too skinny."

A snort popped out of Khloë. "They're all packed with muscle."

"They are indeed," Martina said with a somewhat dreamy smile. Moving her gaze to Teague, she bit her lip. "So, how's Leo?"

Ciaran frowned at his aunt. "I thought you had a thing for Slade."

Martina grinned at him. "Sweetie, I have a thing for them all. But there's just something about the way Leo looks when he's cracking open a vault . . . My body has no defenses against it."

Teague's lips quirked. "He has a thing for you, too, if it helps."

Martina's grin widened. "Oh, it helps." She cut her gaze to Larkin. "I take it you've met the boys."

"Once or twice," she lied.

Teague looked at her and tucked a stray hair that had escaped her braid behind her ear. "You were a hit with them. I think you were more taken with the dogs than you were my clan." He lightly skimmed his fingertip along the shell of her ear and down to the lobe.

Larkin almost blinked in surprise. *You have dogs?* He'd never mentioned them before.

Five, he replied.

Her focus was yanked from the psychic conversation as flames burst around Asher's plastic cup. The fire quickly died down, showing that the drink had disappeared. A small fire roared to life in the kid's hand, and then there was his cup.

Larkin smiled. She couldn't believe that the pyroporting little dude was four years old. The time had *flown* by.

"Ah, shoot," muttered Martina, grimacing at one of her red acrylic nails. "The tip snapped."

"I got you covered," announced Heidi, producing a designer purse seemingly out of nowhere. A purse that didn't look like one a kid would own. She unzipped it, fished out a tiny nail file, and then passed it to her aunt.

Martina responded with a bright smile. "Thanks, honey."

Harper squinted at the young imp. "Where did you get the purse, Heidi-ho?"

She gave an innocent blink. "I found it."

Stole it, more like.

Asher got to his knees on his chair, wearing his adorable dimply smile. "Daddy, I want to go outside and play."

Knox flicked a look at the kid's half-empty plate. "You haven't finished your dinner."

With a small burst of fire, every piece of food on Asher's plate vanished.

Still smiling, the little boy lifted his hands, palms out. "See, all gone."

Harper's gaze slid to the ceiling. "I *can't* with this kid."

Giggling, he pressed a sloppy kiss to his mom's cheek. She responded by blowing raspberries all over his face.

Larkin would have chuckled at the sight, but then Teague rested his hand on her knee beneath the table. Her pulse jumped. The ass apparently meant to step things up, and that was not whatsoever good.

CHAPTER FIVE

Larkin drew in a breath through her nose. Okay, PDA was one thing when it was a matter of them 'performing'. This was different. And not acceptable.

She almost snarled. *Move it or I'll snap it off.*

He glided his hand up her thigh.

Teague, she reprimanded.

He shot her a quick look of complete innocence. *You said move it, I moved it.*

God, he was such a shit.

She rolled her shoulders. Fine. If he wanted to play games, they could play games.

Larkin took a tip from her demon's book and sent him an explicit telepathic image. One of her fisting his cock right here at the table. She heard him quietly suck in a breath. Ha.

His mind brushed hers, buzzing with amusement. *Ho, ho, ho, my harpy plays dirty.*

The word 'my' should *not* have made her belly clench.

An image shoved its way into her mind. An image of her propped on the table with his face between her legs.

Her core spasmed. Not to be outdone, she telepathed him another explicit image. And as conversation continued around the table and people finished their meals, the mind-to-mind exchange of seriously graphic pictures between her and Teague went on and on.

Removing his offending hand from her thigh, he draped his arm over the back of her chair and grazed her ear with his lips. *You're wet. I can smell it.*

Damn his hellbeast-enhanced sense of smell. Fighting a blush, she discreetly cupped his dick. *And you're hard, so we're even.* He was also as well-endowed as he'd claimed.

Just to be a tease, she gave his cock a quick squeeze before pulling back her hand. Which was exactly when Beck turned his attention to her.

"So, how long have you and Teague been dating?" the burly male asked.

"Several months," Larkin vaguely replied, hoping she didn't look as flustered as she felt.

Martina hummed. "Let me guess. You kept it to yourselves so you could date in peace. I understand. I had to do the same for years, because Richie was always interfering."

Beck sighed. "He only did it to rile you up."

Martina let out a little sniff. "Well, he stopped after I set too many of his things on fire."

Feeling his lips twitch, Teague lifted his glass and took a swig of his drink. Dinner with the Wallis family never failed to make him smile.

Larkin's psyche stroked along his, and then her voice glided into his mind. *What is it with imps and fire?*

He set down his glass. *I don't actually know.* Meeting her gaze, he inhaled deeply, dragging more of her scent into his lungs—the spice of arousal there taunted him. *There's quite a few serial arsonists among them. But they only target those who wrong them. And they generally don't let people burn to death. They usually just get them crispy.*

I suppose that makes it okay, then, she said as she faced forward, her tone sardonic.

He snickered and nipped her earlobe just because. *Don't act like you haven't done worse. I've heard plenty of rumors about you and your demon.* Very intriguing rumors.

"Want to share with the class whatever it is you two are telepathically talking about?" Keenan snarked, glancing from her to Teague.

His demon narrowed its eyes at the incubus, not liking his tone. "You really want to hear what I'm planning to do to her when we're alone and naked?"

Keenan's face went a dark red.

Khloë elbowed her mate. "Cheer up, will you?"

His brow furrowed. "I don't need to cheer up. I'm fine."

"You're brooding," Khloë corrected. "Something I'd ordinarily find amusing. Delightful, even. But you keep snarling at my anchor, and I don't like it. Leave him alone."

Keenan spluttered. "He's all over her. At a *dinner* table."

"All over her?" Khloë echoed. "Not even close. God, you can be so dramatic when you're in a mood."

"You're really okay with the idea of them together?"

"Unlike you, I don't feel a need to come between people and the source of their happiness. All right, that was pure bull. Messing with people's level of contentment feeds my soul. Let me put this another way. I want Larkin to be happy. I want Teague to be happy. Together, they are happy. So yeah, I'm okay with them being together."

The girl was so convincing that Teague almost believed her.

Once dinner was over and everyone had said their goodbyes, they exited the house to find two of Jolene's lair digging a *seriously* deep hole in the front lawn. No one batted an eyelid about it—they were too used to imps doing weird stuff. Jolene, however, was not happy.

It was as he and Larkin clicked on their seatbelts in the truck that the Prime shoved one of the diggers *into* the hole.

Starting the engine, Teague chuckled. "You gotta love Wallis imps."

"You fit in well with them," Larkin noted.

"They're my kind of people." He pulled away from the curb and onto the road. "Say what you want about imps, but they have each other's back. There's loyalty there. A real sense of family. Their personal 'code' might differ from that of most, but when it comes to what's important, they don't let others down."

"True," she agreed. "I didn't really see that until Harper came into our lives and we got to know her family and old lair members. Still, I'm not sure I'd want to live among them like Keenan—he's always full of stories about how he gets home to find that Khloë's been up to all kinds of stuff, and suddenly there are boxes of goods that 'fell out of a van' stacked in a cupboard. Goods her relatives later sell. Speaking of Keenan, I don't think he has as many doubts about us as he did before."

Teague dipped his chin. "Knox still isn't convinced."

"I noticed that. But since he failed to comment on the matter at any point today, I'm thinking he decided to stay out of it."

"That's the feeling I got." Teague paused as he made a right turn. "You know, on a whole other note, you surprised me tonight."

Her brow pinched. "In what sense?"

"You gave as good as you got. I didn't think you would. I

thought you'd blush like crazy and maybe try slamming my face on the table."

"I presume you're referring to how you did your best to get me all hot and bothered."

He smiled at the withering look she fired his way. He loved getting under her skin and watching her facial muscles twitch as she fought to hide just how annoyed she was. He decided there and then that he'd work toward giving her a permanent eyelid twitch—it would suit her. "I *did* get you all hot and bothered."

"Two-way street, Black Beauty." She gave him a prim look and dismissively slid her gaze to her window.

He let out a chuckle. "So, basically, I'm gonna have to up my game if I'm to win this wager?"

Her head whipped around to look at him. "What? No. No, you should just stop playing games."

A slow grin shaped his mouth. "Why? It's fun."

"In *your* book, maybe. In mine, it's simply juvenile."

"Liar. You like tormenting me just as much as I like tormenting you. That's why you're not as worked up now as you were earlier."

That was when it hit Larkin. Hit her like a slap to the face, making her lips part. "You instigated it to distract me because you knew something was on my mind."

"And to give you an outlet. You needed one."

She had. She really had. It was only at this moment that she realized just how much tension had drained out of her system during the evening as she'd mentally sparred with the male beside her. He might have weird ways of dealing with stuff, but they were effective all the same.

"I'm not going to thank you for it," she told him. "As we've covered, I'm hot and bothered. That part I'm not pleased about at all."

His mouth winged up, and she thought he might offer to do something about it; to take care of the itch—particularly since it would, in turn, take care of his own. But he didn't make the offer. He didn't even give her a suggestive look.

The oaths, she thought. He'd given Khloë his word, and he wasn't going to break it.

Understandable.

Also frustrating.

But no doubt for the best, given his penchant for casual hook-ups.

Larkin had nothing against them, she simply didn't find them satisfying anymore. Not emotionally, anyway.

When he finally pulled up outside her building, she took a good, long look out of the front window, sweeping her gaze over her surroundings. It didn't seem likely that Holt would have stuck around, but she wanted to be sure.

"Okay, what's wrong?" asked Teague, angling his body toward hers.

She blinked at him. "What?"

"As soon as I drove into the parking lot, you went tense as a bow. Now you're in full-on hypervigilant mode." His eyes darkened. "Are you expecting trouble of some kind?"

"No. Just . . . unwelcome company." That was as much as she was willing to say on the matter.

He let out a long hum. Then he cut the engine and got out of the truck.

Her brows snapping together, Larkin slipped out of the vehicle. "What are you doing?"

"Walking you to the door."

"I don't need—"

"I'm a chivalrous boyfriend, remember." He splayed his hand on her back and gently ushered her toward the building.

With a sigh, she let him, feeling pretty confident that Holt was gone. She'd have sensed if she was being watched.

When they reached the main door, Teague pinned her with a serious look. "You know you can reach out to me if you need anything, don't you? I won't ask questions. I won't share what you tell me. I'll just assist you in whatever way you need."

Larkin swallowed, her chest feeling tight. "Khloë's lucky to have you as her anchor." And if he ever did claim a woman, she'd be lucky to have him as her mate.

"I know," he said, all arrogance.

A smile pulled at her lips. "Of course you do."

He dipped his head and brushed his mouth over her forehead. "Night, baby."

Her stomach took an excited dive. *Baby?*

He shrugged. *Thought I'd try it out. I like it.*

Smiling, she shook her head. "Goodnight, Teague. Get home safe. And try not to piss anyone off on your way there just for something to do."

"I promise nothing."

Larkin was late arriving at Knox's office the next morning. She'd taken a longer, more complicated route to the Underground, determined to be certain that she wasn't being followed. It was unlikely that Holt would tail her like a damn stalker, but she'd needed to be sure.

Keenan sat at his desk, typing while frowning at his computer screen. Levi stood in front of the row of monitors that provided CCTV footage of the Underground, talking into his cell phone. Knox was lounging in his desk chair discussing something with Tanner, who sat in the chair opposite him.

They all gave her brief greetings as she entered before

refocusing on whatever they'd been doing. Well, no one actually cared if any of them were late by a few minutes or so.

She intended to tell them about Holt's appearance straight off, wanting to get it over with. Her demon snarled at the mere thought of him. It had calmed somewhat—mainly thanks to their friendly, neighborhood hellhorse—but it still longed to tear their joke of a psi-mate into shreds.

While she waited for Levi to finish his call, she shrugged off her jacket and then hung it on the back of her chair. She was about to make herself a coffee using the machine at the corner of the office near the water dispenser, but then Levi pocketed his phone.

Larkin cleared her throat, gaining everyone's attention. "I have something I need to tell you," she said, leaning back to prop her ass on her desk.

"You and Teague are over already?" asked Tanner, looking awfully pleased by the prospect.

She felt her forehead crease. "No."

"Shame," muttered Keenan.

"This has nothing to do with Teague." She wet her lips with a swipe of her tongue. "It's about Holt."

That easily, each male in the room went rigid.

Levi squinted. "What about Holt?" The question was laced with wariness.

She folded her arms. "He's in Vegas."

His jaw tightening, Knox pushed out of his chair. "Are you sure?"

Oh, how she wished she wasn't. "Yes. He approached me in the parking lot of my building yesterday."

An animalistic growl rumbled out of Tanner as he stood so abruptly his chair wheeled backwards. "He *approached* you?"

"Why?" Keenan demanded, his expression dark. "What did the bastard want?"

She dug her teeth into her lower lip. "To form the anchor bond."

"Mother*fucker*," spat Levi, turning away.

Keenan's face scrunched up. "He can't seriously think you'd agree to that, or that you'd ever even think about it."

"That was pretty much what I said," Larkin told him. "But it would appear that he does."

His eyes flat and dead, Knox took a slow step toward her. "What exactly did he say?" His voice was low and so eerily calm it was unnatural—an indication that he was *pissed*.

Larkin gripped the edge of the desk behind her. "That he understands if I hate him; that he's essentially spent years regretting how things played out way-back-when; that he's changed now and wants to both win my trust and claim me as his anchor."

Rising to his feet, a scowling Keenan perched his hands on his hips. "If he's really been regretting it all these years, why didn't he come back for you sooner?" he challenged.

"Yeah, I pointed out that he'd have done exactly that if he'd truly longed to fix the situation. He only said, 'I'm here now'. Like that was what mattered." She let out a low, disgusted snort. "He didn't say much else. I told him to leave and then I headed into my building."

Knox very slowly cocked his head. "How do you feel about Holt being here?" he asked carefully, his gaze probing. "Truthfully? I know you're rightfully angry with him. But is there a part of you that wishes he *could* earn your trust and become a part of your life the way he always should've been?"

She frowned. "No. You know me, Knox. You know that mental doors slam shut in my mind if someone betrays or hurts me. Those doors will never open for that person again." It wasn't something she could consciously control.

"Yes, but Holt isn't just anyone," Knox pointed out. "He's your psi-mate. I don't want you to later regret that you sent him away. No one here would judge you if you gave him a shot to see if he really has changed. We might not like him, but we'd support you whatever your choice. What's important here isn't how we would feel about it; it's that you make the right decision for you. So be honest with yourself. Do you want him in your life? Do you want to form the anchor bond?

Those questions were easy to answer. "No and no. Though I appreciate that you'd support me no matter what."

"And your demon? How does it feel about all this?"

"It's on the same page as me. It would never bond with him. Ever. He did the one thing that the entity could *never* forgive."

"He left you," said Knox with a nod of understanding.

Abandonment was a real hot button for her demon. "Neither I nor the entity are at all moved by the fact that he might actually be willing to make any of the concessions or sacrifices he'd once point-blank refused to make."

Knox slipped his hands into his pockets, twisting his mouth. "I don't see why he wouldn't. There's certainly no reason why he couldn't. He's in a better situation nowadays."

She blinked. "How exactly?"

"I didn't tell you this before now because you don't like to talk about him or hear what's going on in his life. He's no longer a sentinel. He's Prime of his lair."

Her smile held a cutting edge. "Just as he always wanted." Even she heard the bitter note in her voice.

"Now that he doesn't answer to anyone any longer, he has the freedom to play however large a part in your life as he pleases."

No, he didn't. Because she wouldn't allow it. Her demon would fight her on it if she tried. "It also means he'd now want more than ever for me to join his lair and be close to him."

"Yes, he won't want you answering to another Prime," Knox confirmed. "Especially when I have no alliance with him."

Larkin bit out a curse, her grip tightening on the edges of the desk. "I *hate* that he came here. Why couldn't he have just stayed away?"

Levi crossed to her, his shoulders tense. "Why didn't you tell us about this yesterday?"

"I couldn't talk about it. My demon was in a *major* snit. Even hearing his name would have sent the entity into a violent fucking tailspin. I couldn't trust that it wouldn't take over and go track him." Her demon was extremely fond of torture, and it had all sorts of plans for Holt—it had been dreaming up ways to make him suffer for years. "It's a little calmer now. Its anger isn't wild and unrestrained; it's cold and controlled."

"Good." Knox paused. "This is why you were a little tense yesterday at dinner. You were not only wound up over Holt's reappearance, you were striving to keep your demon from losing it."

For the most part, yes. There was also the little titbit that she'd been uncomfortably horny, courtesy of Teague's roaming hands and kinky telepathic images. But she felt no need to share that with her brothers. "Teague deliberately did a good job of distracting me."

Tanner tipped his head to the side. "You told him about Holt?"

"No," replied Larkin. "He just sensed that something was wrong and set out to divert my attention."

Knox let out a thoughtful hum. "You should tell him. If Holt intends to linger, he'll see you with Teague. Holt might even approach him. You don't want Teague to be caught off-guard like that, do you?"

She hadn't considered that might happen. And no, she didn't want the hellhorse to be sucker-punched with the situation. "I'll tell him later."

Keenan reached back and palmed his nape. "Holt might not stick around. He might have returned to Canada by now."

Larkin rubbed at her breastbone. "I did a little research." A little hacking, to be precise. "He's staying at The Charon Hotel. He hasn't checked out yet. His room is booked for three weeks."

"Three?" echoed Levi, his brows hitching up. He muttered a curse of annoyance.

Knox pursed his lips. "Then it would seem he came here with every intention of doing as he said and spending time earning your trust."

Like three weeks would have been enough even if she *had* been interested in letting him into her life.

Keenan turned to the Prime. "But now that he knows she isn't interested in giving him a shot, he might respect her wishes and leave."

"I don't know," said Larkin, doubtful. "This is Holt we're talking about. When has he ever respected my wishes?"

"Never," Keenan allowed. "That said, he might—for once—choose to back off."

She sighed. "I guess. Stranger things have happened. And I did make it abundantly clear that he has no hope of convincing me to form the bond. Plus, he's a Prime now. He can't afford to be away from his lair for long."

Knox rubbed at his jaw. "I could pay him a visit and strongly suggest he leave."

Larkin thought about it for a moment. "It may come to that. But first, I'd like to see if he returns home of his own accord. It could be his intention. But if you turn up at his hotel room and pressure him to get on a plane, he could choose to stay merely to make a point that he owes you no compliance."

Levi looked at Knox. "She's right. You wouldn't react well to another Prime laying down the law, however civilly they did it."

Knox stiffly tilted his head, reluctantly conceding that. "I'll give him a chance to make the right choice." He slid his eyes back to Larkin. "But if he doesn't, if he becomes a problem, I will deal with it—both as your family and your Prime."

Swallowing, she nodded.

Levi sidled up to her and curled his arm around her shoulder. "I'm sorry that you have such a fuckhead for an anchor."

She exhaled heavily. "Yeah, me too."

CHAPTER SIX

I really don't see the problem, said Khloë, her mind brushing his.

Leaning his body just right to make a sharp turn on his bike, Teague agreed, *It is a little unfair to you.*

I know, right? It's not like I asked for a kidney or something.

Disregarding the speed limit, he carefully weaved his bike between a car and a bus, smiling when horns subsequently beeped at him in complaint.

I only want to take Anaïs to get her ears pierced, Khloë added.

Quality time with your kind-of-niece.

Yes! Tanner was all like 'you are not mutilating my daughter'. As if I was gonna start hacking off body parts.

People were weird sometimes. *Total overreaction.*

Amen. Why can't more people be on our wavelength, Teague? The world would truly be a better place. Not saying that parts of it wouldn't be on fire or pure wasteland, but it would still be better.

Approaching an amber light, Teague upped his speed, managing to pass through the traffic lights a mere second before they turned red. *Maybe we should look into global domination again.*

I promised Keenan I wouldn't, she grumbled. *He freaked out when he heard my plans to take over the planet. Like it's some big deal.*

Teague frowned. *You'd make an awesome world leader.*

That's what I said. Keenan insisted I'd eventually get executed by the people under my command after I'd driven them insane.

Maybe, but . . . *Sanity is overrated.*

I couldn't agree more. She paused. *He's back. Gotta go. Say hi to the guys for me.*

Will do, he told her just as he took the turn that would lead him out of the small urban area toward the large sections of undeveloped land that was approximately twenty minutes away from his home.

He'd had to pop out to grab a few things from the local minimart which, due to his camp being smack bam in the middle of nowhere, was a thirty-minute journey by bike.

There was a slight breeze tonight, but it wasn't so cool that he was sorry he hadn't worn his riding gloves. Unlike his demon, he didn't mind the cold.

He passed pastureland, forested areas, and privately owned stretches of land that weren't occupied by people or animals. Soon, he reached the roads that were only really used by those who lived in this area, which was mainly farmers.

His clan had together purchased their own plot of land from a farmer years ago. The human hadn't been keen on selling, but it hadn't taken much to convince him. Especially when they'd offered him more cash than the plot was worth.

A mind again touched Teague's, feminine and familiar. It wasn't Khloë's this time. It was Larkin's.

Just a quick heads-up, the harpy said. *My psi-mate—who I haven't claimed and never will—is unfortunately in Vegas.*

Teague felt his brows lift. He hadn't known she'd found her anchor.

So if a blond guy with a Canadian accent comes up to you and starts asking questions about our 'relationship' or gives you any trouble, let me know, she went on. *I'll deal with it.*

She'd said it all so casually, in a sort of 'by the way, this is no big thing, but just so you know' manner. But Teague wasn't at all buying that she felt in any way nonchalant about it. Who *would* be blasé about having such an ill relationship with your anchor that you never intended to claim your rights as their psi-mate?

Why is he in Vegas? Teague asked her.

Holt wants to form the anchor bond. I don't. He's hoping to change my mind on that.

His name was Holt? Teague disliked him already. He'd never met a person with that name who he hadn't found annoying. Then again, he found a fair amount of people annoying.

I told him I won't agree to his request, but he's difficult and stubborn, so he might not return to Canada straight away, she continued. *As he's now Prime of his lair, he shouldn't hang around too long. He'll need to get back to his demons.*

Teague couldn't help but frown, totally thrown by the whole situation—by her refusal to form the bond, by her clear lack of affection for her anchor, by how she'd rather chance turning rogue than have the male in her life. *Why are you so against claiming him?*

Why is there no record of your past? she shot back.

He felt his lips twitch. He did love it when she used that snarky tone.

Holt probably won't bother you, she said. *I simply wanted to warn you that he's around just in case he decided to approach you.* Her mind bumped his slightly, and then it was gone before he could ask more questions.

And he *did* have more questions. Like was this why she'd been in such a state yesterday evening? Had she somehow found out then that her anchor was in Vegas? And if so, why had she been determined to hide it from everyone at Jolene's dinner table?

He also wondered if there was any chance of Holt talking her into forming the bond. It didn't seem likely, because Teague had come to learn something about his harpy: when she firmly made up her mind on something, there was no changing it.

But then . . . this was no simple situation. This was the matter of her psi-mate; of the anchor bond being her only protection against her demon one day gaining supremacy over her.

Teague had never before met anyone who'd rejected their psi-mate, though he knew it happened. Such a decision wasn't made lightly. He couldn't imagine that Larkin would reject her own anchor without good reason.

His beast rumbled a displeased sound as it wondered if the male had harmed her. Teague highly doubted it. The guy would surely be dead if that were the case—either Larkin or her demon would have seen to that. If they'd somehow failed, Knox would have stepped in. Or even one of the sentinels so that—

Something slammed into the side of Teague's bike, knocking it down. Pain streaked up his leg, arm, and shoulder as the bike went skidding along the road, dragging him with it; making the air ring with the sound of metal scraping gravel.

Shock made him blink. *The fuck?*

He lifted his head, and his insides seized. An all-black human-oid figure stood a few feet away, a ball of hellfire in its hand. A ball that then came flying toward Teague.

He swore beneath his breath. He didn't have enough time or space to duck. He could only brace himself for impact.

The orb hit his helmet hard, sharply jolting his head, sending hot pain lancing up the side of his neck. The helmet suffered no damage, protected as it was by magickal wards, but it heated up *fast*. And, as such, so did his goddamn scalp.

Even as he pitched two high-powered orbs of hellfire at his attacker one-handed, he unstrapped and yanked off the helmet with a pained hiss. One of his orbs hit their target. The other crashed into a tree far behind it, lighting it up and sending bits of bark scattering through the air.

Cursing under his breath again, Teague flicked his hand, easing the flames before they could consume the tree and spread. His beast reared within him, wanting to—

A beam of hellfire soared his way.

He slammed up his helmet to block it. The force of it hitting the helmet made his wrist wrench backwards, causing pain to streak through the joint, but it successfully knocked the beam off course.

Teague threw the helmet aside and quickly but awkwardly pulled his body out from under the bike. He'd no sooner stood than a black swirling orb clipped his head. Solid as a rock, it blazed along the side of his scalp, burning like nothing else. *Hell-acid.*

His furious beast reared up again, kicking its forelegs. Feeling his upper lip peel back, Teague lobbed a flaming ball at the humanoid's own head, going for those pure-white eyes.

A tentacle shot out of the humanoid's front and batted away the orb. Then that same tentacle surged toward Teague, aiming for his throat.

Fuck that.

Calling hellfire to his fist, he punched the tentacle hard. It reared back a few inches. He gripped it tight and sent a surge of hellfire racing up the tentacle too fast to be dodged. The humanoid jerked back in pain, and the tentacle withdrew from his hand in a flash of movement so forceful that it almost made him stagger.

Teague and the shadowkin then went on to exchange blow after blow. Despite his attempts to duck and weave, a few hell-acid orbs landed—one on his jaw, one on his kneecap, another on his chest—and he felt the scalding scrape of a hellfire beam down his arm, burning cloth and skin.

His fast-bruising wounds prickled and sizzled and blistered. The scents of corroding skin, burned cloth, and fresh blood clogged his nostrils. The adrenaline dimmed the pain, but only slightly.

Teague ground his teeth. "Why are you doing this? Why have you come for me?"

A series of telepathic images flickered through Teague's mind, answering his questions. His nostrils flaring, Teague snapped his teeth shut as pure rage clawed its way through him, thick and vicious. *Son of a fucking bitch.*

His demon again bucked within him, rumbling snarls. It wanted to rise, but they were on a public road. There was no way Teague could let his hellhorse free here, where it could be seen by humans.

His entity gave no fucks about that. Not a single one. It violently shoved its way to the surface.

The beast felt a brief whip of pain as it took its own form, appearing in a billow of ash and smoke. The air quickly lost its haze. Holding its head and tail high, the hellhorse pawed the ground as it stared down its opponent.

Anger coursed through the demon, tightening its muscles and making its legs quiver with the need to lunge. The steed would destroy the shadowkin. In doing so, it would also send a message to the humanoid's dispatcher that could not be ignored.

Stamping the ground with one leg, the hellhorse flattened its ears and bared its venom-tipped teeth. Then it charged with a roar-scream.

The shadowkin spun and fled toward the forest. It headed right for a thick shadow that was the silhouette of a large tree. The humanoid was incredibly fast.

But not as fast as the hellhorse.

It slammed its hooves into the demon and knocked it down flat. Giving the shadowkin no chance to stand, the steed kicked and stamped on it again and again and again—going for its head, spine, and legs with scorching-hot hooves.

The shadowkin's signature scent of brimstone and smoke quickly became tainted with notes of fear and pain. The hellhorse drank it in. Reveled in it. Was fueled by it.

When its prey's struggles grew weak, the steed breathed out a powerful blast of hellfire, setting the humanoid alight. The flames quickly and greedily ate its body and consumed its brain.

Puffing thick noxious air out of its nostrils, the hellhorse watched as the shadowkin steadily became a puddle of ashes. Only then did the beast retreat, allowing Teague to resurface.

Cricking his neck, Teague looked down at what was left of his attacker. With a sharp wave of his hand, he eased away the small blaze of hellfire and ground his teeth. God, he was pissed. Not only with his inner demon—who gave a haughty, unapologetic chuff—for surfacing here, but with the shadowkin who'd attacked him . . . and with the bastard who'd sicced him on Teague like a fucking dog.

Once the ashes began to scatter with the breeze, a now-naked Teague returned to his bike. The shift had burned his clothes to cinders, leaving not one scrap of cloth behind.

He righted his bike. It didn't have a scratch on it, since it was protected by the same magickal wards as his helmet. He fished spare clothes out of the saddlebag and quickly pulled them on.

His helmet was no longer roasting hot, but there was no way he was wearing it over the damn acidic burns on his jaw and scalp. Instead, he shoved it into his saddlebag and then mounted the bike.

He'd known that more shadowkin would likely be sent his way. He'd known they'd be forced to attack him while he was away from his territory, since the border of black salt kept them off his land. But he hadn't expected to be blindsided while driving.

As he rode home, each slap of the breeze against his corroding flesh hurt like a mother. The injuries began to heal fairly quickly, but not so quickly that they were gone by the time he arrived at the camp.

Sitting across from each other at the picnic table, Saxon and Leo looked up as he drove into view. So did Gideon and Slade, who had each claimed one of the logs surrounding the firepit. All four males went completely still as they took in the state of him.

The moment Teague parked his bike outside his wagon, Leo slapped his playing cards down on the picnic table and said, "Mother of bleeding Christ, what happened to you?"

Teague tossed him a grim smile. "Shadowkin."

His clan mates cursed, not quite overriding the calls of alarm coming from the ravens perched on the oak branches—they puffed up their feathers and flapped their wings.

His face hard, Slade rose from the log and took stock of him. "Where did it attack you this time?" he asked as Gideon called out to the rest of their clan.

Teague dismounted the bike with a grunt, a few aches from the crash making themselves known now that the adrenaline was fast bleeding from his system. He gave quick pets to the dogs that surrounded him as he replied, "In the middle of the road, not far from here."

Feeling his tee sticking to some of his injuries, Teague whipped it off, grinding his teeth at the fiery licks of pain. A collage of bruises, scorch wounds, blisters, and patches of acidic burns, his body was not a pretty sight right then. "It knocked me off my bike."

The front door of Archer's wagon burst open. He and Tucker stepped out onto the porch, followed by a cloud of smoke and the unmistakable scent of marijuana.

Archer glared at Gideon. "What's with the shouting? *Must* there be shouting? Really?"

Gideon pointed at Teague. "I personally think that another shadowkin attack is something to yell about."

Tucker winced in sympathy and descended the wagon steps. "Damn, T. It hit you with hell-acid, huh?"

Teague grunted in confirmation.

"Where's the little shit now?" Tucker asked.

"Dead," Teague replied, dropping his ruined tee on the seat of his bike. "My demon killed it."

His brows snapping together, Saxon laid down his cards. "Your demon? You let it free on a damn public road?"

"I didn't *let* it do anything." Teague crossed to a log and plonked his ass on it. "It took control before I had the chance to fight it for supremacy."

Tucker scowled at Saxon. "Would you not jump down the poor guy's throat?" There was a slight creak as he sank onto one of the lawn chairs. "He's got hell-acid eating at him as we damn speak."

Saxon shot him an unimpressed look. "Pipe down, little man, I wasn't talking to you."

His mouth flattening, Tucker clenched the arms of his chair. "I'm five-foot-eight, as you well know. That makes me average height, as you well know. Just because the rest of you are taller and bulkier than me does *not* make me short. So fuck you, Van Diesel."

Saxon's face went hard. "I don't look anything like Van Diesel."

"I think his name is Vin," Slade cut in. "Just tossing that out there. Do with it what you will."

His lips quirking in spite of his mood, Teague drew in a deep breath through his nose, inhaling the scents of smoke, pine needles, beer, and coffee laced with liquor. Aside for the glow of the crackling flames and the light beaming through the side window of Archer's wagon, the only source of light came from the battery-powered lantern on the picnic table.

"Did any humans catch a glimpse of your demon?" Saxon asked.

"No, no one saw a thing." Noticing that the dogs were slowly prowling around, unsettled, Teague patted his uninjured leg and whistled to call them over. Too on edge, they continued to prowl and sniff and explore the clearing suspiciously.

Slade pulled two cans of beer out of the chest beside his log and offered one to Teague, who gratefully took it. "Did you learn anything from the shadowkin before it went and got itself dead?" he asked, retaking his spot on the log opposite Teague and flicking open the tab on his can.

"A little," Teague replied, stretching out his legs. "You were right. Vine didn't try to use shadowkin to get me executed. Neither did Zagan, just as Leo predicted. It was the person who now holds my old position."

"And who's that?" asked Gideon, leaning forward to rest his lower arms on his thighs.

Teague felt a muscle in his cheek tick. "Ronin."

Silence fell, thick and taut.

Sitting on the top step of his porch, Archer did a slow blink and raised an index finger. "Ronin as in your half-brother Ronin?"

There was a hiss of sound as Teague opened his beer can. "One and the same."

Gideon's jaw dropped. "No way. Maybe I shouldn't be surprised, but I am. I mean, I know you two never got along—"

"Understatement," Archer chipped in.

Gideon inclined his head. "Okay, so he hates you, Teague. And he was always jealous as hell that you were recruited. But there's a big difference between resenting someone for being born and actively attempting to have their existence erased. Plus, well, you share blood."

"That means nothing to him. Never did." Teague took a swig of his cold beer. "Can't say it ever meant much to me either. He's too much like our father."

Saxon lifted his insulated mug. "Sending someone to execute you is by no means beneath Ronin, but this doesn't fully add up. He always coveted your old position. He finally has it. He'll lose it if people find out what he's doing. Why take that chance?"

Slade shrugged. "I suppose he figures that no one will ever know. It's not like anyone monitors us, is it? We've been left alone since we retired."

"Until now," said Tucker.

Yes, until now. "You know, he often told me that he'd one day see me dead. I never took him seriously."

Leo's forehead creased. "Why would you? He's mostly full of piss and wind."

"But why bother at this point in our lives, when I'm not in the picture?" Teague questioned, rolling back his aching shoulder. "Saxon's right, it doesn't fully add up. It's not like our father's infidelity is rubbed in Ronin's face on a daily basis anymore, is it? He has the luxury of pretending I don't exist."

"It does seem like an overreaction," conceded Leo. "Why come for you? What does he hope to achieve? Ronin is a spiteful piece of shit who hated that the brother he believes shouldn't exist managed to outshine him in every way. But if he now has the two things he always wanted—you off the scene, and the position he currently enjoys—he should be reasonably content."

"Whatever the case, Ronin is nothing we can't handle," Saxon upheld, unworried. "I don't see a reason for us to alter our game plan."

"The best thing we can do is stick to it," said Teague before taking another swig from his can. "With each attack that fails, Ronin will get more pissed. And with each time I fail to retaliate as he expects, he'll grow even more pissed." And as it occurred to Teague that there was a chance Larkin could get caught in the crossfire, his gut knotted.

It wasn't *likely* to happen. Ronin wouldn't want to anger other demons and find himself a target of lairs—not even his position would protect him from the consequences—so he'd order the shadowkin to only attack if Teague was alone or with his clan. The order wouldn't be disobeyed. Still, Teague wasn't comfortable taking that chance.

She could defend herself just fine, yes. She was tougher than most people he knew, and it was no small thing that she had the ability to conjure hell-ice. That stuff was potent. But he didn't want her to get caught up in this fucked-up mess; didn't want Ronin or the asshole's minions anywhere near her.

Maybe it would be better to pull out of their deal. He'd done more daring things than sing naked at a bar. He could claim that he couldn't handle the celibacy—she'd find that easy to believe; wouldn't become suspicious and start poking her nose into his business.

Besides, she had enough going on in her own life right now. That thought made him mentally falter. Her psi-mate, who she clearly had no time or liking for, was back on the scene. More, if Holt was as stubborn a person as she claimed, he might well be a problem. Might refuse to accept her wishes. For all she'd tried to assure Teague that it was no real biggie, it was clear that she was braced for trouble.

What concerned him was that it wasn't unheard of for demons to kill a psi-mate who refused to form the bond. It was rare. But it did happen.

Maybe the guy meant Larkin no harm. But maybe he did. Or maybe he'd one day snap and attempt to harm her if she continued to reject him.

The thought made Teague's lungs contract.

She'd never accept protection from him or anyone else—she was a sentinel, and she'd consider herself to be her own body-guard. As such, Teague could only really look out for her if he kept up their charade, because she wouldn't otherwise spend any time with him.

He'd continue with their act for now, he decided. To pull out of it on the mere basis that his half-brother *might* forget to warn a shadowkin to only attack Teague when he was alone seemed like an overreaction anyway.

"Do you really think Ronin will come here?" Archer asked, snapping Teague out of his thoughts.

Taking another swig of his beer, Teague stroked the hound who came to his side. Barron leaned into the move, his eyes going hooded. Glad to see that the dogs were finally settling and taking positions around the firepit, he replied, "Yes. Ronin won't back down. If the shadowkin continue to fail—and we'll make sure they do—he'll come at me himself eventually to personally see to it that I'm good and dead."

"He won't come alone," Saxon stated. "He won't be satisfied with only ending you. He'll come prepared to take us all out."

"Yup," agreed Teague with an annoyed sigh. "There's no way he'd kill me but allow you all to live. He'd know that you'd avenge my death or, at the very least, alert his superiors to what he's done. He won't risk that."

"How many demons do you think he'll bring with him?" asked

Tucker, using a pocket knife to carve sticks he'd no doubt use for roasting hot dogs at some point.

Teague licked the front of his teeth. "Enough that we'll be outnumbered so he can feel sure he walks away the victor."

"No amount of backup will gain him victory," said Slade, his face hardening. "If he comes for us, he'll die."

"Oh yeah," agreed Teague. "He'll die. And so will whoever he brings with him."

CHAPTER SEVEN

Khloë thumped her shot glass down on the scarred wooden table. "It's a relevant question."

"How is it relevant?" Harper challenged. "Seriously?"

The imp elbowed her cousin. "It is to *me*, okay. I just want to know how Noah could *possibly* have fit two of, like, seven million species on an ark. I mean, how big was this goddamn ark? And where can I get one?"

"What would you do with it?" asked Piper, swaying to the loud music playing over the bar's speakers.

Khloë looked away, pensive. "I gotta admit, I don't know."

Larkin tossed back some of her fruity drink, enjoying the burst of sweetness against her tongue. "I don't think Keenan would be down with you keeping a huge-ass ark in your yard. Just a thought." She set her glass down on a square cardboard coaster, telling herself that she had *not* just drunkenly weaved.

Beside her, Raini frowned, her amber eyes a little glassy, and pulled the plastic stirrer out of her mouth. "You still haven't finished your drink."

Larkin felt her nose wrinkle. "I don't think it would be a good idea for me to get blitzed."

"Well, let me tell you, that ship has *sailed*," Khloë told her with a swipe of her hand. "You left sober at the door hours ago."

Larkin grimaced. "I was afraid of that." *Dammit.* "How did it even happen? I didn't drink as much as you guys."

"But you were ordering pretty strong drinks," Harper reminded her. "And you were mixing them."

"Why is it a big deal, Lark?" asked Devon, sitting on her other side. "Your shift is over. A girls' night is so much more fun when we're plastered. And some bodyguards are hanging around, so you don't have to worry that you'll need to leap into action if shit goes down."

Larkin only let out a low hum. When the girls had invited her to the Xpress bar, she'd agreed to go, needing the distraction. Her demon had encouraged her to 'let go', have fun, drink to excess, and forget about Holt for a while. Larkin and the other women had had fun talking, laughing, drinking, dancing, and snapping pictures with their phones.

This particular bar was one of the upscale hot spots within the Underground. Neon, strobe lights slashed through the dark space and beamed through the fog. People were everywhere— the bar, the tables, the dance floor, the stage where the DJ performed.

It was always busy and it could get plenty rowdy to the point where the patrons would dance on speakers or tables, or even on the long bar. Khloë had been guilty of that many times.

"Are you worried that that asshole anchor of yours might turn up?" asked Khloë. "Is that why you didn't want to leave 'sober' so far behind?"

Larkin had told the women about him earlier, and they now predictably despised him. "He probably wouldn't come near me unless I was alone, but it seems better to have all my wits about me just in case I'm wrong."

She hadn't seen anything of Holt since he'd showed up at her building three days ago, but he hadn't checked out of his hotel room. He was still in Vegas. It would only be a matter of time before he approached her again.

As such, lobbing back mounds of alcohol wasn't the wisest thing for her to do. But it had been a while since she'd downed such strong drinks, and she'd forgotten how hard they hit.

"If Holt shows, we'll pounce on him as a group," said Khloë, playing with two lemon wedges, bitch-slapping each with the other. "As for you not wanting to be so blitzed, I have a solution: More shots."

Piper's brow furrowed. "I'm not seeing how that's a solution. What am I missing?"

"We could drink ourselves sober," the imp suggested. "It's a thing."

Raini raised a hand, once more removing the plastic stirrer from between her teeth. "I am *all* for this. But I want a rum and uh, you know, that thing . . ."

"Coke?" supplied Harper.

Raini clicked her fingers. "That's the one." Shoving her pink-streaked blonde hair over her shoulder, she gave the sphinx a bright, grateful smile. "I can always rely on you to have the answers to my problems."

Khloë put a hand to her chest. "Aw, that's such a sweet thing to say. Why don't you say it to *me*? I give you advice."

"You give me advice that will *cause* me problems," said Raini. "And you do it because you find the aftermath entertaining."

"It doesn't mean I don't love you."

"I know. And I love you too."

"For realsies?"

Raini wrapped her arms around the imp. "For realsies." She let out a happy sigh. "You smell like chocolate."

"Oh, I had a white Hershtley bar earlier ... or whatever they're called."

Harper pulled a face. "They don't *really* count as chocolate."

Khloë blinked. "Huh?"

"White chocolate is just cocoa butter mixed with sugar and dairy milk and sweeteners like vanilla," Harper expanded. "It doesn't have the cocoa solids that are in both milk and dark chocolate."

Khloë let out a disbelieving snort. "You talk such bullshit at times."

"It's true!" Harper insisted.

"Uh, yeah, okay."

"It is! How can you so strongly doubt *that* yet fully believe that the moon's made of cheese?"

"I trust my source. Aunt Mildred—"

"Ain't real," Devon cut in. "And neither is white chocolate."

Khloë slammed up a hand. "Whatevs, bitches. Now I want shots." She looked at the succubus who was still hugging her. "You coming?"

Raini let her arms slip away from the imp and then leaned back in her seat. "Leave me here. I'll only slow you down."

"No shots for me," said Larkin. "I'm sticking to water for the rest of the night."

Harper nodded. "Water it is." She, Piper, and Khloë then made their way to the bar.

Devon took a sip of her cocktail. "If it makes you feel better, Lark, you're not as hammered as Raini. I don't think anyone in this bar is as hammered as Raini is right now."

"Why *is* she in such a state?" From what Larkin had observed, the succubus wasn't a lightweight.

"She made a rookie mistake and drank on an empty stomach. I told her not to, but she wouldn't listen."

"I hate it when people don't listen. And when they won't go away. And when they screw you over and think you'll simply just let it go." Like Holt. Who she wasn't supposed to be thinking about. Ugh.

"I can't imagine how hard it must be to have a psi-mate you'd prefer to shoot in the dick than bond with." Devon idly stroked her fingertip down her highball glass, smudging the sheen of condensation. "How come you never told us about him before?"

Larkin lifted her glass. "Don't take it personally. I make a point of not talking about him with anyone unless I absolutely have to. I prefer to pretend he doesn't exist." Cubes of ice clinked against the glass and bumped her lips as she took a sip of her drink.

"I guess I can understand that. It's just that I'm sitting here remembering all the times I gushed about how much I adored my anchor and am grateful for how fabulous he is. The whole time, it must have hurt you to hear it."

"No, no, it didn't, I swear. Don't get me wrong, when people talk happily and proudly about their psi-mates, I sometimes find myself thinking just how different things could be if my anchor hadn't been Holt. But I never feel jealous of others or resent what they have."

"Then you're a better person than I am, because I'm pretty sure I'd be green-eyed with envy and want to go—Jesus, Raini, get off the floor. What are you doing down there anyway?"

Flat on her ass, the succubus glanced around, confused. "I don't know. I was on my chair. And then I wasn't. Like magic."

She grinned at her martini glass. "But look, I didn't spill my drink."

Devon gave her a thumbs up. "Impressive."

"Here, I'll help you." Larkin carefully assisted the succubus in returning to her seat—not the easiest thing in the world, since Larkin wasn't too steady herself.

"Thank you." Raini leaned into her. "You're the best harpy in the history of the universe. Don't let anyone tell ya different." Closing her eyes, she settled right there against Larkin's side.

"How about we shove aside the subject of your wasteless anchor and talk about how things are going with you and Teague," Devon proposed.

"I'm all for the first part of your suggestion," replied Larkin. "But I ain't giving you details on my relationship with Teague." She hadn't seen him since dinner at Jolene's house, but she'd really, really wanted to.

Strange though she found it, she'd missed him. A little. Sort of. In a sense.

"I know you're a private person but *come on* tell me something."

Larkin shook her head at the hellcat. "You are so damn nosy."

"But in an endearing way, right?" Devon put a hand on her arm. "I just want a few juicy details and then I'll let it go. Until then, I'm gonna keep pestering you. I will not be distracted. I'm definitely not gonna—ooh, shots." She sat up straighter as Harper placed a tray on the table.

Retaking her seat, Khloë nudged Raini. "Hey, wake up."

The succubus's eyelids flickered open, and she righted herself . . . only to weave and bump into Khloë. "Hey, watch where you're walking."

"I'm not walking," said the imp. "*You're* not walking either."

Raini looked down at herself. "Oh yeah. You coulda told me

sooner." She lounged back in her seat, and her eyes once more fell shut.

"She'll be fine," Khloë decided. "So, what are we talking about?"

Devon opened her mouth and then frowned. "I don't remember." She looked at Larkin. "Do you?"

Actually . . . "No. But let's think of something we could talk about. Something deep. Meaningful. Intriguing."

Piper's eyes gleamed. "Ooh, like what?"

"I have something," Khloë announced. "Okay, do we think that invisible pink unicorns really exist?"

Harper tipped her head to the side. "If they do, they're invisible. So we wouldn't know."

"But we can speculate," Khloë pointed out. "So let's speculate."

They did that for a little while, right up until Raini's head snapped up and her eyes flipped open like she'd been dealt a slap. "Hmm, Maddox is coming for me in a minute," the blonde announced, sitting upright.

"So is Knox." Harper tapped her temple, adding, "He gave me a telepathic heads-up not too long ago." She swept her gaze over Larkin, Piper, Khloë, and Devon. "He said that your guys are on their way, too."

"Our guys?" Larkin echoed.

"Yup."

Surely not. Larkin telepathically reached out to Teague. *Are you heading to the Xpress bar?*

His mind touched hers, and then his voice poured into her mind like a river. *I figured I better had, since Tanner telepathed me to say you were blitzed. It was obviously a test to see if I'd come take you home.*

Freaking interfering hellhound. She might have missed Teague, but she would rather he didn't see her while she was wasted. If she did or said something dumb, he'd never let it go. He'd tease her about it for all eternity.

Maddox materialized on the spot between Khloë and Raini's chair. It had to be said that the man. Was. Fine. Tall and dark with striking Prussian blue eyes.

His sentinel, Hector, appeared behind him, at which point Raini's bodyguard sidled up to him.

The succubus smiled up at her mate, looking the epitome of lovestruck. "Hey. You're taller than I remember."

Maddox's lips twitched. "You're more plastered than I thought you'd be."

"Funny how things work out, huh?" Raini awkwardly stood. "Bye girlies."

Hugs and air-kisses and waves were quickly exchanged before Maddox, Raini, and their bodyguards teleported out of there.

Knox and the male sentinels appeared only moments later. Both Harper and Piper immediately stood to greet their mates, but both Devon and Khloë remained slumped on their seats.

"What's wrong?" Keenan asked his mate.

Khloë pouted. "I can't find my lipstick."

"It's in your drink," he told her.

She blinked down at the small tube floating in her half-empty glass. "Huh. How did that happen?"

Tanner squeezed Devon's shoulder. "Come on, kitten, up you go."

"Someone stood on my foot," whined the hellcat. "It hurts."

"To stand?" he asked.

Devon shook her head. "No."

Tanner flicked a hand. "Then get up."

Piper snorted at him. "Dude, you are stone cold. Carry her or something. You're supposed to be her white knight."

"Speaking of white, Harper keeps saying there's no such thing as white chocolate," Khloë groused to her mate, using a napkin to dry her lipstick.

Keenan sighed at Harper. "Did you really have to tell her that? She's gonna whine about it all night, and *I'll* be the one who has to listen to it."

The sphinx grinned. "You have fun with that."

"Teague!" hollered Khloë, waving.

Her pulse skittering, Larkin tracked the imp's gaze. Striding toward their table, he flashed his anchor a grin that made Larkin's stomach churn with jealousy; her demon didn't like it either. But then his gaze slid to Larkin, and his grin widened as it became something else—something sexy and warm and purely for her.

Stopping in front of her chair, he stroked her hair. "Hey there, baby."

Larkin smiled, unable to pretend to herself that she didn't like his use of the endearment. "How's it going, Black Beauty?"

"Better now." He helped her stand, chuckling when she stumbled. "Easy." Ignoring her insistence that she could do it herself, he slipped her jacket on her. "Now let's go before you pass out."

Affronted, she huffed. "I won't pass out."

"Uh-huh."

The hand on the small of her back steered her away from the table and out of the bar. As they all walked to the elevator, she sniffed at the sight of her friends leaning against their guys ... only to frown when she realized she was letting Teague take some of her weight.

Too tired and mentally fuzzy to care, she didn't push away from him. Or step back when he held her close in the elevator. Or argue when he insisted on helping her climb the basement stairs of the club.

But she *did* telepathically tell her demon to stop sending her images of him fucking her hard.

The entity, being the little bitch that it was, didn't listen.

Outside the club, Teague guided Larkin straight to Saxon's truck. He'd never seen her drunk before. She was cute as fuck. Sniffing and huffing and frowning. He should have guessed that his prickly harpy would turn even pricklier when smashed.

He wasn't surprised when she passed out during the journey to her complex. She was gonna be pissed about that tomorrow. The idea made him smile.

When he arrived at her building, Teague lifted her out of the car and hoisted her up. She slumped against him, her arms dangling over his shoulders. As he carried her to the main door, he couldn't help but chuckle to himself. She was going to be mad at herself for this, too.

Tanner held open the door for him while keeping his mate plastered against his side. Teague tipped his chin in thanks and breezed into the lobby. There, Levi and Piper were walking into the elevator. Teague followed them inside, closely followed by Tanner and Devon.

Teague didn't miss how the other two males watched to see which button he'd push on the panel. They clearly wanted to see if he knew where Larkin's apartment was—that would be a clue as to if she truly was his girlfriend.

As it happened, Teague would have had no idea what apartment she lived at if Piper hadn't telepathically told him mere moments ago.

A short elevator ride later, he strolled along the hallway toward Larkin's front door. Piper came to his rescue again, fishing the harpy's set of keys out of her jacket and then unlocking the door. Teague thanked her, took the keys, and then carried Larkin inside, closing the door behind them.

Her apartment smelled like her. Rich and heady and feminine. The living space was bright and spacious. No bold colors or frills. The tones were gentle and earthy—mostly pastel shades that gave it a calming feel.

Walking along the hall in search of her bedroom, he saw that the 'gentle and earthy' look continued throughout. Finally reaching his destination, he carried her inside. The space was soothing with its crème and lavender color theme. There were no throw pillows or unnecessary accessories on his harpy's bed. That made pulling back the duvet easier.

He placed her keys on her nightstand and then laid her carefully on her bed. Her head lolled to the side, but she didn't otherwise move. He managed to remove her jacket and shoes without jostling her too much. Not that it disturbed her sleep— she was totally out of it.

Suspecting she might be uncomfortable sleeping with her hair braided—okay, fine, he wanted to see that glossy curtain free around her face just once—he gently removed the hair tie and then carefully unraveled as much of the braid as he could reach.

The strands were so soft and sleek they almost felt cool to the touch. Like silk. And when her curls were fanned all over the pillow, he felt his gut clench. It took everything he had not to bury his hands in them.

Teague stared down at her. Fuck, she was beautiful. Everything he looked for in a woman—fearless, confident, badass, accepting, strong-willed. If their situations weren't what they were, if things had been different . . . But they weren't different. Never would be.

He gently squeezed her leg. "Sleep well, harpy."

He turned on his heel and strode toward the door, his libido firmly protesting and—

"I did not say you could leave."

He halted. That wasn't Larkin's voice. Well, it was. But it wasn't. Her tone was never flat and emotionless, unlike the one he'd heard mere seconds ago. Which meant that it wasn't Larkin who spoke; it was her demon.

Teague slowly pivoted on the spot. The demon was sat upright, its pure black eyes focused on him. It slinked off the bed, fluid as a snake.

His own demon pushed close to the surface and watched as hers began to circle him. A predator appraising him somewhat objectively. As if he were an object as opposed to a person.

There was a light of something not quite sane in the dark orbs that stared at him. That light intrigued both him and his beast. But, not about to be continually circled as if he were prey, Teague flicked up a brow and asked, "Should I be flattered that you can't seem to look away?"

The demon came to a stop in front of him and cocked its head. "I like the shape of your skull."

He blinked at the matter-of-fact statement. A statement that was also a clear indication that the demon was contemplating what part of him it might keep as a trophy if it chose to kill him. "Uh, okay."

"You and I must talk."

Sounded ominous.

It backed him into the bed, pushed him down, and then straddled him.

Well, all right.

He splayed his hands on its thighs. "What do you want to talk about?"

The demon traced his hairline with a fingertip. "He will be trouble."

"He? Your psi-mate, you mean?"

Something ugly rippled in its eyes. "He *would* have been my anchor if he were not worthless. I want to obliterate him so completely that it will be as if he never existed. But my killing him would create problems between the two lairs unless it is a matter of self-defense."

"You want to provoke him," Teague sensed, nodding in approval.

"It will be easy. He wants more than an anchor bond from her. Much more." The demon poked his chest. "You will help me make him jealous. Then he will attack. And I will then shatter every bone in his body one by one, until he is a twisted, disfigured mess. It will be somewhat epic."

Teague couldn't help but smile. He really liked this demon. "Can I watch?"

It pursed its lips. "Perhaps. If you are still alive."

"Still alive?"

"It may be that you have betrayed her between now and then. People seem to enjoy betraying her one way or another. If you join them in that, I will destroy you. But I will leave your skull intact and strip it down to the bone. It will make a nice ornament."

He chuckled. "A nice ornament, huh?" His beast let out an amused chuff as it paced just beneath his skin, riveted by the entity, wanting its attention. "That's not a compliment I've been paid before."

Its head twitched to the side. "You do not fear me. Pity. I like the smell of fear. I like to see it dance in a person's eyes."

"I like whales."

Its mouth slowly quirked, and then it giggled. The creepy sound trailed down his spine like icy fingers and made an honest to God's shiver wrack his body.

"You are fun," it said. "How strong is your pain threshold?"

"You want to torture me?"

"I would not kill you. Or break your mind. I would just like to see how you look when terror lights your gaze. It is such a shame that the emotion bleeds out of a person's eyes when they die, or I would keep all their severed heads on shelves."

A slow smile spread across Teague's face. "I have to say, you fucking *fascinate* me."

"Then you will sign up for a session in torture?"

He snorted. "Uh, no. Your assurances aside, I don't trust that I'd definitely escape it alive."

"Wise." It frowned, adding, "She will soon wake. There is one thing I must do before I go."

"What?"

It closed its mouth over his and sank its tongue inside. The demon palmed the side of his neck as it kissed him hard and wet and deep. Then the flesh beneath its hand began to prickle. Heat. *Burn.*

Teague hissed but didn't pull away. Not only because what should have been pain instead became pleasure, but because he knew the demon wasn't trying to harm him.

No. It was branding him.

Entities could rise and brand a lover if they felt possessive. But he had the distinct feeling that he was being marked for a whole other reason. A ruthless reason he *very* much approved of.

The demon ended the kiss and then admired its brand with a pleased hum. "As I said, you will help me make him jealous."

Oh, Holt would seethe at the sight of the mark if he did in fact have none-too-platonic feelings for Larkin. "She's gonna be furious about this. You know that, right?"

"She will pretend to be furious. Secretly, she will like the look of it on your skin." The entity fingered his collar. "Do hurry and seduce her. I would like you and your demon to fuck me."

A grin shaped his mouth. "I just love how direct you are."

It nipped his lower lip. "We shall speak again soon." Its eyes fell closed, and the warm female body on his lap melted against him as the entity clearly withdrew.

Larkin began to stir within seconds, making sleepy little moans that tugged at his gut. Finally, she sat upright, her eyelids flickering. As her situation hit her, the harpy's brows snapped together, and she went absolutely rigid. "Why am I sitting on you?"

He cupped her hips, his hold undeniably possessive. "I didn't put you here, if that's what you're thinking. Though I like having you where you are, so feel free to stay. I was about to head home, but then your demon wanted to have a little chat with me."

"A chat?" she echoed, clearly confused.

"Yeah. While straddling me."

She squinted. "What exactly did it want to speak to you about?"

"A few things. There was some talk about its likes—the smell of fear, torturing people, seeing terror dance in a person's eyes. Stuff like that. Oh, and there was the kiss."

Her eyes widened. "Kiss? Why did—*oh my God, what in the fuck?*"

He smiled as she gawked at the side of his neck. "So. Yeah. It branded me."

CHAPTER EIGHT

Larkin jumped off his lap like he'd burned her. She shuffled backwards, vigorously shaking her head. Her demon had *not* branded him. It hadn't. She was dreaming. Or hallucinating. Maybe she'd been slipped a drug at the bar.

Her entity snorted, practically sitting back and buffing its nails, all smug and shit. It telepathed her images of how it had kissed him—which did *not* ridiculously cause jealousy to knife through Larkin—and marked him while he remained still, reacting only with a hiss of pain.

Larkin swiped a hand down her face. God, the entity really had marked him. Like a complete idiot. And now Larkin would have to deal with the consequences, would have to … She frowned at Teague. "What are you doing?"

Adjusting the angle of the swivel mirror on her vanity desk, he said, "I want to see what the mark looks like."

She could tell him what it looked like. Bold, in a word. A beautifully detailed harpy wing spanned the side of his neck.

Pure black, it shimmered slightly, as if wet. It looked edgy and cool and not one little bit subtle.

As he checked it out, his mouth curved in appreciation. "I like it. Your demon is creative."

Larkin could only stare at him. He should be mad. Why wasn't he mad?

No one would ever be blasé about being branded by an entity that had zero right to put a mark on them. But here he was, smiling and even complimenting her demon. *Complimenting* it.

People who'd come face-to-face with her demon didn't pay it compliments, they made their excuses to leave. Even her brothers were wary of her entity. She understood why, couldn't blame them for it. But, well, it still stung sometimes.

Teague, though? He wasn't the slightest bit unnerved, despite the fact her demon had apparently easily shared with him all its sadistic likes and dislikes. No, he'd had no issue with it chatting to him, straddling him, kissing him . . . or branding him.

Seriously, what the hell?

He mentally approached things from abnormal angles a lot of the time, sure, but even he should be somewhat peeved about the brand.

She was peeved about it.

She thrust her hand into her hair—and when had her braid fallen out, please?—seriously annoyed at herself. Why? Because even though she didn't want to like the sight of him marked, she did. That thought made her entity smirk.

Christ, what had it been thinking? It had done weirder things when bored, but *still*. "I would seriously slap my demon if I could."

He turned to look at her. "Why? Your demon is fucking awesome."

It grinned in delight. But Larkin again found herself staring at him in complete wonder. "What?"

A slow smile curved his lips. "I fell for it the moment it asked how strong my pain threshold is. It really would torture me for the entertainment value, wouldn't it?"

"And you ... like that?"

"What's not to like?"

Okay, she didn't understand him. Never would. Ever. But that he so easily accepted her entity made her chest feel all warm.

"Has it always been a little bit nuts?"

She usually didn't tell others much about her demon. But then, they asked questions because they feared and wanted to 'fix' it. Teague, however, seemed simply intrigued. He gave not one tiny fuck that her entity clearly had issues.

"Not from the very outset," she replied. "But it was ... different, even when I was an infant. Colder and more entitled than most entities. Also much more distant, so it formed attachments to very few people."

It couldn't love—the emotion simply wasn't on its emotional spectrum. The same went for all demonic entities. But just because they couldn't love others didn't mean they wouldn't grow attached to them. In such cases, they *never* let that person go. Typically, anyway. Her demon was an exception to that rule, but Larkin suspected it was because the entity had never fully connected with anyone.

"The darker aspects of its personality didn't creep in until I was six, though." But Larkin didn't want to go into the whys of that, so she swiftly changed the subject. "I don't get it, why aren't you mad about the brand? It's one thing for an entity to mark someone they're sleeping with. This is something altogether different. The brand might not be permanent, but that doesn't change that my entity had absolutely no right to mark you."

His brows dipped. "It had good reason for doing so," he

insisted in a somewhat defensive tone, seeming a little offended on her demon's behalf. Apparently they'd bonded or some shit.

"I'm not seeing how that could truly be the case."

"It's of the opinion that Holt has a thing for you. It wants to make him jealous." He returned to where he'd been sitting on the end of her bed. "It feels that this'll do the trick."

A thing for her? No. Nu-uh. "Why attempt to make him jealous?"

"So he'll do something stupid that will allow your demon to kill him without it resulting in repercussions for your lair."

A heavy breath slipped out of her. Larkin rubbed a hand down her face. "Maybe I should have expected my demon to try to provoke him in some way, but I never thought it would involve you." Pausing, she bit her lip. "I'm sorry."

Teague frowned. "Why?" He seemed genuinely confused.

"As we've already established, my demon is using you to provoke Holt. That isn't fair to you. You're not a pawn in a game."

He gave a careless shrug. "I don't mind."

Larkin cocked her head. "You really don't, do you?"

"No."

"Your demon must mind, surely."

"Nah. It's just now more determined than ever to convince me to bite you."

She narrowed her eyes. "We've covered that that won't be happening."

He only smiled. As did her demon. God, they were so weird.

Larkin palmed the back of her head. "No wonder it was urging me to get blitzed tonight. It wanted me to pass out so it could have some time unmonitored to do what it pleased. It no doubt suspected that you'd collect me from the bar as part of our act, since the guys always pick up their mates. I really can't believe it went this far to anger Holt."

"Your demon positively loathes him." Teague braced his hands on the mattress behind him. "Tell me about the guy. You were vague when you first mentioned him. I didn't intend to push you for more info, because I respect that this isn't my business and I have no right to your secrets. But your entity has pulled me into this matter. And if Holt truly has a thing for you, he *will* come at me—even if only to verbally warn me off. Tell me what I'm dealing with."

Larkin sighed. He was right. Her demon had unjustly dragged him into this, and it would be unfair of her to not arm him with more information.

Puffing out a breath so hard she was surprised her lips didn't rattle, she took slow, hesitant steps toward the bed and then sat on the edge beside Teague. "He's a cambion. One as powerful and dangerous as he is calculating and selfish. He's also a complete stranger to the concept of loyalty. More, he's the Prime of a Canadian lair." She stretched out her legs and dug her heels into the carpet. "He was a sentinel when I first met him."

"When was that?" asked Teague, a soft note she rarely heard in his voice.

"Over thirty years ago. He came to Vegas for a weekend trip with some demons from his lair."

"How did you meet him and come to realize he was your anchor?"

"I was at a club in the Underground with some members of my lair's Force—it was a sort of work night out. He kept trying to catch my eye. I kept ignoring him, not in the mood to be hit on. He touched my mind and telepathically offered to buy me a drink. And then our psyches just lunged for each other. I knew at that moment we were psi-mates."

"But you didn't let the bond form there and then?" There was no reproach in the question, only curiosity.

"No. I wasn't comfortable with psychically binding myself to a complete stranger. I'm not criticizing those who do it," she hurried to add. "It just isn't for me." She slanted her head. "Did you and Khloë fight the pull of the bond initially, or did you just go for it?"

"We didn't fight it. But we weren't strangers to each other. Some members of my clan are . . . work associates of a few of her imp relatives, so we'd met quite a few times before we realized we were anchors. If I hadn't known her in advance, it might have played out differently."

Larkin swallowed. "It must have been nice to realize that your psi-mate is someone you know and like."

"It was. Were you initially happy to find your anchor?"

"Yes. Holt claimed to be just as thrilled. He wasn't pleased that I wanted to get to know him before we formed the bond, but he agreed to prolong his stay in Vegas so we could spend time together." Feeling a heaviness settle over her chest, Larkin rubbed at it. "In the beginning, he was a regular white knight. He focused on me to the exclusion of all else. Love-bombed the fuck out of me, too."

Teague's brow creased. "Love-bombed you?"

"Oh yeah. But I never thought of him *that way*. He accepted that—or claimed to. But it didn't stop him from repeatedly tossing declarations of love my way. And it made me uneasy. Suspicious."

"Suspicious?"

"Holt wasn't only pushing me to hurry and form the bond. He wanted me to join his lair *and* move to Canada."

"He asked a whole lot of you," Teague noted, not liking it. Of course it was natural for demons to wish to be close to their anchor. But it was also natural for them to ensure their psi-mate's wellbeing, not demand too much of them. Holt had literally asked her uproot and leave pretty much everything behind—her home, her career, her family.

"He got pushier and pushier, which achieved nothing. So I wondered if maybe he was trying to haul me into a relationship so I'd do what he wanted; that the love-bombing was pure manipulation. I'm still not convinced he ever truly felt that way about me, no matter what my demon believes."

She could well be right. The cambion sounded devious and self-centered enough to employ such a trick to get what he wanted. "Did you ever consider moving to Canada?"

"I thought about it. Knox told me I could remain part of our lair if I did, I just wouldn't be able to keep my sentinel position because it wasn't feasible, but that the position would always be open to me if I decided to come back. I didn't want to leave the US, though. I'd have been too far away from the only family I have."

"Understandable."

"Not to Holt," she said, her voice tight. "He didn't see why it would be such a problem, even though he wasn't prepared to make that same sacrifice."

Teague felt his jaw harden. "So, in addition to everything else, he's a two-faced fucker?"

"Yup. I didn't ask him to join my lair or move to the US. I would never have asked him to give up so much. He brought up the subject, saying there was no sense in him making the transfer. And he was right."

"In what sense?"

"He would have lost his position of sentinel, and then he would no longer have been in the run-in to become a Prime. Knox *might* have one day made him a sentinel if he'd switched to my lair, but that was all Holt would ever have been—there's no way he could have usurped Knox. Holt ain't *that* powerful. So it was best for him to remain in his lair."

"That doesn't mean he should have expected you to make all the sacrifices, especially if you weren't demanding things from him." His ambitions weren't more important than her welfare—it was that simple.

"That's not how he saw it. In his view, there was no reason at all why I shouldn't make the transfer—I didn't want to become Prime, so it shouldn't matter to me if I lost my position of sentinel. And, you know, it wasn't like the guys are my 'real family', they're just 'friends and colleagues'."

Fuck, this guy was something else. "It was really *all* about him."

"Very much so. I suggested that we both remain as we were. It wasn't like we *needed* to be part of the same lair or live near each other. We could still have had regular contact."

Teague nodded. "Not all anchored pairs answer to the same Prime or reside in the same country."

"I pointed that out multiple times. But Holt doesn't like to compromise, he likes to get his way—full stop. So he kept pushing. And I kept saying 'no, let's stay as we are'."

"I'm surprised that Knox or one of the sentinels didn't interfere." This didn't seem like something that they would overlook, given how protective they were of her.

"I made them promise not to step in, just as I'm sure you wouldn't have wanted anyone to interfere in your business with Khloë."

Touché.

"But I could see that they were close to breaking their promise. *Then* I overheard a damning phone call." She absently rubbed at her thighs, her expression pinched. "Holt was talking to his Prime, telling him that he needed a little more time; that he *would* lure me to their lair and turn my loyalties. They wanted to ferret out all Knox's secrets."

Teague felt his jaw drop. "Son of a bitch. He planned to use you like that?" It was goddamn *reflexive* for a demon to prioritize their psi-mate. The mere idea of exploiting or fucking Larkin over should have gone against everything in Holt. "What did you do?"

"I confronted him. He swore he'd only said that stuff to his Prime to shut the guy up. As if that would have made it any better, considering it would have indicated that he didn't care enough about me to speak up." She gave a slow, disbelieving shake of the head. "I didn't believe his excuse. We argued. Big time. He then said I shouldn't have a problem revealing Knox's secrets anyway, because my loyalty should be to Holt and only Holt."

Teague felt his brows fly up. "This is coming from a guy who didn't display one ounce of loyalty toward you? Jesus, he's one hypocritical motherfucker." Teague could honestly snap his neck and think nothing of it.

"I threw that very fact in his face. The argument got so heated that I walked away, saying we could talk the following day when we'd both calmed down. But when I went to his hotel room the next morning, I discovered that he'd checked out and gone home." A sour, humorless smile plucked at her mouth. "No warning, no note, no goodbye text, nothing."

"You are fucking kidding me," Teague breathed.

"Nope. I think he thought I'd chase after him."

Teague felt his face scrunch up. "Why would he think you'd even *want* to pursue him? He'd essentially turned his back on you." Demons didn't do that to their anchors. Ever. They were there for each other through thick and thin, no matter the situation. If there was a problem, they hashed it out and resolved it. They didn't desert each other.

"But in his mind, *he* wasn't the one being unreasonable. No, by insisting on a compromise, I was being selfish and unfair."

The male was ungoddamnbelievable. "No wonder your demon despises him."

"I used to loathe him just as much. I let the emotion go, refusing to cling to it, but I don't want anything to do with him. Neither does my demon. We never will."

"No one in their right mind would. It's bad enough that he behaved the way he did. But for him to have just waltzed out of your life without a word as if you mean nothing, and then for him to later stroll back into it like he has every right ... You deserve better in an anchor, Lark."

"I do. I'm hoping he heads home without pushing this."

"Do you think he will?"

"It's possible. He walked away easily enough the first time."

Well, consider Teague fully invested in making the Prime so jealous he couldn't breathe with it. And if Holt reacted by trying to harm Larkin, Teague would help both her and her demon make him suffer.

Teague curled his arm around her shoulders and tugged her close.

She tensed. "I don't—"

"Shut up. I'm comforting my girlfriend."

"I'm not really your girlfriend."

"Semantics."

Larkin thought about pushing away from him. But ... she didn't want to. She instead found herself resting her head on his shoulder. Odd though it was, given his habit of testing her sanity, he was easy to be around.

Maybe it was because there were no mind games with him, no need to read between the lines, no façade to have to see past. That stuff could be tiring, not to mention irritating.

Teague had his secrets, but he didn't present a false face to the world. What you saw was what you got.

He was so much the opposite of Holt. Direct. Frank. Trustworthy. Respected people's loyalty to others. Didn't have unfair expectations of people.

In that sense, Teague made a person feel that they didn't need to have their guard up all the time. That they could relax. That, though he might push their buttons for fun, they were emotionally safe with him because he'd never deliberately hurt them.

Maybe that was why it had been so easy for her to tell him everything. Larkin was self-contained a lot of the time. Private things didn't merely *spill* out of her—she tended to hold back with others. Revealing too much made her feel exposed.

Tonight, she hadn't held back. She'd offloaded her worries and pain onto Teague. And she felt better for it.

"You're unusually quiet," she said without lifting her head. "What are you thinking?"

"I'm wondering if you're as good a kisser as your demon."

That matter-of-fact statement took her totally off-guard. It also made her stomach do an excited little flip.

"I feel like I should know," he added, all innocence. "I mean, as your boyfriend—"

"*Fake* boyfriend."

"—I should know something like that, shouldn't I?"

Uh, no. But she didn't say that, because the idea of tossing aside all her hesitancies and finally giving into the need she'd harbored for him for so long made her blood heat.

Her demon urged her to give in, reminding her that he could help them 'forget'. But that wasn't what tempted Larkin to follow the entity's urgings. She didn't want to use him. She wanted to *be* used. Wanted to not be in control for just a little while. And if there was any guy who'd give no fucks about her difficulty with relinquishing control, it would be Teague.

He wouldn't hold his hands up in surrender. He wouldn't let

her call the shots. He wouldn't crap in his pants if her demon rose and gave him attitude.

No, he'd insist on having his way. Insist that both Larkin and her inner entity gave up control. Which, in all honesty, was what they both wanted. They simply didn't do it easily.

However, Larkin didn't have the luxury of being able to explore that because . . . "You made oaths to Khloë, remember?"

"But even she'd agree that it makes sense for you and me to kiss at least once in private. Otherwise, it would be awkward for us to do it in front of others as part of our act. And it's probably going to come to that, if we're to really make this believable. Right?"

Okay, even she knew that was a bullshit excuse. But she heard herself reply, "Right."

"Then it makes sense for us to have a practice run, doesn't it?"

"I suppose." Righting her head, Larkin inwardly cursed. God, she was freaking weak when it came to this male. It made her feel a little vulnerable, which should have unnerved her; should have made her want to push him away. It didn't. Because she trusted him.

He grazed her ear with his lips, making the tiny hairs there prick up. "Then let me taste you." It wasn't really a request, so she wasn't surprised when he gripped her jaw and turned her mouth to his.

She swallowed. "Make it good."

His lips slowly canted up into that sexy smile she loved, and then he swooped down and took her mouth. Teague did not fuck around. He dived right in, boldly sweeping his tongue inside, devouring her with a ravenous kiss that scorched her. Like a brand. A claim.

Pure carnal need violently tore through her like claws. Her thoughts and reservations scattered. Her body sprung to life like it had been zapped by electricity.

She wanted more. A lot more. With a moan of demand, she drove her fingers into his hair and scratched at his scalp. Bumps rose on her flesh as a growl poured down her throat—she could almost taste the wildness of it.

He roughly snagged her nape as he angled his head and sank his tongue deeper. She moaned again. The kiss kicked up a notch, becoming so wild and unrestrained their teeth clicked.

Teague broke the kiss with a soft curse but didn't release her. She didn't release him either. She kept her fingers in his hair as they sat there, striving to catch their breath.

His eyes—dark and thrillingly hot with naked want—fixed on hers with laser-focus. His grip on her nape tightened almost to the point of pain. He bit out a harsh curse, and then his mouth latched on to hers again.

Larkin eagerly met his kiss, her breath catching as he dragged her onto his lap. He shoved his hands into her hair, holding her head in place so he could feast all he wanted. That was when all her higher functions seemed to shut down.

Larkin scooted forward to straddle him good and proper, settling herself against the growing bulge in his jeans. Urgency humming in her blood, she whipped off her top. He unclipped her bra, and they tossed both garments on the floor. Then he closed his hands over her breasts, blatantly possessive, and a little snarl tore out of her.

She needed him in her. Now. *Right* now.

Larkin yanked open the top button of his fly, but she didn't get the chance to complete the job, because he lifted her onto her knees and sucked a nipple into his mouth. Holy hell, every hard tug on the taut bud went straight to her clit.

She gripped his shoulders tight, arching into him. Even as he licked and suckled, he quickly and deftly unbuttoned the fly of her slacks. She tried pulling back, meaning to stand and shove down her pants and underwear.

His hand clamped around her hip and hauled her against him. "Where are you fucking going?"

"To get these damn slacks off."

Banding an arm tight around her, Teague stood, pivoted, and then unceremoniously dumped her on the bed. He dragged off both her pants and underwear in one smooth move. His eyes raked over her as he fisted the back of his tee.

She knifed up, ready to help him undress, but then the shirt was gone—revealing a whole lot of hard muscle and gorgeously tanned, inked skin—and she sort of just stared at him dumbly. Her gaze dropped when he shoved down his jeans and *holy shit* he truly did have a beast of a cock.

Teague knelt on the bed and then lowered his body over hers, pressing her down to the mattress, lighting up her nerve-endings with the amount of skin-to-skin contact. "I want to take you ungloved. You got an issue with that?"

"No." She tried flipping him over, but he rested more of his weight on her. She frowned. "I want to ride you."

"I don't care." He clamped his hand around her pussy. "You don't want me to care what you want. You want me to do whatever the fuck I please. Which is good, because that's exactly what I'm gonna do." He jammed two fingers inside her.

The shock of it made Larkin go still. For all of a damn second. Because then he starting suckling on her nipple while pumping his fingers hard and fast.

God, that felt good. Nonetheless, her need to fight for control rose up hard. It wasn't in her nature to give in so easily.

She tried rolling him over once more. That had zero effect.

She shoved at his head to dislodge his mouth from her breast. That also had zero effect.

She pushed at his chest *hard* so she could slide her hand down to fist his cock and turn the tables. Again, zero effect.

Teague paid her struggles no attention whatsoever. He didn't try to keep her still or warn her to stop. No, he just went ahead and did what he wanted—much as he'd said he would.

It didn't irritate her anywhere near as much as it incited her. All that strength and tenacity and dominance switched her best levers. Her inner entity totally got off on it.

Add in the mouth toying with her breasts and the fingers plunging into her pussy and, yeah, Larkin was very soon desperate to find her release. "Teague—" She jolted as a third finger sank inside her. "Fuck."

"I can smell how wet you are. It's driving my demon insane."

"Then do something about it. Fuck me. Or at least put your fingers to work a little more; I need to come."

"You need what I say you need." Teague felt a cold breeze sweep up his front and gather around him. He looked up from the breast he'd been licking, unsurprised to see her demon's cold black eyes honed in on him.

"Be very, very careful," it warned.

"No." He wasn't whatsoever willing to give ground—the entity would perceive it as a weakness anyway.

"You do not hold the power here."

"Sure I do. You'll have to deal with it. So will she."

The demon dug its nails *hard* into his shoulders.

He flicked up a brow. "You make me bleed, I'll return the favor with my teeth."

It squinted. "You wouldn't."

"You're welcome to test me on it."

Black eyes gave way to gray-green as Larkin retook control. "No biting, Sullivan."

Teague flipped her onto her stomach. "I'll do whatever I want to you. Thought I'd made myself clear on that." He roughly pulled her up onto her hands and knees and then swept his hand down her sleek back.

"You are *seriously* trying my patience."

"Don't care." Curling his body over hers, he pressed the head of his cock against her entrance and groaned. "Drenched."

The sweet and spicy scent of her need made his demon feel drunk on her. Teague wanted to taste her, but he couldn't wait to be inside her any longer. He needed to take her so bad it was an ache in his teeth, his bones, his cock, his fucking soul.

He pushed his hips forward, lodging a mere inch of his dick inside her. "This might hurt." He fisted her hair tight, snatched her head back, and slammed home.

Slick, rippling, blazing hot muscles clamped down on his cock. A groan slid through his gritted teeth. "Fuck, Lark."

He didn't give her time to adjust. He just took her. Fucked her like he'd needed to fuck her for years—hard, deep, unrestrained.

He'd known before he kissed her earlier that he'd be flirting with his self-control if he let himself taste her. He'd thought he could pull back. Which he had.

Though not for long.

Maybe if she hadn't kissed him back with so much hunger, he could have resisted another taste. And then maybe he wouldn't now be ramming his cock balls-deep inside her over and over. Or maybe he'd never stood a chance of fighting his need for her in the long-run; that this would have happened eventually at some point.

Realizing she was braced on one hand, he batted the other away before it could get near her pussy. "I didn't say you could touch yourself, did I?"

"Fuck you, you prick. It's *my* clit—"

"Not right now it's not. It's mine. I say who gets to touch it." Larkin cursed as he planted a hand between her shoulder blades and pressed down, pinning her upper body to the bed. Her pride dictated she should call him fit to burn, but she'd be lying if she claimed she didn't like how he maneuvered her exactly how and where he wanted her.

Larkin never liked when guys tried exerting control by teasing her or denying her orgasms. It only annoyed her. Teague didn't do that. No, he asserted himself by quite simply *taking*, rough and bold and unapologetic. She dug it. And it was something else about him that her demon got off on.

Her breath caught as he angled his hips, pounding his cock even deeper than before, hitting until-now-unexplored nerve-endings. God, she really did love his dick. Truly. It overstretched her walls, spicing each powerful thrust with an exquisite burn that was dangerously addictive.

And she was going to come any second now. Any second. It— She came.

Whips of hot pleasure streaked through her, intense and blinding. She screamed, fisting the sheets, slamming back onto the cock that pounded deep again and again and again. Then he exploded with a half-growl half-groan, emptying every bit of his come inside her.

She slumped to the mattress, spent, weak, panting. He fell on top of her, catching his weight on his elbows, each warm pant fanning the crook of her neck.

Finally, he withdrew his softening cock from her pussy and rolled onto his back with a sated sigh.

Deliciously sore, Larkin moved to lay on her back as well. Staring up at the ceiling, she cleared her throat. "I'm pretty sure you just broke your oath to not sex-up any of Khloë's friends." And if he started fretting or expressing regrets, Larkin would *not* be pleased. It would be understandable, but it would sting all the same.

"Nah. We were just practicing in case we ever have to have sex in public."

Her lips quirked. Why she thought he'd react normally, she had no clue, since she knew better. "Yeah. It's best to be prepared. Just in case."

"Exactly. And now if we ever have to fuck in public, it won't be awkward."

A silent laugh shook her shoulders. "Yeah, not awkward at all."

CHAPTER NINE

The next morning, Teague stepped out onto the porch of his wagon, a mug of half-empty coffee in hand. He usually prepped his breakfast and then ate it in the clearing, where the entire clan typically gathered each morning just as they had now. But today, he'd eaten alone, knowing that—since the others would for sure shower him with questions the moment they noticed the brand, interfering with his ability to enjoy his food in peace—he'd have otherwise struggled to chomp his breakfast down without it going cold.

Just thinking of the brand made him automatically remember all that had followed last night. It turned out that there had been plenty of substance to his prediction that a single taste of the pretty harpy would intoxicate him.

He hadn't lingered at Larkin's place after fucking them both raw. Not that she'd coldly tossed him out, or that he'd felt the need to leave in a hurry. There had simply been no reason for him to hang around. She'd made that clear shortly after their orgasms had fully subsided . . .

"So, how long do hit-and-run guys usually stick around after sex?" she'd asked with a teasing smile. "Am I going to come out of the bathroom to find that you've done such a spectacular disappearing act that it'll feel as if you were never here in the first place?"

Already greedy for more of her, despite being utterly sated, he'd stared at her for a long moment before asking, "What if I don't want this to be a one-time thing?"

Her smile had dimmed. "I have zero interest in a no-strings-attached-fling, Teague. Don't get me wrong, I don't judge you for sticking to shallow encounters. I'm simply saying it's not for me. I don't regret what happened tonight, but I'm not interested in a repeat. Besides, you pledged oaths to Khloë. You've already broken one of them once. I'd say it's best that you don't do it again."

She'd moved as if to rise from the bed, so he'd caught her jaw, turned her face to his, and then taken her mouth. She'd kissed him back—no hesitance, no half-heartedness.

Pulling back, he'd then said, "I know I shouldn't have broken my word to Khloë. But I don't wish I hadn't. You were worth it."

As he'd once told her, he didn't 'do' regret. Never had. But even if the emotion didn't elude him, he doubted he could have wished away all that happened.

Snapping back to the present, he took a swig of his coffee. His clan were gathered around the clearing. Archer and Slade sat across from each other near the firepit, munching on food. A humming Gideon lay flat on his back on the picnic table, his arms crossed over his chest like a corpse at rest. Saxon lounged in a deck chair while Tucker gave him an earful about something as he loomed over him.

The latter wasn't uncommon. In many ways, watching Tucker rant at Saxon was like seeing a terrier front a bull mastiff. The terrier would yap and yap as it tried asserting its dominance. The mastiff, so sure of its strength and power, would pay the other dog no real mind.

"Morning all," Teague greeted, descending the steps. He felt his brow furrow as he took in the amount of blood stains on Saxon's face, hands, and clothes. "Rough night?"

Chewing on toast, Saxon shrugged one shoulder. "Something like that."

The assassin preferred up-close-and-personal kills, so he occasionally came home in such a state, but not often.

As Teague sat on a log, Tucker turned to him and then gestured at Saxon as he said, "Would you tell him it's unhygienic to cook while covered in gore."

Saxon sighed. "I didn't cook, I toasted a few slices of bread."

"While you have blood all over you," Tucker clipped. "Blood that dripped *onto your plate*."

"You get agitated by the strangest things." Saxon bit into his toast. "I don't get why."

"There's nothing strange about wanting you to wash your damn hands before you eat when they look like *that*. It's just plain common sense. And how can it not be icky to you to touch food while you have someone else's blood on your fingers?"

"It's not like I'm licking it or anything."

"That's not the point."

"Do you even *have* a point?"

Tucker growled, planting his hands on his narrow hips. "Yes, I do. *And you know it*."

A bored sigh slipped out of Saxon. "So determined to be aggressive and imposing. The little man syndrome is at work again."

"I do not have—" Cutting himself off, Tucker threw his hands up. "You know what? I'm not doing this with you."

"Okay," said Saxon with a nod, his voice mild.

Tucker's expression hardened. "Actually, I *am* doing this with you."

"I thought you might," Saxon muttered.

"*Or*," Leo cut in, huddling a bowl of cereal against his chest, "we could all just calm down and use our indoor voices."

"We're not indoors," Archer pointed out, placing his empty plate on the ground beside him.

"Yes, I noticed that," said Leo, his tone dry. "I'm saying I'd prefer it if we all talked at normal volume."

Tucker snorted. "It's not like I'm bellowing or anything, I just ... Hey, Teague, what's that on your neck?" He squinted, leaning to the side to get a better look. Moments later, he jerked back like Teague had taken a swipe at him. "Jesus Christ on a cross."

On the bench, Gideon knifed up. "What? What is it?"

"A wing," Tucker replied. "But not a wing tattoo. No. Our boy here got branded."

"Branded?" Slade echoed, standing. "No way." He crossed to Teague and took a good look at his neck. "Shit, yeah, that's a brand all right."

"I take it that Leanne's demon marked you," Saxon guessed, clearly displeased.

"Her name is Larkin. And yes, her entity—who, on a side note, is adorably nuts—branded me. But it wasn't an act of possessiveness." Still, Teague's demon felt very much self-satisfied by the knowledge that he now wore her entity's mark.

"Then why did it do that?" asked Gideon, his nose wrinkling.

Teague stretched out his legs. "To sum up the situation, Larkin's anchor—a man who is one sorry excuse for a psi-mate, abandoning her years ago rather than claiming her—has reappeared on the scene. Her demon doesn't like it. It wants to provoke him so he'll give it a valid excuse to kill him that won't rebound back on its lair. And since he has a thing for Larkin . . . "

"He'll hate the brand and possibly lose his shit," Slade finished, retaking his seat.

"That's what the entity is banking on. It's a loon. Wants to torture me for fun." Teague smiled. "It said it likes the shape of my skull."

Gideon's mouth curved. "Aw, that's sweet."

"Her anchor might come at you," Saxon said to Teague. "You know that, right?"

Teague hoped the cambion did, because he'd be more than happy to pound the fucker into the ground. "It won't be anything I can't handle."

"Who is he?" asked Leo.

"Holt something." Teague knocked back the last of his coffee. "He's a cambion. And a Canadian Prime."

"I'll look into him." Spooning some of his cereal, Leo added, "If I find out anything of interest, I'll pass it on."

Teague dipped his chin in thanks and then set his cup down between his legs.

"So," began Archer, his eyes narrowed on Teague, "I've never been branded, but I'm pretty sure it happens during sex, right? Does that mean you fucked Larkin?"

"We weren't having sex when the branding was done," replied Teague. "Like I told you, it wasn't an act of possessiveness on her entity's part."

"Which answers my first question, not my second," Archer noted.

Saxon narrowed his eyes at Teague. "You fucked her, didn't you?"

Teague only twisted his mouth.

Slade let out a soft curse. "You said she wouldn't want to get close to you."

"And she doesn't," Teague assured him. "Sex is just sex. She made it clear that though she has no regrets, she only wants it to be a one-time thing."

"What about you?" Slade challenged. "Are you good with that?"

"No, as it happens. But it's not a matter of whether I'm good with it or not, is it? It's a matter of us having secrets to protect. So I'm not going to push for more than one night, which means you can unclench. Our secrets will remain secrets."

Tucker sank into the empty deck chair. "I wouldn't recommend that you tell Khloë you slept with Larkin. It's not something the imp *needs* to know. And it'll only make her mad."

"Why would she be mad?" asked Archer.

Leo dropped his spoon into his empty bowl. "By sleeping with the harpy, Teague went back on his word. Some people are weird about stuff like that." He shrugged, not getting it.

Gideon slipped off the table and crossed to Teague. Taking a closer look at the brand, he smiled. "It's actually pretty cool."

Teague couldn't hold back his grin. "I know, right?"

Saxon carefully braced his plate on the armrest. "You're entirely too smug about that mark. How does your beast feel about it?"

Truthfully ... "It wants to bite her really, really hard. At least twice."

Leo's mouth twitched. "So it's feeling a little territorial?"

"And frustrated, because she's seriously against being bitten."

Archer frowned. "Why?"

Leo looked at him. "She's not a hellbeast, so his venom would hurt her."

"It wouldn't kill her, though," said Archer. "She'd be fine after an hour or so. Maybe longer. I'm not seeing the problem."

"But it's best that Teague's demon doesn't bite her—the beast would feel even more possessive if its venom was flowing through her veins," said Saxon before sliding his gaze back to Teague. "It might be better to quit playing the role of her boyfriend."

Teague couldn't stop his expression from hardening. "Not while her psi-mate is being a pain in her ass. And it's not like bowing out would change anything, is it? My demon was slightly possessive of her before now. Keeping my distance wouldn't alter that. Seeing the mark fade will likely do the trick, though." Because it would symbolize that her entity had lost interest in them.

Slade folded his arms. "What if it doesn't fade?"

Teague felt his forehead crease. "Of course it'll fade." And no, he wouldn't like it much.

"Don't be so sure," Slade cautioned. "Harpies have similar tendencies to birds like magpies and crows. They collect shiny things. If her demon collects you, that brand will go nowhere irrespective of whether you two part ways."

Unable to envision that ever happening, given Larkin's comment that her demon was very distant and tended to avoid attachments, Teague shook his head. "No, the mark will fade eventually. As will my demon's possessiveness."

"Let's hope so." Saxon grabbed his plate and then stood. "I'm hitting the sack. Unless there's an emergency, don't come knocking on my door. I need sleep. Lots and lots of sleep."

"What you need is to wash your hands," Tucker snarked.

Saxon gave him a dismissive look. "Back to that, are we, little man?"

"My name is *Tucker.*"

"Really? It's not Frodo? Hey, don't growl at me, short-ass."

"I'm not short! And you might have a few inches extra on me in height, but *my* extra inches went on my dick." Tucker gave him a cocky smile. "So, guess who wins here."

"The little guy with the Napoleon complex?"

"I'm *not* little!"

As Larkin stepped into the busy bakery with Piper, making the bell above the door chime, a familiar male mind nudged hers. A mind that hummed with agitation.

Keenan's voice then rushed into her head ... *Tell me it's bullshit.*

She felt her brow furrow. *What?*

Tell me your demon didn't brand Teague.

Larkin sighed, which caused Piper to raise a questioning brow. Larkin tapped her temple and mouthed 'Keenan'. News traveled fast in the demon world, so she'd known the incubus would hear about the brand relatively soon. She'd also anticipated that he wouldn't take it well. *How did you find out?*

Wait, so it's true? asked Keenan, the pitch of his telepathic voice shooting up a notch.

Yes, it's true. Rolling her eyes at the string of curses he let out, Larkin joined the long queue with Piper as she scanned the shop. Unfortunately, there were no vacant tables or booths as of yet. It was no shock, given that this particular bakery within the Underground was often crowded in the mornings.

How did you find out? she repeated.

Teague telepathed the news to Khloë, who then told me. But let's face it, he likes to bullshit people for reasons only he understands, so I thought he might be lying.

Well, he wasn't. I'm not sure why you're so surprised by this. You know my demon can be pretty territorial. That might not be what had driven the entity to brand him, but it nonetheless felt that way toward him.

I didn't think it'd be possessive of him. Dammit, Lark, I want better for you than a damn player.

She felt her brow flick up. *Uh, excuse me, Mr. Hypocritical, you did your fair share of playing the field before Khloë. Now go find something better to do than whine at me.* She closed a mental door on him, uninterested in listening to more. She'd reopen it later.

Larkin then psychically reached out to Teague. *You telepathed Khloë about the brand?* She hadn't expected that. She'd thought he'd just let her find out in her own sweet time.

His mind slid against hers. *Don't you think it would have looked weird to others if I hadn't bragged to my psi-mate that my girlfriend branded me?*

Not whatsoever liking that her pulse stuttered at the mere sound of his telepathic voice, she asked, *Did you tell her about everything else that happened last night?*

You mean that I fucked you until you screamed for me?

Her face was *not* heating. *Yeah. That.*

Not yet, but I will. Don't worry, she won't be as furious with me as you're thinking she'll be.

Larkin highly doubted that. The imp had a temper, and the breaking of a vow was no small matter. *If you say so.*

Pulling her mind away from his, Larkin dragged in a steadying breath, taking in the delicious scents of fresh bread, cinnamon, coffee, honey, and warm chocolate.

For such a small shop, the bakery could be loud. It wasn't just due to the murmurs and chuckles of customers. There were also the clatters of plates, the whirring of the industrial mixer, the background music, the scraping of cutlery against dishware, and the beeps coming from timers and the cash register.

"Everything okay?" asked Piper.

"Keenan learned about the brand via Khloë and felt the need to moan at me." She'd already told Piper about how her entity took it upon itself to mark him.

"I still can't believe your demon did that. I mean, *my* entity is devious. But it ain't that devious. You're lucky that his demon didn't mark you right back."

Larkin felt a frown tug at her brow. "It has no actual reason to."

"And why would you think that'll matter to a hellhorse? They don't require their actions to make sense."

Okay, there was that to consider. "Still, I doubt it will do anything like that," she said, keeping an eye on the small sitting area. The moment a table or booth became available, they'd need to pounce.

"Maybe not. You know, while I'm surprised by what your demon did, I'm not surprised that you fell into bed with Teague. The chemistry between you two is, like, *whoa*. It just kept building and building over time. Now that you're sleeping together—"

"We *slept* together. Past tense, not present. We're gonna leave it at that."

Piper jerked, her expression baffled. "Dear God in heaven, why?"

"Are you forgetting the oath he made to Khloë about not getting his freak on with her friends?"

"He already broke that promise once. Is there much difference in him doing it again?"

Larkin opened and closed her mouth. She wanted to say no, but she wasn't certain it would be for the right reason; wasn't certain that it wouldn't be a mere case of her selfishly giving herself the green light to go another sexual round with him. "I guess it doesn't really matter, does it? I'm not interested in a fling." Seeing a couple rise from a table, she quickly gave Piper a nudge. "Go grab that empty table before someone else does. I'll place our order and then bring it over."

"I want my usual," said Piper, making a swift beeline for the table, grinning when she beat others to it.

Larkin knew the nightmare's 'usual' well, since they often

came to the bakery on mornings when they were going on a girls' day out. On this particular day, they had plans to go shopping at the mall.

Larkin adored all the women in their group, but she had a soft spot for Piper. They'd fast become close friends—something that wasn't typical for Larkin. By her own admission, she didn't click with people well.

Just then, Tanner's psyche clashed with hers mere moments before his voice breezed into her mind ... *Your demon branded the hellhorse? Seriously?*

Rolling her eyes yet again, she proceeded to have with him a shorter version of her conversation with Keenan. She did the same with Levi very soon after that.

Finally, she reached the stainless steel counter. Many employees pottered around, dressed in aprons and hairnets. Behind the glass case was everything from sandwiches and bagels to donuts and cupcakes.

Larkin placed her order, resisting the temptation to greedily add one of the pre-prepared white boxes of cupcakes. The latter were her weakness, and she was feeling inwardly unsteady after the branding business and her one-nighter with Teague.

Her demon, on the other hand, was still feeling so self-satisfied about it all that it had been smirking all morning. It wasn't annoyed that Larkin intended for there to be no repeat of last night. Purely because it didn't believe she'd hold out against him. Honestly, Larkin couldn't promise that she would.

She moved to the cash register and paid for her order before heading to the collection point on the far left of the counter. She took a seat on one of the stools at the small bar there ... which was right around the time that she felt someone's eyes on her.

Larkin instinctively glanced to the side, her lips thinning when she saw Holt slowly heading her way with two males close behind him. That quickly, her demon's smirk died a fast death. She blanked her expression as she reached out to Piper. *Don't move from the table.*

The woman's psyche all but clashed against hers. *Is that blond dude him? The motherfucker who has the nerve to call himself your anchor when he's been anything but that to you?*

Yes, unfortunately. Stay where you are while I get rid of him.

Fine. But if he or his goonies make any unwise moves, I am so heading over there.

The aforementioned goonies took up positions around the bakery, hyper-alert. They were clearly sentinels. Holt, however, came to stand in front of Larkin.

Her psyche lunged toward his with such force she inwardly winced, but she'd been ready for it; had already shored up her mental barrier to prevent the bond from forming. That annoyingly didn't stop its call from pounding through her brain, shoving at her willpower.

Even as anger rose up inside both her and her demon, she didn't allow her expression to change. Nor did she slip off the stool so that he didn't have the height advantage. It wasn't an advantage that he could use—Larkin didn't worry for a moment that she couldn't take him down if necessary. "I would have thought you'd be back in Canada by now."

He gave her a pointed look. "I won't be so easy to get rid of, Larkin. I could see that I'd given you a shock when I showed up at your place a few days ago, so I gave you time to get used to the fact that I'm back. Now we need to talk."

"No, we really don't."

His jaw briefly tightened. "I don't blame you for not wanting to make time for me. But I'm not going anywhere. Not until I've fixed things between us."

"You *can't* fix things."

"I don't accept that," he said, inching up his chin slightly. "There were so many hurdles for us when we first met. They aren't there now. I don't have a Prime who's giving me shit and threatening to take away my position if I don't turn your loyalties. *I* lead my lair now. I'm not under pressure to bring you into it. I can visit you here in the US as much as I want."

"Oh, so you don't care that I would never move to Canada or switch to your lair?" Doubtful.

He hesitated, poking his tongue into the inside of his cheek, and she got the feeling that he was being mindful to choose his words carefully. "I wouldn't say I don't care," he finally said, speaking slowly. "Of course I'd rather have you close so I can better protect you. But if you wish your circumstances to remain as they are, I'll respect that."

Her entity let out a disbelieving snort. "So you being Prime of your lair is what's made the difference? That's why you feel we can finally form the bond?"

"Yes."

"Huh. Weird." She scratched her cheek. "I mean, you've been Prime for five years now. Yet, you stayed away until recently."

Surprise flashed in his eyes. If he hadn't expected her to do a little research on him, he was dumb as a rock.

Hearing her order number be called, Larkin edged off the stool, intending to cross to the collection point. But the dickhead in front of her blocked her path. "You need to move, Holt. *Now*."

"I told you, we have to talk."

"What's the point when you're not even willing to be straight with me? You claim you're here right now because you ascended from sentinel, but there's more to it than that, isn't there? Here's what I think happened. See, I learned that you came to Vegas a month ago on a trip of some sort."

Again, surprise quickly came and went in his eyes.

"I think you saw me from a distance while you were here," Larkin went on. "I think your demon reacted rather enthusiastically. I think the entity has been giving you trouble ever since, driving you to seek me out and form the bond. And I think you've had enough of fighting it. So you came back to Vegas and, well, here we are." The only thing she didn't get was why he'd thought she'd agree to what he wanted.

He licked the inside of his lower lip. "I saw you, yes. You were with Tanner, Keenan, Levi, and who appeared to be their partners. But you . . . you looked so alone. I know that feeling. I've felt that way since I left you."

And then realization smacked her in the face. "Oh, I get it. You asked around, heard that I was the last unmated member of my circle, and you thought you could use that; take advantage of it. You thought I'd be feeling lonely and the odd one out. Thought it would make me more willing to turn to you and maybe even transfer to your lair."

His back teeth locked. "I'm not asking you to do that," he calmly reminded her.

"Not now. But you would. You'd push for it eventually. Pushing is what you do. You'll hate the idea of me being under another Prime's rule."

"As I said before, I'd of course rather have you close. I'd say that's natural," he added in that oh so reasonable tone that plucked at her patience. "But all I'm asking of you is to give into the pull of the anchor bond."

She shook her head. "It's never going to happen. Even if I was up for it, my demon wouldn't be. It loathes you with a pathological, blinding passion."

"I'm standing right here telling you—"

"Whatever you think will get you what you want," Larkin

finished. "Maybe you do regret that you walked away years ago. But if so, you don't regret it for my sake. And it doesn't change anything because *you* haven't changed. You're still every inch the predatory opportunist. You thought I'd be emotionally vulnerable, and so you pounced."

A muscle in his cheek flexed. "It wasn't like that. I saw that you were in pain. I wanted to make it better."

"I'm not in pain. Far from it." She'd been lonely, but not hurting.

Just then, someone unexpectedly materialized at her side. Someone who looked the epitome of relaxed but was likely far from it.

Teague's mouth bowed up slightly as his hand slipped beneath Larkin's braid to palm her nape. "Hey, baby." He dropped a soft, brief kiss on her lips that made her nerve-endings sing despite the current situation. "Sorry I'm late."

Holt's sentinels appeared behind him, their eyes narrowing on the newcomer.

Teague glanced from her to Holt, his brow creasing as if he'd only then noticed the tension in the air between them. "If this is lair business, I can wait with Piper," he offered.

"No need," Larkin told him. "I'm done here."

Holt's gaze dropped to the harpy wing on Teague's neck. A number of emotions rippled across his face in fast succession— rage, bitterness, jealousy, resentment. Unexpectedly, he held out his hand and said, "Holt Wilks. And you are?"

The hellhorse shook his hand. "Teague Sullivan. But you already know that."

Holt's brow winched up. "Do I?"

Teague tipped his chin toward one of the sentinels. "Your friend there tried tailing me," he said, and the sentinel in question flushed. "Is there a reason for that?"

Holt didn't respond.

Infuriated that he'd have someone follow Teague, Larkin gave Holt a hard, flinty look. "You and your demons need to stay away from me and mine."

Holt's nostrils flared. "It doesn't need to be this way, Larkin."

"Yes, it does. And the only person you have to blame for that is yourself." She quickly skirted around him, strode over to the collection point, and grabbed the waiting tray.

Conscious of Teague following her, she headed straight to the table where Piper sat drumming her fingers. Setting down the tray, Larkin lifted a brow at her. *I take it you called Teague here.*

She sniffed. *Holt the Horrible needed to see that brand. Well, now he has.*

As Larkin and Teague took a seat, he draped his arm over the back of her chair and asked, "You all right?"

Aware that—in the process of making his way to the exit—Holt was within hearing range, she aloofly replied, "Yeah. Just waiting to hear why it is that you're late."

"I got held up," Teague told her. "Jerking off isn't always a quick process."

A chuckle slipped out of Piper.

Larkin shot him an exasperated look that was completely spoiled by the smile pulling at her mouth. "I don't know why I expect serious answers from you."

His brows dipped. "Just because it wasn't the response you were expecting doesn't mean I'm not serious. It's your demon's fault."

Larkin frowned. "What?"

"One look at this brand in the mirror is enough to make my dick so hard it hurts. I can't just leave it like that."

Shaking her head, Larkin began unloading the cups and plates off the tray.

"They're gone," Piper announced, her eyes on the exit.

A relieved breath slid out of Larkin.

"What did he say to you?" asked Teague.

"To sum up"—Larkin sipped at her coffee, thankful the bitter brew was still hot despite Holt delaying her attempt to collect it—"now that he's Prime, nothing stands in his way so we should form the bond. Oh, and he'll respect that I wish to remain here and not switch lairs."

Teague's brows snapped together. "The only thing that ever stood in his way is his own selfishness."

Piper gave a hard nod, cutting into her slice of apple pie. "Totally."

"Him becoming Prime wasn't the catalyst to his decision to pursue the anchor bond or he'd have showed up five years ago." Larkin bit into her donut, and the vanilla cream filling burst on her tongue. "He saw me from afar while in Vegas last month and it stirred up his demon. He also discovered that I was the last unmated member of my group."

"So he thought you'd be lonely and, as such, easy prey for him," Teague surmised. "Motherfucker."

"Absolutely." Larkin took an angry bite of her donut.

"He's *irate* about the brand." Piper popped a chunk of pie into her mouth. "Jealous, too. He tried to hide it, but . . ."

"Irate and jealous but not shocked," Teague remembered, thinking it strange.

Licking some vanilla cream from her lip, his harpy gave him a questioning look. "Hmm?"

"He showed no surprise." Teague twisted his mouth, feeling his eyes narrow. "I think he knew about it."

Her gaze lost focus for a few moments. "You're right, he didn't look in the least bit taken aback."

"I'd say that he's had people watching you," said Teague. "Probably studying your routines and seeing who you associate with. If he had one of his men staking out your building last night, they'll have seen me leave it with a brand of a harpy's wing on my neck."

Chewing more pie, Piper hummed thoughtfully. "It would explain why he felt motivated to make a move this morning, Lark. He'll feel threatened by Teague; Holt will want him out of the picture so he can more easily wangle himself *into* the picture."

"*And* because he wants you as more than his anchor," Teague told the harpy. "I know you doubt that, but I don't. Not after the flash of jealousy I just saw in his eyes." An emotion that his beast—not a fan of the male—had fed on.

Larkin's nose wrinkled. "It doesn't mean he wants me. Anchors are possessive of each other. Jealousy often comes into play." She pinned Teague with a look. "If he confronts you at any point—"

"I will tell you," the hellhorse assured her ... though he wouldn't until afterward. He wasn't going to call her to his side if the asshole made an approach.

Larkin gave a satisfied nod and bit into her donut again before turning back to Piper. "We can cancel our shopping trip, if you want."

"Hell, no." Piper lowered her cutlery to her plate. "My shopping mood is in no way broken." Lifting her latte, she took a quick sip and then set the cup back down. "And we both need new dresses for the party on Friday."

"Party?" Teague echoed.

Picking up her knife and fork again, Piper tilted her head at Larkin. "You didn't invite him?"

"I planned to; I only heard about it an hour ago." Larkin cut her gaze to his. "Raini's lair is throwing a party. As descendants, they don't welcome outsiders, but they don't mind extending invites to her family and friends. You'll be my plus-one."

"I'll be there." He used his thumb to scoop up a tiny blob of vanilla cream from the corner of her mouth. "What time shall I pick you up?" He sucked the cream from his thumb, watching as her eyes flared.

She cleared her throat. "Actually, we're being teleported there by Ciaran as it's a long-ass drive. Be at my place for seven pm. From there, he's going to 'port us three plus Devon, Khloë, my Primes, and the other sentinels to the party all in one swoop."

"Will the descendants have karaoke?" he asked.

Her brow puckering, Larkin tossed the last of her donut into her mouth. "I don't know. Maybe."

"I hope they do. It will be good practice for you, since you'll soon be treating us all to a naked performance."

"You're not dropping that wager?" asked Piper with a chuckle, forking more pie.

"And miss the chance to see her sing while butt-naked? No way."

Her demon rolled its eyes, amused. Larkin didn't find the wager so damn funny, nor did she like that he assumed she'd be the loser in this scenario. "Look, if you want to believe you'll win the wager, feel free to do so. It'll make it all the more fun for me when you lose."

"You're *that* confident?"

Her fingers sticky from the sugary glaze, Larkin tore open the small, square packet on her tray and pulled out the wet wipe. "I'm *that* confident."

"Hmm. Guess I'll have to up my game a little when we're at the party, then," he mused.

She paused in wiping her fingers. "What does that mean?" But she had the feeling she knew exactly what it meant: he intended to sexually taunt her just as he'd done during their dinner at Jolene's house. Only this time, he'd take things up a notch. *Shit.*

He gave her a mysterious smile. "Don't worry, pretty harpy. It won't be anything you can't handle."

Honestly—and somewhat annoyingly—she wasn't too sure of that.

CHAPTER TEN

His head tipped back, Teague stood beneath the stall's overhead shower with his eyes closed as the hot water pattered down on his tired muscles and still-healing injuries. Steam hazed the air, laced with the stadium's complimentary sandalwood-scented shampoo.

Weekend races tended to be more intense. This particular Friday had been no exception. The afternoon race he'd just competed in—and won—had involved incredibly nasty hurdles. He'd come away with plenty of wounds, and all were stinging like a bitch. They were further aggravated by the soap suds and shampoo, since it had been impossible to ensure that every single injury avoided contact with the silky bubbles.

Despite the loud whirring of the fan above him, Teague could easily hear the many sounds that echoed throughout the locker room—laughter, playful smack-talk, the splatter of water on tile, the gurgle of pipes, the hiss of spray cans, the squeaking of shoes, and the clang of locker doors slamming shut.

With their enhanced sense of smell, his inner demon wasn't fond of locker rooms. There were too many astringent scents, such as body spray, bleach, and citrus air freshener.

The hellhorse racing stadium naturally had a plentiful amount of locker rooms, given how many races took place per hour. Whenever competitors arrived at the stadium, they were assigned the same locker room as the other hellhorses of their gender who'd be competing in their race.

Some might think that such a thing was a bad idea since racers might not be all that nice to their competitors. But although on the track they might go so far as to pull dirty moves that included harming each other, that shit got left behind once the race was over.

There was a sense of camaraderie among hellhorses ... though not always the most pleasant kind. As evidenced by the guy in the neighboring shower who persisted in singing *really* badly and letting out an evil laugh each time one of the others complained that their ears were bleeding. Another hellhorse was whining because there was no toilet paper in his stall, begging someone to toss a fresh roll to him, but the others only teased and laughed at him.

Yeah, in a bad situation, hellhorses often weren't all that helpful.

As the water steadily drummed down on him, Teague's attention drifted to the upcoming party. He figured it would be a blast, so he was looking forward to it. Some didn't like descendants and considered them mutts, but he'd never understood why it mattered that their breed only came into being after fallen angels mated with demons. Who gave a fuck?

What he was most looking forward to was seeing Larkin. Touching her, kissing her, playing with her sanity.

He hadn't seen her since they talked at the bakery a few

days ago. He'd telepathically checked in with her daily, though. Not only to check that Holt hadn't again approached her, but because he just liked talking to her. He saw no need to lie to himself about it.

Teague had hoped that Holt would at some point seek him out. It had to be killing the cambion to stay away, given how furious he was about the brand. But he had apparently decided to be on his best behavior to appease Larkin, because he'd not only kept his distance from Teague, he'd also ordered his minion to cease following him. It was a crying shame, really.

Having rinsed off the shampoo and soap suds, Teague turned off the spray and then pushed open the frosted glass door. The cool air whispered over him, making little bumps rise on his flesh. Stepping out of the stall, he swiped a cotton towel from the shelf, dabbed his face with it, and then wrapped it around his hips.

Crossing to the countertop, he swiped a hand over the steamed-up wall-mounted mirror and took stock of his wounds, probing each one. They were healing well, and the bruises were already a faint yellow.

Heading for the rows of narrow metal lockers, he padded along the beige tiled floor, leaving faint wet footprints behind; passing the sinks, urinals, and toilet stalls.

There were a few other hellhorses still lurking, talking and readying themselves to leave. One, Azaire, was leaning against the concrete wall with both a t-shirt and a roll of toilet paper in hand, grinning like a fool.

"Just pass me some fucking toilet paper!" hollered a voice from within the nearest stall. *Beau*.

Azaire let out a put-upon sigh. "Fine." He threw the shirt over the door. "Here."

Beau spluttered a curse. "That's my tee, asshole."

"It'll feel nicer than any paper, I can tell you that," said Azaire.

Shaking his head in amusement, Teague walked past them and turned down a particular aisle of lockers.

One of the two guys there, Felipe, looked up from dabbing some kind of ointment on his burned arm. He smirked as he said, "Nice brand, Sullivan."

Teague grinned. "Ain't it, though?"

"So it's true, huh? You're dating Knox Thorne's sentinel?" Felipe let out a low whistle. "You're a ballsy bastard."

So he was often told by guys whenever they glimpsed the brand.

Stopping at his locker, Teague twisted the dial this way and that to unlock it, and then pulled open the door. He wondered if Larkin knew that a lot of males had avoided dating her because they feared Knox so much—to hurt her would be to piss the Prime off, and few people were tempted to do that.

Teague wasn't the type to let others keep him away from what he wanted, no matter what the consequences might be. Hence why he'd broken his word to Khloë. Which he hadn't yet fessed up about, but he would.

He retrieved his duffel from the locker, slid an abandoned granola bar wrapper further along the wooden bench out of his way, and then dumped his bag on said bench. Speaking of granola bars, he was pretty sure he had one in his duffel. He was always both thirsty and hungry after a race. He'd already downed a full bottle of water, along with two power bars.

Gripping where he'd knotted his towel, Teague sat on the bench beside his duffel. He dug out a snack and a sports drink and then got to work on both.

Person after person left as he ate, until there weren't many guys lingering.

Somewhere, a toilet flushed. Soon after, there was a gale of laughter followed by a full-on rant. Teague looked to his left as a chuckling Azaire and a furious Beau made their way to the door. Since Beau was wearing his tee, there was a good chance he hadn't first used it to wipe his ass.

Probably.

After he'd demolished his drink and snack, Teague chucked both the wrapper and empty bottle in the nearby trash can. That was when Felipe and his brother said quick goodbyes to Teague, their shoes squeaking against the tiled floor as they crossed to the door.

Alone, he dried himself off and fished his set of fresh clothes out of his duffel. Once fully dressed, he dumped the towel in the bin that was set aside for used ones. He then zipped up the duffel, gripped the handles—

Smoke and brimstone.

Both Teague and his demon froze at the scent.

A shadowkin jumped out of the murky corner ... quickly followed by a second humanoid.

Motherfucker.

They didn't give him a moment to react. One attacked instantly—hitting him with an orb of hell-acid that caught him right on the face—while the other vanished behind the row of lockers.

Gritting his teeth with the searing pain, Teague pitched three balls of hellfire right at his attacker's chest. Within him, his demon went postal. He bolstered his mental defenses, not willing to let his beast take over this time. Why should it get to have all the fun?

He half-turned his body so that his back was against the lockers. If the other shadowkin thought it could come at him from behind, it was wrong.

As the first humanoid recovered from the hellfire orbs, Teague effortlessly lifted the bench and hurled it through the air. The bench whacked the shadowkin hard, sending its head whipping back as it promptly hit the floor. He might not be able to injure this breed with an everyday object, but that didn't mean they wouldn't feel the pain from the impact.

Sure enough, the other humanoid appeared at the other end of the aisle, its white eyes laser-focused on him. But he was ready for it. The ball of hellfire he'd conjured sailed through the air with a whoosh of sound and crashed into its chest. He hurled two more, but the bastard lurched to the side, causing both orbs to smack the concrete wall behind it.

The bench scraped the floor loud as the first shadowkin shoved it aside and jumped to its feet. Then both shadowkin glared at Teague, each holding a black swirling orb in one hand.

Great.

Wicked fast, he tore the door off an open locker and slammed it up, using it as a shield against one orb while he deflected the other with a ball of hellfire. More orbs came his way, and he pulled the same move each time—shielding and deflecting.

It didn't always work. Patches of burning skin soon blistered courtesy of both hellfire and hell-acid. And when a flaming orb smacked right into a still-healing wound on his thigh, reopening it, he felt his upper lip curl back.

His inner demon didn't push for supremacy this time; it merely sent Teague telepathic advice of what move to make next. And one particular image made him smile. Yeah, he could do that.

He flicked a look at his 'shield'—the metal door was corroded badly from the hell-acid that fairly dripped from it. He threw the door like it was a frisbee. It sailed through the air and smacked the humanoid in the throat, splattering hell-acid right at the fucker.

The shadowkin staggered back in what appeared to be

both pain and shock, shaking its head as if it could also shake off the pain.

His demon chuffed, rather pleased.

Teague's peripheral vision screamed at him in warning.

He ducked, narrowly avoiding the thick tentacle that then smacked into the locker above him. Rising sharply, he gripped the tentacle tight and, ignoring how it burned his palm like a bitch, he yanked *hard*.

The humanoid wasn't expecting that, wasn't braced for the move; it fell to its back and skidded along the wet floor, writhing in pain as hellfire blasted from Teague's fist all the way down its tentacle and into its body.

While the other shadowkin attacked with more hell-acid, Teague concentrated on the humanoid that was already at his mercy, volleying orb after orb of hellfire at such close range that the little shit stood no chance. Teague kept going, even as hell-acid slammed into his arm, shoulder, scalp, and leg, eating through cloth and flesh.

Finally, the humanoid went limp. *Dead*. Teague dropped the tentacle and turned to the second shadowkin ... with just enough time to dodge the beam of hellfire that would have otherwise buried itself in his throat.

He and the remaining shadowkin then went at each other hard, neither willing to lose. The air rang with the hissing of flames, the sizzling of acid, and Teague's grunts and curses.

As another beam came toward him, he leaped to the side, inadvertently placing himself in front of the other wooden bench. The humanoid planted itself at the opposite end of the bench, braced as if to jump on it.

That was the shadowkin's mistake.

Teague slammed his foot down hard on the bench, making it lurch up like a see-saw. The other end caught the humanoid beneath its chin, sending its head snapping backwards with such force that its neck would have broken if it had bones.

Then Teague was on the little shit, taking advantage of its distraction. He launched ball after ball of hellfire. Its body flinched and arched again and again with each impact.

Finally up close to his attacker, Teague snapped his flaming fist around its throat and hit it in the chest with a high-powered orb. And another. And another, causing flames to spread along its body.

It jerked and bucked and kicked its legs.

Until it didn't.

He dropped the corpse to the floor and lit it up with yet more hellfire, wanting no trace of it to be left behind. The other humanoid was already mostly ashes.

Teague took stock of himself, cursing. He was covered in blisters, scorch marks, and bad burns. Patches of his clothes were corroding and charred. He not only had a fresh bunch of wounds, but some of his earlier injuries were now worse than before.

Fucking wonderful.

He glared down at the corpse at his feet, noticing there wasn't much of it left. Good. He didn't—

His head snapped up at the sound of excited voices. Two tall males barged into the locker room. Taking in the situation, they stopped dead.

The blond frowned. "What in the delightful fuck went on in here?"

"Some demons teleported in and went at me," said Teague, grateful there was no way to tell at this point that those demons were shadowkin—it would raise too many questions. "Probably lost a bet and didn't like it."

The second hellhorse rolled his eyes. "Typical." And then

they went back to their conversation. Well, his kind weren't fazed by much.

Still, his clan were going to be *pissed*.

Standing in the center of her living room, Larkin exchanged an exasperated look with Harper as the females sitting either side of the sphinx squabbled like kids. The argument had sparked to life after Khloë brought up her Aunt Mildred—a woman who Devon insisted did not exist. It didn't matter to the hellcat that Khloë, Jolene, *and* Ciaran repeatedly stated she was mistaken. No, Devon insisted they were bullshitting her. And since imps took such joy in dicking with people, there was every possibility that she was right.

Knox, Keenan, Tanner, and Ciaran stood near the floor-to-ceiling window, ignoring the squabble while discussing mundane topics. As soon as Teague, Levi, and Piper arrived, Ciaran would teleport them all to the monastery. The male imp would likely stay, despite not being invited. His kind didn't let stuff like that get in the way.

Really, Knox didn't need to be teleported anywhere—he had a similar gift that allowed him to travel in such a way. However, it was a gift he only used around the few people he most trusted, and those didn't include the descendants. Demons generally weren't open about all their abilities, particularly Primes.

Neither Asher nor Anaïs would be coming along to the party. It was one thing to be allied with a lair, it was another thing to trust them with your young. So both sets of parents had chosen to leave their child with babysitters at Harper and Knox's home. Their estate was impenetrable. In their position, Larkin would have made the same call.

If she was honest, she wasn't sure she'd make a good mother. She liked kids, she just wasn't maternal by nature.

The first time she'd been given a doll, she'd stared at the plastic infant, not entirely sure what she was supposed to do with it. She hadn't at all liked its overly wide eyes.

So she'd buried it.

Not normal, no, but it had made perfect sense to her back then. Well, Larkin had let her inner demon guide her a lot in those days. And when said demon discarded something, it did it in a definitive fashion.

This included people.

It was even more unforgiving than Larkin. If someone in their life messed up, the entity no longer had any time for that person—they ceased existing for the demon. As proven by how it had literally zero interest in its own psi-mate due to his betrayal.

She hadn't seen or heard from Holt since their little confrontation at the bakery. Predictably, Knox and her fellow sentinels had been furious about it. As had their mates, who'd all agreed that Holt should be drawn, quartered, skinned, and decapitated—and preferably all while alive and sobbing.

Her demon was certainly up for it.

She knew that, despite his betrayal, some would still struggle to understand how her demon could want to harm its own anchor. *Wish* him dead, sure. But be prepared to kill him? Not so much. After all, it went against every instinct a person had toward their psi-mate. But her entity's supremely vindictive nature completely overrode those instincts.

Of course, its aforementioned nature made relationships difficult for Larkin, because everyone made mistakes. Nobody was perfect. That didn't matter to her demon. It would discard people just as easily as Larkin and her entity had once been discarded.

On one level, she was glad of its reluctance to trust and connect. Because it meant that its habit of collecting pretty things didn't extend to collecting people. That was good, since it was pathologically possessive of whatever it owned and point-blank *refused* to share those belongings with others.

She suspected this came from growing up in a children's home. You didn't have many things that were purely yours, and people tried to snatch from you whatever you *did* have. As such, her demon was something of a hoarder and stashed its belongings in hidey holes around Larkin's apartment.

You couldn't exactly stash people, but you could certainly monopolize their time and attempt to isolate them. She worried that her entity would attempt such a thing with any person it chose to collect. That would be bad, so it was better this way even if it did make relationships complicated for Larkin.

A knock came at the front door, pulling her out of her thoughts.

She crossed to it, opened it wide, and felt her pulse briefly stutter as she found Teague stood there. He looked all self-assured and sexy and business-casual in his gray shirt and black slacks. Her ovaries got a little faint, and her demon slinked closer to her skin.

He gave her one of his slow, languid smiles. "Hey, baby."

Her belly did an excited roll at the endearment, even though there could be no real feeling behind his choice to use it. "Hey."

He didn't wait for her to step aside to allow him entrance. He stalked forward, pushing into her personal space and forcing her to back up. Cupping her hips, he mule-kicked the door to close it and very blatantly eye-fucked her.

Her hormones pathetically aflutter, she resisted the urge to tense under his scrutiny. The others—who she could feel staring at them—would easily see it.

"You look incredible." He swept his gaze over her once more. "I do like that dress on you. I'd rather it was off, though, so I can do wicked, wicked things to you."

Tanner cleared his throat. "We're *right here*," he clipped.

Teague blinked at him. "That's ... nice."

Larkin snickered.

"Settle down, pooch," Devon told her mate. "You promised Larkin you'd leave him be tonight so they could enjoy the party, remember?"

Tanner clamped his mouth shut. His gaze lowered to the harpy wing brand, and he gave a disapproving shake of the head. Keenan and Levi looked equally unapproving.

See, this was why Larkin had extracted a promise from them to behave. They would otherwise have bitched about the mark. It was one thing to *know* it existed, it was another thing to *see* it for themselves. Knox was the only one who seemed to have little interest in the matter. *Seemed* being the key word.

"Hey, Teague!" Khloë gave him a big wave from her seat on the sofa.

He flashed her a warm smile. "Hey there, gorgeous."

Keenan looked at Larkin, his lips pressed tightly together. "It really doesn't bother you that he calls another woman 'gorgeous'?"

Khloë shot the incubus a look of annoyance. "Stop trying to stir the pot. That's my job. I like it. You can't have it."

As the mated pair began to argue, Teague returned his focus to Larkin and lightly dragged the tip of his nose up her throat. "Damn, you smell good." *You smell even better when you're wet for me*, he telepathically added.

Her stomach did another crazy flip. *Oh, so that's how tonight is going to go?*

Releasing her hip, he slid his hand up her side. *If you're asking if I intend to dedicate some of our evening into taunting the holy hell out of you, the answer is yes.* As if to emphasize that, he swiped his thumb over the outer side of her breast through her dress—the touch was featherlight but made her nipples tingle. *You made it clear that I needed to step up my game. I'm a man who rises to every challenge.*

I didn't challenge you. It's all in your head. "We're just waiting on Piper and Levi. They should be here any—" She cut off as a rhythmic knock sounded on the door. "And here they are."

Shortly after Larkin let the couple inside her apartment, Ciaran teleported their entire group to the outside of the monastery. The building was tall and wide, constructed of pure stone. There was a beautiful cathedral nearby, along with what looked to be an expansive cemetery.

The double doors leading to the monastery's massive hall were wide open, and two descendants were manning them. Offering them hellos and tips of the chin, Larkin and her group filed inside the dimly lit space.

The party was already in full swing, so maybe someone had decided to start it early. If it wasn't for the music blasting, the array of food on the long-ass tables, and the demons gathered on the makeshift dance floor, it would not have been easy to guess that there was a celebration going on.

There were no banners or fairy lights on the white, rough-hewn stone walls. No balloons stretching up toward the high-vaulted ceiling that boasted broad beams. No foil party curtain that dangled down the arched opening on the other side of the large space.

There were some lanterns and votive candles here and there, along with stunning floral centerpieces that were made up of red and black roses, but that was pretty much it.

Sidling up to her, Teague planted his hand *low* down on her back, resting the heel of his palm right above her butt. The bold touch was a little too proprietary for her liking, but her demon had no issues with it.

Larkin shot him a quick look. "Watch where you put your hand." She wasn't going to let him take advantage of their necessity to engage in a little PDA.

His gaze locked on the aforementioned hand, he said, "I *am* watching. You have no idea how many fantasies I've had about your ass."

"Just my ass?"

He shrugged, meeting her gaze. "The rest of you is all right, I guess."

Larkin discreetly elbowed him hard, but he only chuckled.

Pulling her flush against him, he put his mouth to her ear. "I think I proved the other night that it isn't only your—"

"We're not going to talk about what happened the other night."

He bit her earlobe. "Why not?"

She dug her nails into his chest. "Because I said so."

"Why do you say so?"

"Because I don't want to talk about it."

"Why don't you?"

Larkin pinched his side, her lips flattening when he chuckled even as he flinched. "Behave." She glanced around, taking in the many guests. Most were descendants, but there were some imps hanging around.

The Black Saints were also there, including their president, Viper. The fallen angels had formed an MC club straight after falling over a year ago, from what she'd learned. There wasn't much *to* learn about the Black Saints.

She knew they were allied with Maddox and Raini's lair, and she knew they owned a club that had quickly become quite popular. While it was rumored that Viper could be a fallen archangel—perhaps even one of the infamous seven—he'd allegedly never confirmed or denied it.

Teague slid his hand all the way up her spine and then idly plucked at the wispy little curls on her nape, his own gaze scanning the hall. There was nothing sexual about his touch. And yet, her skin began to heat and prickle.

Annoyed by how frazzled her body got around him, Larkin huffed at the big bastard. "Would you give me some space?"

"Why, you feeling faint from all the seductive pheromones I'm giving off?"

God, he was a loon.

He gave her a sympathetic smile. "I have that effect on women. I wish it wasn't so, but yeah, it happens all the time."

"Sometimes, you make me want to scream right in your face. Do you know that?"

He shrugged. "You'll get used to it."

"You're an idiot."

"You'll get used to that, too."

Larkin was about to pinch him again, but then Khloë materialized in front of them.

"Girl, you gotta stop bitching at him," she told Larkin. "The guys are noticing, and they think he's upsetting you. Tanner's debating storming over here."

Even as Larkin planted a smile on her face and leaned into him, she said, "I can't help it, Khloë. He does and says things that drive me to rag out his hair. And mine."

His lips curved, he nuzzled her temple. "You don't know how happy you make me."

Larkin barely fought the urge to grind her teeth. "See what I mean?" she asked Khloë.

"Hey, I was being nice," he said, all innocence.

When he dipped his head as if to kiss her, she planted a hand on his chest. "Nu-uh."

He grinned. "Why? You don't trust that you won't lose control and jump me? Or are you more worried that you'll swoon right here in front of everyone?'"

"Yeah, that's what it is," Larkin deadpanned. She turned back to Khloë, who was glancing from her to him.

The imp perched her hands on her hips. "You guys have fucked, haven't you?"

Larkin scratched at her cheek while Teague twisted his mouth.

Khloë gaped at him, her nostrils flaring. "I can't *believe* you."

He frowned at the imp. "It's your fault."

Khloë's brows flew up. "Excuse me?"

"You wanted me to play her fake boyfriend. It's important that everyone buys that the relationship is real." He gestured from himself to Larkin, adding, "How else could we have been sure we wouldn't feel and look awkward having sex in front of other people unless we first practiced in private?"

Her lips parted, Khloë stared at him for a moment. Then her hands slipped from her hips as she inclined her head. "Valid point."

"Thank you."

She looked at Larkin. "Remember, ease up on the bitching." With that, she headed back to her mate.

Staring after her, Larkin felt her mouth drop open. Had that actually just happened? Seriously?

She'd expected yelling and threats and curses and finger-pointing. Instead, Khloë had actually accepted his bullshit excuse. And it *was* bullshit. At least to Larkin. But to those two crazy-ass demons, it apparently held merit. And she didn't see how.

"Valid?" Larkin echoed, her gaze snapping to Teague. "How is it *valid* when there'd never come a time when we'd have sex in public even if we were an actual couple?"

"There are lots of situations in which that might happen."

"Give me *one*."

"A dirty game of Truth or Dare."

Okay, he had her there. Demons took that to the next level, so things could get out of hand fast—she'd witnessed that for herself. "Give me another."

"There are a few clubs in the Underground where people fuck right out in the open. Private parties are even held in those places. I'll bet you've been to at least one of those clubs in the past."

Actually, she had. "I'm done with this conversation."

"In other words, you can't deny I'm right and you don't want to hear more examples that prove it?"

"In other words, we need to find Raini and Maddox so we can thank them for inviting us and all that courtesy jazz," Larkin corrected. Well, lied.

His brow creased. "We can grab some food first, right? I'm starving."

So was she, as it happened. "Yeah, we can do that."

They crossed to the nearest table and each grabbed a paper plate. They shuffled along, piling bits of food onto their plates. Sensing someone come up on her other side, Larkin glanced to her left. Recognizing Raini's father, she tipped her chin and said, "Hey, Lachlan."

The imp gave her a nod. "Nice spread they've got going on, isn't it? Teague, I didn't expect to see you here."

"I'm with my girl," he told Lachlan, likely having no idea that his comment made her belly feel all warm. "Where's your mate?"

"Over in the corner lecturing Martina on the evils of stealing wallets from unsuspecting descendants." Lachlan shook his head in judgment. "You can't leave Martina alone for five minutes. Typical Wallis female."

Just then, Raini appeared with a beautiful smile. "Larkin, Teague—thanks so much for coming. I really appreciate it. I know descendants aren't the most welcoming toward outsiders, but I am *determined* to make them mingle just fine with my friends and family." She turned that smile on her father. "Behaving yourself?"

Lachlan let out a tired sigh. "You don't have to keep an eye on me. I already promised I wouldn't purloin anything."

Raini's brow flicked up. "I just watched you stuff a gold goblet in Mom's purse."

"For safekeeping. It's only wise to hide it from your Uncle Bram. You know he likes collecting goblets."

"What I know, dear father, is that you're full of shit."

Affronted, he bristled. "This is your lair. If I steal from them, I steal from you. Do you honestly think I'd ever do that?"

"Well, you've done it before, so don't give me that wounded look. I can't count the number of times my stuff mysteriously disappeared when I was a kid. Bikes, video games, DVDs, stereos."

"You'd outgrown them."

"How does one outgrow a TV?"

Lachlan shrugged. "Don't ask me. I don't question these things. Anyway, I only did that to keep your skills sharp. It's a standard Campbell exercise. And I always replaced what I took with something better."

Larkin frowned. "Keep what skills sharp?"

"Booby-trapping, of course," he replied. "If you're going to protect your things from being taken, you need to lay clever traps. My Raini is excellent at it."

Larkin suspected that by 'things', he meant 'ill-gotten goods', since imps often kept them stored in warehouses and would lay all kinds of traps. "I guess there's no one more paranoid that they'll get robbed than an *actual* thief."

"You got that right," muttered Raini.

A short time later, Larkin and Teague slowly walked around

the hall, eating and talking with whatever cluster of people they came across. Well, *he* talked more than she did, being that he was a social butterfly.

She very soon learned that, though descendants might by nature be wary of other demonic breeds, they were clearly big fans of Teague. They smiled at him, pulled him into conversation, talked about his races, and even asked for damn selfies.

A few women tried discreetly ogling him, but Larkin didn't fail to notice. She knew those bitches would be *all over* him if it wasn't for the brand on his neck. And, unfair to him though it might be, she was at that moment terribly glad that her entity had marked him.

Her demon smirked at that, though said smirk faded as one particular female leaned a little *too* close to Teague.

Worse, the brunette touched his arm, saying, "I don't know if you remember me; we met once years ago. Anyway, I was hoping—"

"If you touch him again I'll stab you in the fucking eye," Larkin told her, her voice as calm as it was flat.

The descendant's gaze danced from her to Teague. "Oh, you two are ... ?"

"Yeah," Larkin replied, considering throwing her empty plate at the woman.

The brunette stepped away with a respectful nod. "Got it. Backing off right now."

Wanting to get away from this particular group, Larkin crossed to the nearby trash can and binned her plate.

Following her, Teague did the same, a grin toying with the edges of his mouth. His mind brushed against hers. *You're hot when you get all possessive.*

I'm not possessive of you. It just would have looked strange if I hadn't reacted that way. Ha, what a load of ole shit.

His lips tipped up. He telepathed her an image. No, not a mere image. It was a *memory* of her sitting naked on the edge of her bed, staring at an equally naked Teague with pure feminine possession in her gaze.

Feeling her face heat, she lifted a brow. *What's your point?*

His smile widened. *If it makes you feel any better, you're not the only one feeling possessive.*

Oh, her demon liked that. Annoyingly enough, so did Larkin. Which made her growl.

Another snapshot of a memory appeared in her mind. One of Larkin on her hands and knees, his cock—all slick and shiny—half-buried inside her.

No. No, they were not doing this. They were not going to torment each other this way like they had at Jolene's house. Because Larkin feared she'd be a sexual mess at the end of it.

CHAPTER ELEVEN

Teague bit back a smile as his harpy's face went bright red. Emotions whirled in her dilated pupils—need, aggravation, impatience, and unease.

"No, I'm not playing this game with you," she declared.

Oh, but she would. She just needed a little push first. "All right," he easily agreed. But then he telepathed her another snapshot—this time of her on her knees and elbows, one side of her sex-drunk face pressed to the mattress. It was a memory that made his cock twitch.

She snarled. "You're such an asshole."

Chuckling, he leaned into her, looking her dead in the eye. "You can huff and bitch and growl at me all you want, pretty harpy—I happen to enjoy it." So did his demon. "But you're not fooling me. I know you like me."

She exhaled heavily. "I actually do. And I can't explain it. With logic, I mean."

His beast let out a low nicker, pleased. "Brave girl. I wasn't sure you'd admit you're falling for me."

"I didn't say I was *falling*—"

"You don't need to, it's written all over your face." He curved an arm around her shoulders and pulled her close so that her body was perfectly aligned with his. "Don't worry. I'm here for you. We'll get through this together. LarTea all the way."

Exasperation rippled across her face, but a smile pulled at her mouth. "Do you never get tired of being a freaking weirdo?"

"It's being normal that's exhausting."

"You wouldn't know what normal was if it fucked you in the ass and called you Judy."

"Why Judy?"

She spluttered. "Because."

"Gotcha. Makes sense."

Shaking her head fast, Larkin threw up a hand. "Stop talking."

"Well, that was rude."

"Do you care?"

"That you were rude? No. If you want to flirt with my beast that way, go for it," Teague invited with a shrug. Lowering his head so that their mouths were mere inches apart—and barely resisting the urge to close that small distance—he warned, "Just remember that you'll only make the demon more determined to bite you."

She tensed in his arms. "Just remember that that won't be happening. And before you complain about it, let me point out that I don't see *you* lining up to be tortured by *my* demon. I'm no masochist either."

He felt his brow crease. "Whoa, my entity doesn't want to torture you or yours." Where was she getting that from?

"Your venom would likely put me through a shitload of pain the likes of which could make me pass out."

He pursed his lips. "I'm not sure what you're getting at."

She poked his ribs hard.

Laughing, Teague breathed her in, letting her scent settle him. His demon was still tightly wound after the attack earlier. His clan hadn't taken it well either, and there had been some talk of eradicating the entire shadowkin race at some point. But now that he had Larkin's body all snug against his own, her scent in his lungs, her gorgeous eyes glaring up at him, he felt the rest of the day fall away.

Dropping his gaze to her lips, he said, "You haven't kissed me tonight yet."

"The only thing I want to do to your mouth is punch it."

A chuckle rumbled out of him. "Oh, how you lie." Before she could protest, he telepathed her another image. Not a memory this time, but a picture of her spread out beneath him on her bed while he feasted on her pussy.

Heat flared in her eyes, and she swallowed.

He hadn't teased her too much through the evening up until this point, wanting to wait until she was good and agitated— that was when her defenses fell and she was more likely to play with him.

"Don't, or I'll retaliate," she warned, fisting the sides of his shirt.

"I'm counting on it." He sent her another image—one of him lying on top of her, pinning her down with his weight while he held her wrists above her head.

Her cheeks flushing, she psychically struck fast.

An image of her on her knees sucking him off popped into his head . . . and went straight to his cock, making it begin to thicken. He smiled slow and wide. "I do love it when you play dirty."

At that moment, Harper and Knox appeared.

The sphinx gave them a winning smile. "Hey, kids, I—Jesus,

Teague, what did you do to put that look on her face? Tell me you haven't been purposely riling her. She looks ready to pounce on you—and not in a good way."

"I'm struggling to make him understand that it would be bad if he or his demon bit me," Larkin fudged. "Which wouldn't be so annoying if it was the first time we'd had this conversation. But it's not. And I could roll my eyes if he was being obtuse. But he's not. He genuinely doesn't see the issue."

Harper scratched at the back of her head. "Yeah, I'm not surprised, given the amount of pain he and his beast willingly put themselves through during every race."

His expression neutral, Knox studied Teague with a probing gaze. "There's one thing your demon could do to limit your venom's effect on Larkin. But I'm sure that both you and the entity already know that, so I have to wonder why it hasn't done it; why you haven't urged the beast to do it."

Yes, there was something Teague's demon could do to spare her any pain from the bite. Something the entity *wanted* to do. But as the relationship was fake, Larkin would hate it. Neither he nor his beast wanted to see the abhorrence on her face that she'd inevitably feel. However, this wasn't something he could explain to Knox.

Instead, Teague shrugged and said, "Her demon wouldn't take kindly to being branded yet. It isn't ready. Both me and my demon sense that, and we respect it."

Approval gleamed in Knox's eyes. "Good."

Larkin's mind brushed Teague's, and then her voice was in his mind ... *Wait, a brand would minimize my body's reaction to your venom?*

Yes. It would still sting a lot, but that's all. Being marked is not something you or your demon would want, though. His entity was a law unto itself in many ways, but Teague didn't worry that it would brand her regardless—it wouldn't do anything to Larkin that would upset or repel her.

Wanting to switch to a lighter topic, he added, *We'd also like to do this to you.* He telepathed her an extremely filthy image that made her face flush.

No way. That's an exit-only zone.

Even as the four of them fell into a conversation, Teague and Larkin continued their telepathic war, exchanging explicit image after explicit image until his cock was hard and his demon was ready to mount her right there.

At one point, Harper's brow puckered as she observed them closely. "You two okay? You look . . . tense. And distracted."

Teague explained, "Larkin and I are having a somewhat filthy telepathic conversation—"

"*Teague,*" the harpy hissed, flushing.

He widened his eyes. "What do you want me to do? Lie?"

"It's what you do on plenty of other occasions," she sniped.

"And you're the one who wants me to be more honest, remember? That's what I'm doing."

Unsuccessfully stifling a smile, Harper said, "Well, I guess Knox and I will leave you to your dirty chat."

The male Prime cleared his throat. "Yes, that might be best."

After the mated pair walked away, Larkin cast Teague another hard glare. "Are you trying to give me an ulcer? Is that what this is?"

"No." He snaked his hand up her back and palmed her nape. "I mean, I am pushing toward my goal of giving you a permanent eyelid-twitch—I think it'll look good on you—but all I want here and now is to make you wet for me. And you are." He could smell it. It was driving his demon nuts in the best way.

"A permanent eyelid-twitch?" she echoed, evidently choosing to ignore the rest of what he'd said.

"Yes." He lowered his head to breeze his lips over hers. "But I'm more interested in discussing how wet you are and just how badly I want to lick you clean."

The need glinting in her eyes bloomed, turning the gray-green pools a little glassy. The rising sexual tension was an incessant pulse in the air between them, impossible to ignore. It held his body captive, and he could see that she was no less affected. But his harpy stubbornly shook her head.

"Why bother talking about it when it's never going to happen?" she questioned. "We agreed that the other night would be a one-off."

He hiked up a brow. "Did we? As I recall it, you told me we needed to leave it as a one-time thing. I don't share that opinion. I made no secret of that."

"And I was clear that I'm not interested in being anyone's booty call, nor do I want a cheap fling. If that doesn't matter to you, think of Khloë. She might have excused you from breaking your oath, but that's only because she bought your bullshit that it was a practice run. She wouldn't excuse it again. So just drop the whole thing."

"Not sure if I can," he admitted, his voice pitched low and deep, "since I've thought of little else but fucking you again since moments after I first had you."

An aroused flush creeping up her neck and face, she cursed. "Do you have to be so difficult?"

"Yes."

"Is there a reason for that?"

"Not one that wouldn't irritate you." He gently nipped at her bottom lip, his teeth barely grazing it. "You can hiss and spit, but I know you're thinking about it. Thinking about how it felt to have my cock balls deep inside you. Thinking about how you want it to happen again." He tightened his hold on her waist, tugging her lower body closer so she'd feel how hard he was. "You were so hot and tight. You took my dick like you were born for it."

"I get that from guys a lot," she said, her tone airy yet meant to provoke. As if he were that easily riled.

"You really want to go down that road? I mean, we *could* talk about our past sexual experiences, I guess. There was this one woman—" He stopped as her eyes bled to black and the temperature cooled in an instant.

Her demon glared at him. "Push her buttons all you please. I would, after all, prefer that you wear her down. But I will not listen to stories of your past exploits." Its gaze dropped to his neck, as if something caught its eye. It poked its finger beneath his collar and tapped his gold chain. "Can I have this?"

He felt his lips twitch. So easily distracted by something shiny. "No."

Its frown was almost childlike. "But I want it."

His beast nickered, amused. "Tough shit. I'll buy you one, though. How's that?"

Humming, it skimmed its fingers through his hair. "Have you ever been waterboarded?"

His lips twitched again. "No."

"I think I would like watching you fight for breath."

God, he fucking *loved* this demon. "What else would you like to do?"

"To you? Many things." It nuzzled his throat. "Some you would enjoy. Some you would not. I would very much like to see how much pain you can take; to see you covered in bruises and welts."

He full-on smiled this time. "Cruel little shit, aren't you?"

It only shrugged one shoulder, uncaring. "Do not forget the chain." Then it retreated, and Larkin's striking eyes were once more locked on him.

He skated a hand down her braid. "Your demon would totally waterboard me if it could, wouldn't it?"

"Often," she admitted with a sigh.

"It's sadistic in an almost clinical way, right? It's not that the entity is evilly bloodthirsty. It simply likes to put people through pain and terrify them to see how they handle it."

"Pretty much, yeah. But it would have no fun playing with masochists. It wouldn't get any satisfaction from giving pain to those who crave it. It wants to experiment on those who don't; to push them to their limits and watch them break."

"Makes sense."

Her brow furrowed. "It does?"

"Yeah. Where's the enjoyment in torturing someone who'll welcome it?" He loosely fisted the end of her braid. "Can I watch next time your demon puts someone through the ringer like that? I'd like to see it at work."

Her eyes all but delved into his. "You're not even kidding, are you?"

"I don't know why you'd feel that I should be."

She sighed again. "Of course you don't."

"Larkin!" Piper called out, waving her over to where the nightmare and the rest of the women stood.

Larkin let her arms slip away from him. "I'll be back in a sec."

"I'll go grab us both a drink while I wait."

"All right. A mojito will do nicely. Try not to cause havoc while I'm gone."

He grimaced. "Yeah, I promise nothing."

She rolled her eyes and then disappeared.

Teague made his way toward the makeshift bar, whistling along to the upbeat tune that played over the speakers. Skirting the end of the table, he came to a stop as he almost bumped into a tall, dark, well-built male who was fairly cloaked in pure power.

The president of the Black Saints shot him a lopsided grin. "Teague," he greeted. "Nice brand. I noticed you're cozy with Knox Thorne's sentinel. Bit risky, isn't it? I mean, you wouldn't want him to learn that . . . " He trailed off, a glitter of mischief in his eyes.

Teague didn't tense, confident that the male wouldn't finish his sentence. "How you doing, Viper? Or should I call you . . . ?" He trailed off, reminding the guy that he wasn't the only one privy to secrets that weren't his.

Viper's mouth curved a little more. "I haven't seen you or your boys at my club in a while."

"We've been sort of preoccupied lately."

The president's gaze sharpened. "Anything you need help with?" The MC club had a loose alliance with Teague's clan— one they'd formed shortly after the fallen angels made an appearance on Earth. It was an unlikely alliance, in truth, but it made sense in a way that no one outside the club or clan would understand due to the secrets they kept.

"Nah, we're handling it."

"If that changes, be sure to let me know."

"Will do." Teague gave him a curt nod and then crossed to the makeshift bar, where he ordered a beer for himself and a mojito for Larkin. As he grabbed both drinks and turned to seek her out, Levi materialized at his side, an odd look on his face. Teague frowned at the reaper. "What?"

Levi cocked his head. "You smiled," he replied, sounding both impressed and baffled.

Teague's frown deepened. "What?"

"You smiled at Larkin's demon."

"Why wouldn't I? That creature is a hoot."

After a long moment of staring at him, Levi let out a heavy exhale. "All right. Fine. I'll back off."

"Huh?"

"You might not know this, but Larkin's demon has scared off many guys she's dated. I think it simply meant to test them, but it's equally possible that the entity was bored and decided to fuck with them just for something to do."

Teague gave a slow nod. "It's hard to fight that kind of temptation, to be fair."

Levi snickered. "Yeah, I guess you can relate to the fulfillment it gets from messing with people," he mused. "It no doubt tried to scare you off, but it didn't succeed. You're still here. And you smiled at it, talked to it, touched it, and even let it nuzzle you. I personally wouldn't want that callous entity anywhere near my throat." He paused. "If you can accept Larkin's demon so fully, I'll just as fully accept you."

Twisting his mouth, Teague shrugged. "All right."

The reaper eyed him for long seconds. "You don't care either way, do you?"

"No, not really."

Smiling, Levi clapped him on the back. "You'll do, Teague. You'll do."

Later on, Ciaran teleported most of their group back to Larkin's apartment. It was only the Primes, Khloë, and Keenan who he took elsewhere, teleporting them to their prospective homes.

With a nice buzz going on, Teague slumped onto the sofa and watched as Larkin hugged Levi, Tanner, and their drunken mates before ushering them out of her apartment.

Shortly after Levi had given Teague his acceptance earlier at the party, the drinking had *really* gotten started. He'd knocked back beer and whiskey and even the last of Larkin's final cocktail—she'd had a fair few of those, so she was pretty tipsy.

She was also still intent on ignoring the tension that had

throbbed between them all night. A tension he'd fed each time he'd teased her with wicked promises, none-too-casual touches, and telepathic images of the many things he wanted to do with and to her.

At no point had he given her a reprieve, determined to make her face that it was too late to try reversing back over platonic lines. They'd never manage it. They'd end up in bed together again sooner or later. It might as well be sooner, in his opinion.

Right then, she closed the front door but didn't move away, her eyes on the wall-mounted clock. She was giving the others time to get back to their apartments before she tossed him out, Teague knew. Well, it would have looked strange to them if she'd refused to allow her boyfriend to stay over, wouldn't it?

Finally, she turned to face him. "Now you." She pointed at the door.

He pouted. "But I like it here. And you don't really want me drinking and driving, do you?"

"I'll call you a cab."

He patted the sofa cushion. "I can sleep on this couch—you won't even know I'm here."

"No."

"Just admit you don't trust that you won't seduce me while I'm asleep," Teague dared, delighting in the long, suffering sigh she let out.

"Get moving, Sullivan," she pushed, once more pointing at the door.

With a heavy exhale, Teague pushed to his feet. "Fine." He prowled toward her, slow and purposeful, his demon *so close* to the surface as it eyed her like she were prey. "If you want me to go, I'll go." Reaching her, he towered over her, liking how nervous she looked. "Although I'm not so sure you truly do."

She swallowed, averting her gaze. But that gaze flew back to him as it turned pure black, and a slight chill wafted over him.

Her demon trailed its finger along his jawline. "Let's chip away at her stubbornness, shall we?" It palmed his nape, pulled his head down, and kissed him hard.

With a low growl, he wrapped its braid around his fist as he kissed the demon back. Their tongues tangled. Their teeth gnashed. Their hearts pounded almost in sync.

His cock hardening, Teague backed the entity into the wall and caged it there with his lower body. Its fingers dug almost painfully into his sides as it arched into him, all but eating at his mouth. But then it stopped.

Teague opened his eyes and found Larkin staring back at him. Their mouths barely touching, he winged up a brow. "Well, am I going or am I staying?" he asked, his voice thick.

She muttered a curse, gripped his hair, and then latched her lips fully on to his.

Taking that for the answer it was, he closed his hand around her breast as they kissed like goddamn savages. There was no restraint, no hesitancy, no attempt at finesse. Just an explosion of need and hunger and desperation.

Pulling back, he peeled off her dress in one fluid movement. As she tackled her bra, he dropped to his knees, caught the waistband of her underwear, and then roughly dragged them down. Inhaling deeply, he nuzzled her pussy. "I swear the scent of your need could make me high." He lifted her leg, planted her foot on his shoulder, and then dived right in.

Her taste bounded into his system, sweet and warm and spicy. He couldn't get enough of it. As if it latched on to him with claws.

He sank his tongue inside her over and over, pausing occasionally to swipe it between her slick folds. His scalp stung from the death grip she had on his hair, but he didn't care. Didn't care about anything but gorging on her taste and making her come. So he kept licking and stabbing, loving how she bore down on his tongue as if desperate to have it deeper inside her.

When he sensed she was close to coming, he wrapped his lips around her clit and suckled gently. She gasped, arching into his mouth, her thigh muscles trembling. He shoved two fingers inside her.

And she fractured.

Feeling her tight inner walls ripple around his fingers made Teague groan. He wanted to feel them around his dick. Needed it. Now.

Withdrawing his fingers from her pussy, he lowered her foot back to the floor and then shot to his feet. He tore open his fly with a snarl. "I'm gonna fuck you so hard." His cock jutted out, aching and throbbing. Her glazed eyes dropped to it, and she licked her lips.

Too intent on getting inside that pussy, he didn't give her a few seconds to recover from her orgasm. He gripped her ass, lifted her, and pressed her body against the wall. She'd barely had the chance to wrap her legs around his hips before he slammed her down on his cock.

Her head shot back, her eyes snapping wide open, her brow creased with pleasure and pain. "Jesus, Teague."

He groaned. "Fuck, you feel good."

She righted her head and tugged at the back of his tee. "Take this off."

"No."

Larkin swore as he began railing her hard, his fat cock mercilessly overstretching her. There was a burn to each deliciously deep thrust, but it didn't dim the pleasure. Not in the slightest.

Curling her legs tighter around him, she locked an arm

around his shoulders and thrust the fingers of her free hand into his hair. She'd done a lot of pulling on those strands tonight, so his scalp was gonna be tender tomorrow. She kind of liked that thought.

Without losing momentum, he shifted his angle. She gasped because, oh God, each slam of his cock now brushed over her clit. A clit he'd earlier flicked and rubbed with his wicked, fabulous tongue that could give a masterclass on how to please a woman.

One thing she loved about sex with Teague was that there was no teasing, no dragging out foreplay, no orgasm denial. There was only taking and giving and demanding. "Stop scraping your teeth on my face."

"No."

There was that, too. A habit of ignoring her orders and doing as he pleased. But she loved that as well, so she couldn't really complain. "If you dare bite me, I'll rip your dick off."

He went still, and then the air cooled as his demon surfaced. It narrowed its black eyes at her and rumbled an animalistic sound.

Larkin licked her lips, admittedly a little nervous. All demonic entities were cruel and dangerous, but hellbeasts? They were on another level. Because they weren't civilized or reasonable, too primitive in their way of thinking. They were more beast than man. More monster than animal.

Teague's demon rubbed its nose along her cheekbone, letting out a low and rumbly nicker. That nose ghosted down her cheek, over her jaw, and down her neck. The entity set its teeth around the thick vein in her throat—a blatant assertion of dominance.

It didn't bite down, and she didn't get the sense that it meant to. No, this was more of a message that it *could* so easily hurt her and so she should watch her step.

Snorting, Larkin tugged hard on its hair. "What the fuck ever, Applejack."

Without withdrawing its teeth, it let out an annoyed chuff, sending a waft of warm air at her neck.

Then it began to fuck the holy hell out of her.

A startled gasp burst out of Larkin as the demon powered into her like the wild beast it was, chasing its own pleasure, uncaring of her own. Weird though it might be, there was something about the moment, about flirting with the danger of being bitten, about being *taken* by an entity that gave no fucks what she wanted, that somehow incited both her and her demon.

She would have arched into the brutal thrusts if the hands on her ass weren't clenching so tight. The entity held her perfectly still, forcing her to take only what she was given.

All things considered, it was really no wonder that Orgasmville was already so close, making her inner muscles spasm.

Snarling, the demon roughly upped its pace, ramming into her so hard it hurt. It clamped its teeth a little tighter around the vein in her throat—not nicking the skin, but taunting her with how she was at its mercy right then. God help her, the reminder of danger only shoved her closer to Orgasmville.

Mere moments later, she was there.

Pleasure burst through her in an electric wave so damn blinding she lost her breath. The demon snapped its hips upward faster, harder, and deeper. Then, with one last slam, it exploded.

Panting and trembling, she felt its teeth slide away from her throat. The demon dragged its tongue along the vein with a soft nicker, and then she sensed the entity withdraw.

Teague lifted his head, his striking eyes all lazy and warm. "Applejack? Really?"

She felt her lips quirk. "Your demon didn't like being referred to as one of the My Little Pony characters, huh?"

"No, it didn't." He carried her to the bathroom, where he propped her on the counter. He swiped a small flannel from a shelf and used it to clean her up. Once he'd dumped it in the hamper, he set a hand on the counter either side of her. "It'll happen again."

She sighed, unable to deny that it was highly likely—particularly since her demon would continue to help him wear down Larkin's defenses. Those defenses were already ragged at the edges where he was concerned. But . . . "I told you, I'm not into shallow flings."

He hummed. "You complicate things by tossing out labels. Booty calls. Hook-ups. Flings. Bed-buddies." He scraped his teeth over her chin. "The core of the situation is much simpler. I want you, and you want me. That's it. Where's the negative in that? There's no reason we can't just let ourselves enjoy it. No reason we have to put it in a neatly marked box that gives it rules and boundaries and limitations."

Spoken like a true hellbeast. They were much more elemental in their sexual way of thinking. Which, honestly, she envied. There had to be freedom in that.

He seemed to be forgetting something, though. "I'm pretty sure that although Khloë didn't get mad about our 'practice run', as you termed it, she didn't give you the green light to fuck me whenever you pleased."

He waved that away. "She knows that practice makes perfect."

A silent laugh shook Larkin's shoulders. He came out with the weirdest stuff.

"You know, we're similar in some ways."

She felt her brow pucker. "We are?"

"Yeah. We both make a point of not getting close to people, particularly when it comes to relationships."

"That's not true. I avoid—"

"Sweet and short flings," he finished. "And bed-buddy arrangements. And one-night stands. And long-distance relationships.

And just about anything that doesn't involve total commitment. See what I'm getting at? You demand everything from your partners—it's all or nothing. Generally, guys don't agree to 'all' straight off the bat. It's a way for you to hold people back."

Her demon gave a hard nod of agreement. Larkin only stared at him, mentally floundering. She'd never looked at the situation like that before. But yeah, he was spot on.

Feeling a little vulnerable and defensive, she folded her arms and fired a scowl his way. "Are you going somewhere with this?"

"You're using my tendency to avoid 'complicated' to keep me at arm's length. Why bother, Lark? Like I said before, the situation is simple—I want you, and you want me. Can't we explore that and take it day by day? Do we have to define, label, and put a time restriction on it?"

A sigh slipped out of Larkin. She *had* been overcomplicating it, hadn't she? Of course, she knew why. She'd done it because she feared letting him too close.

The problem was that, in truth ... it was too late for that. Teague was already under her skin. She'd refused to admit it to herself, scared of the power it gave him, but it smacked her in the face right then like a two-by-four.

He might annoy her like no one else, but she felt more alive around him than she ever had around anyone. More, she felt *accepted*. It didn't matter to him that her demon was a loon. He wasn't put off by it, or by how snarky she was, or by her having four meddling brothers that would fry him on the spot if he upset her.

He also made her feel safe. Larkin could take care of herself just fine, of course, but that was *physical* safety. Feeling at ease and comfortable with someone, being confident they'd never purposely hurt you, was something else altogether. Few people had made her feel that she'd be emotionally safe with them.

Teague, she realized, was one of them.

He'd never abandon someone who mattered to him. Never be anything but loyal and protective of them. Never consider his own wants more important than their wellbeing.

And, well, she kind of wanted to keep him. Something she hadn't consciously acknowledged until this moment.

Her demon grinned, satisfied that Larkin had finally faced the reality of the situation. It felt that he made a good partner and intended to keep him around.

Staring into his hazel eyes—so languid and piercing and utterly focused on her like nothing else mattered—Larkin decided that, yes, that wouldn't be a bad idea at all.

Of course, there were two issues at play . . . One, he didn't do permanence. Two, Khloë would never condone it anyway.

Larkin would somehow convince her otherwise. She would talk the imp into releasing him from his promise, just as she would coerce Teague into shedding his 'flings only' attitude. Because whether he saw it or not, their fake relationship wasn't entirely fake anymore. They had something. It was fragile and made up of very strange components, but it was there.

She couldn't point any of that out to him, though. If he knew she intended to keep him, if he saw that they'd inadvertently crossed the 'fake' line, he'd undoubtedly react by backing away. And that basically meant she'd have to be sneaky about coaxing him further over that line.

Luckily, Larkin wasn't a woman who needed a guy to do all the chasing and seducing. In fact, there'd be some fun in subtly chipping away at the defenses of this bastard who'd already found his way around hers. There'd be humor in trying to force him out of his comfort zone like he'd pushed her out of her own.

He'd probably crap himself when he finally realized they were in a real relationship.

Yeah, this would be fun for sure.

She was crafty enough to pull off shattering his defenses, though she wouldn't be able to give it her all until she'd dealt with the Holt situation and kicked him out of the picture. *Then* she could pour her full concentration into the much more interesting project of luring Teague into accepting his fate. Her demon was *all* for it.

Unfolding her arms, Larkin rubbed at her thighs. "Okay, we just take it day by day and enjoy the simplicity of it." She'd let him think her intention was for them to simply test the endurance of the bedsprings some more.

His mouth curved. "That's my girl."

Yes, yes, she was. He just didn't know it yet. Ha.

He dropped a quick kiss on her lips and then straightened. "I'm staying here tonight."

"Are you? Thanks for letting me know."

"You're welcome."

She huffed, rolling her eyes. "You're an idiot."

"Like I said earlier, you'll get used to it."

CHAPTER TWELVE

Chewing on a chunk of fluffy pancake the next morning, Teague eyed Larkin from where she sat opposite him at the kitchen island. "You keep looking at me weird."

Coffee mug in hand, she arched a brow. "I do?"

"Yeah."

"Weird how?"

"Like a predator watches another predator, looking for weaknesses and blind spots." And she was very much aware that she was doing it.

His demon squinted, unsure how it felt about this. Being the center of her focus pleased the entity. But this feeling of being studied and hunted? Not so much.

It also made no sense.

He was certain of one thing. "You're plotting something."

A smile shaped her luscious mouth. "I am," she readily admitted.

He leaned forward slightly, intrigued. His demon pricked up

its ears, equally interested. Joining forces with her could be fun. "Let me in on it."

"No."

He felt his forehead crease. "Why not? My input would be invaluable."

"Probably. You are, after all, a devious little shit."

Seriously, she came out with the best compliments. "So clue me in. Take advantage of my expertise in this area."

His harpy pursed her lips. "Nah."

"Ah, come on."

"Don't worry. You'll eventually learn what I'm plotting."

Straightening, he sliced into his half-eaten pancake, asking, "When will 'eventually' come rolling around?"

"I don't have an estimated date for you, unfortunately."

That wasn't vague at all. "I'm not a fan of suspense. Just tell me."

"How about *you* tell *me* why there's no record of your past?"

"But I like being mysterious."

She snorted, throwing him a derisive look. "You like keeping secrets."

He didn't really have much choice *but* to keep things hidden. But, obviously, he couldn't explain that to her. He wouldn't have done anyway, because he saw what she was doing. "You're just trying to distract me from questioning you about whatever it is that you're planning."

Pausing, he forked a piece of pancake and dipped it in the sweet maple syrup that had trickled onto the plate. "It won't work. I use this trick all the time. I'm immune to—Jesus, Lark."

The little minx had whipped off her camisole, revealing her gorgeous breasts perfectly cupped in a neon pink lacy bra that gave her some *wicked* cleavage—his harpy had a whole drawer full of colorful, sexy underwear. And then she took a casual sip of her coffee, like she did this all the time.

He smiled. "Bravo. I'm officially distracted."

One corner of her lips tilted upward. "Typical boy."

A phone chimed from somewhere within the apartment.

She set down her cup. "I'll be back in a minute." Her stool legs scraped the tiled floor as she pushed out of her seat.

"Be braless when you get back."

She only rolled her eyes and strode out of the room.

Raising his fork to his mouth, he bit into the large chunk of pancake. Damn, the woman could cook. *Really* cook.

When they'd taken a break from their sexual marathon halfway through the night, she'd whipped up the most *amazing* stir fry. His stomach was in love with her.

She was stacking up points fast. She cooked like a pro, stocked his favorite beer, liked watching sports, knew her way around a spectacular blowjob, and made him come harder than any woman ever had.

Yeah, he needed to wangle himself some future invites. It might not be easy, despite the agreement they'd made last night. Because Larkin was skittish at the best of times and liked to have her space. But then, he was good at pushing himself into it. He'd been doing it for years.

As he chewed on yet another piece of pancake, he wondered what exactly she could be plotting. Maybe it was related to Holt. Maybe she wanted Teague to agree to something that would further agitate her idiot of a psi-mate.

If so, Teague would be up for it. The sooner the cambion did something stupid, the sooner Teague could watch her demon obliterate him. He had the feeling that it would be one hell of a show. His beast was looking forward to it.

He used the last chunk of his pancake to sweep up what was

left of the syrup. Wolfing it down, he glanced around the kitchen. It was spacious, not to mention contemporary with stainless steel appliances, dove-gray cupboards, and bright white wall tiles. It was also immaculately clean like the rest of her apartment.

There were no crumbs or spilled sugar on the countertop. No old sauce splatter on the tiles above the stove. No overflowing trashcan or cup rings on the wooden surface of the island.

His kitchenette was clean, but not so much that it damn sparkled. His countertop boasted scars, a little clutter, and a couple of ring stains that no amount of scrubbing had ever removed.

Just as he lowered his cutlery to his empty plate, he heard the sound of steady footfalls. Soon, Larkin came strolling into the kitchen.

"You're still wearing your bra," he complained.

"And I have no intention of taking it off. Deal with it."

"Well, that was rude, but I'll let it go because those pancakes were *awesome*." He lifted his mug, and the fragrant steam of his coffee wafted his face. "Do you have a cleaner?"

She returned to her stool. "Nope."

Huh. Who would have guessed she was something of a neat freak? Then again, she didn't have any needless accessories or sentimental objects lying around to keep tidy. There wasn't even a single plant or herb pot on her windowsill.

"You have a junk drawer, don't you?"

Her brows flicked together. "What?"

"No one's kitchen is this tidy unless they have somewhere to stuff their clutter."

She shook her head. "No junk drawer."

Also, no real personality to the space. The only personal touches were the childlike drawings that had been attached to her double-fridge with magnets. He tipped his chin toward them. "I'm guessing Asher was the artist."

The set of her mouth softened. "Yeah, he was. And that reminds me ..."

He arched a questioning brow, sipping at his coffee.

"What are your plans for today?"

"I've got a race coming up this afternoon, and then nothing. You?"

"It's my day off. I'm having lunch with the girls. That's the extent of my plans until later—I'm on babysitting duty tonight. So are you."

His head jerked back slightly. "What?"

"You're helping me babysit Asher." Larkin almost smiled at the flash of panic on his face. She knew from Khloë that though Teague liked kids, he had a huge aversion to babysitting—the thought of being responsible for young living beings made him uneasy, which was why he'd never agreed to babysit Khloë's younger siblings. "The other sentinels and I take turns. It's now mine."

"What does that have to do with me?"

"People in relationships babysit together." Sort of. Larkin simply wanted to rope him into spending as much time with her as possible so she could begin to subtly sneak beneath his guard and eat away at his 'no relationships' stance.

His brow pinching, he flicked his head to the side. "They do?"

"Yup."

"Huh." He chewed on the inside of his mouth. "I didn't know that."

"Why would you? You've never been in a relationship."

"I came close to it once."

Jealousy flared inside Larkin, and her equally green-eyed demon flexed its fingers. "Really? What happened there?"

Exhaling a sad sigh, he lowered his cup to the coaster. "Not much. She and I didn't have much in common. I'm loud and social. She was quiet and inflatable. It was never going to work out."

Crossing her eyes, Larkin felt a smile curve a mouth. "You're insane."

"Proudly." He propped his elbows on the island. "When does the babysitting gig start?"

"Six-thirty. Meet me here. We'll head to Harper and Knox's home together."

He gave her an odd look. "You sure they'll be fine with this? I mean, they don't know me very well. They might not want me in their home and around their kid without them there to supervise."

Her demon's jaw hardened, and Larkin felt her expression firm. "If they're not okay with it, they can ask someone else to babysit. Either we both go, or neither of us go." She wasn't going to have *anyone* make him feel on the outside of their group.

Teague smiled, slow and sexy. "Aw, look at you being all protective. It's sweet. I'm touched. I really do have the best girlfriend."

"Yeah, you do. And don't forget it."

He chuckled, apparently not unnerved by how she hadn't done as she usually did and stated that she was his *fake* girlfriend. It was good that he'd read nothing into it—he might otherwise clam up and pull away. His cluelessness was also somewhat amusing for both her and her entity. The poor hellhorse had no idea that he was the focus of a harpy on the hunt.

It was shortly after they'd finished their coffees that he announced he needed to leave. Her demon predictably pouted. It would no doubt sulk for a while, but whatever.

After pulling on her camisole, Larkin walked him to the front door and pulled it open. As he stepped out into the hall, she shuffled forward and said, "Good luck with your race. Not that you need it." He never did.

He crooked his finger at her. "Closer. I want to leave here with your taste in my mouth."

Her stomach fluttered. "Then come get it."

Grinning, he moved toward her, dipped his head, and then kissed her. It was a deep, drugging kiss that went on and on. Giving her wrist a little squeeze, he drew back. "Later."

"Later."

They both turned their heads as Levi's front door opened. The reaper strolled out of his apartment, quickly followed by his mate. Piper gave Larkin and Teague a wave, beaming. Levi tipped his chin at them and greeted, "Morning."

"Morning," Teague returned.

Larkin, however, merely stared at the reaper's back as he stalked off with Piper.

"What's wrong?" Teague asked her.

Nothing, it was just that . . . "He didn't glare at you." Nor had he given the brand a dirty look.

"Ah, so, he's apparently decided he'll accept my place in your life, since I accept your crazy-ass demon." Teague gave a fluid shrug. "That's what he told me last night, anyway."

God, she loved Levi. She really did. Her demon actually blew him a kiss.

Sure that Knox, Tanner, and Keenan would follow the reaper's lead, Larkin smiled as she said, "Good." Pausing, she pointed at Teague. "Six pm. Don't forget."

Backing up, he saluted her. "I'll be here."

Returning inside, Larkin closed the door and then telepathically reached out to Knox. *I want to bring Teague with me later when I babysit Asher at your place. Will that be a problem?*

Her Prime's mind lightly clipped her own. *I had a feeling you'd want to bring him.*

Is it going to be an issue?

I don't see why it should be. I trust that you'd never ask this if you weren't positive that he would never be a threat to Asher. And, as it happens, I don't believe Teague would ever be a threat to any child. Plus, I'm quite sure you could put him on his ass if necessary.

Larkin's lips tilted upward. *I totally could.* Though the hellhorse would probably disagree.

Levi told me that Teague and your demon seem to get along quite well.

They have a few things in common. Namely, they're both incredibly disturbed and like to make people feel uncomfortable.

A vibe of pure male amusement touched her mind. *I don't think your demon would have settled for anyone who was well-adjusted.*

Probably not. I'll see you tonight. She broke the psychic contact with a pleased sigh. Levi had accepted Teague, and apparently so had Knox.

Two bros down, two left to go.

As a lean, graying male urged Larkin and Teague into a huge-ass mansion with a polite smile later that day, Teague gestured for her to enter first. He followed closely behind, stepping into a gleaming marble foyer. His demon's nostrils flared as it inhaled the smells of floor wax, freshly cut flowers, and scented candles lacing the air.

He'd heard that Knox and Harper lived on a grand estate, but he hadn't known it was so expansive. He'd only gotten glimpses of the front, but that was big enough with its sprawling landscape, huge mansion, a sizeable garage, and also a gatehouse. He suspected there were more buildings at the rear of the property.

High brick walls bordered the estate, though he supposed that was more for privacy than security. Because the entirety of it was surrounded by a psychic shield that was invisible to the naked eye and impossible for demons to penetrate. An orb of hellfire would bounce right off it, and any attempts by strangers to teleport inside would fail.

Only people who were psychically 'keyed' to be allowed entrance could bypass the shield, arriving either via the tall, metal security gates or by some means of demonic travel. Larkin was one of those people.

As the butler who Larkin referred to as Dan led them further into the house, Teague saw that it was as opulent as its exterior. Not pretentious, though, which he liked.

Dan led them into a vast sitting room. Harper was perched on one of two half-moon upholstered sofas that framed a coffee table. The latter was the same light pine as the wooden flooring. Asher sat cross-legged beside his mother, his gaze locked on the TV.

Knox stood in front of the fireplace, his feet planted on the blue Persian rug beneath him as he spoke into his cell phone. Behind him, mismatched knick-knacks lined the fire mantel.

Spotlights beamed down from the high ceiling that also boasted a crystal chandelier. Similar spotlights were embedded in the walls alongside striking paintings, framed family photos and a tall antique mirror.

The three Thorne demons looked up as Dan announced the arrival of Larkin and Teague. The butler then melted away as greetings were quickly exchanged.

Asher crossed to Teague, swinging his arms. "You're gonna stay with me while my mommy and daddy go out and make kissy faces at each other."

"What?" asked Teague.

"Ciaran said that's what mommies and daddies do on date nights." The wrinkling of Asher's nose made clear what he thought of that. "He said he'd tell me more when I'm older, and we'd talk about bees and birds. But I don't know why he wants to talk about those."

Knox looked at his mate. "Our son will not be having such a conversation with an imp. God knows what they'll tell him."

Harper smiled. "My dad's version of *that* particular talk was teaching me all about artificial insemination, saying I should stay away from boys because if I kissed one I'd grow fangs."

Larkin snickered.

A Hispanic woman inched into the room. "Would either of you like something to eat or drink?" she asked both Larkin and Teague.

"Thanks, Meg, a soda would be great," Larkin told her.

"I'm good, thanks," he told the woman.

With a smile, Meg nodded and then disappeared.

Once Harper and Knox were ready to leave, she cupped Asher's chin and said, "Now, you be good for Larkin and Teague. Okay?"

The kid gave her a dimply smile. "'Kay."

She dropped a kiss on his head. "That's my good boy."

Asher disappeared in a roar of flames, only to reappear in front of Knox. "I want a hug," he told his father.

Knox lifted him, gave him a tight squeeze, and kissed his temple. "You know what to do if you need me or your mom, don't you?"

Asher gave a curt nod. "I 'path you and say *hey, get your butts home.*"

Humor lit Knox's eyes. "Something like that."

A loud, high-pitched *toot* filled the air, and then Asher dissolved into a fit of giggles.

Knox sighed. "That was why you wanted a hug, wasn't it? So you could fart on my arm?"

Asher didn't respond, too busy laughing.

Harper snatched him from his father with a playful growl, tickled him mercilessly, and then set him down on the sofa. "You are trouble in its purest form." She grabbed her purse from the table. "Thanks so much for this, guys, we appreciate it," she said to Larkin and Teague.

"Contact us if you have any problems," Knox told them, slipping his arm around his mate's waist.

"We will," Larkin assured him.

"Bye!" Asher yelled, bouncing on the sofa.

"Dammit, kid, stop jumping on the couch," groused Harper.

He only giggled again.

Then the Primes were gone. Meg entered the room mere moments later, handed Larkin her soda, and then once more vanished.

Larkin took a swig of her drink as she turned to Asher. "So, what do you want to do while we wait for your mom and dad to get back?"

He scuttled off the couch and dashed to Teague. "I wanna ride the horsey."

Uh, yeah, no. He hoisted the kid up. "How about we just do this instead?"

"Do what?" asked Asher.

In answer, Teague dangled him upside down by one ankle. Asher squealed in delight, kicking his free leg.

"I have an idea," said Larkin. "How about we go play in the backyard?"

"Yes!" agreed Asher. "The horsey can take me outside!"

"I'll give you a piggyback ride—that's the best deal you're getting," Teague told him.

The kid dedicated a good ten minutes into trying to change Teague's mind. When it didn't work, he agreed to the piggyback ride.

After placing her soda on the coffee table, Larkin led the way as they walked out of the room and through the mansion.

"I like the blue-tinted windows," said Teague.

"They're bulletproof," she told him, confirming his suspicion. "Despite the shield encompassing the estate, Knox has extra security measures for the mansion. He takes no chances."

As they walked out of the rear patio doors, he felt his brows lift. "Some backyard." There was a BBQ area, an outdoor bar, a massive cabana complete with a widescreen TV, and a currently covered swimming pool.

Various smells scented the air. Chlorine, sun-warmed stone, stagnant pond water, and all the freshly mown grass that sat between the patio area and a large playground.

As soon as Teague stepped foot on the playground's spongy rubber flooring, Asher pyroported from his back to the floor. Then he raced off.

"Sweet little play area he's got here." There were swings, a slide, a tube maze, a sandbox, a see-saw, a jungle gym, monkey bars, and a rock climbing wall. Like the rubber flooring, the equipment was brightly colored.

Larkin nodded. "His parents don't do anything by halves."

"Teague, come push me," Asher urged, perching his butt on a swing.

"Not too high," Larkin said to Teague. "Go easy."

He smiled. "Well, *obviously*."

Larkin spent the next hour with her heart in her throat. Why? Because Teague didn't know the meaning of *go easy*. He was as much of a daredevil as Asher.

So during the time the two dudes made full use of the playground, there was one moment after another where she was sure the kid would fall and split his head open. But Teague would be at his side *super*fast, steadying him in an instant. Which was the only reason she didn't put a stop to it and instead hovered close just in case she was needed.

When Asher finally settled down in the sandbox to play with the toys there, Teague sidled up to her and said, "That boy is a whirlwind of energy."

"You're good with kids," she noted.

He shrugged. "I like them. Sort of."

"Sort of?" she asked with a chuckle.

"I mean, it depends on the kid."

"So I take it you're not in a rush to have any of your own?"

His mouth curved. "Keenan insists that it would be better for the world if I never breed."

Larkin shook her head. "Some would say the same about his mate, so . . ."

"What about you? Do you want your own brood?"

"Maybe not a brood. One or two would be enough for me." She paused as they both crossed to the nearby bench and sat. "Why haven't you joined Jolene's lair?"

His head twitched. "That came out of nowhere."

She shrugged. "I've always wondered why you didn't. I know she offered for you and your clan to join. How come you said no?" It would have made sense for them to snap up Jolene's offer. The demon world could be brutal, and strays were easy targets.

He twisted his mouth. "I'm not the type of person who'd do well at answering to others."

Yeah, she could see that. "Do you have any family?"

He blinked. "Family?"

"Yeah. You know. Parents. Siblings. Extended relatives."

Leaning slightly away from her as if to better study her face, he offered her a wary look. "What's with the questions?"

Ah, always so cautious. "What's with the evasiveness?"

"*You're* no more open than I am. You rarely answer my questions."

That much was true. "Okay, ask me something."

He slowly sank back onto the bench and then draped his arm over the back of it, his hand brushing against her shoulder. "All right. I heard that you, Knox, and the other three sentinels grew up in a children's home for demonic orphans. Is that true?" By the look on his face, he didn't expect her to answer.

But she did. "It is. It's how we all met and formed a family of sorts."

"How did you end up an orphan?" Again, he didn't seem to be expecting a response.

Again, she gave him one. Because although she didn't like revisiting this time in her life, she needed to make an effort to be open with Teague if she truly meant to keep him. "I was a stray once, like you. So was my mom, Belle. I don't properly remember the attack on our lair—I was only a toddler back then—but it decimated most of our numbers. The survivors sought a place in other lairs. Except for my mom. She didn't want to."

"Why?"

"I'm not sure. She never said." Larkin pulled in a steadying breath through her nose. "Anyway, one day—I was four, I think—she took me to the local forest so we could pick berries like we sometimes did."

Pausing, Larkin swallowed as she remembered how her mother would always sing and dance and laugh like a wood nymph. "On the way home, she said she needed to stop off somewhere to speak to a friend. She took me to this huge building and told me to wait in the reception-type area while she spoke to the person in charge. She kissed my forehead, gave me a trembly smile, disappeared down the hall . . . and I never saw her again."

Teague's brows snapped together. "The building she took you to was the orphanage?"

"Yes." Her chest tightening painfully, Larkin let out a shaky exhale. "I didn't realize she'd left at first. She didn't say goodbye.

Just went on her way like she was dropping me off at daycare." That was when her demon's issues had come into play.

Teague's face went rock hard. "She *left* you? Just like that?"

"Just like that." She swallowed. "When the Ramsbrook staff told me that she wanted me to live there now, I didn't believe them. I was sure she'd never abandon me. But I was wrong."

Threads of red-hot anger crisscrossing in his belly, Teague softly cursed. "You had no clue she meant to leave you there?"

"No." Clasping her hands tightly in her lap, his harpy sucked in her lips. "I never saw it coming. It wasn't as if Belle was a neglectful mom or anything. She told me every day that she loved me, and I believed her. But I don't know how you can abandon someone you love like that."

Angling his body toward her, Teague rested a hand on her nape. "What about your other relatives? Your father? Grandparents? She couldn't have at least put you in the care of a family member?"

"I never met my dad—I was the product of a one-night stand, and he had no interest in me. I learned that much from eavesdropping. As for my other relatives ... they died during the attack on my lair, I barely remember them. Belle and I only had each other. Until we didn't."

The way her voice broke on the latter word made his stomach hurt. Furious on her behalf, he slid closer to her. "Did the staff at the orphanage explain why she took you there?"

"They had no explanation to give me, because she gave none to them." Larkin licked her lips. "I could seek out the answers if I want to. She's still alive."

"You looked her up?"

Larkin nodded. "She's happily mated with two adult children. She and her new family live in Atlanta."

Jesus Christ. He couldn't imagine how it would feel to be

tossed aside like unwanted goods so that your parent could essentially start over. That was how the situation came across to him. Belle wanted a fresh start after losing her lair; wanted to shed her daughter so she could once again be single, childless, and carefree.

No wonder Larkin and her demon had no willingness whatsoever to forgive Holt. He'd done what her mother had done: Left with no warning, and never looked back. Or, at least, he hadn't until now. But it was too little too late for Larkin and her entity.

She looked off into the distance. "I thought about confronting Belle when I first tracked her down, but I see no reason why I should give her that level of emotional importance. She walked away. She turned her back on me. She deserves nothing at all from me. So I chose to instead embrace my future rather than chase my past. Knox, Levi, Tanner, and Keenan are my family. They'd *never* do to me what Belle did."

Anger skipping along the surface of his skin, Teague did what he did at her apartment when she told him about Holt. He curled his arm around her shoulders and pulled her toward him. She didn't stiffen this time; she melted into him, resting her head on his shoulder.

His demon's blood boiled. The beast was stomping and letting out rumbly neighs, outraged that she'd been let down and abandoned by the two people who should have most wanted what was best for her.

He understood now why she so rarely opened her world to outsiders. The less people who were in it, the less chance she had of anyone again leaving her.

Though he appreciated that she'd been so open with him, he couldn't return her honesty with his own. Not fully. There was too much he needed to hide. But he could give her some details.

"I haven't seen my mother in years. We lost touch after I went my own way. We were never close, so I doubt she's any more affected by that than I am." They loved each other; they just hadn't bonded.

Loosely fisting his tee, she raised her head from his shoulder. "And your dad?"

"The man is a dick. And no father to me." Personally, Teague didn't believe that Soren was built for parenthood. "I have one sibling. A half-brother. He hates me just about as much as his mother does."

Larkin's brow knitted. "Why?"

"Our father was in a relationship with his mother when he impregnated mine."

She winced. "That wasn't your fault."

"No, but I was a reminder of his infidelity." He cleared his throat. "So, in short, I'm not in contact with any of my biological relatives. Like you, I formed my own family."

"Self-made families are the best," she proclaimed with a faint smile.

"I gotta agree with you there."

A short time later, Asher became bored and so they went inside. The sand was the kind that you could easily shake off, but Larkin nonetheless changed him into fresh clothes.

All three of them gathered on one of the sitting room sofas to watch a movie that Asher chose. They were around halfway through it when he fell asleep lying across both Larkin and Teague's laps.

"I think he tired himself out running around the playground," said Teague.

Larkin hummed. "He'll probably only nap. He's old enough now that he doesn't need to sleep every night, but he still has the occasional nap. So ... how are you finding babysitting? Is it as terrifying as you thought it would be?"

He pulled a face. "Worse."

"Liar. You enjoyed racing around outside with the little man."
She rubbed her chest, adding, "I still can't *believe* you had him
jump off the top of the climbing wall."

"No, I asked him to pyroport himself down. He chose to
instead jump. But I caught him, didn't I?"

"Not before he took two years off my life."

"Now *that* is one heck of a brand," said a new voice.

Teague watched as a familiar male wearing a tatty red cap, a
faded Metallica tee, and a pair of scuffed jeans strolled toward
the sofa. *Lucifer himself.* A being who was nothing like the devil
that humans spoke of.

Lucifer—who went by Lou—might lack a conscience, but
he was not a creature of darkness. In fact, he was more of an
antisocial, moody, psychopathic child who happened to have
OCD and liked only one person on this Earth: Asher. Hence
why he occasionally appeared at the mansion uninvited, able to
somehow bypass the shield.

Lou smirked at Larkin. "Your demon sure is possessive of
Teague, huh?"

She grunted, folding her arms.

The devil's smirk didn't whatsoever dim. "Still mad at me?"

"Yes."

Teague narrowed his eyes at him. "What did you do?"

It was Larkin who explained, "The asshole picked a fight with
me while I had the hiccups."

Teague managed to stifle a smile. Barely.

Lou plonked himself on the sofa opposite them. "I could try
to be a better person. But why bother? It's not like I'm going to
heaven. Been there. Done that. Wasn't feeling the vibe."

"So you chose to embrace evil instead," muttered Larkin.

"I highly recommend it," said Lou, completely serious.

"There's more fun to be had in the dark than in the light. Trust me on that."

"I'd be a fool to trust you in anything."

"That I will concede." Lou glanced from her to Teague. "So, I'm guessing this is a result of Harper's matchmaking efforts."

Larkin squinted. "How do you know about the matchmaking?"

"I heard Harper talking to Knox about it when I last came to visit my delightful nephew." Lou pouted as he looked down at Asher. "It's a bummer that he's asleep."

"Don't wake him."

"I wasn't gonna. I'm happy to spend some quality time with one of my besties."

Larkin frowned. "We're not friends."

"You gotta stop fighting it, Lauren."

"That's not my name. And you're not supposed to be breathing my air—we've been over this."

Lou smirked at Teague. "I *adore* how bitchy she is. People concentrate far too much on being nice and approachable and smiley. Sounds exhausting."

"I'm with you on that one," said Teague.

Larkin grunted. "You two sing several lines from the same hymn sheet."

Lou made a weird face. "Nah, I steer clear of hymns. So done with all that's holy. Though I do have a beautiful singing voice. Want to hear it?"

"No," she told him.

Lou shrugged. "Just as well. The only lyrics I know are downright filthy. It would be horribly awkward for Teague if I got you hot under the collar."

"There is like *zero* chance of that happening," said Larkin.

"Beelzebub's consort said the same. And yet . . ."

Larkin's phone began to ring. She fished it out of her pocket and frowned at the screen. "I need to take this." She carefully scooted out from under Asher and then left the room.

Lou leaned toward Teague, his eyes bright. "She doesn't know the truth about you, does she?"

Teague tensed. "No."

"Are you gonna tell her?"

"No. And neither are you."

Lou straightened. "Honesty is the best policy. Or so they say. I personally think that lying your ass off is the best way to go. Makes things more interesting."

"I mean it, you say nothing to her."

Lou flicked a hand. "Don't worry, I'm a whizz at keeping secrets. The friends I share them with? Well, that's another matter."

"You don't have friends. You don't want friends. You alienate as many people as you can."

"It's my calling."

Asher stirred with a mumble, rolling onto his back. His eyelids flickered open, and languid dark orbs took in the room. Those eyes widened when he spotted the newcomer. "Lou!"

"Hello, my favorite nephew." Lou caught the little boy who launched himself at him. "Have you been causing mischief and mayhem?"

Asher nodded. "Uh-huh."

"Good, good." Lou cocked his head. "So, when are you and I gonna get around to ending the world?"

Asher's face scrunched up. "I wanna rule it for a bit first."

Lou's mouth spread into a wide grin that held a huge dose of pride. "That's it, boy—think big."

Just then, Larkin returned. Looking from Lou to Asher, she asked, "What are you two talking about?"

"Ice-cream," they both replied in unison.

She narrowed her eyes. "Lou, if you're trying to encourage him to destroy the Earth again, I *swear* . . ."

Lou gave her a look of wide-eyed innocence. "You're always so quick to think badly of me."

"And there's every reason in the world why I should," she said, returning to her spot on the sofa.

"That hurts, bestie. But it's fine. Whatever." Lou held Asher a little closer. "As long as my nephew here loves me, all is well."

A high-pitched, drawn-out *toot* rang through the air.

Lou grimaced at Asher, who burst into a round of giggles. "Jesus, kid, that *reeks*. What have you been eating?" Lou stretched his arms out fully, holding the kid away from his body. "Dan! We need air freshener in here! Pronto!"

Teague felt his mouth curve. "I'm starting to think he's learned how to fart on cue."

Lou's lips flattened. "If he has, he probably learned it from Jole—" He cut off as another fart rang out. "No, Asher, no— *Look lively, Dan, and bring us some air freshener!*"

CHAPTER THIRTEEN

One week later, Teague parked his bike outside his wagon and fluidly dismounted off it. As usual, with the exception of a sleeping Hugo, the dogs padded over for strokes as he removed his helmet.

The rest of the clan were gathered around the clearing eating breakfast and sipping from mugs. Well, all but Gideon—he stood in front of a bird box, his hands set on his hips.

"This isn't funny," Gideon snapped.

A raven's beak briefly peeked out of the box's hole. There were a few deep squawks and angry chirps.

"I'm not arguing with you about this," Gideon declared. "Just give it back."

More squawks. More chirps.

Gideon growled, balling up his hands. "Don't make me come in there."

"What's going on?" Teague called out, stuffing his riding gear in his saddlebag.

Gideon turned to him. "One of the ravens swiped the last bit of my toast."

"And you want it back?" *Ew.*

"It's the principle of the thing."

"Ravens are thieving little shits," Leo chipped in from his seat at the bench, earning a squawk of complaint from the bird perched on a sleeping Hugo's head. Leo tossed it a frown. "Well, it's true."

"They're just bored," said Saxon before biting into a bagel, ignoring the Alpha bloodhound that sat in front of him, licking his muzzle. The dogs were fed three times a day but never failed to 'beg' when others were eating.

Cupping his mug with both hands, Slade shifted slightly on the log beside Saxon as he eyed Teague carefully. "Spent the night at the harpy's place again, did you?"

Yes. Just as he had every other night since he and Larkin had come to their agreement a week ago.

On a deck chair, Tucker shook his head. "This ain't good, man."

"Yeah, fucking her on the regular is one thing," said Archer, sitting on a log across from Slade and Saxon. "Spending time with her outside of sex isn't a little bit wise."

Teague inwardly sighed. "I haven't told her anything, and I won't."

"We're not saying you have or ever would," Saxon assured him. "But the more she's around you, the more chance she has of picking up on something she shouldn't."

Tucker dipped his chin. "You don't want that, T. We don't want that." He snatched back his foot as the raven who'd skittered its way from Hugo's head to Tucker's chair began plucking at the lace of his sneakers.

"She's not going to pick up on anything, I'm careful." And

utterly unwilling to walk away from her just yet, so they'd need to deal with it.

"You've never had a problem taking such precautions before." Finished his cereal, Leo drank what milk was left in his bowl. "What's different this time?"

"You *like* her like her," Gideon sensed, sinking into a deck chair.

Teague palmed the back of his head, exhaling heavily. "I do, yeah." It seemed impossible for him *not* to. Everything about her drew him, compelled him, appealed to him. His inner entity coveted her just as much.

Leo placed his empty bowl on the table. "Look, I'm not trying to be an asshole here. The last thing I want to do is tell you to distance yourself from someone who you really like. But she's Knox Thorne's sentinel."

"I know that," Teague gritted out. "Don't need the reminder. And if there comes a point where I feel she's at risk of figuring things out, I'll back away. Until then . . ." He turned to head inside his wagon.

"Wait, before you go, we need to run something by you," Gideon announced. "Something completely unrelated to the harpy."

Teague slowly pivoted on his heel. "What?"

It was Leo who explained, "We've been tossing ideas around. And we think it would be good to set a trap for the shadowkin."

Intrigued, Teague folded his arms. "What kind of trap?"

Slade smiled, setting his cup down on the ground—a cup Baxter immediately began sniffing. "One you're gonna like." He rubbed his hands together. "So, we were thinking that, given you killed the two shadowkin that came for you, Ronin is probably going to send even more shadowkin next time."

Teague gave a slow nod. "I've considered that."

"It makes sense for us to ensure that the next attack happens in a contained environment where it will go your way," said Slade. "And what better contained environment than our own territory?"

"They currently can't so much as step foot on it, thanks to the black salt," Teague reminded him. "They have no way to penetrate the invisible shield it has created."

"Ah, but we can change that." Saxon ate the last of his bagel. "We can sweep aside just enough black salt to give them an opening, making it seem like an animal or breeze disturbed it— it's highly probable they search our border periodically, hoping for such an opportunity. If you're sat out here alone, they won't hesitate to take advantage."

Slade nodded. "They'll step through the shield, unaware that we're ready and waiting to close the gap behind them. Then they'll be trapped and totally at our mercy."

Teague swept his gaze over his entire clan, taking in the eagerness that glimmered in their eyes. "You feel left out of the action."

"Yes," Leo admitted.

Gideon nodded. "Absolutely."

"It's almost painful," Archer added.

In the reverse situation, Teague would have been as keen to involve himself. He rubbed at the back of his neck. "Providing not too many shadowkin are sent for me, we should be able to kill them quickly and cleanly."

"Where would be the fun in that?" asked Tucker.

And then realization dawned on Teague. "You don't want to simply trap and then swiftly dispatch of them. You want to play with them."

Slade lifted a finger. "If by 'play with them' you mean we hope to overpower them to such an extent that they flee in search of another opening in our border—thus giving us the chance to hunt them—then yes."

Gideon shivered, excited. "I'm getting tingles just thinking about it."

A sense of anticipation swirled inside Teague and roused his demon. It had been a long time since they'd hunted anything. Both had missed it.

The problem was that . . . "I don't know if they'll take the bait. They'll be suspicious if I'm alone out in the open like the perfect target. They might be animalistic in their way of thinking, but they're not stupid."

Saxon frowned, thoughtful. "One of us could hang with you. You won't be such an easy target then, but you'll be vulnerable enough for them to feel that they can collectively take you out."

Teague twisted his mouth. "That could work."

"It *will* work." Tucker tapped the armrest of his chair. "I say we do this tonight. I gotta feeling they'll show later. We know not to ignore my feelings."

Gideon bit down on his bottom lip. "You know, we don't have to kill *all* the shadowkin. We could maybe release one of them; could have them send Ronin a message that will make him confront you that much sooner."

Teague licked over his front teeth. "It's a good idea, but I don't know if our demons would pull back enough to let one live."

Gideon's nose wrinkled. "Yeah, there is that."

"So, you up for this plan or what?" asked Slade.

Teague felt his mouth curve. "I'm up for it."

Leo gave a nod of satisfaction and rubbed his hands. "Then let's discuss it all the way down to the finer details, gentlemen."

*

Standing in front of Knox's office desk, Larkin looked from her Prime to Levi, who stood not so far behind him like a sentry. Their expressions were hard to read.

Although Knox mostly worked from the Underground, there were times he utilized his many other offices. As an owner of several hotels in Las Vegas—including the one they were currently in—along with countless other businesses, Knox had offices scattered here, there, and everywhere.

She'd been called to this particular office by Knox himself, who'd been pretty vague about the purpose of the meeting. He also seemed hesitant to explain, so she prompted, "Is everything all right?"

"Yes," Knox replied, adjusting the lapels of his dark-gray suit jacket. "As long as you discount the fact that Holt contacted me and pushed for an in-person, one-to-one meeting. Hearing his voice tends to sour my mood considerably."

Anger bubbled in Larkin's stomach at how Holt had *dared* request anything of her Prime. "I can relate." Big time. "Did he say why he wants to meet with you?"

"No, but I don't think it would be a stretch to assume that he wishes to talk about you. I've consented to the meeting for one reason only."

"You mean to intimidate him into flying home," Larkin guessed, having suspected it was coming, given Knox's lack of patience where Holt was concerned.

"Yes, because he doesn't appear to have any intention of listening to you." The Prime's dark eyes turned flinty. "I will not have him harass you. I want him gone."

"Don't we all," mumbled Levi.

Larkin planted her feet. "I want to be here for the meeting."

"He might not speak freely if he knows you're here," Levi pointed out.

She flicked a look at the attached bathroom. "I'll wait in there so he's oblivious. I'll be able to hear the conversation clearly."

Knox gave her a firm look. "I'll allow it on the condition that you remain out of sight. I respect that this is fully your business, but he won't take kindly to my insistence that he leave Las Vegas. No Prime would. He may dig in his heels out of pride alone. If you are there, he will definitely resist—he won't want to look weak in front of you."

"I'll stay in the bathroom and keep quiet," Larkin promised. She had no desire to speak to Holt anyway. And as Knox had already pointed out, the cambion wasn't *hearing* her when she advised him to give up the ghost and leave. Maybe he'd listen to Knox. "When is the meeting?"

"In half an hour, so I'd imagine he's on his way here."

Good. She'd rather have it over and done with. "Then we wait."

It was twenty minutes later that Knox was informed of Holt's arrival. Larkin went straight into the bathroom and closed the door. As Knox's bodyguard, Levi remained with him.

From her hiding spot, she heard her Prime woodenly welcome Holt and one of his own guards inside the office. The sound of the cambion's voice made her demon peel back its upper lip in distaste. The entity hoped he did something stupid enough to get himself killed by Knox. Their Prime would for certain allow her demon to join in the fun.

There was a creak of leather as Knox sank into his chair behind the desk and invited Holt to take the seat opposite him.

"I hope all is well with you and your lair," said Holt, oh so very formal.

"Do you?" It wasn't a question from Knox. It was a bored statement that rang with skepticism.

A male sigh. "I'll cut to the chase, shall I?"

"That would be best," Knox told him.

"I'm here to talk about Larkin."

Even though she'd suspected that would be the case, she felt her lips flatten. Likewise, her demon huffed at his nerve.

"I gathered that much," said Knox, his tone clipped.

A long pause. "I realize that you're likely as angry with me as she is. You may even share her opinion that I should simply return to Canada and leave her be. But you have an anchor, Knox. Can you imagine not having her in your life? Is there anything that anyone could do or say that would make you agree to keep your distance, to forsake the bond?"

"Admittedly, I cannot imagine not having my psi-mate in my life. No one—not even her—could make me stay away. But you *did* stay away from your anchor, Holt. You turned your back on Larkin and the bond over thirty years ago, and you've clearly had no issue being out of her life all this time."

Larkin's thoughts exactly.

"Not true," Holt objected. "It was incredibly difficult to keep my distance—"

"And yet, you did," Knox pointed out. "You managed it well enough."

"There was nothing easy about staying away from her," Holt refuted, a hint of impatience breaking into his voice.

"Perhaps not. But you did it anyway. You placed your personal wants and needs before Larkin, before the anchor bond, and before what your demon must have wanted. No way would the entity have been content with being without her. You probably made it a promise that you'd one day find her; probably dangled that promise on a string to keep your demon from taking the situation into its own hands."

"I always intended to come back—my entity knew that. It understood that we merely needed to wait until our old Prime was out of the picture. He made things difficult."

Uh, no, *Holt* made things difficult. *He* was the reason they were in this situation. And Larkin didn't believe that he truly had always meant to return. But she'd bet he'd assured his entity that he would in order to keep it under control, just as Knox accused.

"My demon is not going to let me walk away from her again. Not that I will, in any case," said Holt, the words pure steel. "I won't deny that I was selfish, or that I fucked up majorly years ago. I won't even dispute that she deserves a better anchor than me. But whether you like it or not, Knox, I'm the only psi-mate she's ever going to have."

"So?"

"So my hope is that you will facilitate a meeting between me and Larkin. My attempts to speak with her in public were fruitless. She might be more inclined to hear me out if she is in a place where she feels safe. If you wish to be present, I will not object. I merely wish to talk to her in an environment where we won't be interrupted."

That motherfucker. He thought to go *around* her like this to get his way? Thought he could manipulate her Prime into pushing her to talk to him?

Knox's mind touched hers. *I don't suppose you're open to that?*

Not in the slightest, she replied.

"She would never agree to it, and I won't force her," Knox told him.

"You don't know for sure that she wouldn't consent," Holt objected. "And I'm not asking that you force her. Only that you speak with her. She listens to you."

"She does. But why would I tell her to give you time out of her day? What have you done to earn that?"

"Not one thing. But I'll do what it takes to make up for that." He said it like it would be easy enough.

Larkin could only shake her head in wonder. It was like he had no true concept of how significant psi-mates were, or no real grasp on why his past actions should have upset her so much. She wasn't sure exactly what blocked him from fully appreciating the situation, but it was something.

"If she was to agree to a meeting, her partner would wish to be there," Knox tossed out, no doubt to see how Holt would react.

Seconds of silence went by. "If that's what she wants, I won't object," Holt finally said, a slight strain to his voice. "You can throw any number of conditions at me, Knox. I'm not going to be difficult about this. The important thing to me is that I get to speak with Larkin. That is all that matters."

"If only you were so determined to bond with her all those years ago . . . "

"As I said, I was selfish back then. I didn't make her my priority. I regret that more than you can ever know."

"I'm not so sure you do, or that you'd make her your priority now either," Knox told him, echoing her thoughts. "From what I can see, your personal situation might have changed, but you haven't. If you hadn't seen her from afar not so long ago—"

"I still would have come for her," Holt insisted.

"Maybe. But I fail to understand why you seem to think that's all that counts. It has no meaning for Larkin at all."

"If I could just speak to her—"

"You'd try to manipulate her, just as you did when you returned home years ago without first bonding with her," Knox finished, a distinct chill to his voice. "You thought she'd chase you. Back down. Make concessions. You thought that leaving would put you in a position of power in terms of negotiations. Only it didn't, did it?"

Holt hesitated. "I expected her to contact me, yes. But

my leaving wasn't an attempt to manipulate her. My Prime called me home."

"A Prime who intended to use her to learn all my private business. What did he promise you in return?"

"Nothing." Holt paused. "He indirectly threatened to demote me if I failed to turn her loyalties."

"And instead of protecting her from him by urging her to remain in my lair, where he couldn't reach her, you did as he asked. In doing so, you tried using her to get what you wanted . . . just as he did."

Exactly. Holt might claim to look down on his ex-Prime, but he was really no better than that power-hungry, people-using old bastard. He just didn't seem to see it.

"It wasn't like that," Holt asserted, his voice hard-edged.

"Oh, that was exactly what it was like," said Knox.

Silence fell, rubbing her impatient demon's nerves raw.

"She could turn rogue without the bond," Holt threw out. "I'm her one chance at ensuring that it *never* happens. Surely you'd like for her to have that assurance. You know as well as I do that her demon is bolder and stronger than most. So if you won't try to facilitate a meeting as a favor to me, one Prime to another, at least do it for her. It's in her best interests, and you know it. The sooner she and I hash things out, the sooner we can move forward. Dragging it out isn't helping anyone, least of all her."

"You don't get it, do you?" There was another creak of leather, and she wondered if Knox had leaned forward in his seat. "You're fighting a losing battle, Holt. She doesn't want you. She doesn't want the bond. Neither does her demon. Both would sooner live with the risk of turning rogue. *That's* how badly you fucked up. There's no fixing it, no going back."

"If she and I could only have a proper conversation—"

"It would make no difference."

"You don't know that," Holt clipped, his words thick with irritation. "Knox, she needs me."

Larkin gaped. *Needed* him? What planet did he live on?

"No, Holt, she doesn't," Knox stated. "Plenty of demons never find or bond with their anchors, they deal with it and manage to still lead full lives. So will Larkin. Besides, she has a different sort of anchor. Not a psi-mate, but a person who steadies her and her demon in ways that only partners do."

Larkin suspected that Knox only made the claim to poke at Holt. But in truth, Teague actually did give her that balance, just as Khloë did for Keenan, and Devon did for Tanner.

"Maybe that's the case right now, but it won't last much longer," said Holt, a gritty quality to his voice. "Everything I've learned about Sullivan tells me that he's never in it for the long haul. He prefers the sowing-of-oats lifestyle."

"He may not have a good track record where relationships are concerned, but he isn't a man who struggles with commitment," said Knox. "He's fully committed to the people in his life who are important to him, including his own anchor—one to whom he is also utterly loyal and incredibly protective of. You know, you could learn a few things from Teague."

Larkin felt her lips tip up, knowing Holt wouldn't have taken the latter comment well.

"I didn't come here to discuss the hellhorse," said Holt, curt.

"No, you came here in the hope of gaining my support. You thought that, what with you being a fellow Prime, I'd be inclined to play nice with you." Knox paused. "I don't play nice with people who hurt those who matter to me." The words were delivered in a silky smooth tone but dripped with malice.

A heavy exhale sounded that vibrated with annoyance. "Then this was a waste of time."

"As was your coming all the way to Vegas. Larkin doesn't need you, Holt. She's perfectly happy as she is. You should have just left well alone."

There were more creaks of leather, and she got the sense that both males had risen from their seats.

"Now," began Knox, "I suggest that you, your bodyguard, and any other demons you may have brought with you go book yourselves a flight home. And by suggest, I mean insist."

"I can't oblige you in that," Holt stated, a defiant edge to his tone.

"Oh yes, you can," her Prime insisted. "And you will. Because you wouldn't want to face the consequences."

A pause. "You're threatening me?" The words came out soft and low but were laced with anger.

"I would have thought the answer to that was clear. I didn't butter it up, did I?"

Another pause. "It's a mistake for you to be so confident that you'll walk away the victor if you and I come to blows. You're not the only demon who wields a lot of power."

"Oh, there are others," Knox allowed. "You're not one of them. A duel between us would end badly for you, and that show of weakness on your part would lead to you being usurped. You made a lot of sacrifices to become Prime. It would be stupid of you to throw your position away. But, by all means, do exactly that. Making you suffer will be most cathartic, and I'm sure Larkin's demon will enjoy assisting me in that."

Long moments of silence went by. If she had to guess, she'd say that Holt was struggling to admit to himself that, yes, Knox was right. The cambion was no match for him.

"Go back to Canada, Holt. Forget about Larkin. Focus on yourself. It shouldn't be too difficult. You've been doing it for years."

Larkin smiled at that.

There were two sets of footfalls, the opening of a door, the mutters of voices, and then the door once more closed.

"You can come out now," Levi called.

Larkin exited the bathroom, her gaze immediately seeking out Knox. "Well, that was unpleasant. Do you think he heard you? That he'll heed you?"

Her Prime twisted his mouth. "I got through to him. *That* I'm certain of. But it's difficult to say if he'll heed my warning or not."

Levi scraped a hand over his jaw. "Did anyone else find it weird that Holt—a Prime who would never willingly look weak—basically threw himself on the sacrificial altar?"

She nodded. "Oh, it was definitely weird. He's proud and arrogant. He'd want Knox to view him as an equal. But he came in here, admitted all his failings, and asked for help with a personal matter. That's not very Holt-like, or Prime-like."

"It's possible that he isn't pursuing the anchor bond for the reason he claims," Knox mused. "He's an incredibly ambitious demon. We all know that. We know he uses people. We know he plays power games."

Larkin narrowed her eyes. "Why do you suspect he's truly here? What do you think this is really about?"

Knox dragged his teeth over his lower lip. "Politics. I learned yesterday that he's been having some difficulties with other lairs. Bigger lairs who seek to overtake his. He has alliances with Primes, but not many. He knows he'd never get an alliance from me, even if you two were bonded. I would never trust him. But I think he believes that him being bound to you would at least make the other lairs back off."

Having a total 'aha' moment, Larkin nodded. "They'd think that you wouldn't like anyone screwing with my anchor; that you'd defend Holt. And the idiot probably figures he could also be sure that you'd never act against him if he was psychically linked to me."

"Unless the situation was extremely dire, I would never harm your anchor if you were bound to him," said Knox. "Because to do that would be to harm you emotionally. I would want to preserve our familial relationship even if you switched to his lair. He will know that."

Feeling her lips press into a tight line, she folded her arms. "This is why he's acting so reasonable and self-flagellant and offering to make all the sacrifices. He's in a real hurry to get me to cooperate. He won't be prepared to lose his seat of power—he spent too long striving to get it."

Levi rubbed at his nape. "As much as I hate to say it, yeah, I think Holt is mostly here for political reasons. That's not to say I think you don't matter to him, Lark. I believe you do on some level. It's just that—as it was before all those years ago—his ambitions matter more."

Maybe it should have hurt Larkin to realize that *her anchor* yet again sought to use and manipulate her for his own gain. Her demon was outraged but, honestly, Larkin only felt tired. She was just so done with his bullshit.

"You don't have to give me pitying looks," she told Knox and Levi ... because that was exactly what they were doing. "I'm not upset."

"And your demon?" asked Knox.

Larkin licked her lips. "It's thinking up yet more ways to make him cry."

"Can't say I blame it." Knox licked over the edges of his upper teeth. "What I said to him sank in. He really did hear me when I said that you don't—and never will—want anything to do with him."

"So you think he'll cut his losses?"

"I do. He's tenacious, but he's not delusional. He won't waste his time or energy on something that will amount to nothing. And he'd be a fool to stay away from his lair too long when there are other Primes coveting it." Knox put a hand on her shoulder. "It may be that this is over; that he finally leaves you in peace." A dangerous glitter entered his eyes. "And if he doesn't . . . well, we'll together make him wish that he did, won't we?"

Oh yes, they damn well would.

CHAPTER FOURTEEN

How's the mysterious clan thing going?

Teague didn't outwardly react as Larkin's voice slinked into his mind later that evening. He remained sprawled in the deck chair with his eyes closed and his arms folded, feigning sleep. *Not as eventful as I'd hoped*, he replied.

For over three hours, he and Leo—who was lounging in the chair beside his, also pretending to be out for the count—had waited impatiently for some shadowkin to attack. The rest of their clan were taking cover in the nearby shadows, ready to act at a moment's notice. As ordered, the dogs lay near the pit, but they were tense, likely sensing that some shit might go down if Tucker's 'feeling' could be trusted. Which it usually could.

What, there aren't enough strippers?

Teague let out a telepathic snort. *I told you earlier, it isn't a party.*

When he told her that he wouldn't be able to see her

tonight as he had 'a clan thing to attend', she hadn't been annoyed or upset. Larkin never made attempts to monopolize his time. But when she'd asked a few general questions about 'the clan thing' and he hadn't expanded, she'd gotten somewhat suspicious.

His harpy had prodded and poked at him a little more, fishing for details. He'd continued to gently bat away most of her enquiries and painted a very vague picture. That she hadn't at all appreciated. Something she'd expressed by fisting his tee, hauling him close, and biting his jaw hard. She'd then told him that he wouldn't find it so easy to hold her at bay, which his demon had liked a whole lot.

Teague should have panicked at the thought of her pushing for more room in his life. Instead, he'd felt a smile build inside him. Because if things were different, yeah, that was exactly where he'd want her. Unfortunately, it would never happen, though.

You said there'd be beer, games, and laughs, Larkin added. *Sounds like a party to me.*

Do you really think hellhorses would throw low-key parties?

No. Hence my strippers question.

Teague wrestled back a smile. Her comment had been lighthearted, but there was a possessive bite to her voice. He didn't normally like women feeling territorial toward him, but he had no issue with it when it came to Larkin. It meant that the scales were balanced, because he was equally possessive of her.

There are no other women here, he swore. *I'm not having even half as much fun as you seem to be thinking. Truthfully, I'd rather be at your place with you.*

I'm not home right now, so you'd be hanging there by yourself.

Teague caught himself before a frown could tug at his brow. *Where are you?*

Not far from your territory, actually. One of the demons from my lair caused something of a stir at the little hellbull village. Tanner and I are handling it.

I take it there's a lot of sniffing and posturing going on with Tanner and the bulls.

You hellbeasts are always swinging your dicks around. It's tiring.

Teague again stifled a smile. *What can I say? We—*

A twig snapped. The dogs stirred. He went rigid.

Anticipation began to beat inside Teague, kicking his pulse into gear. He subtly drew in a long breath, and there it was—the distinctive scent of smoke and brimstone. His inner beast edged close to the surface, knowing the plan, eager to track and kill its prey.

There was a faint rustle of leaves, and then a whistle of alarm rang out.

Teague opened his eyes as he jumped to his feet. Four shadowkin stood several feet away. One had whirled to face Gideon, who was closing the gap in the shield with black salt. The other three humanoids were braced to lunge, their pure-white gazes sweeping over the men now surrounding them.

The dogs danced from foot to foot near the pit, awaiting the go-ahead to move and attack. Likewise, the ravens in the trees restlessly flapped their wings as they waited for an order to act.

We, what? Larkin prodded.

There's something I gotta deal with, Teague told her as he and Leo joined the rest of the clan in surrounding the trespassers. *I'll speak to you again later.*

Is everything okay?

Everything's fine.

A vibe of wariness touched his mind. *You're lying.*

Seriously, all is good. I'll talk to you soon. Pinning his entire focus on the shadowkin before him, Teague clenched and unclenched his fists. It was easy to sense their panic by the tension in their bodies and the way their gazes couldn't keep still. Yeah, they knew they were fucked, knew there'd be no escape, knew that death would soon take them.

"It was good of you to join us," Teague told them. "Not very smart, though."

One of the humanoids narrowed its eyes, and then an image of Ronin flashed in Teague's mind.

"You're merely following orders, I know," said Teague. "But you're not mindless puppets. You made a choice to obey Ronin. You came here with the intent to kill me. Go ahead and do it." He paused, letting his mouth curve. "If you can."

The humanoid squinted even more, and then it conjured an orb of hellfire. The crackling ball arrowed through the air with a *whoosh* of sound, heading right for Teague.

He dodged it, hearing it slam into something solid—likely a tree—far behind him. Everyone then sprang into action.

Flashes of amber and red broke up the darkness as orbs of hellfire sailed back and forth. Barks and squawks came from the waiting animals, the sounds almost overriding the hissing of flames, the sizzling of hell-acid, and the grunts and curses and laughs that flew out of the clan.

At first, the shadowkin tried focusing on Teague, apparently deciding to at least complete their mission so that their upcoming deaths wouldn't be meaningless. And they got a good few hits in—landing balls of hellfire on his ribs, thigh, and shoulder. But the clan bombarded them with so many blows that it forced the humanoids to divide their attention to defend themselves.

The clan made no attempt to kill the intruders, only to wound and weaken them. But that didn't mean they went easy on the shadowkin. They inflicted maximum pain, and they did it with no mercy.

A tentacle shot out of a humanoid's side and whipped at Teague and Leo, knocking them both right off their feet. That same tentacle surged toward Teague's throat only to be caught by Saxon—the male snapped his hand around it and then slammed it with a ball of hellfire.

The shadowkin sharply pulled back the tentacle in what was no doubt excruciating pain—a hit at such close range would be agonizing.

Teague and Leo sprang to their feet, both conjuring—

Hell-acid smashed into Teague's chest. White-hot agony stole his breath and made the flaming orb in his hand wink out. A hiss escaped through his gritted teeth as the sizzling acid ate at his flesh almost hungrily. His beast puffed out an angry breath, making all sorts of violent plans of retaliation.

Glaring at the offending shadowkin that was now being attacked by Leo, Teague pitched a ball of hellfire through the air. The humanoid saw it coming and weaved, but not fast enough. The orb wacked its jaw, making its head snap back.

Teague grinned, and his demon let out a satisfied nicker. But then an unbearable heat clipped his ear as another of the shadowkin targeted him with hellfire. God, these little fuckers were gonna die *hard*.

As blisters pebbled his scorching-hot ear, Teague quickly threw one, two, three, four flaming orbs—not aiming for any humanoid in particular, just wanting to pile on the pressure and push them into tucking tail and running.

A few minutes later, he got his wish.

One humanoid fled. Two quickly followed it. The fourth backed away, blindly launching hell-acid orbs at the clan, but then it swiftly pivoted and ran.

Teague's beast bared its teeth in disgust at their cowardice even though it was pleased they'd fled.

Smirking, Slade cricked his neck and did a languid stretch. "About damn time. Gotta say, I'm gonna enjoy this." He flicked his hand, making any hellfire flames die away so that the fire wouldn't spread.

"Let's give them a five-minute head start," suggested Tucker, whipping off his tee, getting ready to shift.

Removing his own tee, Teague winced as the burned cloth pulled at his rapidly healing wounds. He whistled at the dogs, who rushed to his side with whines of excitement. He pointed in the direction of the fleeing shadowkin. "Track."

The hounds let out eager barks, and then they bolted.

Looking up at the ravens circling above him, Teague waved a hand. "Go."

The flock disappeared in a rush, fast overtaking the dogs.

Naked, Teague took stock of his injuries. Patches of his skin were red-raw and peeling. Other patches sported blisters and scorch marks. They were healing, but not fast enough for his liking.

"I'd say the shadowkin have had enough of a head start," claimed Archer.

Teague nodded his agreement. "Let's go have our fun."

Unease bolted through Larkin as Teague abruptly withdrew from their telepathic conversation. He hadn't sounded anxious or hurt; hadn't said anything that should concern her. But there'd been an undercurrent of *something* in his voice. A sense of battle-readiness that surely shouldn't have been there.

Apprehension pricked at her nape, making the fine hairs there stand on end. Her inner demon slithered close beneath her skin, not liking this situation at all; not liking that his clan event might in fact be something dangerous.

She turned to Tanner, who was directing members of their

Force to take away the demon they'd detained. "I have to go." He didn't need her—the matter was now resolved.

He frowned. "What? Where?"

"To see Teague," she fudged, forcing herself to seem casual, not wanting to involve him. "Holler if you need me."

Calling on her ability to switch forms, Larkin planted her feet. Smoke bloomed around her as everything that was her—clothes and all—seemed to whirl and melt before reforming and, in doing so, taking the shape of a harpy eagle.

Larkin gave her avian body a quick shake, fully settling into her alternate form, and then took to the sky. The cool air washed over her as she sliced through it like a bullet.

She wasn't far from Teague's territory. At the speed she could fly, it would take her mere minutes to arrive. Although she'd never been there, she knew exactly where to find it.

An aerial satellite view of the clan's territory would reveal nothing—it seemed like an untouched stretch of land. But that was a mere glamor trick. And if you knew to *look* for glamor, knew how to spot it, it wasn't so difficult to pick up the signs.

Larkin winged through the sky, skimming over treetops, her stomach churning with nervousness. It was very possible that she was overreacting. Possible that maybe two of his clan members had gotten into an argument and he'd simply broke off his conversation with her to handle it. But her gut believed differently, and she wasn't about to ignore it.

It occurred to her that, whatever the case, he might not be so pleased she'd ventured to his territory to check things out; that he'd consider the situation a 'clan matter' and believe she had no right to involve herself. He wouldn't be wrong. She was an outsider, after all. But she was also his girlfriend—which yeah, okay, he wasn't yet aware of. That was beside the point, though.

The fact of the matter was that if he was fronting danger, she intended to have his back. Simple. He'd just have to live with it.

When she arrived at his territory, a slight buzzing sensation vibrated along her feathers as she passed through the repellent bubble of glamor. That was when, as if the bubble kept noise contained, ominous sounds reached her. Sounds of *battle*.

With an inward curse, she flapped her wings harder and upped her pace. She glided through the trees toward a clearing, able to make out with her eagle-enhanced eyesight—*what the hell?*—four shadowkin in the near distance quickly hightailing it out of there. The entire clan stood around, but none moved to pursue. They *smirked*.

"About damn time. Gotta say, I'm gonna enjoy this," said one of the clan.

Uh, what now?

Her gut reared up and insisted she not reveal her presence just yet. Subtly landing on a thick tree branch not too far away from the clearing, she took in the scene up ahead of her. Took in the pack of bloodhounds, the large ravens, the wounded but *happy* hellhorses.

"Let's give them a five-minute head start," said another.

Head start?

A whistle from a stripping Teague had the dogs darting to his side. Dogs he *sent after* the shadowkin. Her head twitched in surprise when he did the same with the ravens. It was bizarre and unnatural . . . and . . . and . . . Oh, fuck.

Larkin's feathers puffed up as realization hit her. Like a sledgehammer. Hard, fast, heavy. Every piece of the puzzle that was Teague slotted firmly into place as it all became clear. And it mentally knocked her sideways.

Her inner demon blinked rapidly, struggling to process it. Very few things took the entity off-guard. But this? Yeah, this rocked it.

"I'd say the shadowkin have had enough time," proclaimed one of the clan.

Teague nodded slightly. "Let's go have some fun."

Almost as one, the seven men shifted in clouds of smoke and ash.

The hellhorses swished their tails and scraped the ground with their hooves. And then they were galloping away.

Larkin took to the sky again, staying high overhead where she wouldn't be seen. She watched as the hellhorses split into four groups and dispersed. Two groups followed the sounds of baying hounds while the others tracked the squawking of the ravens.

The animals were circling each of the shadowkin in separate spots, she soon realized. The four humanoids hadn't stuck together on fleeing—they'd split as they sought a route of escape. Why they hadn't vanished through shadows and couldn't seem to leave the clan's territory, she had no idea.

The hellhorses expertly descended on the shadowkin and savaged them—biting, stomping, breathing fire, exhaling noxious smoke—in what seemed like a rehearsed fashion ... as if they'd done it a thousand times before. And for Larkin, there was no denying that she'd been right in what she'd concluded mere minutes ago.

She circled back, leaving the clan to their 'fun'. She didn't leave the territory, though. Didn't even consider it. No, she and Teague had some talking to do.

Would he *want* to talk? Likely not. At least not in regard to the subject matter she had in mind. But she wouldn't be blown off this time.

She landed at the camp and changed back to her true form. Absently plucking at her tee, she drank in her surroundings, taking in everything from the wagons and the firepit to the hammocks and the small barn.

She'd expected to find cabins sprawled around the property; that each of the clan would want their own space as opposed to living close together like a herd. She *really* wouldn't have guessed that Teague lived in an old traveler's wagon.

But then, she also wouldn't have guessed that he . . . God, this whole thing was surreal.

Perching her butt on a log near the pit, she rested her elbows on her jeans-clad thighs and rubbed at her face. So many times she'd pondered what Teague could be so determined to keep hidden. She'd explored endless possibilities; considered countless scenarios. But none came close to the actual truth of the matter.

Did she now understand why he guarded his secrets so closely? Yes. Absolutely.

Did she now understand why he hadn't even hinted at those secrets despite that she'd parted with some of her own? Yes. Yes, though it nonetheless stung, she did get it.

Her inner demon, on the other hand, wasn't so understanding. It had never liked that secrets stood between them and the hellhorse like a stone wall, and it felt entitled to know his private business. Which was totally unfair, but hey, that was how the demon rolled regarding Teague. It didn't respect his boundaries because it didn't want him to *have* boundaries when it came to her or the entity.

The demon wasn't unnerved by what they'd learned about him. Nope. Now that the shock had worn off, the entity was simply somewhat miffed that it was only learning of this *now*.

Muffled voices and laughs drifted through the air.

Larkin slowly straightened and casually splayed her hands on her thighs as she waited. What happened next probably wouldn't go well. The clan as a whole was *not* going to like that she was no longer in the dark.

Not that she worried they'd hurt her. Well, they were welcome to try. They'd die in the doing of it, though.

The ravens appeared first. Spotting her, they let out cautioning calls. The distant laughing cut off. The talking stopped. The footfalls hastened.

Larkin didn't move from the log. She instead watched as the ravens settled on nearby branches, purposely surrounding her.

Soon, seven naked males prowled into the camp with panting but highly alert dogs walking among them. Quiet curses were spat and wary looks were exchanged as the hellhorses spotted her. They couldn't yet know how much she'd seen, but they'd certainly be apprehensive all the same.

Larkin only really had eyes for the man in the center of the group. Teague's own eyes were pinned on her. They were somber, dark, unreadable.

She'd rarely seen Teague without a half-smile on his face. Generally, he was *all* emotion. Now, he appeared closed off and devoid of feeling.

He looked at her as though she were a stranger. As if they stood on the opposite sides of some metaphorical fence. He made her feel shut out with his gaze alone.

Teague had made her feel many things over the years, but never shut out. Not even when he danced around her questions or diverted their lines of conversation—that had always been done in a playful manner.

There was nothing playful about him right now.

Her demon hissed, annoyed. It wanted to kiss him so hard his lips would bleed and he'd cease looking at Larkin that way. Not a bad idea.

Coming to a stop in front of her, he stared down at her. "How long have you been here?" His voice didn't have its usual breezy tone. It was completely flat.

Larkin lifted her chin. "Long enough. You were never going to tell me, were you?"

Teague's face remained carefully blank. "Tell you, what?"

She ran her gaze along the seven males. "That you were all once members of the Wild Hunt."

CHAPTER FIFTEEN

Fuuuuuuck.

Teague pressed his lips tight. Had it been naïve of him to think that it would never come to this? Maybe. But he hadn't expected her to ever show up here—least of all at a time when a very telling event would go down.

Yes, Larkin was incredibly protective of those inside her circle. But despite that he'd failed to telepathically convince her that all was fine, he hadn't for one moment thought she'd hurry to his side. Granted, he wasn't entirely outside her circle anymore. But nor was he in it. It was more like he hovered on its border. Evidently, he'd been wrong to think that that would mean little to her.

As she steadily met his gaze, Teague instantly dismissed the idea of spouting denials. He had no clue what she'd seen while on his land, but it had clearly been enough for her to make all the right conclusions—her utter certainty was lined into her face. There would be no making her doubt herself.

See, this was why he'd kept his distance from her all these years. It was why he should have continued to keep his distance. But he hadn't, and now he and his clan were fucked.

He understood why she'd feel compelled to relay what she'd learned to Knox—he was not merely her Prime, but her family. Nonetheless, for Teague, it would feel like a betrayal. Like she'd chosen Knox over him.

"That's why I can't find any record of your past," Larkin continued. "There is no record. You're all hell-born. You spent the prior portion of your lives in that realm."

Tucker blew out a quiet breath. "Knew this was gonna happen sooner or later," he muttered to himself, solemn. "Just knew it."

Ignoring the sting of his injuries, Teague began pulling on his clothes, and the others followed suit.

"I get why you got yourselves some dogs and seem to have tamed some local ravens," Larkin added. "You're used to having animals."

Humans had strong misconceptions about the Wild Hunt. In truth, it was a unit of hell's army. A unit that tracked down and returned any souls who escaped from hell, which wasn't an easy feat, considering those souls might have sought refuge in any number of realms. It was much like looking for a needle in a whole bundle of haystacks.

In that sense, they were the Dark Host's bounty hunters. Their performance reflected on its strength, so every member had to be *beyond* good at what they did. As such, training was brutal, and mistakes were unacceptable.

Members of the unit—which always consisted of seven hellhorses, five bloodhounds, and five carrions birds—would serve for six whole centuries before retiring. At that point, they could do whatever they wished. Including making a home in another realm.

Larkin shook her head, her gaze still locked on Teague. "No wonder you glossed over any mention I made of how I'd like to meet your clan. You never intended to introduce me to them or to bring me here. Never intended to let me fully into your life."

His gut clenched at the pinch of hurt in her eyes. Now fully dressed, he set his hands on his hips. "Why did you come here?"

Her brow flicked up. "That's what you want to focus on?" A scathing snort popped out of her. "You're not going to distract me this time, Teague."

Yeah, he could see that. "You have to know why we keep our pasts to ourselves."

She dipped her chin. "No one in this realm much likes having hell-born demons around. You grew up with a different set of rules, a different set of ethics, a different idea of priorities. As such, you're often ... problematic."

Even Teague could admit that that was something of an understatement.

"You also tend to pull all kinds of crap and think you're entitled to get away with it; that you shouldn't have to answer to 'lesser demons.'"

"That doesn't apply to us. We don't view Earth-born demons as less."

"I know that. I know *you*. And I would have thought you knew me well enough to know that I wouldn't hold where you were born against you." That pinch of hurt in her eyes was back.

"I never thought for a second that you would."

"And yet, you kept me in the dark. More, you had no intention of *ever* telling me the truth of your past."

"I knew you'd feel obliged to inform Knox. That will lead to a shitshow, Larkin. He's not going to like that hell-born demons are around. Because anything born in hell will take one look at him and know *what he is*." Teague took a slow step toward her. "It's something he strives to keep secret—and for good reason. As such, he'll want us gone. And by gone, I mean dead." He shouldn't have to spell all this out.

Her brow creased. "Why would you think I'd feel obliged to inform him?"

Was she being serious right now? "He's your Prime. As his sentinel, you need to keep him apprised of anything that affects him."

"This *doesn't* affect him."

"It's something he'd want to know."

"Probably. But it isn't something he needs to know. So I'm not sure why you think I'd expose you."

Teague's mouth snapped shut. Wait, what?

Again, there was a twinge of hurt in her eyes. "I'm a lot of things, but I'm not unnecessarily cruel. Nor am I someone who'd take a dump all over a person who matters to me. Which you do. Sort of. At times." Her cheeks reddened. "Don't read anything into it."

Teague's chest went tight. Damn if that snippily spoken confession didn't get to him. And damn if she didn't look so fucking cute, all red-faced and flustered.

His beast wasn't the slightest bit surprised by her words, or by her intention to guard their secrets. In the entity's opinion, both her declaration and demonstration of loyalty were only to be expected.

"Wait," began Leo, raising a hand, "you don't plan to tell Knox?"

Her gaze sliced to Leo. "No. It would be different if I thought you were a threat. But if any of you meant to blab his secret, you'd have done it long before now. You've given him no trouble. You're not callous, self-entitled assholes who treat Earth-born demons as mere toys for you to play with and break at your leisure. So what reason do I have to warn him that you're hell-born and, in doing so, condemn you? None."

Pausing, she returned her focus to Teague and fixed him with a hard glare. "And don't think I'm not pissed at you for believing I'd fuck you over like that."

God, he wanted to kiss her stupid right now. It was going to happen. Soon.

"I thought he was only your pretend boyfriend," said Archer.

"You don't have to be in a relationship with someone for them to mean something to you," she pointed out.

"You expect us to buy that you'd keep this from your Prime?" asked Saxon, folding his arms.

Larkin bristled, feeling her expression morph into a glower. "Yes, actually, I do. I don't say what I don't mean." She paused to flick a look at the bird that kept repeatedly flying above them in a figure of eight. "If that raven shits on my head, we're gonna have problems."

A male who she knew from her research was named Leo scratched his temple and said, "It's more likely to try stealing any jewelry you're wearing. They're all thieving little bastards." At a loud screech, he looked up at the raven and lifted his hands. "I didn't say that was a *bad* thing." He returned his gaze to Larkin. "They're touchy, too."

She'd heard that hellhorses had an infinity for animals and could form such a deep connection with them that it not only enabled the hellhorses to communicate with them, it allowed the animals to understand them. Apparently it was true.

"So you're *really* not going to tell Knox?" a red-headed male asked her, looking cautiously hopeful. *Gideon*.

"No, I'm not." Even if Teague hadn't mattered to her as much as he did, she wouldn't have doomed him in such a way when it would be totally undeserved. "Regardless of what you all seem to think, I don't tell him every little thing. That goes both ways."

"This is no little thing," said a guy she knew brawled in the Underground's fighting pit. Slade Something Or Other.

"No, it isn't," Larkin allowed. In fact, a part of her still struggled to process it. "But it's your business to share or not to share. Of course, if any of you ever suddenly decide to screw over Knox, I'll return that favor in a fucking heartbeat and then hunt you down to execute you," she warned. "But I'm hoping it won't come to that."

Silence reigned as the seven hellhorses stared down at her for long moments.

The one she recognized from her research as Archer extended a small, brown paper bag toward her. "Mushroom?"

She felt her nose wrinkle. "No, thanks."

"Good. I don't like sharing them." He bit into one. "I'm Archer, by the way."

Gideon raised a hand, a lazy smile now curving his mouth. "Gideon." Gesturing at the others, he added, "That's Leo. And then you have Tucker, Slade, and Saxon."

Rather than explaining she already knew their names, she gave them a curt nod and said, "Larkin." She then refocused on Teague, asking, "Why were shadowkin here?"

He didn't answer. He unabashedly stared at her, his body no longer still and tense. Just the same, his gaze was no longer grim and distant. Far from it. There was a blatant and super-intense possessiveness there that made her demon grin and her belly do a slow roll.

"Come here," he said, his voice pitched low and deep.

She felt her brow knit. "What?"

"Come here."

Still unhappy with him for believing she'd expose him, she sniffed. "You want something from me, you better come get it."

Teague closed the space between them, took her hands, and tugged her to her feet. Then he slanted his mouth over hers and kissed her. Hard and deep and long.

She broke the kiss with a nip to his lip. "Don't think I'll forgive you in a hurry for thinking the worst of me. Asshole." She would have slapped his chest if she hadn't spotted the burns there before he slipped on a tee.

His lips canted up. "I do like it when you're all huffy with me."

She rolled her eyes. "I will not be distracted. Tell me why shadowkin were on your territory. I can't help if I don't know what's happening."

"Help?"

"Yes. Help. You're clearly dealing with a major situation here. If you think I'm going to overlook that, you're out of your mind."

He gave her hands a gentle, reassuring squeeze. "It's nothing we can't handle."

"I'd imagine so. But I still intend to help." She sighed in annoyance when he looked like he'd argue. "Teague, don't make me hurt you. I won't enjoy it—at least not a lot—but I'll absolutely do it if you don't start talking."

Archer chuckled. "I like her," he told Teague. "My beast wants to bite her, so I get why yours is having that problem."

"There'll be no biting," she asserted.

Archer frowned. "We'd watch over you while you recuperated."

"That isn't really a comfort." She turned back to Teague. "Talk, Black Beauty."

Keeping possession of her hands, he backed up, pulling her with him. "Come with me. We'll talk inside."

Larkin let him guide her toward a slim ladder that led to a burgundy wagon. She ascended the creaky steps and then moved aside so he could join her on the small porch. Once he'd opened the glass-paned front door, he urged her inside.

She felt her lips part as she took in the beautiful, cozy interior. The intricate gold carvings were out of this world. And that china cabinet would look so good in her apartment, though probably not as good as it did here.

Turning toward Teague, she planted her feet and shot him a haughty, expectant look.

His lips twitched. "You really are mad at me."

"Of course I am. You thought *I'd send you to your death*."

"I didn't mean it as an insult." He settled his hands on her hips. "You're an exceedingly loyal person, Larkin. Not to mention very protective of those you care for. And you take your sentinel role hyper-seriously. Can you really blame me for thinking you'd be inclined to report to your Prime that there are hell-born demons hanging around?"

No. But she wasn't going to say that out loud, because she didn't want to admit that he had a point—she wasn't done being angry yet. She folded her arms and said, "I don't hear you explaining why shadowkin were here."

He sighed. "Sit."

She settled on the built-in cushioned seat, finding it surprisingly comfortable.

Opposite her, he leaned against the countertop behind him. "Basically, they were here to kill me."

Anger whipped to life in Larkin's stomach. "*Just* you?" she asked, her demon instantly developing a total hate-on for the dead shadowkin.

"Yes. They were ordered to do so by the demon who's presently Master of the Wild Hunt."

She cocked her head. "Why?"

"He has very personal beef with me." Teague crossed one

ankle over the other. "Remember I told you about the half-brother who resents that I exist?"

"*He's* siccing them on you?" What a little fucker.

"Yes. By all appearances, Ronin has very simply decided that it's time I breathed my last." A muscle in Teague's jaw jumped. "He keeps sending shadowkin to do his dirty work."

"Keeps sending?" she echoed, squinting. "So that wasn't the first time you were attacked by them?"

"No, it was the fourth."

"*Fourth?*" Her demon cricked its neck, fairly vibrating with the same fury building within Larkin.

"The first attack came on the night you and I agreed to pretend-date."

She spat out a bunch of harsh expletives. "I get why you never told me, but it still pisses me off that I didn't know your life was in danger all these weeks." She'd known he was keeping things from her, but she hadn't imagined this. "How do we get your brother to bring his ass up here so he can be dealt with?"

"By killing every minion he sends until he feels he needs to take care of the issue himself. Which is exactly what I've been doing. Tonight, my clan helped."

"You trapped the shadowkin here somehow, didn't you?"

He nodded, pushing away from the counter. "Black salt works a treat when it comes to them. It forms a shield they can't cross, no matter what side of it they're on. It serves to contain them, preventing them from disappearing through a shadow." He moved to the cushioned bench. "We lured them inside the shield by creating a small opening."

"And then you closed it."

"Yes," he replied, taking a seat beside her.

"Does Khloë know about all this?"

"She knows about my history. She doesn't know about my

current shadowkin issue. You're the only person outside of my clan who does."

Larkin frowned when he dragged her onto his lap so that she straddled him. "Idiot, you have wounds on your thighs," she said, straining to get up.

Holding her in place, he shrugged. "I heal fast, remember? They're almost gone." He pressed a lingering kiss to her pulse that made it skitter. "They don't hurt anymore."

Larkin carved a hand into his hair as he licked a line up her throat. "We're supposed to be talking."

He slipped his hands under her tee and gripped her waist—they were so big, they almost completely spanned it. "I'm just getting more comfortable." He lashed her earlobe with his tongue.

As the feel of his hot breath washed over the wet lobe, she almost shivered. If he was trying to distract her again . . . well, it was working. Dammit.

"What's your plan for dealing with your half-brother when he surfaces?" she asked. "Tell me you have one."

"We have one." He swiftly peeled off her tee and dropped it beside him on the bench.

"Hey!"

"I'm simply making sure you don't overheat." His eyes went dark with need as they locked on her cleavage. "You really do have spectacular breasts."

She pulled lightly on his hair. "Tell me about your plan."

He coasted his fingertips along the swells of her breasts and then flicked open the front catch of her bra. "What plan?"

She let out a low growl.

His gaze snapped to hers, and he smiled. "Do that again."

She fisted his hair tight. "Sullivan, you are testing my patience in a major way."

"I can't focus worth a damn right now," he said, parting the cups of her bra. "Which is all your fault. If you weren't flashing your rack at me—"

"*Flashing?* I'm not flashing anything."

"—and I didn't have your nipples staring at me—"

"They're not eyes, dickhead."

"—I'd be able to keep track of the conversation. Now what were we talking about?"

Larkin gasped as he filled his hands with her breasts. "I really think I might kill you one day," she clipped even as she arched into his hold. "We were talking about—"

"Me fucking you hard?"

Her inner muscles fluttered. *Oh, piss it.* "Yeah. Yeah, that."

His mouth descended on hers as he shot to his feet, keeping her pinned against him. His tongue plundered her mouth as he backed her toward the bedroom area. But then he stopped. Spun her. Pressed his front firmly against her back.

Panting, Larkin watched as he planted her hands on the edges of the doorjamb.

His lips grazed her ear. "Hold on."

Ordinarily, she might have put up a fight for the heck of it. But though his wounds were healing fast, it wouldn't be too hard to reopen them. She didn't want to hurt him. So instead of protesting, she gripped the edges of the doorway.

He hummed, pleased. "Good girl." With quick movements, he removed the rest of her clothes, leaving her completely naked. "Don't move." He stepped back, and then there were the sounds of shoes being kicked off and clothing being shed.

She waited, her body strung tight, her pulse racing, her nerve-endings on fire with anticipation. Then he pressed his front against her back once more, and the skin-to-skin contact made her break out in a shiver.

His cock aggressively throbbed against her. It was hot and hard, and the sooner it was inside her the better.

Teague planted a hand on her stomach, his fingers spread, taking up maximum space in a very territorial gesture. "See that bed over there? I've never fucked anyone in it." He slid his hand down, down, down, and slipped two fingers between her slick folds. "I'm gonna pound you into that mattress later." He jammed two fingers inside her.

She jolted, her head flying back, her inner walls clenching and rippling.

"But right now"—he snaked his free hand up her body to palm her breast—"I want to take you right here."

So hard he ached, Teague began pumping his fingers inside her. He groaned in the back of his throat as she moved into his thrusts, rubbing against his cock each time. He loved pleasuring her this way. Loved feeling all that wet heat pulsing around his fingers. Loved hearing her breath catch each time he zeroed in on a certain spot.

He mattered to her. The thought kept circling around his brain. It also filled him with a very male contentment that fed his possessiveness and taunted him to take, use, fuck.

He wasn't sure he'd mattered to many people, despite having lived a long life during which he'd met many. It wasn't a small thing to him that he meant something to this woman. A woman who intended to guard his secrets, protect them, protect *him*; who'd put his safety before what she knew her Prime—her family—would want.

Feeling her slick inner muscles tighten, he upped the pace of his thrusts. "Get ready to come for me." Releasing her breast, he skimmed his hand down her body and rolled his fingertip around her clit once, twice.

She came, groaning hard, her pussy squeezing his fingers tight and bathing them in more hot liquid.

He didn't stop thrusting, drawing out her release. "Yeah, keep coming."

Once her orgasm passed, she slumped back against him.

He slowly withdrew his fingers and then sucked them clean. "Straighten up for me a little. I need to be in you. That's it."

He reached down, fisted his cock, and then wedged the head inside her. Gripping her hip tight, he began to push in. Slow, smooth, insistent. Until every inch of him was crammed inside her. "Hold tight to the wall. I'm not gonna go easy on you."

A delicate sniff. "I don't recall asking for easy."

He felt his lips hitch up. "You might wish you had." And then he powered into her. Harder and faster than he ever had before, burrowing impossibly deep every time.

She didn't flinch away. Didn't complain. She arched to meet his thrusts, her soft moans and hoarse rasps drifting through the air.

Possessiveness beat in his blood, fueling his pace. She felt so insanely good he wished he never had to stop. That he could be in her, taking her, twenty-four/seven. It would probably kill them both, but there was no better way to go.

He licked over the curve of her shoulder. "A bite mark would look good on you right here. My mark." He put his mouth to her ear. "I want my venom in you. Want it flowing through your veins, where you'll never get it out."

Ignoring the part of her that was all for that, Larkin shook her head. "Not happening. Ever."

He went still behind her, and then cold air wafted up her back.

Crap. "No," she told the demon, "I can't keep doing this with you. Biting is *out.* Deal with it."

The entity nuzzled her throat, its chest rumbling with an animalistic sound of warning. The hand on her breast squeezed tight enough to make her gasp, and then she was being savagely fucked.

Larkin tightened her hold on the doorframe. It was that or go flying from the force of the thrusts. The demon took her how it always took her—with little finesse, with a sense of entitlement, with a mind selfishly focused on chasing its own pleasure. Yet, it was a ride that neither she nor her demon could help but relish.

It wouldn't be long before she came. Her release was already close—a coiled force in her core that could explode outward at any moment.

She reared back to meet every powerful lunge, needing more, needing its cock *deeper*. If she could—

The breast it was holding suddenly felt a little too warm. Her skin quickly heated to an unbearable height, yet the pain was somehow pleasure. *Oh hell*, the demon was branding her. And quite honestly, that knowledge only shoved her closer to coming.

Her inner entity all but clapped, delighted. And as her skin cooled and the thrusts hastened, the force in her core wound tighter.

The demon fisted her hair, wrenched her head to the side, and bit into her shoulder. Hard. Driving its teeth down deep, piercing the skin.

And injecting its venom into her.

She hissed at the burn and came. *Fuck*, she came. The white-hot bliss violently thundered through her, making her eyes go blind and her mind go blank because the pleasure left no room for anything else.

She bucked. She screamed. She lost herself in the moment, barely noticing when the demon found its own release.

Finally, her orgasm subsided. Her unsteady breaths sawing at her throat, she leaned back against the solid body behind her. A tongue laved the bite as a rumbly nicker fanned her shoulder.

The demon released her hair, nuzzled her throat yet again, and then . . .

"You sure know how to press my beast's buttons," said Teague.

"Press its buttons?"

"Like you don't know that your 'no biting' statements only came across as a challenge to it."

Okay, yes, she had known that. "I didn't expect it to act on that, though."

"More fool you for thinking it was safe to taunt a hellbeast," he said, slipping his softening cock out of her. "Their minds don't work like ours."

"*Your* mind doesn't work like anyone's I've ever met."

"Aw, thanks, baby," he said with a smile as he scooped her up.

"It wasn't actually a compliment."

He carried her into the small bathroom. "Sounded like one to me." Setting her on her feet, he got a good look at the brand on her breast. His mouth curved, so he seemingly approved. "You're purposely not looking at it," he noted. "Why? Are you pissed about it?"

That depended on what the brand looked like. "Your demon didn't give me a third nipple or something, did it?"

He laughed. "A third nipple?"

"You have a weird-ass sense of humor, so it struck me that your entity might be the same."

His shoulders shaking, he used a washcloth to clean her up. "It's not a nipple." He gently turned her so that she faced the wall-mounted mirror and then he cupped her still-smarting breast. "Look."

Her eyes dropped straight to the black horseshoe-print on her breast. Her lips parted. It wasn't like a drawing, no, it genuinely looked as if she'd had a hellhorse step right on her and leave a print of its hoof behind. It was basically a stamp of ownership. Something her demon rather liked.

"Your beast is pretty territorial."

He hummed in agreement, sweeping his thumb over the brand, looking mightily pleased with it.

"So are you."

His eyes flicked to hers, dancing. "Which makes us even." He guided her out of the bathroom and over to the bed. A bed that turned out to be extremely comfortable.

"I'm staying here tonight," she told him. Well, *he* made those sort of statements when he felt like it. It was only fair that she could, too.

"Thanks for letting me know," he replied, echoing the response she typically gave him whenever he made the same declarations.

Recalling his answering phrase on those occasions, she repeated: "You're welcome."

He grinned. "I'm a bad influence on you and I can't tell you how much I love that." Smoothing his hand up her arm, he studied her face. "So. I matter to you, huh?"

Larkin felt her cheeks flush. She hadn't originally intended to tell him so soon. But she'd blurted it out in a moment of anger, and now she'd need to be careful he didn't sense that her wants had changed where he was concerned. That meant playing things down. "A little bit."

Still smiling, he brushed the tip of her nose with his. "Two-way street, harpy."

A grin shaped her demon's mouth, who gave her a smug 'Did you hear that?' nudge. Yes, she heard it. She couldn't lie, it hit her in the feels. It was also a relief.

"It doesn't bother you that I'm hell-born?"

She frowned, not seeing why it should matter. "No."

"What about that I was once Master of the Wild Hunt?"

"What about it?"

His smile widened. "Good response."

"Speaking of the Wild Hunt, I have a lot of questions." She was super curious about it. "First, though, I want to know what your plan is for dealing with your half-brother."

He swiped a hand over his jaw. "All right. It goes like this . . ."

CHAPTER SIXTEEN

Walking out of his bedroom area the next morning, Teague found Larkin using her fingertip to trace the swirly patterns that were ingrained on the doors of his china cabinet. Her gaze slid to him, pure black, and he realized her demon had taken the wheel.

"I want this," it told him.

Smiling, he crossed to the entity. "Well, you can't have it."

"Why not?"

"Because it's mine, and I intend to keep it."

"But I want it." The childlike statement was flatly spoken yet rang with a sense of self-entitlement that amused his demon.

"I have something for you." Teague returned to his bedroom and walked to the chest of drawers. He grabbed a jewelry box from a particular drawer and then made his way back to the demon. "Here."

Its eyes twinkling with interest, it took the box and opened it. Delight rapidly replaced the intrigue in its gaze. "You kept your word," it said, tracing the gold chain that was a feminized version of his own.

"I don't break my promises."

The entity took the piece of jewelry from the box and clipped it on.

"Like it?"

"Yes." It skimmed its fingertip over the part of the brand that peeked out of its tee shirt. "I also like this."

"So do I." A little too much.

"As does Larkin." The demon splayed its hands on his chest with a hum. "I want to carve her name into your skin."

He couldn't lie, the utter seriousness of that statement weirded him out almost as much as it tickled him. "That won't be happening."

"I would make sure the blade was clean."

"You know, funnily enough, whether or not I'd get an infection wasn't my main concern." He took its hand. "Come on, my little sadist. You can officially meet my clan." He led the demon outside and down the wagon steps.

Slade, Archer, Tucker, and Gideon were gathered around the firepit while Leo and Saxon lounged in the deck chairs. All were talking, drinking, and eating breakfast.

Teague and Larkin had eaten an hour ago, since they'd woken early. *And* fucked like there was no tomorrow. "Everyone," he began, "this is Larkin's demon, as you can see."

The males looked up and gave it wary nods. Well, her entity had quite a reputation.

The dogs swarmed it, sniffing at its hands and circling it while its black gaze eyed them closely.

The demon then looked up at Teague. "I like the shape of their skulls."

Jesus. "You're not killing the dogs."

"I would make it quick."

He tugged on its hand and pulled it toward the firepit. "Stop trying to freak me out; it's working."

The entity giggled.

Archer shuddered, almost spilling his coffee. "Jesus, that sound," he mouthed.

"I know," Teague mouthed back, sitting down on a log beside Tucker. The rest of the clan seemed similarly creeped out by the damn giggle.

Larkin's demon sat on Teague's other side and slowly swept its eerie gaze along their surroundings, exploring every inch.

Tucker cleared his throat, his attention on the harpy. "I think I speak for all of my clan when I say that—"

"Don't," Saxon told him, lifting a slice of bacon as if to ward off the comment. "You're likely the only one thinking whatever it is."

Tucker arched a brow. "So no one else is thinking that we never expected to meet Larkin's demon, let alone her?"

Leo spooned some fruit loops. "Well, I'm thinking it *now*."

"I like their feathers," her entity announced, watching two of the ravens perched on a tree branch.

Teague narrowed his eyes. "You're not killing the ravens."

It pursed its lips. "I suspect I could de-feather them without killing them."

"You're not stealing their feathers either."

"But they are so shiny."

Tucker bent down, grabbed a stray feather from the ground, and then reached across Teague to hand it to the entity. "Here."

It smiled. "Thank you, small man."

Saxon burst out laughing.

"I'm not short." Tucker bit harder into his slice of toast than necessary.

Watching the demon happily pocket the feather, Teague asked, "You're really going to keep that?"

"Yes." Its gaze abruptly turned inward, and its head twitched to the side. "Larkin wants to surface now. You and I will talk again later." Then it retreated.

Larkin double-blinked at him, her eyes now gray-green. "You shouldn't have bought it a gift. It'll expect more."

Teague shrugged one shoulder. "I don't mind." He thought he might enjoy spoiling it.

"Don't take this the wrong way," Archer said to her, setting an empty cup on the ground, "but your demon is creepy as hell."

She flapped a hand. "No offense taken."

"Would it really kill the dogs?" Gideon asked.

"Only if they hurt it," she replied. "So don't let them hurt it."

Leo rested his bowl between his spread thighs on the chair. "Off the subject ... We're out of black salt. Someone needs to buy more."

"I'll pick some up from the Underground before my race," offered Teague.

Larkin looked at him. "What time does your race start?"

"Noon. Why, you planning on being there?"

"I might as well go cheer you on." She gave a nonchalant shrug. "A girlfriend would do that."

"You're better than me at this pretend dating thing."

"Teague, I'm better than you at a lot of things."

He full-on smiled. "That was wonderfully bitchy."

"I mastered bitchiness as a kid." She glanced at each face. "Did you all know one another before joining the Wild Hunt?"

"Teague and I did," said Saxon. "We grew up in the same town."

She tilted her head. "What's hell like?" she asked no one in particular.

"Very different from here." Slade took a swig of what was likely liquor-laced coffee. "There's lots of barren land, lots of desert, lots of perpetual warzones. There are some kingdoms where peace *mostly* reigns, but there's still plenty of fighting and drinking and mayhem there."

"The town where Saxon and I grew up was in the middle of nowhere," Teague told her. "It was like something you'd see in a Western movie. People settled most things with violence. Fights were always to the death." He shrugged. "It's just the way of life there."

"Yeah, I've heard that. Tell me about Ronin."

"He's a dick," said Archer.

Larkin twisted her mouth. "I was really hoping for a little more detail."

Teague stretched out his legs. "He's eight years older than me. Strong. Powerful. Motivated. And his loathing for me is a twisted, infinite, obsessive thing."

"A lot of it stems from resentment," Leo chipped in.

Larkin looked at Teague. "You're living proof that his father cheated on his mother."

"Yes, and he didn't have the luxury of pretending I don't exist. Our town was very small. It wasn't possible for him and his mom to completely avoid me and mine." A part of Teague had felt bad for them. "Every time his mother laid eyes on me, pain would flash across her face. He saw it. Hated it. Hated me *for* it."

"Not his father, though," said Saxon. "Ronin never blamed Soren for her pain. He blamed Teague's mom; focused all his spite and scorn on both her and Teague."

It was as if Ronin hadn't been able to allow himself to think badly of his father, so he'd projected all his negative feelings onto Teague and his mother. "He idolized Soren. The old bastard was once a commander within the Dark Host. A highly decorated and well-respected commander. Ronin was extremely proud of that. But I was his reminder that his hero wasn't quite so perfect."

Saxon rested his empty plate on one thigh. "Soren had originally tried joining the Wild Hunt, but he was never accepted. I guess he thought he could live it through his son, because he pushed Ronin to apply to join; began training him when he was just a kid. I don't know if Ronin truly wanted it for himself or if he caved under the pressure to walk that path, but he pursued it all the same."

Teague nodded. "Every time a scout from the Dark Host turned up to watch one of the hellhorse races that took place in our town, you can bet your ass that Ronin ensured he took part."

"I'm guessing you also took part in them," said Larkin.

Teague had rarely sat out races. "I also always beat him."

"That's part of Ronin's issue with Teague," said Saxon. "Jealousy. Soren had literally nothing at all to do with Teague, but the asshole liked to take credit for his speed and strength and grit—he would brag to his buddies at the tavern that his blood would always make a man strong. Dumb shit like that.

"More, Soren would try motivating Ronin by taunting him that his 'little bastard brother' was showing him up. But using Teague as a measuring stick did nothing other than feed Ronin's hate for him."

"That hate hit new heights when a Dark Host scout recruited me for the Wild Hunt," said Teague. "Ronin took it real badly. Pitched a fit the likes of which you've never seen."

Saxon's mouth curved. "It was quite a sight to behold."

"To Ronin's credit, he didn't throw up his hands and accept defeat." Teague had thought he might. "He chose to instead sign up to be a general soldier within the Dark Host. Over the years, he bounced from unit to unit and worked his way up—which takes a lot longer than you might think. Promotions aren't given easily. But he wasn't content with that. He wanted to be part of the Wild Hunt. And he apparently got what he wanted after I retired."

"How soon after you retired?" she asked.

Puffing out a breath, Teague shook his head. "I have no idea. Ronin might have been assigned the position immediately after I left, or other demons could have filled it before him. Typically, units serve for centuries. But that length of time might well have passed for Ronin. For me, it's been over sixty years since my retirement. But, as I'm sure you already know, the times of the various realms aren't in sync. It's possible that, to him, I left hell only yesterday."

Pausing, Teague gave a slight shrug. "Whatever the case, he feels motivated to use his position of authority to have me killed. The Master of the Hunt can direct shadowkin."

Larkin frowned. "Won't his superiors be a little pissed about it?"

"They will if they learn of it, yes." It would seem that they hadn't yet done so. "Retired hunters are respected. For someone to think to repay their service by having them assassinated ... He'd lose his position for sure."

Larkin looked away for a moment, pensive. "If he spent so damn long fighting to get that role, why would he risk throwing it away like this? I know he hates you, but would that really be enough to make him do such a thing?"

It was Slade who answered, "We're not so sure. It seems senseless to us, but maybe not to Ronin. Is there anyone on this Earth who you hate with every cell in your body?"

She bit her lip. "There are people I'd happily see dead, but I guess that's not quite the same thing."

"Ronin has detested Teague since the moment of the guy's conception," said Slade. "And he has lived a *very* long time.

Centuries upon centuries. Imagine spending so long a time investing such a level of hate in another person—it would become imprinted in your system. It would root itself deep and spread like an infection. You'd never be able to get it out, no matter what you did."

Leo nodded. "Ronin might have always had his eye on becoming Master of the Wild Hunt, but remember that it was never really *his* ambition. It was Soren's. And that probably hit him square in the face when he stepped into the position and didn't feel the satisfaction he thought he'd feel."

"And we have to take into account that hell is a place where dark emotion reigns," said Teague. "To take a person's life is no big thing there. Depending on the circumstance, you may be punished. But then you may not. My point is that murder isn't the huge deal that it is here. It's often a way that someone settles their emotions. Like therapy. Duels to the death are far from uncommon."

Larkin hummed. "I'm surprised he never challenged you, then."

"He came close to it a few times when we were young, but he never went through with it. He knew I'd kill him, so he allowed people to talk him out of it." Ronin was a good fighter, but not *that* good.

"But you're sure he'll come here to take you out himself?" she asked.

"He won't agree to a one-on-one." Teague paused as Barron came to sit beside him. Stroking the dog, he went on, "He'll likely turn up with his entire unit, or maybe a group of mercenaries. Whatever the case, he'll have plenty of backup. But we'll deal with them in the exact fashion I told you last night."

"And I'll be participating in the exact way I told you last night," she tacked on.

Tucker blinked. "You're gonna fight with us?"

Larkin frowned, quite frankly affronted that he'd assume differently. It was as if being part of such an inclusive group for so long meant they didn't expect others to have their back. "Of course."

Gideon grinned. "Awesome. Can you really shoot hell-ice?"

She dipped her chin.

"But not high-powered hell-ice, right?" asked Archer. "I mean, the chips you shot Teague with didn't hurt him bad."

Only because she hadn't wanted them to. And at close range, they were deadly. "Don't worry, I'll be far from a weak link."

"She isn't wrong." Teague cast her a hard look. "She is, however, gonna be damn fucking careful not to get killed."

Larkin shot him a raised brow. "The only reckless one of the two of us is you."

His brow creased. "I'm not reckless."

"You purposely poke at a harpy on a daily basis. How is that anything but reckless?"

He looked away from her. "I don't like it when you make good points."

Gideon chuckled. "You're like two kids in a toy box."

"Sandbox," Archer corrected.

Gideon's brow furrowed. "What?"

"You mean sandbox," said Archer.

"No, I meant toy box."

"Then you're just stupid."

Gideon jerked back, almost falling off the log. "Hey!"

"It's all that alcohol." Archer gave him a superior look. "It's eating at your brain."

Gideon spluttered. "Those mushrooms won't be doing good stuff to yours."

"They give me clarity."

"They make you high."

"It's the same thing."

As the two males fell into an argument, Larkin turned to Teague and said, "I like your clan. I mean, they're weird, but I like them."

A smile wrenched at Teague's mouth. "Yeah, so do I."

A short time later, everyone was gathering their dishware and retreating to their wagons. Once she and Teague grabbed their things, they returned outside and made their way to his bike. She watched as he pulled on his gear and then mounted it.

"We might as well ride to the Underground at the same time," he said. "Where's your car?"

"I didn't drive here. I flew." She planned to take her harpy eagle form again and—

"Then I guess you'd better hop on."

Shock slapped her. "Hop on?"

"Yeah." He removed his helmet and gave it to her. "Put this on."

"Wait, your demon's good with me riding on the back of your bike?"

"More than."

Warmth built in her chest and then spread through her like thick honey. She swallowed. "Well. Okay, then."

She clung tight to his body as he drove them to the Underground. Many times she'd wondered what it would be like. Now she knew. Thrilling. Exciting. Invigorating.

Once in the Underground, they headed straight to a particular store where black salt could be purchased. It was run by two of Levi's friends, Ella and Mia. Both were incantors, meaning they were demons who could use magick.

The store sold a whole lot of stuff, most of which were either enchanted in some way or could be used when practicing magic.

Teague grabbed a few tins of black salt from a particular shelf, and they then made their way to the counter.

Behind it, Ella looked up from her e-reader and flashed them a smile. The leggy redhead was seriously pretty with her inky-blue eyes and rich ruby-red hair. "Hey, you two. So the rumors that you guys are an item are very much true."

"How are you?" Larkin asked.

"Great, thank you." She rang up Teague's purchases and then bagged them. As she placed said bag on the counter, her eyes drifted to something behind them. She frowned, blinking hard.

Larkin tracked her gaze and saw several males gathered outside. "You know the Black Saints?" she asked Ella.

The redhead's brow furrowed. "I've heard of them. They're fallen angels who formed an MC, right?"

Larkin nodded.

Ella's gaze again darted to them, and her forehead creased.

"Everything okay?"

Ella returned her attention to Larkin, her frown smoothing away. "Yeah. Yeah. It's just, for a minute there, I thought I recognized the guy in the middle of the group."

"That's Viper, the president of the club," Teague told her.

"Huh." Ella gave her head a fast shake. "Anyway, you two have a great day. And Teague, I do hope you'll one day tell me why one little clan would need so much black salt."

He smiled. "Maybe one day."

She softly snorted. "Liar. You'll tell me *shit*, just like always."

He chuckled and turned for the door.

Larkin gave Ella a nod. "See you around." She then followed Teague out of the store.

The Black Saints instantly looked their way. The president tipped his chin at them, his mouth bowing up. "Teague, I was gonna find you at some point today. You and I should talk."

Larkin narrowed her eyes. There was no veiled threat in the guy's voice, no trace of hostility or dislike. And yet, her protective instincts rose. "Is there a problem?"

Viper looked at her, seeming surprised by her question. "No problem. I just need a few minutes of his time."

"I've got a race coming up shortly," Teague told him. "Come find me afterwards."

"Will do."

As Larkin turned to leave, she noticed Viper cast a look at Ella through the window. Her instincts stirred. Something about his eyes at that moment, about the way he looked at the incantor ... It wasn't the way a man would look at a stranger.

Huh. Weird. She made a mental note to revisit the topic of Viper with Ella at a later date. Right now, Larkin had a few things to do. More specifically ... "I'm going to pop into Urban Ink to check on the girls. I'll make my way to the stadium afterward."

"You want to show them the brand," Teague guessed.

She lifted one shoulder. "Maybe."

Amusement gleamed in his eyes. "You like the thought of your brothers finding out second hand, because it'll get them all riled up," he correctly surmised. "I really am a super bad influence on you."

She rolled her eyes at the delight in his voice. "I'll see you soon. Good luck with your race." With that, they parted ways.

Roughly ten minutes later, she was strolling into Urban Ink ... just in time to watch Anaïs karate-chop Levi in the throat with a baby book, *hard*. The reaper sucked in a breath, rearing back. He coughed like a chain-smoker, shoving her into Tanner's arms.

While the hellhound admonished his daughter as he strived to pry the book from her hands, Piper patted the back of a still-coughing Levi. She was also doing her best not to laugh. Harper, Khloë, and Raini were making no such effort. Even Knox was smiling.

Flushing, a sheepish Devon offered Levi a smile of apology. "Anaïs didn't mean to hurt you, she doesn't know her own strength yet, she was just playing—"

"Save it," Levi bit out. "Don't you dare laugh, Piper, it isn't funny." He coughed again, which only made his mate turn away, her shoulders shaking with a silent chuckle.

Grinning, Larkin crossed to the group. "That was one *hell* of a karate-chop."

Harper knuckled away a tear. "I know, she hit him like a pro."

"She didn't do it on purpose," Devon insisted, but everyone just cast the hellcat a disbelieving look.

Larkin swept her gaze over the males as she said, "I didn't expect to see you all here."

"We decided to stop by on our way to the rodeo show," said Tanner.

Devon rounded on him. "You're taking our daughter to a *rodeo* show? You want her to watch people get flung around by wild bulls? Seriously?"

He lifted his shoulders. "It always lulls her straight to sleep."

The hellcat's jaw dropped. "You've taken her before? How many times?"

Tanner cleared his throat. "Once. Maybe twice. Okay, six or seven times. But it's hard to make her fall asleep. My opinion? Whatever works." He turned to the rest of the group. "Am I right? We do what we must when . . . Is that what I think it is?" He leaned toward Larkin, trying to get a closer look at the parts of the brand that her tee failed to hide.

"Is what, what?" asked Harper, sliding closer to her.

"If you think it's a brand, yes," Larkin told Tanner.

Devon's eyes went wide as she fairly shoved her friends aside to get a better look. "Oh my God, oh my God!"

Khloë came out from behind the desk and skirted the two males who'd been blocking her view. "I want to see, I want to see." The imp's brows shot up when Larkin pulled aside her collar a little to expose more of the brand. "Is that a hoof print?"

"Yup," replied Larkin.

Raini hummed. "Well, now."

Piper nodded. "Teague's demon likes to make a statement."

"Mine is no better, so . . . " Larkin looked at Knox, Tanner, and Levi, finding them both staring at what little they could see of the brand. All three looked surprised, but not in a *bad* way. That was a relief, because if they had started to complain or anything she'd have been pissed.

Knox's gaze lifted to hers. "As his demon branded you and you're seemingly fine with it, I take it that your fake relationship somehow became real."

Larkin's lips parted.

"Which means my sneaky plan worked." Smirking, Khloë nudged Piper. "Told you it would."

Larkin spluttered. "Plan? What plan?"

Looking rather pleased with herself, Khloë folded her arms. "Remember the oaths I made Teague take? I did that to avoid ending up in a situation where he hurt one of my friends by making them feel used or something. But I would never have minded if he was serious about them. And I could see that he was *totally* into you. I could also see that it wasn't a one-way street. I wanted you guys to have a shot at building something. You suit in a way that wouldn't be obvious to people who don't truly know him.

"But he avoids relationships like he's allergic to them for a few reasons. He was never going to break that habit easily. So when

Piper was like 'oh, Larkin, use Teague as your fake boyfriend', I saw an opportunity. I figured a case of forced proximity would make him cave. When he broke his word to me, I knew then that it was more than just sex for him. That brand shows that the same applies to his demon."

For long moments, Larkin just stared at her, shocked. "I should have seen that you were plotting something—I mean, it's not like that's not usual for you. But I didn't see it."

"Neither did I." Frowning, Harper looked from Devon to Raini. "Did either of you?"

They shook their heads, looking equally unhappy about it.

"How come you told Piper but not us?" demanded Raini.

Khloë gave an aloof shrug, her lips pursed. "I didn't feel like it."

Her mouth tightening, Harper set a hand on her hip. "You didn't feel like it?"

"No," replied Khloë, letting her arms slip to her sides. "And it wasn't like you needed to know or anything."

"It would have been nice for us to have known, though," Devon clipped.

Khloë's forehead wrinkled. "Why would you think I care about what you'd find nice? It's like you—stop hissing at me!"

As Raini worked to soothed Devon, Levi turned to fully face Larkin. "Knox kept telling me that you and Teague were just acting, but for a while there I thought it might be real. You played me well."

"I was annoyed about the matchmaking," she explained. "I wanted you all to get off my case."

He sighed. "Yeah, I get it. So, Khloë's plan really worked? You and Teague are an actual couple now?"

"Yes." Larkin bit her lip. "But he doesn't know that yet, so I'd appreciate it if you didn't tell him."

Levi laughed. "How can he not know that you're a couple?"

"He thinks it's all pretend."

Tanner gave her a skeptical look. "I doubt it."

Khloë snorted. "Teague has *no* idea what a relationship is. It's very possible it hasn't hit him yet that he's smack bam in the middle of one. He'll cotton on to it soon enough."

Piper materialized at Larkin's side. "How does your demon feel about all this?"

Larkin couldn't help but smile. "It's perfectly content."

"Are you going to request that he join your lair?" Khloë asked her, her expression uneasy. "He *might* do it for you. But it would make him unhappy."

Larkin already knew the latter. "I have no intention of asking that of him. Nor do I have any intention of leaving my lair to be a stray like him. I don't see how either of those things could affect us. It's not like we answer to different Primes. He doesn't have one. He doesn't answer to anyone. His clan has no leader."

Pausing, she turned to Knox. "I will only ever answer to you, you'll always have my unswerving loyalty, but . . . my loyalty will first and foremost be to Teague."

Knox nodded. "As it should be. And it doesn't concern me, if that's your worry. I don't believe that Teague would ever ask you to betray your lair. I won't insist that he join, or that you leave. I only ask that you still keep certain things to yourself. Being loyal to someone doesn't mean you need to share the secrets of others with them."

She knew *exactly* what secrets he was most interested in keeping quiet—the majority were related to Asher. "I would never share someone else's secrets without their expressed permission. Lair business will always be lair business, not Teague's. By the same token, his clan business will always be clan business, not yours."

Knox inclined his head. "Fair enough."

Levi crossed his arms over his broad chest. "You know he might try to exit this relationship once he realizes you maneuvered him into one, right?"

Her entity snorted. "He can try. It would come to nothing. My demon won't let him go anywhere."

"It formed an attachment to him?" asked Raini.

"Oh, yeah." A very strong one. It was the first time her demon had ever truly connected with anyone. "It intends to keep him. So do I. He'll get used to it."

Devon grinned. "I love how you quite simply decided you'd keep him. Like he's a hat you found on the floor. And now he's committed to you for life but has no clue. It's just great."

"Typical harpy—you're all collectors," Tanner teased.

"Personally, I don't envision him trying to walk away," said Piper.

"Neither do I," Larkin told her. "He gave me a ride to the Underground on his bike this morning."

Levi's brows hiked up. "Then I'm no longer skeptical, because that is no minor act for a hellhorse."

Khloë gave an excited nod. "It means that he and his demon trust you with their lives. That's *huge*."

"Yep," agreed Raini. "He's totally caught in your web. I can't wait for the moment where he realizes he's been shepherded into a relationship. I hope I'm there to witness it. If not, I'm going to want every detail."

Larkin chuckled. "Maybe I'll be kind enough to relay them, maybe not." Ignoring Raini's groan of complaint, she added, "Right, I'm off. Teague's racing soon. I'm going to grab myself a spot near the finish line, which means getting there early."

"Tell him we said congrats." Piper shrugged. "It's a given that he'll win."

"I'll tell him. See you all later."

CHAPTER SEVENTEEN

Making his way to the stadium, Teague sighed. Ordinarily, his beast would be in a good mood right now, given that a race was imminent. But it was currently in a funk. Why? Because Larkin wasn't at their side.

It didn't want her to head there separately, it wanted her where it could see her. *Clingy bastard.*

The intensity of its possessiveness hadn't cooled now that she wore its brand. No, that territorialism had kicked up several notches. There was no doubt in Teague's mind that his beast would mark her again. She'd be covered in them, if the entity had its way.

It was her own fault. If she'd only reacted as expected to all she'd learned the previous night, if she hadn't proven that they could wholeheartedly trust her, the beast wouldn't now view her as inside its circle.

Part of Teague was still reeling over how she'd not only taken his being hell-born in her stride but had rolled with his revelations about his past profession.

Also, she liked his clan. He hadn't expected that. Larkin held herself apart from strangers, not giving herself the room to feel either like or dislike. But she had been the opposite of distant and aloof toward them, and he knew she'd done that solely for him.

Last night, he'd tried talking her out of involving herself in the Ronin business, but it was impossible to change her mind once she'd firmly made it up. Eventually, he'd let it go and instead pulled her into his plans.

She'd won over his clan without consciously seeking to do it. That she'd demonstrated such loyalty to him had been enough. Once they'd realized she was determined to fight at his side, they'd gone from 'I think I could like her' to 'Teague, you should keep her'.

Well, it was mostly Gideon and Archer who'd telepathically expressed the latter opinion, but the others had made similar comments. His beast had the same attitude. And, to be honest, so did Teague.

But Larkin was 'all or nothing'. She'd want a real relationship. He didn't know if he had it in him to build and sustain one. Didn't know what exactly it would entail.

Would she expect him to move into her apartment? Leave his clan to join her lair? He could never agree to those conditions; could never abandon his clan.

Given her own hot buttons regarding abandonment, Larkin might not insist on it. But he could be wrong on that. Couples were supposed to make compromises and sacrifices, right?

Teague wouldn't know how to integrate himself into a lair. He'd existed outside of a hierarchy for too long, and he *liked* it that way. He had no wish to change it. He was ...

Teague's thoughts trailed off as he caught sight of three familiar demons hovering not far from the stadium's entrance. Holt and his sentinels. *Motherfucker.*

His beast's lips peeled back. Larkin had mentioned that Holt had paid a visit to Knox the previous day, asking that the Prime intercede on his behalf. She hadn't elaborated beyond that except to say that Knox had urged the asshole to leave Vegas or suffer the consequences. He'd clearly decided to ignore that warning.

Teague could have bypassed him, but then the cambion might linger, intent on getting an opportunity to speak to him. If Holt did that, there was a possibility he'd come across Larkin when she arrived. Teague didn't want him near her.

As such, he didn't skirt around the trio. He came to a smooth halt in front of Holt, ignoring the guy's companions, and met his unblinking stare full-on. This kind of posturing really fucking bored him, but it was the only language some demons spoke.

The Prime regarded him with a blank expression, saying not one word. It was only when his gaze dropped to the harpy wing on Teague's neck that he showed any emotion. A flash of hot anger that came and went so fast you could almost believe you'd imagined it.

Teague spoke, "The brand isn't fading, if that's what you were wondering." It would have been an indication that her demon was losing interest in him.

Holt's eyes bounced back to his. "Why is it that you're investing so much of your time and attention on Larkin?"

The unexpected question dented Teague's brow. "What?"

"I've looked into you. Everything I've learned has told me that you have no interest in serious or long-term relationships. So I'm confused."

It was no lie, Teague detected. The guy truly felt that Teague must have some kind of 'angle' here; that he was slyly using her to gain or achieve something. "You're judging me by your standards. We don't all have devious motivations behind the things that we do."

"Does she know that there is no record of your past? I think she would find that interesting. Suspicious, even."

"She already knows. Nonetheless, she's in my bed. What does that tell you?"

"That she hasn't yet sensed why you're really making a place for yourself in her life. Are you hoping that Knox will invite you to join his lair due to your being his sentinel's boyfriend? If so, it is a foolish plan. Oh, he may grant you a place, but he would toss you out once the relationship ended. And it *will* end. Something that, if the brand is anything to go by, may hurt her deeply." Holt took a small step forward. "And if it does, I will come for you."

Teague's mouth curved before he could stop it. "Come for me?" That was precious.

"Without a doubt. I'll be leaving Vegas soon. Only for a short time, so you need not get excited. I have a few things to attend to."

It seemed more likely to Teague that the guy had chosen to heed Knox but was saying this bullshit to save face.

"I will have people watch over her while I am gone. If you make a wrong move, I will find out, and I will end you."

"Oh, I do hope you try." It would make Teague's week—hell, his whole month. "If I were you, I wouldn't bother coming back. You won't get what you want."

Holt's brow winged up. "Larkin convinced you that she has no intention of ever forming the bond, did she? It hasn't occurred to you that she is testing me? That she is pushing me hard to see if I mean it when I say that I won't leave her again? That a part of her also wants me to feel how she felt years ago—angry, rejected, hurt?"

"Actually, no, I don't find any of that feasible." Not when he knew Larkin as well as he did.

"You should."

The guy wasn't a fan of reality, was he? "When is it gonna get through your head that you fucked up too spectacularly to fix it? Larkin didn't send you away from her out of spite. Or to test you. Or to hurt you. Or because anger is coloring her decisions. She simply wants nothing to do with you."

Holt's eyes narrowed. "You like the thought of that being the case. Which only illustrates that I'm right in thinking you care nothing for her. If she mattered to you in any way, you would want her to have her anchor in her life. You wouldn't be so keen to get me out of the picture."

"If Larkin wanted to form the bond with you, I'd support that. But when it comes to you, she has no interest in doing anything but putting you on a plane."

"You really shouldn't be so sure of that."

"Oh, but I am. And you know something? I think you are, too. I think you've come to realize that you're fighting a losing battle here—it's written all over your face." Teague could see it clear as day. "So why haven't you left already?" And why had the cambion bothered to seek him out?

Teague didn't get it. There appeared to be no real point to the conversation. Holt might truly have doubts as to why Teague was around Larkin, but it seemed a poor excuse to confront him like this. Plus, Holt had issued his little threat—it was done and dusted; there was no need for their chat to continue. Yet, the Prime hadn't walked away. He was still here.

"Why track me down for a chat? What's the purpose of all this?" Teague stared hard at him, searching his eyes, studying his expression. "Are you trying to provoke Larkin into contacting you?"

Holt's eyelids flickered.

Teague nodded, certain he was right. "That's it. That's why you're here. You know she won't like that you've come anywhere near me. You know that she'll want to deal with you personally. You think this will make her come to you." Unbelievable. His beast puffed an annoyed breath out of its nostrils, tired of this male who just couldn't stop playing games.

"I have no reason to need her to come to me. As you said, she has no interest in me."

At least he was admitting it. "But you want to talk to her all the same. Maybe to give it one last shot at convincing her to see things your way, or maybe even just to have an opportunity to curse her out for rejecting you." Teague didn't see that it mattered why, because it wouldn't work.

Of course . . . "It would have been a good plan if she was so easy to manipulate, but that's not the case." Teague tilted his head. "I would have thought you'd have picked up on that long before now. It's not exactly hard to sense."

"You talk of her with such authority. You think you know her so well." There was a mocking note in Holt's tone.

"I know her far better than you do—that much is clear, or you wouldn't have bothered pulling this stunt. You would have been well-aware that it was pointless."

Holt's eyes flared. "Trust me, Sullivan, I understand my anchor well."

"No, you only *think* you know her. The truth is, you never bothered to try. You did what all manipulators do—you set out to learn just enough about her for you to know what buttons to push to get your way, that's all. And that's what you did. Pushed her buttons over and over. You're still doing it now, even though it gets you nowhere. I guess you just know no other way to get what you want from people."

Holt looked away, sighing. "It would seem she has painted me as a real villain to you." He gave his head a quick shake and then returned his gaze to Teague. "I may have hurt her, but I'm not the enemy here. I'm trying to do right by her."

"If that were true, you'd be back in Canada now. You'd have respected her wishes; you'd have put them before what you want. But you haven't. You won't. So don't bother claiming to be misunderstood and brimming with good intentions—it won't fly with me."

Holt's mouth tightened. "You don't understand me as well as you think you do."

"Sure I do. I've met people like you many times before. You all think you're so very clever. But you're nothing special. And you bleed like everyone else—*that* is something you might want to remember. Because if you come back to Vegas again, you won't leave it intact. If I don't see to that, Knox will. And neither of us fuck around."

Done with the asshole, Teague shrugged past him and walked straight into the stadium. His beast jerked up its head with a snort of derision. Why the universe thought that that dick out there would make a good anchor for Larkin would forever remain a mystery.

There was one thing that Teague could be certain of: she wasn't going to take this well. Not even a little.

"I don't get why Khloë finds it amusing," said Teague. "What's funny about my demon branding you?"

Cocking her head, Larkin watched from her seat at his table while he stood at the counter, stirring their coffees with a tea-spoon. "She said it was funny?"

"No. She telepathically reached out to me just before my race. She said she saw the brand and likes it. Told me it's great that my beast is happy to help you and me make the fake dating seem real. But I'm pretty sure she was mocking me."

Khloë was likely entertained by how he hadn't yet realized that the whole thing wasn't fake anymore when his beast clearly had. "Did you ask her what she found funny?"

Teague plonked the teaspoon on his counter. "Yeah."

"And?"

"She laughed at me and then ended the conversation."

Larkin stifled a smile. "Well, that's Khloë for you. She's always chuckling over things other people see no humor in."

He placed two mugs of coffee on the table. "Hmm, I guess." He took the seat across from her. "It's good that Knox, Tanner, and Levi didn't give you a bucketful of shit over the brand."

She'd told him most of what got said during her visit to Urban Ink, but she'd obviously left out that the reason the guys were fine about the mark was that they'd sensed things were now truly serious between her and Teague. "It is. Keenan took it pretty well, too."

Initially, the incubus had given her a short *'I knew you were bullshitting us and I'm so hurt that you lied'* spiel. She'd cut that off with a *'Stop whining, I know that you're nowhere near as wounded as you claim, so now who's the bullshitter?'*

He'd grunted, before then going on to express his amusement at how Teague had no clue he was the target of a harpy on the hunt. Mollified by the brand—or, more to the point, what it represented—Keenan had even then wished her luck in permanently 'snaring' Teague.

Noticing that the hellhorse had an odd expression on his face, she asked, "What?"

Cradling his mug, he idly tapped his fingers along its side. "There's something I need to tell you."

Tensing, Larkin narrowed her eyes. "How very ominous that sounded." If he announced he wanted them to part ways, she was gonna kick his ass right here in his own wagon. Her demon would paint the walls with his blood. "Well, spit it out."

He raised a hand. "First, I need you to promise that you'll hear me out all the way before you react."

"You're serious?"

"Super serious. Promise me, Lark."

She let out an annoyed breath. "Fine. I promise. Now cough it up."

He straightened a little in his seat. "I saw Holt today."

She went rigid. "*Saw* him?"

"To be specific, he was waiting for me outside the stadium before my race."

Her eyelid twitched, and her inner demon stirred with a snarl. "What did he say to you?"

"In sum . . . I must have an ulterior motive for being in your life, and I'm mistaken in thinking that you won't bond with him eventually. Oh, and he'll be gone from Vegas for a short time, which I think you'll agree is good news."

Good news would be hearing he'd been dropped into a vat of boiling hot oil and then set alight by the flames of hell. Larkin flexed her fingers as anger curdled in her belly. "I warned him to stay away from me and mine." She especially hadn't wanted him in even Teague's general vicinity.

"And he knew you'd be pissed. That was why he did it. He didn't truly want a conversation with me. He wanted to provoke you into contacting him."

"Did he touch you?" The question came out through her teeth.

"No."

"Did he threaten you?"

Teague hesitated, twisting his mouth.

Larkin leaned forward and laid her hands flat on the table. "Don't lie to me, Rainbow Dash."

"If that's another My Little Pony character—"

"I want the truth. Now."

Sighing, he scratched at the back of his head. "He said he'd come for me if I ever hurt you, but that was pretty much it."

Spitting a curse, Larkin pushed out of her chair. Filled with a dark restless energy, she began to pace up and down. The whole time, her inner demon fumed.

It wasn't bad enough that Holt had come here thinking he could use Larkin to deter his enemies from dicking with him, was it? No. The sack of shit had threatened the man in her life. A man who was barely *in* her life and could very well think *I don't need this crap* and then go on his way if Holt pushed hard enough.

"It wasn't much of a threat, Lark," said Teague. "No cursing or snarling or anything. It was more like a casual statement."

"I could give a shit how he phrased it. He threatened to harm you."

"It didn't do anything but amuse me."

"*So* not the point."

Knowing better than to touch a harpy who was firmly in the grip of anger, Teague didn't give into the urge to get up and go to her. Instead, he angled his body to fully face her and said, "I wasn't bothered by that, I was bothered that—" He ceased speaking as her demon abruptly surfaced.

Freezing in place, it pinned him with a black gaze that swam with fury. "I should have killed him long ago, consequences be damned."

"Why bother? He's irrelevant. To you. To Larkin. To me. And he knows it. He did this to try to make himself relevant."

The entity's hands balled up. "I want to dice up his eyeballs and feed them to him. Then his fingernails. Then his toes. Then his teeth."

"I'm pretty sure he'd vomit several times."

"I'd make him eat that, too."

The delightful little freak really would. "This isn't worth getting worked up over."

"I disagree."

"If you go to him, you'll be giving him what he wants. He did this for a reaction. He's trying once again to manipulate both you and Larkin. Don't let him do it. Or do you want him to have that power over you?"

It squinted. "Now *you* are trying to manipulate me."

"No, I'm simply pointing out the facts of the situation. I want you to look at it from every angle and not react out of anger. You'd later be pissed at yourself for letting him win."

The entity sneered at him. "I don't wish to speak to you right now. You're making too much sense." That fast, it subsided.

Larkin bent her head far to the side until her neck cracked. "My demon's not much interested in being rational right now."

"I got that impression. What about you?"

She sighed, rolling back her tense shoulders. "I know you're right. I know that to pay him a visit would do nothing more than make him feel smug. But I'm *so fucking done* with his shit. You know, what really annoys me is that he won't even be all that disappointed if I don't go to him, because he'll still have the satisfaction of knowing he pissed me off just like I pissed him off by trampling over his cunning little plan."

"There's a cunning little plan?"

"I didn't see it at first; it was Knox who pointed it out. Holt is predominantly here for political reasons. He's having issues with other Primes. He'll never get Knox on side, but if he's bound to me . . ."

"The Primes on his ass will likely back off," Teague understood.

"Exactly. Holt doesn't want to claim me as his psi-mate for the right reason. I don't think he ever did. Total asshole, isn't he?"

"Of the worst variety." Teague rose from his chair, crossed to her, and curved an arm around her neck to tug her close. "I get why you don't want to let this go, but what I said earlier about going to him being a bad idea still stands. How about you send someone else to deal with him? And by deal with him, I mean kill him."

Her brow pinched. "Send some of my lair's Force to take on a Prime? I'd never put them in that position."

"Who said anything about your lair members?"

"You're offering to take care of him?"

Teague shrugged. "You want him gone; I can make that happen. Just say the word and I'll bury the fucker." With relish. Plenty and plenty of relish.

"No."

"What, you think I can't handle him?" His beast snorted in affront.

"I have no doubt that you can handle him. But you'd struggle against his entire lair. They'd sniff out who killed him. They'd come for that person. If you were part of a lair, they'd need to request the permission of your Prime to execute you. But you're a stray, so they wouldn't be required to seek permission to administer a punishment. They'd sneak up on you when you least expect it."

"And then they'd die." It would be epic.

"Probably. Given your past occupation, I am sure that you and your clan are quite equipped at killing. But that would only lead to more demons coming your way seeking revenge. It would be a never-ending cycle. Trust me, I've seen it happen."

"You're making too much sense," he complained.

"And *you're* so similar to my demon it's eerie."

He smiled. "I'm putting that in my mental 'favorite compliments' drawer."

She rolled her eyes. "Yeah, do you that."

He rubbed his nose against hers. "So how do you want to handle this?"

Some lines of tension smoothing away from her forehead, she threaded her fingers through his hair. "I'm just going to take a moment to say how I appreciate that you don't try to override my decisions."

"I want to work with you, not against you."

"I know, I like it." She blew out a breath. "With regards to Holt, I don't think that sending others to deal with him would achieve anything. He's not stupid, he'll expect a visit—if not from me, then from someone on my behalf—so he won't even be in his hotel room while he waits. He'll be somewhere close, monitoring who enters and exits the building. He might recognize who I send, he might not. Either way, he won't give them a chance to harm him."

"Why have you let him remain at the hotel? Surely Knox could have had him kicked out." The Prime wielded a shitload of social power here in Vegas.

"I felt it better to know where he was. It made it easier to keep an eye on him."

"Ah, gotcha. It wouldn't surprise me if he's checked out already. Like you said, he'll be expecting a visit. And he means to return to Canada anyway."

"Hopefully he'll stay there."

"It would be nice."

Larkin didn't think it would be so unrealistic of him to do so. Knox felt certain that he'd gotten through to Holt, so the cambion knew he'd be wasting his time if he stuck around. Plus, he had troubles with other lairs to handle.

His demon might not like that there'd be no anchor bond, but it would surely be so angry with her for repeatedly rejecting it that it wouldn't fight Holt on leaving. And maybe with time and distance from her, his entity would feel less inclined to push him to form the bond. *Fingers and toes crossed.*

Teague toyed with the end of her braid. "Is your demon any calmer?"

"It's currently making a mental list of torturous methods it would like to use on Holt. Does that answer your question?" It also cast Teague a disinterested look, unmoved by his concern. "It's still miffed at you for talking sense earlier."

He gave her a look of complete understanding. "I've got to admit, I'm not a fan of 'sense'. But I didn't want you or your demon doing something you'd later regret. I mean, I might not know what regret feels like, but people seem to really hate it."

"It's not an enjoyable emotion."

"Seems synonymous with 'weak' to me."

Larkin snickered. "Of course it does."

He rubbed a hand up and down her back. "What can I do that will help you and your demon calm down?"

One thing was guaranteed to work. "I need to spar with someone. I won't use my abilities, it'll just be combat."

"Slade will be good for you to spar with, then." He let his arms slip away from her. "I'd offer to be your sparring partner, but let's face it, I'd just get all worked up seeing you hot and sweaty, and then I'd end up wrestling you to the floor so I could fuck you."

Larkin felt her lips curve. "Wrestling me to the floor?" she echoed. "You're cute."

His brows shot up. "You don't think I can put you on your back?"

"I know you can't."

"You're wrong."

"Oh, yeah? Prove it." She'd barely gotten out the latter word before he lunged for her—*fast*. She sidestepped him, did a swift turn, and brought her hand down sharply on his ass.

He slowly pivoted on his heel, looking reluctantly impressed. "You're sure quick on your feet, baby."

"I know." She raised a challenging brow. "Spar?"

"Yeah, all right. Let's go outside and do this. But you know I'll fuck you afterwards, right?"

Walking toward the door, she glanced at him over her shoulder. "Not in front of your clan, you won't."

"But a little exhibitionism can spice things up. LarTea is all about spice."

Concerned by the level of seriousness in his voice, she halted and then turned to face him. "We're not having sex in public," she firmly stated.

"Why not? We practiced for this."

"Maybe *you* had it in your head that we fucked in private so we'd be okay doing it in front of other people, but I didn't." She lifted a hand when he would have argued. "No, it's not happening."

"Ah, come on. It'll be fun. My clan will egg us on and everything. Maybe even eat popcorn. It won't get weird."

"The mere idea of it is weird."

"You said you had sex in that club in the Underground that can get a little raw."

"That was different. It was dark. And people weren't sitting there watching me."

Pursing his lips, he lifted his shoulders. "I can ask them to stand up."

"You're not right in the head. You're just not. It's like . . ." She trailed off as realization dawned on her. "You're doing that thing again where you help me get out all my frustration by bickering with you."

He grinned. "It never fails to work." Crossing to her, he tapped her chin. "But you *would* enjoy some exhibitionism."

"I would not."

CHAPTER EIGHTEEN

Stepping out of the shower stall a few days later, Teague wrapped a towel around his waist and padded into his bedroom. Drying himself off, he glanced at the wristwatch he'd placed on his dresser. 5pm.

Larkin would be here in half an hour or so. They often ate dinner together at her place, but Saxon had announced he'd be throwing a BBQ tonight for the entire clan. No real reason; he just felt like it.

When Teague had telepathically let her know about the BBQ, she'd said, "I'll be there." Like he'd invited her. Which he hadn't. And she knew it.

Call him weird, but he liked how she simply *stated* what she'd be doing in a deal-with-it voice.

As it happened, he'd fully intended to invite her. Still, he might have teased her that it was a guys' night or something—which would no doubt have earned him an uncaring snort followed by a "See you soon." But he hadn't had the chance, because she'd psychically withdrawn from the conversation without a goodbye.

The sound of barks splitting the air made both him and his beast stiffen. Knowing his clan members were outside, he tuned into their telepathic channel and asked, *What's wrong?*

Not sure I'd choose the word 'wrong', said Leo. *More like 'surprising'. You're not going to believe this, but Vine is here.*

Teague blinked at the mention of their old commander within the Dark Host. *Vine?*

Yeah, and a few of his legionnaires. He wants to speak with us all.

Swearing under his breath, Teague began to quickly dry himself off. *About what?* It had been years since Teague had last seen the commander. The demon hadn't contacted them after they left the Wild Hunt. It wasn't usual to keep in touch with retirees.

It was Slade who responded, *He hasn't said yet.*

I doubt I'm the only one thinking he somehow found out that Ronin has been sending shadowkin after Teague, Archer chipped in. *He could be here to assure us that the attacks will come to an end.*

It did seem the likeliest scenario. Dry, Teague started dragging on clothes.

I don't think we need to worry that any shit is about to go down, said Tucker. *Vine's all smiles and back-claps, and he doesn't have a large force with him.*

True. Vine knew it would take more than four demons to bring the clan down. For him to have brought along only a few legionnaires, Vine was deliberately attempting to not appear threatening.

Once dressed, Teague exited the wagon. None of the clan were sitting—a sign that, despite their easy smiles and relaxed postures, they weren't feeling so blasé. In fact, they'd all stationed themselves around the clearing, boxing Vine and his three demons in.

It wouldn't have gone unnoticed by the commander, but he didn't seem annoyed by it. He sat at a log near the firepit with his companions, chatting amicably with Gideon, who was dumping dry wood in the pit to feed the fire.

The dogs slowly and casually circled the camp, not looking in the least bit predatory. But Teague knew that each were on high alert and would pounce at a moment's notice, much like the silent and still ravens.

He lifted a brow at Saxon, who was leaning against one of the wagons, and asked, *Everything still all good here?*

So far, yes, the other male replied. *Vine and his boys are a little on the tense side, as if unsure of their welcome—not exactly unexpected, given we requested that we be left alone when we retired and we're not exactly giving them a gushing reception—but they've been friendly enough.*

Good, I'd rather not have to kill Vine, said Teague as he clambered down the stairs.

The creak of the wood made the commander turn his upper body slightly, and his mouth curved into his usual shark's smile. Vine pushed to his feet—the guy was tall, bulky, and dark-skinned with black-ringed blue eyes that were as sharp as they were unusual. "Teague, good to see you. Shit, none of you have aged one single bit."

Teague walked to him and shook the hand he held out. "It's only been roughly sixty years since we settled in this realm."

"That all? Centuries have passed down below."

"That explains the gray streaks in your hair."

Vine shot him a droll look. "Don't remind me of them." He introduced his three companions, who all gave Teague respectful nods.

Teague settled on a log, and the four visitors then returned to their spots across from him.

"How's retirement suiting you?" asked Vine.

Wanting the male to get to the point, Teague only said, "Well enough."

"You haven't found yourself bored after so many years of adrenaline rushes?"

"At first, it took some adjusting to. But now? No, not at all. It's hard for a hellhorse to get bored." They could find the smallest thing entertaining.

Vine's lips kicked up. "True."

"But I don't think you came all the way here to ask how retirement is treating us."

Vine leaned forward, braced his elbows on his thighs, and brushed his hands together. "How would you feel about returning to the Dark Host?"

Shock tightened Teague's muscles, and his beast jerked its head in surprise. It was literally the last thing that he'd expected the commander to say. "Returning as what?"

"As Master of the Wild Hunt, of course. I'd like you all to come back."

"Why?" The question came from Slade, who stood beside the steps of his wagon.

"The hellhorses that formed the unit after you left . . . Let's just say they were nowhere near as good as yours," Vine prevaricated. "They retired a century early."

Saxon squinted. "By choice, or by persuasion?"

"The latter, but it wasn't difficult to convince them." Vine grazed his fingertips over his jaw. "We formed another unit after that, but they too struggled to keep up with the demands of the job. As for the current unit, their record is even worse."

A low telepathic whistle of surprise sounded down the clan's mental channel—one that came from Leo, who then said, *Okay, this conversation is going in a direction I hadn't expected.*

Maybe he doesn't actually know what Ronin's been up to, mused Gideon.

Let's not enlighten him, said Teague. *If we do, we'll be the prime suspects when Ronin drops off their radar and can't be found. The clan would ensure there'd be nothing left of him to find.*

"We had high hopes for them," Vine continued. "They're excellent trackers and have plenty of experience within the Dark Host. They're also by no means weak. Your half-brother, Ronin, actually leads them, Teague." Pausing, he rubbed at his brow. "But he fast buckled under the pressure of the job, just as the others did."

Teague's brows lifted in a surprise he failed to hide.

Vine sighed. "Yes, I hadn't expected that from Ronin either. He'd pushed to join the Hunt for so long that I assumed he'd be ready for all that would come with it. You know yourself that being part of it demands much from a demon. It's not simply a role; it's a way of life. There's little to no downtime. No way to be a real partner or parent, which means making sacrifices that demons often don't realize will bother them until they're in that situation."

"What, Ronin wants to breed?" Archer cut in, leaning back against the picnic table. "I wouldn't consider it a good thing."

Vine's mouth quirked. "No, that's not what ails him." He paused. "The seven of you are massively respected within the Dark Host. In all of its history, few units have performed and functioned as well as yours. You never failed to capture who you were sent to track, you never left any trace of yourselves behind, you never took too long to complete a mission. You were a team in the truest sense of the word. An excellent team.

"The units that came after yours weren't able to come close to matching that record, let alone surpass it. In all three cases, a very big issue was that the Master huntsman didn't have what it took to lead the Hunt." Vine cut his gaze to Teague. "Ronin has been constantly compared to you by others, and he's not measuring up in their estimation."

Tucker puffed out a breath. "Ronin can't like that much."

"He doesn't," Vine confirmed. "What he likes even less is that Zagan threatened that if his unit's performance didn't improve, we would ask you all to return and replace them."

Teague blinked. He did, what?

Well, shit, said Tucker.

"Zagan thought it might light a fire under Ronin's ass. It did. But it hasn't made him any better at his position. He still struggles to handle the pressure, as does the rest of his unit." Vine blew out a breath. "I think the problem is that you all made it look easy. The reality of the situation was therefore a shock to those who came after you."

"So you intend to persuade the current unit to retire as well?" asked Leo, sitting on the log beside Teague.

"Yes." Vine straightened. "A weakness in the Wild Hunt is a weakness in the Dark Host, and it reflects badly on the army as a whole. We can't have that."

Leo nodded. "Does Ronin or his unit know you're here?"

The commander shook his head. "But they'll learn of it if you return with me. And I'm hoping you will. There are, of course, other hellhorses eager to join the Hunt, but I don't wish to take my chances on another bunch if there's a possibility that you all might be willing to come back."

Teague hadn't ever anticipated that such an offer would be made to them, since it wasn't common for ex-huntsmen to be asked to come out of retirement. But despite being flattered by it, he couldn't say he was at all tempted to grab onto the offer. His years in the Wild Hunt . . . it felt like another lifetime. One he'd moved on from and had no wish to revisit.

Just the same, his beast had no interest in returning to that time in their life. Or to hell, for that matter. It was settled here in this realm now, as was Teague. Neither could imagine leaving their current life behind, or people such as Khloë and, yes, even Larkin.

Teague rubbed at his nape. "I can't speak for the others here, only for myself. Though I appreciate that you'd make this offer, I have to respectfully decline. As you rightly pointed out, the Hunt demands a lot from a person. I had no life outside of it. Now I do. Now I know how it feels to be free and able to do as I please. I enjoy that far too much. I couldn't go back to a time when I didn't have it."

"Same applies to me," said Slade, and the others echoed his sentiment.

Vine exhaled heavily. "I was afraid that would be the case. There's no way I can change your mind? No offer I could make that would appeal to you? I've been given the go-ahead by Zagan to promise you whatever you want."

Teague gave him a wan smile. "My hunting days are over."

His clan made similar comments.

Vine twisted his mouth, grim. "I can't lie, I'm disappointed. Zagan won't be pleased either. But I can understand why you would make such a decision." He stood, and his companions did the same. "If you change your mind, you'll be welcomed back into the Dark Host without hesitation."

Teague gave him a curt nod. "I appreciate that." Sort of. Not really.

Goodbyes, back-pats, and nods were exchanged. Vine then opened a portal through which he and the legionnaires left. It shut with a *whoosh* of sound.

Sinking into a deck chair, Gideon looked at Teague. "Now we know why Ronin sent shadowkin after you—if you're dead, there's no way you can replace him as Master Huntsman."

Leo nodded, absently plucking at the golf glove he'd removed. "It makes sense now that he'd be prepared to risk losing the position by targeting you," he told Teague. "He's going to lose it anyway—it's just a matter of when. He wants to make sure he doesn't lose it *to you.*"

Yep, because that would only add insult to injury. "Once he's officially demoted, he'll lose the ability to direct the shadowkin. That's when he'll come for me personally."

"Definitely," agreed Slade, taking a seat at the picnic table. "That you don't intend to be reinstated as Master Huntsman won't stop him from wanting you dead. And I don't just mean because as long as you live there's a chance you'll take Zagan and Vine up on their offer. Ronin will feel the need to prove once and for all who's the biggest, baddest brother. He'll seek to do that by taking your life."

"He'd be dumb *not* to try it in any case," began Archer, "considering he'll know by now there's a good chance that Teague's aware he sent the shadowkin. Ronin will want to cover his tracks."

"Yeah, he won't want to chance that Teague alerts Vine," agreed Tucker before sliding his gaze to Teague. "You didn't tell the commander about it just now, sure, but Ronin might not learn that Vine came here. Either way, Ronin won't want it hanging over his head."

When Reggie nosed Teague's thigh, he took the hint and began petting him. "I didn't expect to be offered our old positions. You really didn't want to return to them?"

Slade shook his head, his brows drawing together. "Like you, I couldn't go back to following orders."

"Me neither," said Leo. "I make my own rules now, and I like it that way."

Archer stretched. "I've done enough tracking and killing to

last me a lifetime. Plus, they don't have mushrooms in hell. I'd miss them."

"I'd miss the weed here," said Tucker. "It's way better."

Saxon folded his arms. "I can't lie, I enjoy hunting. I enjoy killing. But I do that here with my current profession, so . . . "

Gideon pulled a small flask out of what seemed like nowhere. "I don't think I'd be as good at hunting as I used to be. I've been inactive too long. I'm used to late nights and not waking up at the crack of dawn. I'm not inclined to give that up. I'd rather . . . " He trailed off at the sound of an engine rumbling in the near distance. "Someone's here."

Teague's beast flicked its ears. "It'll be Larkin."

"She might as well eat with us," declared Saxon. "I'm going to fire up the grill now."

The others headed to their wagons to retrieve foods and drinks for the BBQ. Teague waited on the log for his harpy to arrive. Her car soon pulled up behind Saxon's truck, and then she slid out.

He felt his brow crease. "You have blood on you." A lot of it.

She waved that away and stalked toward him. "It isn't mine."

That was usually Saxon's line. "Whose blood is it?"

"Some idiot from our lair who thought that breaking the rules would be tolerated. As if that's ever been a thing." She propped her delectable butt on the log beside Teague and landed a quick kiss on his mouth. "I doubt he'll repeat that mistake—at least not in a hurry. My demon shook him up."

Teague frowned. "And you didn't invite me to come watch it at work?"

She looked at him, her brow furrowed. "Uh, no."

"But I want to see it make someone cry."

"That's *your* mental damage to deal with. I'm not touching

or accommodating it. Besides, it's lair business. Just like your business is yours. Right?"

He snapped his mouth shut. *Valid point.* He hated when she made those. "Come on, you can help me grab some bits from my wagon for the BBQ while I tell you about our recent visitor."

By the time they were placing the last of said 'bits' on the outdoor table, he'd relayed the details of his visit from Vine.

"That explains a lot," she said. "Being told you might replace him will have been a real hit for Ronin. To then be threatened that you'd be brought back to take over from him has to have been his tipping point."

Saxon dipped his chin. "His bitterness has been brewing for centuries. He'll hate that he's struggling where Teague didn't." He placed a platter of buns on the table, his gaze sliding to Teague. "You shone in that position. He's done the opposite. And if people have been comparing his performance to yours, that has to not only gall him but remind him of how Soren used you as a measuring stick."

Leo folded his arms. "All those years he impatiently waited to take over your old position, he probably had it in his head that he'd be better at it than you; that he'd earn a level of respect that *way* surpassed yours," he said to Teague.

Nodding, Tucker pulled a lid off a pot of potato salad. "He's such a damn tool he probably convinced himself he'd go down in history."

"He will," said Teague. "He'll be known as the Master Huntsman that mysteriously disappeared, because that's how it will be made to look after we kill him."

Larkin tilted her head. "I take it you didn't tell Vine that Ronin's been sending shadowkin after you."

"Of course I didn't," Teague confirmed. "If I had, he'd have later suspected me of being responsible for Ronin's upcoming disappearance."

Glad he'd thought of that, Larkin gave a satisfied nod. Well, it wasn't as if he *always* had his thoughts straight. His version of 'common sense' differed from that of most people.

Taking a knife, she began sawing open the bread buns. "Is it typical for huntsmen to be asked to come out of retirement?"

"Not as far as I know," he replied.

"You weren't even a little tempted to return to hell and pick up the mantle you once lowered?" Not that she'd have let him. She'd have stopped him. Somehow.

"Fuck, no. I'm good as I am." He swept his gaze over his camp. "The life we lead is simple and unexciting, but that's the point. I know some people seem to struggle with retirement; with having no demands on them or their time. Not us. We like it that way." He shot her a slow, lazy smile. "Why, would you miss me if I left?"

She sniffed. "Maybe a little. At first. Then I'd get used to you being gone. Might even eventually forget your name. But I'd think back on your cock fondly."

He chuckled. "You'd miss me."

Totally. "Yeah, well, you'd miss me."

"*And* your demon. It cracks me up."

Her entity practically preened. "I'm pretty sure you're the only person other than me who actually likes my demon."

His brow knitted. "Really? People are so weird."

Eyeing him, Larkin nodded. "Yeah. Yeah, they are."

Stepping closer to her, he said, "I have an idea."

"Will it disturb me?"

"Possibly."

She reluctantly invited, "Go on."

"I could convince Gideon to let your demon torture him," he

began, his eyes lit with excitement, "and then I'll have a front seat to what will surely be an amazing show."

Torture him? She placed down the knife. "How, pray tell, could you convince Gideon to agree to that?"

"I'd get him shitfaced first. That won't be hard. He loves his whiskey. Add in a few glasses of brandy and he'll. Be. *Plastered.* He doesn't handle mixing his drinks well." He rubbed his hands. "So, what do you think?"

She supposed she shouldn't be surprised that he'd suggest something like this, or that he'd believe she might be up for it. "I think 'no'."

The light faded from his eyes as a disappointed frown pulled at his brows. "Why?"

"*Why?* Lots of reasons. It's immoral. Mean. Sly."

"I'm not seeing the issue."

She felt her eyelid twitch. "Go help Saxon flip burgers or something." She went back to slicing open the bread buns.

"So it's a definite no, then?"

"A definite, *huge* no. Really huge. Like . . . it couldn't be bigger."

"A no to what?" asked Archer, sidling up to Teague.

"I said we should get Gideon so blitzed he'd agree to let her demon torture him so I can watch," Teague explained.

Archer's brow dented. "Why do we need his agreement?"

Dropping the knife again, Larkin flicked her gaze upward. They could *not* be for real.

Teague lifted his shoulders. "I thought it might make her feel better about the whole thing."

Larkin planted her hands on the table. "What will make me feel better is if we end this conversation."

Archer leaned into Teague. "Maybe it will help if we get *her* drunk, too."

"I heard that," she told him.

Archer gave her a reprimanding look. "It's rude to eavesdrop."

"It's not eavesdropping if you're *right there*, where I have no choice but to hear you," she pointed out, admittedly snippy. "And something tells me you don't care about 'rude' anyway."

He slapped a hand to his chest. "I'm offended that you would—"

"Don't. Just don't."

The asshole chuckled.

A few hours later, after the BBQ was over and she was seriously bloated, she and Teague were heading into his wagon.

Peering down at the duffel she'd pulled out of the trunk, he asked, "What's that?"

"My overnight bag." She dumped it on the cushioned bench.

His brows inched up. "You're staying over?"

"No, I brought it for absolutely no reason," she deadpanned.

He smiled. "Snarky." The word rang with delight. "It's like you want my demon to bite you again."

Rolling her eyes, she took a seat at the table and placed a hand on her full stomach. As he opened the window, she glanced around. "I like your wagon."

He shot her a sideways look of surprise. "I would have thought you'd find it confining. You're used to your big-ass apartment."

"I like my home. But it's not cozy. I prefer cozy over spacious."

He tipped his head to the side. "How come you don't live in a smaller place, then?"

"It's easier to have Knox as a landlord. I don't have to pay rent or worry about human bullshit. Plus, my complex is super secure. And it means I'm near Levi, Tanner, and their mates. Though the latter isn't always a positive, because the guys like to be up in my business, despite having busy lives."

Casting her duffel a quick look, he said, "I almost forgot to tell you, you left some of your stuff here last time."

"I did?"

"A comb and a hair tie."

Humming, she casually stretched her legs out. "I wondered where the comb was. Remind me to toss them in my bag before I leave."

He crossed to her, his eyes narrowed, his mouth curving. "You know, Gideon has a theory."

"I'm almost afraid to ask what it is. In fact, I don't want to know."

Teague's smile widened. "He thinks you left your stuff here on purpose. That you did it to put your mark on my territory."

"Because a hair tie and a comb make a *real* statement," she mocked, her voice bone dry. But in the privacy of her own head, she had only one thought: *Busted*. "Take your jeans off."

His forehead wrinkled. "What? Why?"

"It'll make it easier for me to blow you."

Teague pressed his lips together, squeezing one eye shut. "I really feel like you're trying to distract me, but I don't have it in me to choose pursuing this line of conversation over having your lips wrapped around my cock again."

Success. "Then the jeans need to go. So get to it."

CHAPTER NINETEEN

"I don't know why you keep glaring at me," said Teague the following day, sitting across from her at a table in one of the Underground's ice-cream parlors.

Larkin didn't credit that ridiculous, bullshit statement with a response. She did, however, pause in devouring her waffle cone to shoot him a sneer of disgust.

He responded with a mocking oh-so-innocent look. She'd slap it right off his face if he wasn't careful. Which he likely wouldn't be. Because this was Mr. Who Cares About Self-preservation?

Larkin went on to irritably lick at her honeycomb ice-cream, scooping up some caramel syrup and chocolate chips with her tongue. A sucker for such treats, she'd ordinarily be enjoying the moment. But at present, she was feeling too antsy to properly relish its icy smoothness and the slight fizz of the honeycomb chunks.

In no way edgy, her demon wanted Larkin to playfully tease him with some sexually suggestive licks of her ice-cream. The entity wasn't a little bit bothered by the current situation, unlike her.

"It's not my fault people are staring," he added, his eyes still wide-eyed with faux innocence.

No, it was his demon's fault. But Teague was fully responsible for the fact that *he kept smirking*. There was nothing funny about this matter. "Keep pushing me and I *will* hurt you."

"What? Why? My beast is the one in the wrong, not me."

She scowled. "Don't act like you think your demon did anything bad. You're not one little bit bothered by any of this. It's all one big source of amusement for you."

"At no point have I laughed."

"You did it this morning. Twice."

"I wasn't laughing at you, I was laughing at . . . I can't actually remember, but it definitely wasn't you." His eyes dancing, he dipped his plastic spoon into his bowl and scooped up a dollop of chocolate ice-cream mixed with cookie dough, chopped nuts, and toffee syrup. "I swear it on my mom's grave."

"Is she dead?"

"Uh . . . well, no."

Larkin ground her teeth. If she could reach one of the metal scoopers behind the glass case, she'd honestly hit him with it. Hard. Probably more than once.

He scoffed down his spoonful of dessert. "I'd like to point out that we're in the same boat. *Your* demon branded *me* again as well. You don't hear me complaining about it."

The same boat? Seriously? "*Mine* didn't leave a barcode on your ass or a tribal horse-head on your goddamn face."

Though she was not *whatsoever* impressed by the barcode, she was more annoyed by the facial tattoo. There might as well be a note on her cheek that read, 'Chattel of Teague Sullivan's Demon'.

Not that the latter brand wasn't pretty. Feminine and loosely detailed, it almost looked like someone had stylishly doodled it on her skin. It would definitely work as a logo. Yeah, she liked it. *But it was on her face.*

On. Her. Face.

It bore repeating.

He gazed at the brand, clearly stifling a smile. "It's really not that noticeable."

Larkin managed to hold back a hiss. Reminding herself that he wouldn't look so pretty with a broken nose, she resisted slamming her palm into his face—*barely.* It was a close call.

She took in a steadying breath, inhaling the scents of caramel, vanilla, chocolate, ozone, and fresh fruit.

It didn't help.

Pinning him with yet another glare, she delved back into her ice-cream. As it was her day off work, they'd last night planned to hit the Underground together for a few hours today. But that was before his demon had pulled its asshole move.

Knowing the facial brand would earn her plenty of startled looks, Larkin had pushed to cancel their day out. Call her odd, but she wasn't fond of being stared at. Teague, though, had been determined that they go out as planned. He'd teased her and poked at her when she'd resisted, calling her a chicken—which her demon happened to agree with.

Larkin's response had been to twist his balls, but the weirdo had laughed even as he groaned in pain. She'd eventually relented, as he'd been right in something he said—people would see the brand sooner or later, so canceling their plans wouldn't achieve anything. Not a procrastinator by nature, she'd chosen not to delay exposing the brand to one and all.

However, as they'd walked around the Underground for the past few hours—browsing the market stalls, eating lunch at the man-made park, betting on hellhound races—she'd found herself wishing she'd stayed at his wagon. She'd been on the receiving end of so much staring that her skin actually crawled and itched with discomfort.

Something like that would normally irritate her demon, but the entity was smug that his beast was feeling so possessive.

It wasn't often that an entity would brand a person's face. Only extremely territorial demons tended to do so, and they generally only did it when intent on making a very clear 'mine' statement that no one would fail to notice. So yes, his beast branding her was indeed a good sign. After all, Larkin couldn't keep Teague unless she also managed to win over his demon. That appeared to be working. But she'd still much rather it had branded her neck or something.

Then again, the mark would have gained people's attention in any case. Because Larkin had never been so visibly branded before, and Teague wasn't known for being at all possessive. Which was why the chatter had stopped when she'd first walked into the ice-cream parlor. The guy chopping strawberries behind the counter had almost dropped the knife in surprise. One of the women who'd been scanning the various tubs of ice-cream behind the glass-covered case had spat out a "Holy hell" that had made Larkin's demon smirk.

Well, at least someone was finding it funny.

Larkin had arched a haughty brow, and people had looked away fast. They'd also started muttering about the mark. Still were. She could hear them even over the music playing low, the hum of the air conditioning, and the whir of the blender.

Larkin didn't like being the focus of so much attention. She preferred to fade into the background; to be the one doing the watching. And she *especially* didn't like being the subject of gossip, but it was plain unavoidable now.

She'd bet that by the time she arrived at Devon's apartment for the upcoming movie evening in a few hours' time, the girls would already have heard about the brand. No doubt they'd have plenty to say about it, too.

"Personally," began Teague, spooning more ice-cream, "I would have thought you'd just be thankful that, out of the two brands, it's the horse's head that's on your face. It could have as easily been the barcode. Which I actually would have preferred."

"Because I'd have looked ridiculous?"

"Because you'd have looked well and truly owned," he replied, his eyes heating.

Ignoring the little flutter in her stomach, she licked at her ice-cream again, scooping up the last few chocolate chips. "I'm totally gonna encourage my demon to put 'Village Idiot' on your cheek, by the way."

"Your entity wouldn't do that." He flashed her a cocky grin. "It likes me."

"I don't know why that makes you feel smug." Most people didn't even want to be on her demon's radar. It was understandable, really.

"How can I not be smug about it? Your entity doesn't like many people. Same as you." He pointed his spoon at her, adding, "But you like *me*. You're falling for me fast, just like I said you would."

Oh, he had *no* idea just how true that was. But she didn't let that show on her face. "If I told you that you were right, you'd shit your pants and run."

He frowned. "What?"

"You're well-known for reacting badly to women claiming they care for you." She gave him a smile of mock sympathy. "Hey, it's okay. It's not your fault that feelings scare you."

"Okay, first of all, I don't run from women who say they care for me. I just speed-walk." His tongue flicked out and collected the stray nut that had stuck to the corner of his mouth. "Second of all, it's not because feelings scare me, it's because these people are talking a load of tripe."

"Why would you think they don't mean what they say?"

"How *can* they mean it? None of them know me. They only see the surface."

Larkin let out a thoughtful hum. "Maybe that's your fault, seeing as you make a point of not letting people close."

"Whatever. The point is their 'feelings' for me aren't real."

"So what you're saying is that if a woman's feelings for you *are* ever real, you will stick around and try to build something with her?"

He opened his mouth, squinting. "Not quite."

"Then we're back to you being a scaredy cat. So maybe stop saying I'm falling for you. You don't want to tempt fate, now, do you?"

Larkin looked away, inadvertently locking eyes with another starer. She shot him a dark look. He shrunk in his seat, holding his waffle cone in front of his face as if it would protect him, and then glanced up at the wall and pretended to admire the ice-cream parlor's cheery, colorful fifties décor.

She returned her gaze to Teague. "The staring is getting old *fast*."

"Enough with the scowling at me, I won't be held responsible for what my demon does."

"I'm not glaring at you because I hold you responsible. I'm glaring at you because I'm annoyed that you find this amusing."

"No, I don't."

"Then why are you laughing?"

"I'm a nervous-laugher, and you're making me nervous with the way you're trying to kill me with your eyes." Teague felt his mouth curve as she made one of those low, raspy growls in the back of her throat. "Best sound ever, I swear."

Her eyes narrowed. "Fuck off, Shadowfax."

"I hear the adoration in your voice," he teased.

There was a loud crunch as she bit unnecessarily hard into her cone, her fingers flexing around it.

He stiffened ever so slightly. "You're imagining throwing that ice-cream at me, aren't you?"

"Yes," she all but grunted.

He couldn't say he blamed her.

He resisted teasing her again while they ate. But there was no way to fully stifle a grin each time she glared at him. Luckily, they managed to finish their desserts without him getting anything flung in his face.

Cleaning her fingers with a thin napkin, she spared the wall clock a quick glance. "I need to head to Devon and Tanner's place or I'll be late for her movie-evening thing. Not that we'll actually watch a movie. We never do."

His beast let out an unhappy snort at the idea of them parting ways. It didn't want her going anywhere unless it was accompanying her. As if its possessiveness increased with each brand that it put on her body. That should concern Teague and make him sternly insist that the beast cease marking her.

Later. He'd do it later. Maybe. Not that his demon was likely to obey him or anything.

One thing mollified the entity—she wouldn't be staying at Devon and Tanner's place long, since she was coming to the Underground's pit later to observe one of Slade's brawls.

"Why call them movie nights, then?" Teague asked, dabbing his mouth with a napkin.

"We always start out *intending* to watch one. But we get distracted by all the talking and laughing, especially when the drinks start flowing. And, of course, Khloë will try drawing on people with a sharpie, which usually leads to arguing, since she tends to draw dirty stuff."

Frowning, he dumped his napkin in his bowl. "Dirty stuff? I thought she drew animals. Cute ones. Like Fritz the baby hippo."

"Fritz is not a hippo. It's a doodle of a cock complete with hairy balls."

"No, it isn't."

Her brow flicked up. "So you've seen one of her Fritz sketches?"

"A few. I know he doesn't look like average hippos—"

"Because he ain't one. You know it. I know it. So let's not do this." Rising to her feet, she threw her balled-up napkin at him.

He caught it fast, smiling. "Such violence."

"Such idiocy."

Chuckling, Teague stood and then guided her out of the parlor with a hand on her lower back. He had to smile at how quickly people looked away if she caught them staring at her. He perversely liked that so many were scared of his woman. Fake-woman. Whatever.

In an effort to distract her from all the looks she was receiving, he engaged her in general conversation as they made their way out of the Underground and through the club that concealed its entrance. Okay, by 'general conversation', he meant he pushed her wonderfully sensitive buttons until it got to the point where she tried whacking him over the head. Expecting it, he dodged her strike, which earned him one of her growls.

Outside, he escorted her to her car.

"I'll meet you at the pit later," she told him as she pressed the button on her key fob.

Teague nodded. He wasn't sure if she knew, but it was no small matter that Slade had invited her to come watch one of his fights. It meant that the hellhorse was beginning to view her as an extended member of their clan. Which was yet another thing that should concern Teague, and he should probably talk with Slade about it.

Later. Teague would do it later. Maybe.

He fisted her tee, hauled her close, and took her mouth, sipping and licking and nipping. Humming, he pulled back. "You taste good. Like caramel and honeycomb and chocolate." He cast her a wolfish grin. "We really need to put some of that icecream on your—"

"Stop."

"What? I was going to say shopping list." He fought a smile as her eyelid twitched. Again. That permanent eye-twitch he was aiming for was *totally* gonna be a thing soon.

She tugged her tee free of his hand. "I will see you later. Try not to cause any trouble while you're unsupervised."

"You talk like I'm five."

"You act like you're five." She poked his chest. "Later."

His mouth kicking up, Teague waited until she'd driven off before he crossed to his bike and mounted it. Before long, he was driving into his camp.

The entire clan was outside. Gideon was removing laundry from the hanging line. Slade was battling with Dutch for possession of a branch. Leo was using a hammer to refix a bird box to a tree while Archer held the box still for him. Tucker and Saxon were bickering about something or other. Well, it was more like Tucker was posturing and snarking at Saxon, who remained completely calm in that way that drove the other hellhorse crazy.

Teague unmounted his bike and petted the dogs that came to greet him. Removing his helmet, he nodded at Gideon as the male clambered up the stairs of his wagon with a pile of laundered clothes. After shoving his protective gear into his saddlebag, Teague then crossed to Saxon and Tucker, who were *still* bickering.

Sitting on a log, Saxon paused in carving a stick and looked up at Tucker. "I don't know why you persist in getting yourself all worked up," he said, his voice calm.

Standing over him with his hands set on his hips, Tucker scrunched up his face. "How could I not?"

"No one else here is," Saxon pointed out, gesturing at the others. "Just you. It's only ever a case of *just you.*"

Teague looked from one male to the other. "What's the problem?"

Tucker turned to him, his mouth tight. "This fucking sicko here is carving sticks with a knife that's crusted with the blood of his last kill. Sticks he thinks we should be totally okay with using to roast marshmallows later." He rounded on Saxon. "I mean, what in the love of hell goes through your damn, hairless head? Because it can't be anything good."

Exhaling a bored sigh, Saxon looked at Teague. "Basically, the little man syndrome is at work again."

"Little ma—" Tucker cut himself off, pressing his joined hands against his mouth. He took in a long breath. "I cannot keep doing this with you."

"So stop," Saxon suggested with an airy shrug before going back to carving the stick.

"I would if you'd stop calling me short, Van Diesel."

"It's Vin," Slade piped up.

Tucker snarled at him. "I don't care!"

"You know," began Leo, strolling over to the table with Archer, "ancient warriors liked painting their face with the blood of their prey."

Tucker's brows snapped together. "They didn't want their goddamn marshmallows covered in it, though." He refocused on Teague. "Where's Larkin? *She'd* back me up."

His back feeling a little stiff, Teague did a long stretch. "She's meeting us at the pit later."

Leo set his hammer down on the table and slid Teague a look. "You know she's collected you, right?"

Teague frowned. "What?"

"The harpy. She's collected you." Leo airily waved a hand. "It's what her kind do."

Choosing to ignore that he might like being collected by this particular harpy—another thing he'd *maybe* address later—Teague forced a nonchalant shrug. "She's possessive, that's all."

"It ain't as simple as that," Slade insisted, relinquishing the branch to Dutch. "You matter to her. She openly told you that right in front of us all."

"Who told who what?" asked Gideon as he stepped out of his wagon and onto his porch.

"Larkin told Teague that he matters to her," Archer elaborated, taking a seat on a log.

Gideon smiled, clambering down the steps. "Yeah, that was sweet."

Teague only grunted.

Tucker tilted his head. "You don't believe her, T?"

"I believe her," replied Teague, rubbing at the side of his neck. "She's given me every reason to think I should. But various people matter to her. That hasn't been enough to make her collect them, so there's no reason for us to assume that she's collected me." His demon snorted at that, feeling quite positive that he was very much mistaken.

"And if you're wrong?" asked Gideon, perching himself on the log beside Archer. "What, then?"

"Yeah, what will you do?" Leo folded his arms, his expression expectant . . . like Teague owed them answers, which he did not.

Teague frowned as he swept his gaze over his clan. "How is this your business?" he snarked.

His mouth curling, Gideon leaned into Archer. "Ooh, he's getting defensive. Interesting."

"Very," agreed Archer.

Saxon idly traced the blade of his knife. "I saw the brand-new spanking mark that your demon put on her face. I'd have had to be on the moon not to have seen it. Entities aren't usually so bold with branding unless they're playing for keeps."

Teague felt his frown deepen. "How would you know? Has your demon ever marked anyone?"

Saxon pursed his lips. "Well, no—"

"Then you're only going on what you've heard," said Teague.

"So your demon *doesn't* want to keep her?" Leo cut in, settling at the picnic table. "Is that what you're saying? Because if so, I call bullshit."

"As do I," said Gideon.

Tucker raised a hand. "Same here."

The others nodded their agreement.

Teague inwardly sighed. In truth, his beast had every intention of keeping her, regardless of what Teague's own wishes might be. It felt that he'd be stupid to let her go.

To be honest, he could easily envision having something real with her ... though he wasn't exactly sure what 'real' would entail. He stopped himself from exploring the idea too deeply because he had no clue where Larkin was mentally at.

There was a possibility that she wouldn't want to take a chance on a guy who'd never committed to a woman before; that she wouldn't feel she could trust that he'd stick around—much like her brothers didn't. Well, it was worth considering, since she'd found it difficult to believe he'd keep up *fake* dating her for five months.

"What was her reaction to the new brand?" asked Slade, sitting on the bottom step of his wagon.

Knowing that the male would be referring to the horse's head, seeing as Slade would have no idea about the barcode on her ass—which she'd ranted about for fifteen minutes straight earlier, and it had been a glorious sight—Teague replied, "She wasn't happy about it, though she claimed she wouldn't have cared if it wasn't on her face."

That she'd complained had bugged his beast. It wanted her to wear its mark with pride, no matter where said mark was located. But it had been placated by the fact that her demon had branded Teague again.

He now sported what looked like rake marks on his back—rake marks from the talons of a harpy eagle. And he found that he liked them. Liked that her demon was so boldly proprietary.

"But even though she ain't happy about it, she isn't walking away from you," Slade pointed out. "She has to know that facial brands aren't done casually, but she still spent the day with you. She's still coming to watch my fight later. And she's still probably going to end up in your bed tonight. That says she isn't alarmed or put-off by the brand."

"Which is a real good sign," added Gideon. "Her demon can't much care either, or you'd be missing a limb or something at this point."

Tucker dipped his chin. "That entity would not hesitate to work over anyone who even remotely irritated it."

Not sure it was a good thing that hope had firmly planted itself in his gut, Teague flapped his arms and asked, "Why are we having this conversation?"

"Because it's making you uncomfortable," said Leo.

Gideon shrugged. "Because I'm bored."

"Because I like to watch you grind your teeth," added Archer.

Clenching his jaw, Teague gave his head a quick shake.

"I still say you should keep her," Gideon told him, his lips hiking up. "She's loyal, she's good for you, and she fits with us well."

"Yeah, you should definitely hold onto her, T," Archer advised. "But only if she's not going to ask you to join her lair or move into her place."

Gideon gave the male a hard look. "Hey, that's selfish."

"What is?" asked Archer, appearing bewildered.

"Expecting him to remain with us if he'd be happier being part of her lair and setting up house with her. You want him to be happy, right?"

Archer blinked. "Not particularly, no."

Gideon elbowed him hard.

"What?" demanded Archer, lifting his shoulders. "I have other things to concern myself with. Very important things that take up much of my time and attention."

"Name one thing. *One*. That isn't related to mushrooms," Gideon hurried to add.

His gaze turning inward, Archer opened his mouth, but no words came out.

Teague sighed again, raising his hands, palms out. "Just to note, I have no intention of becoming part of any lair at any point in time, or of moving out of our camp."

Archer smiled. "That's all I wanted to hear."

"If you change your mind, Teague, the rest of us will understand." Gideon took in every face. "Right?"

People exchanged looks, twisted their mouths, averted their gazes, or forced a cough.

"*Right?*" pushed Gideon.

Leo scratched his cheek. "I would *try* to understand. How's that?"

"Yeah, we'd give it our best shot," said Slade, to which the others dipped their chin.

Gideon gaped, shaking his head. "You're all awful. Just awful."

"Dude, that's harsh," upheld Tucker. "We just don't want to have to—" He abruptly cut off as the dogs' heads snapped up.

Barron let out a cautioning growl as the hounds then all got to their feet. The fur on their backs rising, they stared at the trees far up ahead of them and bared their teeth. Moments later, a distinctive squawk of warning came from a raven—a warning that they had company.

Falling silent, Teague and his clan went very still. They all exchanged looks, and he felt a grin tug at his mouth as anticipation quickly began to buzz through his veins and electrify the air of the camp.

Welcoming the shot of adrenaline that pulsed through his bloodstream, Teague reached out to his clan using their channel. *It would seem that Ronin's here.* Fucking finally.

CHAPTER TWENTY

Teague signaled at the growling hounds to remain in place. They heeded him, their leg muscles quivering with the urge to pounce. Similarly, he let out a bird call to warn the ravens to hang back and stay alert.

Within him, his abruptly energized beast swished its tail and restlessly kicked up a hind leg. It was looking forward to the battle to come; was anxious for it to begin.

He telepathically reached out to Larkin. *Quick warning, baby: Ronin's come to visit.*

Her psyche touched his, and a low curse drifted into his mind. *I'll be there as soon as I can. No more than twenty minutes.*

Tracking the hounds' gazes, Teague and his clan turned to fully face the section of trees wherein Ronin and whatever backup he'd brought had to be standing. Teague wasn't worried that anyone would creep up behind them—the ravens would alert him if such a thing were to occur.

When none of the intruders showed themselves after long

moments went by, Teague sighed. "We know you're there." He exchanged an eye-roll with Slade.

Leaves crinkled as footfalls finally came toward them, slow and easy; steadily increasing in volume. The whole time, adrenaline continued to pump around Teague's body—sharpening his senses, feeding his anticipation, making his heart start to beat that little bit faster.

His beast was similarly amped up, thrilled the enemy they'd been waiting to confront was finally here. Especially since that enemy was Ronin. For most of its life, the demon had wanted the male's blood. Wanted his fear and his suffering. The entity intended to get exactly what it had sought for so long.

Hell-born bloodhounds spilled out of the trees first, each unhurried step silent and stealthy. Baring their teeth, they came to a halt at the sound of a sharp whistle that came from the wooded area behind them. There were five bloodhounds in total. Far taller than an average dog, they sported red eyes, powerful jaws, and thick, black, ruffled fur.

Five carrion birds came next, noiselessly gliding into view and then settling onto a branch in a neat line. They eyed the ravens cautiously, their feathers fluffing up in affront as said ravens boldly stared at them.

Teague casually widened his stance as seven men prowled into the clearing, fluid and confident. They took only three steps before coming to a smooth stop, apparently intending to keep plenty of space between them and Teague's clan.

Seven males. Five hounds. Five birds. Yeah, Ronin had brought his entire unit.

Teague found his gaze slamming on his half-brother. He hadn't seen him in so long that, honestly, he'd forgotten the guy's face—its features had been a blur in his mind.

Wide, dark-brown eyes that Ronin inherited from Soren were

set into a square face that sported a crooked nose, dimpled chin, and thin lips. His sharp, angular jaw was currently hard and tight as he glared at Teague.

Skimming his gaze along the six men fanned out around Ronin, Teague noticed that two didn't look particularly comfortable with the situation. But neither did they look on the verge of fleeing. The others stood with their chin up, their shoulders back, their posture cocky.

That wasn't all. Oh, no.

Ronin had brought yet more company.

Hellish creatures were slowly pouring out of the trees to gather in a long line behind the unit of hellhorses. All stared at Teague and his clan through eyes that were flaming orbs embedded in over-pronounced eye-sockets. Their lips peeled back in a snarl, revealing long fangs that were coated in blood and thick saliva.

Motherfucker, Ronin had brought goddamn chupacabras.

Teague hadn't seen any since leaving hell. It was rare for one to escape the realm. They resembled overgrown coyotes, though they boasted gray, leathery skin that had only brief patches of coppery fur here and there. Sharp spines protruded from their nape and ran down their back, stopping at the base of their long tail. They gave off a rancid odor similar to that of roasting, dead meat—Teague could smell it from where he stood.

Animals they might be but, like shadowkin, chupacabras were as intelligent as any human. They communicated through telepathy, and packs often offered their services for the right price. Ronin had clearly agreed to pay theirs.

I wasn't expecting the chupacabras, said Archer, speaking through the clan's channel.

They were indeed a surprise. Not that they worried Teague or his demon. The more, the merrier. *Notice that there's no shadowkin. I think we can guess what that means.*

Yeah, Zagan must have lived up to his word and demoted Ronin's unit, said Saxon.

It would seem so. If Ronin had still had authority over shadowkin, he wouldn't have needed or bothered to hire chupacabras.

I've got to be honest, began Leo, *my beast is looking forward to taking on those mangy little bastards. It's been a while since my demon last stomped one to death. It likes the crunching sound it makes.*

At Teague's side, Baxter restlessly danced from foot to foot with an eager-to-get-moving whine. The other dogs let out aggressive little yaps and snarls, equally keyed up.

Laying a hand on Baxter's head, Teague fixed his gaze on Ronin and said, "Maybe I'm being paranoid, but I don't think this is intended to be a friendly visit."

His neck seeming tight with tension, Ronin planted his feet. "You know, I never quite understood what my father saw in your mother. Pretty she might be, but she is so very fragile. Codependent. *Weak.*"

Well aware that the dick only meant to rile Teague up, he didn't take the bait. "And yet, she has so much power over your emotions, doesn't she? You invest so much hatred in her that it close to consumes you. Seems kind of sad, really."

Saxon folded his arms. "I can guess that you're here to kill us," he said, his voice fairly dripping with boredom. "I'm curious as to why."

"But you're not shocked to see me here," Ronin mused, "so I suppose one of the shadowkin made you aware that it was I who sent them, which means you also know that I became Master Huntsman," he added, his chest puffing up.

Slade coughed out a low, scornful snort. "Zagan must have been having a weird day when he thought you'd make a good Master."

A cord in Ronin's neck seemed to twang. "He saw my potential."

"He sure didn't see that you'd abuse the Dark Host's resources by siccing shadowkin on people like dogs to avenge private grudges," muttered Leo. "You don't think it was a chickenshit move to send them after Teague?"

"Chickenshit?" echoed Ronin, his chuckle strained and empty of humor. "If I in any way feared him, I wouldn't be here now."

Gideon raised an index finger. "Ah, but you're not here for a one-to-one fight—you versus Teague. Are you? Nah. You're not even here for a fair-and-square battle wanting to pitch your people against us. You brought mercenaries with you. Which brings us back to the whole chickenshit thing."

"I don't know, Gid," said Archer, scanning the pack of chupacabras. "Maybe it's not that he's a chinless wonder. Maybe he just doesn't think there's a hope of defeating us unless we're outnumbered." He put a hand to his chest. "I personally find that a compliment."

Ronin's upper lip quivered as he looked Archer up and down. "The chupacabras are here for entertainment value." He cut his gaze to Teague. "I will enjoy the sight of them tearing into you."

"*Weakening* Teague, you mean," Tucker put in. "That's what this is about. You want to tire him out so you have an edge over him."

Ronin's eyes flared. "Why would I fear my father's bastard child who never once challenged me, no matter what I did or said?" he countered, all snooty and pompous.

"*You* never officially challenged *me* either," Teague pointed out. "Or have you forgotten that?"

A muscle in Ronin's cheek ticked as he clamped his mouth shut.

"You know, I almost did throw down a gauntlet once. It was

back when we were juveniles, when you constantly pulled dumb crap like egg my house and play knock-and-run. Honestly, all it really did was exhaust my fucking patience. It was the stuff you said to my mother that got to me. I was done listening to you insult her—something you insisted on doing at every given opportunity. There's only one reason I left you alone. Would you like to know what it is?" asked Teague, arching a taunting brow.

"I already know the answer: you weren't confident you could take me."

Teague had to chuckle. "Oh, far from it. The truth is . . . " He paused, feeling a dark smile curve his mouth. "Soren promised he would keep you in line and away from my mother if I swore not to challenge you."

Ronin's lips parted. He spluttered. "Nonsense."

"Nope. Pure fact."

"He wouldn't have spoken to you about anything at all, let alone about me. He had nothing to do with you."

"You were the only son he gave a crap about, yeah." It had never bothered Teague, because he'd felt not one ounce of respect for the man who'd tossed his pregnant mistress out of the little cottage he'd once put her in, making her homeless. "That's *why* he made that deal with me. He wanted to protect you."

"You lie," Ronin ground out, his cheeks stained red.

Teague shook his head. "He sensed I'd hit my limit with you, and he had no faith in your ability to survive a duel to the death with me." Soren had openly admitted it, annoyance and shame coating every word. "So he came to me and made an offer. One I accepted, because I wanted my mother to be left in peace. But I made it clear to him that if he failed to do as he vowed, my own promise would become null and void."

Ronin's lips trembled, almost pulling back into a snarl. "No. He would never have made you *any* offer. He certainly wouldn't ever have doubted that I could end you."

Teague arched a brow. "That so? Then why did he always step in whenever me and you almost came to blows as adults in the tavern? Think back. He told you I wasn't worth your anger, that you should focus on yourself, that you shouldn't give me the satisfaction of a reaction. You backed off every time, just like he intended. Why *would* he have intended it if he was positive that you'd win? It certainly wouldn't have been that he cared whether I lived or died, would it?"

Ronin gave his head a fast shake. "He had complete faith in me. He had none whatsoever in you. He saw you as weak and a shame to his name. It disgusted him when you joined the Dark Host—he said there was no place for you there."

"I'm sensing that you think this will hurt me. I don't know why. I don't give a rat's ass what he thinks about anything; I never did." Teague had never made a secret of that. "It was only you who strived to earn his pride."

"Because you knew you couldn't have earned it, no matter what you did."

"No, because I don't want or need it." Teague slanted his head. "I pity you, Ronin. When you're not living in the past, still focused on loathing me and my mother, you're living for someone else—living their dreams, their wants, their goals. Is it really worth it just to have Soren pat you on the back and say, 'Good job, son?'"

"I'd say no, T," interjected Archer. "He wouldn't be here pursuing a personal vendetta if he was happy with his life. I would have thought the Wild Hunt would have better things to do anyway. *We* sure wouldn't have had the time for something like this when we were huntsmen."

"Our time was very much eaten up by our job." Gideon let out a wistful sigh. "Still, I almost miss it."

Tucker smiled. "We did have our fair share of fun, didn't we?"

"The Wild Hunt isn't about fun," Ronin sniped. "It is about serving the Dark Host."

Slade's face hardened. "It's not about tracking down your half-brother—who's in a whole other realm, minding his own business—to wipe out him and his clan."

Teague nodded. "Then again . . . I suppose I shouldn't expect you to know that, Ronin. I was told that you couldn't cope with the role you were given. Such a shame."

Every muscle in Ronin's body seemed to tense. "Either you are lying, or your source of information was lying."

Teague mock winced. "If I were you, I wouldn't accuse Vine of being a liar—he really wouldn't like it."

"He paid us a visit," Leo added. "He told us you were doing a piss-poor job of being Master Huntsman, Ronin. He also said something about Zagan threatening to have Teague replace you if you didn't buck up."

Teague didn't bother biting down on a smile as his half-brother's face flushed a deep red. "And that's when I understood why you all of a sudden wanted me dead. You weren't going to allow me to take that role from you. You weren't going to suffer that embarrassment and have Soren see you be outshined by me. You weren't—"

"You could never outshine me," Ronin burst out. "*You're* the embarrassment. A product of an affair. You should never have been born."

Teague barely resisted rolling his eyes. "So you've said a million times before. It didn't bother me then. It doesn't bother me now."

His nostrils flaring, Ronin went to take a step forward, but then Hugo growled. Ronin blinked, surprised. And then his mouth curved into a mocking smile. "Oh, he's cute. And soon to be dead. He's absolutely no match for my hounds here. Your little group as a whole is no match for the force you're up against."

"Before the going-up-against begins," Saxon cut in, "I'd like to state for the record that Teague actually said no to Vine's offer. But I don't suppose that will placate you, Ronin. Particularly since I think it's safe to conclude that you've officially lost the job. It would explain why there are no shadowkin here. You can't direct them anymore."

Slade looked at each of Ronin's men. "He convinced you all that we're taking your positions from you, didn't he? That's why you came. You mean to kill us in an act of spite. It's senseless, since we all turned down the offer to rejoin the Hunt."

The men exchanged unreadable glances, stiffening slightly.

"They're lying," Ronin told his unit. "Once they've gotten their Earthly affairs together, they'll be returning to hell."

The males flanking Ronin lost their tension and once more inched up their chins, clearly choosing to believe their previous leader.

Staring at his spineless half-brother, Teague clenched his fists. "If you go through with this, your men—people you're supposed to lead and protect, not use in such a way—will die here tonight. So will your hounds. And your birds. And the pack behind you."

Ronin sneered. "No. Death will come only for you, your clan, and your little pets here."

Teague reached down and began to unfasten Baxter's collar while other members of his clan did the same with the other dogs' collars. The moment said collars were removed altogether, the canines' bodies morphed—becoming larger, more muscular, and sprouting coal-black ruffled fur just as their eyes became a deep crimson red.

Ronin swept a shocked gaze over the hounds before refixing

his attention on Teague. "You took the hounds from your unit with you when you left hell."

"Of course we did." Teague briefly slid his gaze upward as the ravens began flying in circles above their heads. "We brought them as well." They weren't supposed to, but neither Teague nor anyone in his clan ever let anything like rules hold them back. "Oh, and since we knew you'd do something as weak as bring a mini army, we made sure that *we* had backup as well."

Viper and his brothers stepped out of the trees either side of the camp, where they'd been waiting since Saxon—as prearranged—earlier telepathed the president.

Lines of wariness carved into Ronin's face as he took in the newcomers. If he knew that they were fallen angels, he'd be even more unnerved. Especially since this particular bunch weren't a standard breed of angel.

Teague cocked his head. "Are you sure you want to sacrifice your men just to pettily assuage your wounded ego and get some revenge?"

His face hardening, Ronin conjured a ball of hellfire in his hand.

"I'll take that as a yes."

At the telepathic warning from Teague, Larkin shot to her feet, startling everyone in the sitting room. Assuring Teague mind-to-mind that she'd be with him soon, she tensed as the women frowned up at her.

"Is everything okay?" asked Harper.

Larkin blanked her expression and casually straightened her sweater. "Fine," she smoothly lied.

She couldn't afford to alarm them. If she did, they would contact their mates, who would subsequently involve themselves in the situation no matter how much she objected. They would then learn things about Teague and his clan that the hellhorses would prefer remain secret.

"I just have to go check something out," Larkin added.

"Sentinel business, huh?" Raini guessed. "I don't know how you cope with being always on call—it would drive me nuts in no time."

"You get used to it." Ignoring Devon's nosy questions, Larkin forced herself to coolly stride out of the room, despite her demon's urgings for her to *move, move, move*.

Finally out of the apartment, Larkin put on a burst of speed, sprinting down the hallway and all but barging through the door that led to the stairwell. Her stomach rolling with nerves, she called to her wings, clambered onto the iron railing, and then dropped down. Nearing the bottom floor, she used her wings to slow her descent and made a smooth, practiced landing.

Urgency a drumbeat in her blood, she hurried out of the building. It would take her roughly half an hour, maybe forty-five minutes, to arrive at Teague's camp by car. Hence why she dashed to the shadows of the parking lot and, in a haze of smoke, shifted into her harpy eagle form.

After a quick shake of her avian body to settle her feathers, she took to the evening sky, her heart hammering in her chest. She told herself that she didn't need to panic; that Teague wouldn't struggle to protect himself. No one could lead the Wild Hunt for centuries and not be a deadly fighter, could they? Still, dread squeezed her heart like a cold fist.

Her demon wasn't as flustered. Not merely because it was rarely rattled by anything, but because it trusted that he could handle himself. Still, it wanted to be at his metaphorical side, even though he had his clan to back him up.

The Black Saints would also help—something they'd offered to do after hearing from 'a source' that hellish beings were making appearances in Vegas. How they'd tracked the issue back to Teague, she didn't know. Nor did she know why Viper would want to involve himself. She'd asked Teague, but he'd told her that to reply with the truth would have been to expose Viper's secrets.

As she understood and respected that Teague couldn't share another person's private business, she hadn't complained. But she was very curious as to what—

Something closed around her with a snap, squashing her wings against her body. Something tight, wiry, and buzzing with a power that slowly began to lower her to the ground. A net, she realized.

The fuck?

Her heartbeat kicked up even more, the organ battering her ribcage while her demon went nuts. She screeched as she struggled hard, raking at the net with her talons and biting it with her beak. No joy. The net remained perfectly intact.

Her gut tightening and twisting, she inwardly cursed. Unable to use telepathy while in her avian form, she tried shifting so she could sound an alarm. But nothing happened. Not a thing. Her skin didn't even *ripple*.

No matter how hard she tried, no matter how many times she tried, it didn't work. She just couldn't shift. She was stuck in this form, and she'd bet that the net was responsible for that.

She screeched again, furious. Her demon lunged for supremacy … but it couldn't surface. It was trapped, just as she was trapped.

Her body finally touched the ground, settling on a stretch of grass that she recognized as being part of a local park. She glared up at the three male demons that surrounded her. *Holt and his two cronies.*

Oh, they were gonna die *so hard*.

As her waste-of-space anchor stared down at her—his eyes flinty, his face an impassive mask, his posture radiating superiority—she knew she'd been right all along. He hadn't changed a bit, despite his claims. Here and now, he looked so very different from how he'd presented himself each time he recently approached her. He looked like the old Holt. The *real* Holt, to be exact.

"I'm not supposed to be in Vegas anymore, I know." He cocked his head. "But did you really think I'd leave without you?"

Well, yes, actually, she had.

He turned to the tallest of his sentinels. "Put her in the van. And be careful about it."

Van? What v—

Oh. It was idling at the nearby curb.

You could bet your ass that she made it as hard as possible for Holt's little minion to carry her to it. She writhed and screeched and bit at him through the gaps in the net. He swore and stumbled and winced and bled, to her demon's morbid delight.

But he also kept walking, the perseverant bastard.

Holt opened the van's rear doors. The sentinel jumped inside, placed her on the floor of the vehicle, and then disappeared. Holt promptly hopped into the van and closed the doors behind him. His expression still blank, he took a seat on the wooden bench across from her.

She kept screeching. Kept squirming. Kept biting at the net. Kept attempting to shift.

"You can calm down," said Holt, his tone flat, as the van began to move. "There's no need to be distressed."

Her demon blinked in surprise, and Larkin almost did a double-take. She could be *calm?* Just exactly what aspect of this scenario could warrant or allow her to be totally chill?

"I realize how this might look, that you might assume I want revenge for how you so firmly rejected me, but my intention isn't to kill you." It was a statement, not an effort to reassure.

Clasping his hands, he leaned forward and dipped them between his spread thighs. There was a sort of exaggerated casualness with which he moved—it fairly oozed self-satisfaction; showed he was completely at ease. He believed he was on top of the situation and lacked any concern that something would get in his way.

"I wish it hadn't come to this, Larkin. Truly. I never wanted any harm to come to you."

She was finding that a little hard to believe right now, given she was trapped in a goddamn net. Hence why she didn't stop chewing on it.

"All you had to do was agree to form the bond. That's all." His slow, disapproving shake of the head was something an adult might do to a child who'd disappointed them. "I meant it when I said I would have respected your wish to remain part of your lair."

If she could have raised a doubtful brow, she would have.

"Perhaps I would have eventually urged you to switch to mine," he admitted, no hesitation or sheepishness. "But not straight away. I would have waited. I would have given you time. I would have earned your trust." The corners of his eyes tightened. "But you just wouldn't swallow your pride."

She paused in chewing, confused. He thought this was a matter of pride?

"You might not wish to admit it, but that's all this was about for you. It was a hit to your ego when I left you. A hit you never recovered from, because you don't *want* to recover from it. You held tight to your anger all these years so that you didn't have to feel the pain."

Uh, no, not at all.

"You held even tighter to that anger when I showed up recently. You did it so that you wouldn't be tempted to give into me. Pride wouldn't let you back down."

That was honestly what he thought? That she would ever let her ego interfere with a situation so serious? Maybe that was how *he* functioned, but not her.

"Much as I understand it, I can't let it be a factor, Larkin. I can't."

Yes, yes, he could. Absolutely.

She chewed harder on the net, determined to free herself; determined to get to Teague's camp.

The battle would be well underway by now. Did Teague *need* her? Probably not. He was a tough son of a bitch, and he had not only his clan but the aid of fallen angels.

More, Ronin would be no match for him. But *that* was what worried her. If his insistence on sending shadowkin to do his dirty work was anything to go by, he knew on some level that Teague could overpower him. Ronin would do something sneaky to increase his odds, hence why her plan was to do something equally sneaky: Attack while in flight.

Ronin wouldn't expect an assault from above. He likely wouldn't be braced for it. And neither would anyone he'd brought along with him.

But until she got out of this net—which she would, she had to—she wouldn't be attacking anyone.

She also couldn't touch Teague's mind to be certain he was alive. She hoped he didn't try telepathically reaching out to her. If he did, if he found himself touching a psychic barrier rather than her mind, his focus would falter. With any luck, he'd released his demon by now—the beast would get so caught up in the battle and consumed by blood-lust that it would hopefully be too distracted to wonder about her whereabouts.

"You know, when I first found you, I couldn't believe my luck."
A nostalgic smile touched Holt's mouth. "My anchor was the
sentinel of not just *any* powerful Prime, but Knox Thorne. Also,
she was strong and lethal and powerful. I was proud as fuck."

He spoke like she was a trophy. An asset, even. Something
he'd earned. *Dick.* She went back to work on the net, chewing
and raking at it.

His smile slipped. "I didn't for one minute think you would
ask for time before we formed the bond. Or that you'd refuse to
join my lair."

Why? He'd refused to join hers.

"I didn't like that my Prime intended to use you, but I didn't
think it would bother you to share your secrets with me. Not
when you knew it would enhance my standing with him.
Anchors do that," he added, his voice growing sharp. "Help each
other. Support each other. Build each other up."

None of which he'd ever done for her, so she wasn't sure where
he was getting the insane notion that he was in a position to
lecture her.

"But I soon realized that you would never tell me what I
wished to know. That you would choose to protect Knox's privacy over supporting me as you should have." His lips pinched
tight. "My demon felt as betrayed as I did. We wanted to teach
you a lesson; remind you of what was important; spur you into
backing down."

And so he'd walked away like the asshole he was.

"But you didn't come to me. Didn't choose to prioritize me
and our bond. Didn't even send up a fucking smoke signal. No,
you put Knox's secrets and safety first. You chose someone else
over me. So I did something similar—I focused on myself and
on pursuing my goals rather than on you."

Actually, for her, it hadn't really been about choosing Knox over him. She'd told Holt that repeatedly all those years ago, but he hadn't *heard* her. Nor had he realized how selfish he was being, which obviously hadn't changed.

He drew in a slow, controlled breath. "Once my anger drained away, I thought about contacting you. But I didn't. I knew it would have been pointless. That you would never move to Canada or my lair. I chose to instead let you go. But I thought about you often, though I tried not to. So did my demon. You were on its mind practically all the fucking time."

Her own entity kind of liked that—why *shouldn't* they have suffered?

"It never recovered from your betrayal. It steadily became bitter. Scornful. Withdrawn. And then its control began to waver, and it started to push for supremacy more and more. I soon realized that I was on the path to turning rogue."

She went still. Well, fuck.

Unclasping his hands, he flexed his fingers, his gaze turning inward. "I thought I could get a handle on it. Reverse the issue. And when I rose to power, it did help. My demon loves having that power. Loves wielding it. Loves being respected and feared by our lair."

Unsurprising. Things such as power and authority were like drugs to most entities.

His eyes once more became wholly focused on her. "Long before I ever met you, there was something I'd always intended to do on becoming Prime: Heal the breach that my previous Prime caused between him and Knox. I wanted an alliance. I'd never imagined that his sentinel would be my anchor; that I'd have a way *in* when I finally rose into power.

"Things didn't work out that way, though, did they?" A hard, self-deprecating smile curved his mouth. "Oh, I became Prime. But my way 'in' with Knox hated me."

And it appeared that he held Larkin responsible for that. Unreal.

"So I chose to not pursue the alliance. But then I began having issues with a couple of lairs. Issues I knew would come to a dramatic halt if I had the right backing." He straightened. "I knew I would never get an alliance from Knox, but I also knew that my being bound to you would be as much of a deterrent to any Primes tempted to fuck with me. So I thought about perhaps attempting to earn your forgiveness in the hope that we would bond."

Larkin's demon peeled back its upper lip, thinking it a fine idea to bite off his ear.

"You'll twist that; claim I meant to use you."

Uh, his intention *was* to use her.

"But, really, it's natural that anchors aid each other. I simply wanted what was rightfully mine: Your loyalty and support."

Then he should have offered her the same in turn instead of expecting *her* to do all the giving.

"I was still deliberating on it when I came to Vegas on my previous trip. I hadn't yet decided what to do. But the night I saw you from a distance looking so very alone even among your friends, something happened. All the progress I'd made with my demon went sailing out of the window."

She frowned about as much as her avian features would allow.

"It metaphorically dived at you. Went insane with the need to get to you. It fought me for supremacy with such force that holding it back was painful. I had to leave the bar. Fast. But it didn't calm down when you were out of sight. It continued to fight me for dominance."

Larkin couldn't imagine having to battle her inner demon that way. Hey, hers could be a trial at times. It took over at inopportune moments, and it wasn't the most cooperative of beings. But it had never put up *that* kind of struggle.

"I went back to Canada quickly, thinking all would be fine if

I put some distance between you and me. Instead, it only made my demon more unstable. It no longer felt any satisfaction in its power or position. It was no longer interested in working *with* me, or in us being in sync. No, it only wanted you."

He paused, his nostrils flaring. "It wasn't only the pull of the bond I then felt. It was the pull to let go and hand over full control to my demon. I'm not balancing on the knife-edge of rogue," he added, his voice roughening, "but I'm at risk of being overpowered by my entity sometime in the near future. My control over it is precarious at best."

An element of pity swirled in her stomach. To turn rogue was no joke. A person lost the part of themselves that *made* them a person. All that then existed was the demon. It ruled supreme. It wreaked havoc. It killed indiscriminately. Did whatever the hell it wished, basically.

Unmoved by his plight, her demon sniffed. It wasn't feeling even a tiny hint of sympathy for him. Then again, such an emotion wasn't something it generally experienced.

"So I came back to claim you before I lost the fight. At that point, the political advantages of our being bound would have merely been a bonus." A glitter of menace bled into his eyes. "I thought you might delay forming the bond to punish me for leaving, but I hadn't expected you to turn me away so completely. That was a mistake, wasn't it? You'll never agree to form the bond. Not even now, when you know it would save me. Your demon would sooner I perish, wouldn't it?"

Maybe if he'd just told her about his struggles in the beginning she might have been open to it—she wasn't a monster. But he hadn't been truthful or genuine with her. He'd instead tried to trick, manipulate, and provoke her. More, he'd played games and even confronted Teague. And so they'd never know what decision she would have otherwise made.

But right now, considering Holt had caught her with a god-damn net, no, she had no plans to help him. Her demon—just as he suspected—would see him in hell before it would aid him in any way.

"I can't allow that, Larkin. So I've taken the matter into my own hands." He paused, settling his palms on his thighs. "That net is slowly draining you of psi-energy. At some point, you will be so drained that whatever mental wall you slammed up between us will fall. Our psyches will then clash, and the bond will form."

She froze again, and her stomach bottomed out. No. No, no, no, no.

"Unfortunately, since I know you will hate me for it and slit my throat whatever chance you get—even if it means you'll turn rogue in the process—I have no choice but to keep you prisoner." He let out a weary sigh. "My hope is that there will come a day when you understand, when you forgive me, when me and our bond mean enough to you that I can free you without worry that you will harm me or yourself. Until then . . . well, until then you'll exist in a cage in my home. It's really the only way."

CHAPTER TWENTY-ONE

No sooner had Teague said, '*I'll take that as a yes*' than Ronin had hurled the hellfire orb at him. It hissed and spat as it whooshed through the air as fast as any bullet.

Sharply leaning to the side, Teague managed to dodge it. The orb crashed into a tree behind him, causing pieces of bark to clang against one of the wagons.

That was when the tension in the air seemed to explode.

Shedding his tee, Teague emitted a sharp, distinctive whistle and then sliced a hand through the air. His bloodhounds hurtled across the clearing, heading right for Ronin's hounds, while the ravens flew at the intruding flock at top speed.

Similar gestures from Ronin had his own hell-animals moving. Casting Teague a dark grin, he lifted his chin. "I'd tell you to enjoy watching your pets get torn apart, but you'll be a little too busy being torn apart yourself."

Kicking off his shoes, Teague had to smile. "You really think a pack of chupacabras will take us down?" He shook his head and then shoved down his jeans and underwear. "My demon will end whatever stands between it and you. And when you're forced to free your steed in your own defense, it'll ravage your demon until the steed retreats out of terror. Then?" Teague pinned him with flinty eyes. "Then *I'll* kill *you*."

Flushing, Ronin glanced over his shoulder at the waiting pack and called out, "Now!"

Snarling, the chupacabras charged, fast and focused. So fast that dirt clouded the air as they skidded to a non-too-smooth halt when the Black Saints teleported in front of them.

The fallen angels pounced both figuratively and metaphorically. Some wrestled the creatures to the ground. Others slammed them with glowing, ultraviolet balls of fire.

Shift, Teague telepathically ordered his clan, who were now as naked as he was. As one, they released their beasts in billows of ash and smoke.

As the gray haze cleared, Teague's hellhorse flattened its ears and bared its teeth at the intruders. Every beat of its heart pumped rage through its veins. A rage that wound its muscles tight and caused a pounding in its ears.

The steed stared down the leader of the trespassers. *Ronin*. A male the hellhorse had long ago decided had lost his right to live.

He would die tonight. Those who had arrived with him would die. The steed wanted their blood in its mouth and under its hooves. It wanted to bite and tear and maul them.

And it would.

Several chupacabras skirted around the fallen angels. They rushed at the steed's clan, their flaming eyes narrowed, their lips peeled back, their muzzles covered in foam.

Pawing the ground, the hellhorse let out a roar-scream that was a pure battle-cry. The steed then galloped toward the approaching chupacabras, knowing its clan would follow. It went for the broadest creature, exhaling a stream of hellfire.

A high-pitched yelp tore out of the chupacabra as flames engulfed it, causing its pace to falter. But only briefly. It came at the steed again with a vicious growl.

The chupacabra leaped up to bite into the hellhorse's neck. The steed flinched its head back, narrowly missing the creature's jaws, and rammed a hoof into its attacker's chest. A whine gusted out of the chupacabra as it flopped to the ground.

Baring its teeth in a satisfied grin, the hellhorse moved swiftly. It stomped on the creature's skull, neck, and flank, avoiding the sharp spines. Bones snapped and crunched beneath its hooves, and the cloying scent of blood poured into its nostrils.

Dead.

Abandoning the corpse, the steed turned to the nearest chupacabra—it was aiding its pack-mate in attacking one of the hellhorse's clan. The steed lunged and closed its jaws around the chupacabras' head. It bit hard. The skull caved in. Blood squirted into the hellhorse's mouth.

Relishing the taste of blood and death, it dropped the corpse just in time to brace itself for impact—another chupacabra was almost upon it. They collided, all hooves and paws and teeth. The fight was ugly and brutal.

The steed snarled as the burn of sharp claws raked its skin. Feeling warm liquid trickle down its coat, it bit into the creature's muzzle, injecting its venom into its bloodstream. Venom that weakened it fast. Before long, the hellhorse was holding its foe's neck in a lethal, suffocating bite.

It dumped the fallen chupacabra on the ground and then charged at the next threat. With each new enemy, the hellhorse went in fast and hard—its aim to cause maximum damage swiftly. It intended to save its strength for its duel with Ronin's demon.

Around it, the steed's clan battled other chupacabras. Fallen angels attacked the rest of the pack. Airborne birds bit and raked at others. Hounds savaged and clawed their foes.

Ronin and the other trespassing hellhorses continued to do nothing. They remained still. Watchful. Were probably waiting for the clan to be killed, or for them to be so weak they were easy prey for the hellhorses.

A mistake.

Teague's steed *never* made easy prey. Neither did its clan members.

The battlefield was a cacophony of sounds. Hellfire flames hissed and spat. Bones snapped and crunched. Ultraviolet orbs whooshed and crackled. Roars, snarls, yelps, screeches, barks, and grunts blended with the perverse laughter coming from the Black Saints.

The chupacabras were fast and vicious and tireless. They didn't give an inch. Didn't back down. Didn't give mercy. But they stood no chance against their opponents.

Not against the fallen angels' raw power and primitive brutality.

Not against the hellhorses' arsenal of vast strength, incredible speed, lethal venom, noxious smoke, and fiery breaths.

Still, the pack fought on.

Turning away from a dead chupacabra, the hellhorse quickly lunged at another. It savaged the creature with its teeth and hooves; reveled in its yelps, enjoyed its pain, relished the sight of its injuries. The chupacabra weakened more and more under both the pressure of the attack and the effects of the steed's venom. A brutal kick to the head finished it off.

The hellhorse stood still a moment, its sides heaving as its breaths sawed in and out of its throat. It could feel blood dripping down its coat; could feel the heat of many injuries. Bites. Claw marks. Puncture wounds that came from chupacabra-spines.

Amped up on adrenaline and bloodthirst, it shelved the pain and ignored the fatigue that threatened to invade its muscles. It wasn't difficult. Not when each inhale fed its hunger to kill, the air laced with the drugging scents of blood, pain, and fear.

Another chupacabra charged at it. Clashing, they tore into each other. Fierce. Pitiless. Targeting existing injuries. It was—

The hellhorse flinched as teeth sank into its wounded flank. Refusing to remove its gaze from the opponent in front of it, the steed body-slammed its second attacker. It heard a *crack* as the creature collapsed to the ground. In its peripheral vision, the hellhorse saw it attempt to rise; saw it fail as one of the clan pounced.

Satisfied, the steed exhaled a powerful gust of hellfire that swept up the badly injured creature before it. The chupacabra backpedaled, yelping in pain. The hellhorse moved quickly. It clamped its jaws around its enemy's skull and shook it viciously, tasting spurt after spurt of blood.

Something barreled into the hellhorse's side. The jarring move almost knocked it over, causing it to drop the dying creature. It whirled fast, seeking the chupacabra that had dared blindside it. They clashed as they leaped at each other.

They were both brutal in their attack. Skin tore. Blood dripped. Chupacabra-bones cracked. As the creature's wounded rear leg crumpled beneath it, making it topple to the ground, the steed took advantage—pouncing, stomping, crushing its skull.

Once its enemy was dead, the hellhorse puffed a breath out of its nostrils as it took a moment to look around. Its clan and their hounds were wounded but still fighting. Two dead birds from Ronin's flock lay on the ground among feathers, bodies, ashes, and tufts of fur. The number of chupacabras had greatly fallen, but the Black Saints were still standing—*battling*.

As another chupacabra came at it, the hellhorse took a brief moment to wonder where its harpy was. Then it flew at its enemy.

Failing yet again to rip open the net, Larkin screeched in fury. The piercing sound burst up her eagle-form's throat and echoed around the van so loud Holt winced. So she did it again. Louder.

Sighing, he slid his gaze skyward for a moment. "There's no point in trying to tear the net, Larkin. No amount of biting or clawing will damage it." He spoke like she was being childish by fighting to free herself.

He didn't know her at all if he thought she'd sit back and bemoan her situation like a poor little damsel. Just as tenacious, her demon battered at her insides, refusing to admit defeat; intent on surfacing and getting to the male who not only held them captive but acted as though it was his right.

He rolled his eyes when she resumed raking and biting at the net. "Settle down. We'll be at the airport soon enough. I have a private jet waiting there. Unfortunately, it will be an uncomfortable flight for you, since you must remain within the net, but there's sadly nothing I can do about that."

Oh, there was. He could free her, for one thing.

Larkin went very still as she felt Holt's psyche push at the mental wall she'd erected. She would have done her best to strengthen it if it wasn't essential that she didn't waste any psi-energy right now.

His brows slid together. "That barrier of yours should have weakened at this point. You apparently made sure it wouldn't be easy to tear down." His eyes narrowed. "You truly were determined to keep me out, weren't you?"

Absolutely. That was why it worried her that she could feel

her psi-energy leaving her in tiny little dribs and drabs. The wall would soon buckle under the strength of his mental shoves if she didn't hurry to free herself.

Once more vigorously attacking the net with her beak and talons, she ignored his put-out *you're wasting your time* sigh.

He idly adjusted his cufflink. "I will cut away the net once we're at my home. I have a cage in my cellar that prevents telepathic exchange. Once inside it, you'll be able to shift back to your normal form."

Larkin wasn't sure what bothered her more—that he planned to put her in a fucking prison of some sort, or that he seemingly felt she should be thankful that the net would be replaced by a cage.

Well, no one was going to coop her up *anywhere*.

She'd get free of this net. She would. And then she'd go to Teague—no other eventuality was acceptable.

It was *killing* her that she had no way of knowing if he was okay. The battle was likely still waging—she couldn't imagine that it would be over so fast. Not when it seemed inevitable that Ronin would have turned up with a small army, the coward.

"You're no doubt thinking that Knox will suspect me of being responsible for your disappearance," Holt mused, leaning back against the van, still oh so casual and oh so confident that he had the upper hand. "I'm sure he will. Just as I'm sure he will come to my home in search of you."

Knox wouldn't pay Holt a mere visit to look for Larkin if she disappeared. No. He'd shit fury all over this fucker's doorstep, sure to the bone that it was the cambion who held her captive. Knox wouldn't care to ask questions. Wouldn't bother to tread carefully. Wouldn't give one shit that there was a chance he was wrong, because killing Holt would be nothing to him in any case.

In sum, the cambion had signed his death warrant by taking her. If she didn't kill him, Knox would.

"He won't find you. Nor will Tanner, if that is your hope. The cage will even keep a hellhound's nose from sensing your presence." Holt inched up his chin. "Face it, Larkin, you have no way of escaping me. Stop fighting. Accept your fate. Accept that *I am* your fate—always have been."

She had no need to accept anything. Because she knew something he didn't.

He carried on talking, pressuring her to cease opposing him; to resign herself to the situation; to see that this was 'for the best'.

She ignored him . . . right up until his mind once more tried bypassing her protective wall.

Satisfaction flashed across that face she wanted to slap. "Ah, the barrier is not quite as well-fortified as it was before. The process may be slow going, but it is working."

It was, dammit. It was working well.

She squeezed her eyes shut for a moment and then all but *attacked* the net. No, she was *not* bonding with this mother-fucker. She'd be stuck with him for life, even if she never became his captive. Because she wouldn't be able to kill him in revenge. To do that would be to quite possibly kill herself—anchors generally didn't survive the breaking of an anchor bond, at least not without turning rogue, so she'd need to keep him alive.

She couldn't stand the thought of having a connection with him for the rest of her days. It made her skin crawl and her belly do a slow, nauseating roll. Her demon would for sure—

There was a slight *give* in the net. As if a seam somewhere had popped.

Larkin's pulse did an excited leap. She forced herself not to go to work on the material with a renewed, energized effort. It would make him suspicious. She couldn't have that.

So she kept chewing and raking at the same pace as before, letting him think she was merely refusing to accept that her attempts—in his point of view, at least—were fruitless.

They had never been fruitless. He simply hadn't known it.

The truth was . . . a demonic harpy eagle could chew through *anything*, even if that 'anything' was boosted by power or magick.

The same applied to a few other breeds of demon who could shapeshift into avian forms. None of them advertised it, since it gave them an edge in certain situations—such as the one she was in right now.

"You're not going to stop trying to get out of that net, are you?" He sighed, as if disappointed in her. "So stubborn."

She let out a *fuck off* screech. He jumped slightly. Which would have delighted both her and her demon if they weren't too worried for Teague to find any amusement in anything right now.

Holt's nostrils flared. "There is no sense in being angry with me," he snapped, defensive. "*You* are at fault for the position you're in."

Say what?

"It would never have come to this if we had only formed the bond when we first found each other. But you refused. You held back from me—your own anchor—instead of trusting me from the outset like you should have," he reprimanded, as if he hadn't done things that would justify her failure to do so.

God, he was such an ass.

Feeling another testing shove against the wall in her mind, Larkin would have hissed if she could have.

Holt's brows knitted. "The barrier should have cracked by now." He hummed. "You have more mental strength than most people I know. But I don't see why you'd bother putting up such a resistance. You can't possibly sustain it."

Yeah? Watch me, asshole.

There was another *give* in the net. Not as if a seam had popped, but as if a few threads had torn. *Ha.* Soon enough, it would split. It had to.

"If you think I'm wrong, you're lying to yourself. We *will* form the bond, Larkin. There's no avoiding it. There never was. If you had just made your peace with that long ago, things would be so different now. I wouldn't be at risk of turning rogue. You wouldn't have been angry and hurt all these years. In fact, you would be firmly settled in my lair, and we might even be ruling it together."

She stopped chewing, shocked. Together?

"You once accused me of only pretending to care for you, but it wasn't true. My feelings for you were genuine. I envisioned us being co-Primes of my lair." His mouth set into a bitter twist. "But that would never happen now, would it? Too much has passed that tainted what could have been."

There would never have been anything romantic between them, even if he'd been the world's best anchor. She simply didn't view him in that light.

His eyes turned glacial. "And then there's fucking Sullivan."

Not whatsoever liking his scathing tone, she took a moment to shoot Holt hate eyes before going back to chewing the net.

"I saw how you look at him. He means something to you. Matters enough that I think you would actually go as far as to leave your lair—something you refused to do for me—to be with him."

Honestly . . . she thought there was little that she wouldn't do for her hellhorse.

A dark smirk curled Holt's lips. "Unlucky for you, that won't happen. You'll never see him again."

God, it would *really* be great if he would stop talking about Teague, because it was already difficult for her to fully concentrate on the seriousness of her personal situation when she was inwardly obsessing over the hellhorse's safety.

Even as she told herself that Teague would be fine, fear for him curdled in her stomach all the same.

By now, he would have noticed that she hadn't showed yet. He would be wondering why she hadn't yet arrived. She hoped he wouldn't worry that something was wrong. He didn't need to be distracted right now. He needed to—

Her heart jumped as more threads in the net tore. *Yes.* It was only a matter of time, hopefully mere minutes, before the material would split.

Awesome. Except for one thing. The split might be audible.

If Holt heard it tear, he'd move to restrain her. That meant she'd need to be prepared to act *fast.* She'd need to move so swiftly that he'd be unable to get a hold on her or blast her with hellfire.

She didn't think he would kill her. He needed her. Or, more to the point, he needed the anchor bond to ensure that he didn't turn rogue.

But that didn't require her to be unharmed.

Given that he was quite clearly pissed at her for a whole multitude of reasons and blamed *her* for his current near-rogue state, she suspected he'd have little problem causing her pain. Especially if he and his demon were raging over her repeated rejection.

Holt had many aggressive abilities. And she knew what his favorite method of disabling and torturing people happened to be. He liked to utilize his power to generate enough heat in his hands that by merely touching a person he could liquify their bones.

Lovely, right?

It meant there'd sadly be no slow death for him. She didn't

have the luxury of granting herself or her demon that indulgence. She'd need to kill him quickly before his sentinels interfered.

Holt lightly brushed one hand over the other. "You should probably know that, once the dust has settled, I have every intention of wiping Sullivan from this planet."

A screech of rage exploded from her mouth just as her demon's furious scream echoed around her head.

Holt let out a dark laugh. "Oh yes, he really does matter to you."

Angry breaths heaving in and out of her, she glared at him. No way would he get even *the chance* to harm Teague. Holt would be dead soon enough. He just didn't know it yet.

"So sad that it isn't a two-way street," he taunted. "His demon may have branded you—yes, I heard all about it—but that means little. Teague would never have committed to you, and neither would his beast."

Her demon cracked its knuckles, raring to slam its fist into this fucker's dick. Or maybe just pluck out his eye . . . and make him eat it.

Though Larkin wanted to screech at him yet again, she didn't. Because she recognized what he was trying to do: Distract her. Anger her. Tire her out emotionally so that he'd be more easily able to power through the mental wall that stood between them.

Not happening.

Refusing to take the bait, she focused on the net once more.

There was nothing genuine in the look of sympathy he offered her. "I suppose you now know how it feels to want more from someone than they'll ever be willing to give you. Not nice, is it?"

Snarky bastard.

"You may believe I'm wrong; may think that he cares for you as you do him. But even if he does, he wouldn't have claimed you. Hellhorses rarely take mates, and it's been said that Sullivan avoids relationships more than most do anyway. He prefers to simply sample whatever flower in the field he comes across."

More determined to get to the prick than ever before, her inner demon renewed its efforts to surface, beating at Larkin's insides.

"He'll move on soon enough. He might ponder over your disappearance. Might even vaguely worry about it. But he won't grieve it. Won't put his life on pause to look for you. Not that it would do him any good if he did. He'll never find you."

Pausing, Holt leaned forward. "*No one* will ever find you. You'll be with me for all time. Bound to me for all time. There will be no escape. Not physically, not psychically. And whenever you find yourself hating your life, remember that the blame for your situation lies squarely with you."

Material split. Holt froze. The net's buzz of power winked out. And Larkin inwardly smiled.

Sinking its teeth into the vulnerable throat of a chupacabra, Teague's steed heard a voice bark out an order to shift. Its gaze sought Ronin. Narrowed. He and his fellow hellhorses were beginning to shed their clothes.

A sense of twisted anticipation coursed through the steed. It dropped the dead creature it held and turned to fully face its main enemy, conscious of its clan flanking it. The beast snorted in disgust at the cowardice of the invaders, who had waited until their opponents were injured and tiring before acting; until the only chupacabras left were presently toys of the Black Saints.

Panting hard, the steed puffed out a thin cloud of smoke with each breath. The fighting and blood loss had taken a toll on it, and the adrenaline-dimmed pain refused to be shelved any longer. But the thought of finally going head-to-head with Ronin's beast energized the steed.

It yearned to sink its teeth into the flesh of the one who had brought this fight to its land. It was eager to wreak vengeance for every slight Ronin had ever committed throughout the years. Merely recalling those incidences made a red haze cloud its vision and a growl vibrate in its chest.

Naked, Ronin swallowed hard, as if nervous. He should be. His life had reached its expiry date.

Smoke and dots of floating ash began to build around the trespassers. When the smoke cleared, seven hellhorses stood in their place. The beasts shifted from foot to foot, neighing and shaking their heads.

Ronin's stallion was slightly smaller than Teague's demon. Less muscular. But it was powerfully built, and it stood solid and at the ready.

Unintimated, Teague's beast boldly locked its gaze with that of its adversary. It was utterly confident it could take down its foe, even as it acknowledged that it would be no simple win. Teague's steed didn't care that it would be a challenge. It *liked* that.

The chupacabras had been too easy for it to defeat. But against another hellhorse, the beast had no great 'edge'. Its venom would not be lethal to another of its kind, nor would the noxious smoke. This would be a battle of strength, speed, will, and power.

As it glared at its enemy, they both danced from foot to foot, each sizing up the other. Geared up to start the fight, Teague's steed scuffed the earth with its hoof, kicking up a small cloud of dirt—a dare, a challenge, a taunt.

Ronin's demon peeled back its lips to expose its teeth. It charged, its fellow invaders still flanking it.

Teague's steed bucked with a roar-scream. And then it

bulleted across the clearing toward its approaching enemy, jumping over corpses. Its clan followed the steed, heading for the other hellhorses.

The two sides reared up and clashed in a ferocious storm of teeth, hooves, and hellfire. A storm that made the evening echo with roars and growls and the smack of hoof against flesh.

Scorn. Loathing. Fury. Bloodthirst. Vengeance. All of it pounded through Teague's hellhorse and fueled its every lunge and blow and bite.

Ronin's stallion was not as weak as the male with whom it shared its soul. It was strong. Deadly. Trained. Fearless.

It attacked hard. Fought with sheer cunning and viciousness. Targeted existing injuries—deepening bite marks, striking bruises and burns.

Teague's steed was equally brutal. It didn't merely sink its teeth down, it tore out chunks of flesh. Every gush of its enemy's blood tasted of victory and vengeance.

His beast caught its foe's ear between its teeth and gave a sharp twist of its head. The enemy reared back with a pained sound as half its ear was ripped away. Teague's steed spat it on the ground, a feral satisfaction whirling in its gut.

Its sides heaving, Ronin's demon growled low in its throat, scraping the earth with a hoof. Extending its head, it exhaled a blast of hellfire.

Teague's stallion danced backwards to avoid it, but the hot flames licked at its muzzle, searing the skin. The steed vigorously shook its head as if it would shake off the pain. A pain that ramped up its need to vanquish its enemy.

Its nostrils flaring, the hellhorse rushed its foe again. It rammed its scalding-hot hooves into vulnerable spots; hammering at the kneecaps, determined to crumple the forelegs.

Ronin's stallion fought back hard, its own coat now covered

in almost as many patches of blood and charred skin. Blisters pebbled parts of its flesh, particularly that of its face.

Around them, the other hellhorses continued to rear up and attack again and again. The battle was as primal and savage as it was animalistic. Neither side showed signs of backing down.

Fatigue soon began to creep up on Teague's beast again. Its lungs hurt from the noxious fumes, making it hard for the panting steed to catch its breath. Its blood seemed to sting from its foe's venom in its system. The pain added to those of its injuries, distracting it; threatening to weaken it.

The other hellhorse sensed it was tiring. Tried to take advantage, upping its speed. But Teague's demon was still too fast for its opponent to find the opening it needed.

Recalling each of Ronin's slights and crimes, the steed embraced its fury. Used it. Channeled it.

As Teague's beast gave a hard kick to its opponent's badly burned shoulder, Ronin's beast swiftly backed up with a sound that rang with both rage and pain. Its muscles bunching, it breathed out another blast of hellfire.

Teague's demon had anticipated the move and danced aside, evading most of the blast. A little of the flames blazed across its badly blistered flank, leaving a trail of white-hot pain in its wake. Furious, the steed snapped its teeth and charged yet again.

The two demons once more quickly became caught up in a deadly duel, their coats damp with blood and sweat. On and on they fought, ferocious in their determination to win.

Teeth sank down, making blood spurt. Hellfire raced over skin, causing blisters. Red-hot hooves singed coats with every bruising hit.

The reflexes of Ronin's demon steadily became slower. Its

strikes lost some of their force. Its balance began to suffer due to its scuffed and battered kneecaps.

A loud, wheezy yelp sounded. *Baxter.*

Teague's beast faltered. Rage rushed through its system, and a roar of blood thundered in the steed's ears. Snarling, it struck harder. Faster. Angrier.

Ronin's demon began to fall back under the pressure, its attempts to attack becoming attempts to merely defend.

Taking advantage, Teague's demon dove in again and again, its goal—*need*—to maul and dominate. Soon, its foe began to tire even more. Its responses and attacks grew slower and weaker, but Teague's hellhorse didn't let up.

It had a point to make. A message to deliver. A punishment to administer. And that was what it would do.

CHAPTER TWENTY-TWO

Before Holt could think to act, Larkin spread her wings in a sharp movement that ripped open the net. She lunged at Holt, her wings still spread.

He caught her with a muffled oath, trying to rear back out of reach. But there was no evading the long beak that stabbed and bit at his face, or the curved razor-sharp talons that raked through cloth and skin. "Jesus, Larkin, fucking stop!"

She didn't. She went at him like a harpy possessed.

The smell of blood blanketed her senses, fairly intoxicating her demon. It had wanted his blood and pain for *so long* . . .

A loud snarl. "Fuck this." He punched her. Right in the fucking head. Then he grabbed one wing and yanked hard, snapping the fine bones there.

Motherfucker.

Unmoved by her screech of pain, he pulled at her wing even harder, causing more bones to give way with a sickening *crack*.

As his hands turned scorching hot in a telling move that

said he meant to use his ability to melt her bones, she did as her demon craved.

She stabbed his eye with her beak and plucked it right out.

A rough sound of agony tore its way out of him, and his hands tightened painfully on her body.

She spat out his eye and shifted *mega* fast—healing her wing in the process. Larkin then slapped her hand on Holt's head and shot out a blast of hell-ice chips. "Now you're dead, fucker," she spat as the chips sank through his skin, burst their way through his skull, and buried themselves in his brain.

His eyes shot open wide, and his breath stuttered. Feeling his grip on her weaken, she watched with supreme satisfaction as awareness began to fade from his eyes.

Whereas hellfire burned, hell-ice froze. The cold would spread throughout an organ wicked fast, freezing it—a heart, a lung, a brain, anything. And as that unnatural cold right then took over Holt's brain, finally bringing every bit of activity up there to a sharp stop, his gaze turned unnaturally unfocused. He then slumped back, lifeless.

The van screeched to a halt so suddenly she stumbled.

Great. He'd probably given his henchmen a telepathic shout-out before death took him.

She moved off Holt's lap and called to her wings. Large and midnight-black, they snapped out, heavy and so much stronger than those she sported as a harpy eagle.

Feeling no sadness at all about Holt's death, she quickly lit his corpse up with hellfire, sorry that she didn't have the time to watch him burn. He'd suffered too quick a death in her opinion. It majorly disappointed her demon that they hadn't been able to torture him some, but it did love that it got to watch the life leave his eyes.

The van's rear doors were wrenched open.

Larkin didn't give the male demons a moment to take in the scene. She acted instantly—slamming up a hand and projecting a hail of hell-ice out of her palm.

They stumbled back in surprise. One ducked, but the other didn't manage to avoid the onslaught. As the chips sank into his head, he swayed, his eyes hazing.

Before the dying sentinel had even dropped to the ground, the other male straightened and conjured a hellfire orb.

Larkin flapped her wings hard, emitting a bitterly cold, gale-force wind. It put out the orb, knocked him off his feet, and sent him sliding along the ground.

She leaped out of the van and landed in a crouch above him. Before he had the opportunity to attack, she slammed her hand down on his chest and fired a hail of hell-ice. The chips pierced through his skin and ribcage to plant themselves in his organs and veins. In mere seconds, he was dead.

Standing upright, she exhaled a long breath and reached out to touch Teague's mind. Relief whipped through her as she felt that he was alive. *Thank God.*

Eager to get to his camp fast, she quickly dumped both corpses in the van and then lit it up with hellfire. It burned fast, consuming the entire vehicle and the bodies inside.

Done.

Satisfied there was no one around, she bulleted up into the sky and began heading fast for Teague's territory. She flew hard, her pulse beating fast in her throat, her panic so all-consuming she was unaware of the passing of time.

When she *finally* crashed through the preternatural shield surrounding Teague's land, the sounds of battle whacked into her. Jesus, it was *loud*. If it wasn't for the shield, the noise would be heard from miles away, and there would be police gathered in no time at all.

Hovering high above Teague's camp, Larkin drank in the sight below, blinking in surprise at the dead chupacabras littering the earth. *The fuck?*

The clearing was the picture of pure chaos. Hellhorses battled. Fallen angels attacked chupacabras. Hounds tore into each other—and yeah, if Teague hadn't told her the truth about his pets, she would have been shocked at the sight of ten, red-eyed dogs.

Not far away from where she hovered, two flocks of birds were going at each other hard, sending tufts of feathers everywhere.

She frantically scanned the mayhem for—*there*. She recognized Teague's hellhorse straight away. You couldn't miss the scar on its neck. It was locked in battle with who was most likely Ronin's beast.

The fight was *ugly*. There was raw power in every lunge, every bite, every slam of hooves. Muscles bunched and flexed and shimmered with both sweat and blood.

Though Teague's demon was dominating the duel, it wasn't satisfaction she felt. No, a surge of anger swooped through both her and her demon. Why? Because it was a walking mass of injuries.

Its face, neck, and shoulders were covered in bites. Puncture wounds were here and there. Burns and blisters and scorch marks could be seen on the front of its body. And there were also lots of deep gashes, particularly on its muzzle, legs, and flank—likely courtesy of chupacabra-claws.

Hissing through her teeth, she clenched her fists. If it hadn't been a hellhorse—a creature hard to hurt and even harder to destroy—it would likely have been in a terrible state, if not dead.

Ronin *really* needed to die. She had every confidence that he would. His beast was slowly backing up under the pressure of the brutal assault, clearly outmatched. The hellhorses flanking it were also struggling against their opponents. *Good*.

Sure that Teague's demon didn't desperately need intervention, she quickly took another glance around, wanting to be certain that Ronin didn't have any extra minions waiting in the trees. She wouldn't put it past the spineless little shit.

Nobody appeared to be hanging around. The only chupacabra left—there were half a dozen or so—were surrounded by the Black Saints. The fallen angels sported some injuries but were ... well, they were doing a whole bunch of stuff. Mostly just playing with their prey. *Literally* playing with them.

The Black Saints would let them run but then teleport in front of them and either punch their muzzle, wrestle them, or shoot them with crackling weird-ass balls of ultraviolet fire.

They also did a lot of laughing. And occasionally sank their teeth into the creatures' necks, whatever that was about. She didn't *think* they were drinking blood, but it was hard to tell. Surely not.

Basically, they were in no rush to end their fun.

Well, all right.

A pained squawk made her glance to the right. Ravens were still fighting in the air, and two appeared to have fallen to their death. Fuck, she hoped they weren't from Teague's flock—there was no way for her to tell simply from looking at them.

Similarly, she couldn't tell the bloodhounds apart from the ones who'd evidently come along with Ronin. All were covered in puncture wounds and deep gashes at this point. Two were limping, and one was missing an ear.

She didn't try to help either the ravens or the hounds, worried she'd hurt the wrong ones. Instead, she switched her focus to the hellhorse battle. It was still nothing short of ugly. Teeth scraped and sank deep. Hooves kicked and slammed. Hellfire consumed and scorched.

Her demon fairly rubbed its hands, eager to watch Teague's steed and its clan lay waste to the fuckers who'd dared come here to kill them. Wanting to speed things along, Larkin decided to jump in.

Attacking from above, she threw up her palms and let out a volley of hell-ice. The chips zoomed down through the air and sank into the backs and flanks of the enemy-hellhorses. The steeds flinched and whinnied in pain. Her demon drank in the sounds with a sadistic smirk of delight.

Since she was at such a distance away from her targets, Larkin wasn't sure if the chips would embed themselves deep—they might merely settle an inch or so beneath the skin. But they'd still sting and ache like crazy.

A couple of the hellhorses that had been hit peered up and spotted Larkin. She waved, beaming while her demon flipped them the finger. The steeds had no way to retaliate and needed to keep their attention on their battle, so they went right back to it . . . but not before one of them first let out a loud neigh that seemed like a call.

A squawk was the only warning Larkin got before an oversized bird bulleted through the air toward her. Since Teague's flock wouldn't attack her, it could only be one of Ronin's.

Sharply turning its way, she threw an orb of hellfire at it. Missed. *Ugh.*

She emitted a rain of hell-ice chips at the winged fucker, smiling at its screech of pain. Then she rocketed toward it. The raven's pace faltered, as if it hadn't expected her to meet it head-on.

Another raven came out of nowhere and slammed into the side of her would-be-attacker, unbalancing and knocking it aside. The little shit somehow managed not to drop to the ground, but nor did it come at Larkin again.

It didn't get the chance.

A bunch of ravens descended on it. Feathers and pained screeches peppered the air, delighting her entity—it was thoroughly enjoying itself right now, loving the 'show'.

Figuring Teague's flock didn't need her aid, Larkin turned back to Ronin and who were likely his unit. Raising her hands, she targeted them again. Chips of hell-ice arrowed down and burrowed into their flesh. Some flinched and kicked out with their back legs.

Between sending out clusters of hell-ice, she slammed the hellhorses with orbs of hellfire. She paid particular attention to the legs, wanting to ensure said legs failed them fast.

Her peripheral vision caught movement. Two chupacabras had managed to evade the Black Saints and were attempting to flee. Larkin angled her body toward them and flapped her wings hard, emitting a harsh gust of air that flattened them to the ground. She blasted them with balls of hellfire, keeping them pinned in place.

Viper and his brothers were soon on the little shits. After giving her a nod of thanks, they . . . uh, well, they gripped the chupacabras hind legs and dragged them back to where they'd been playing with them. Clearly, they were still in no rush to end their prey.

Deciding she'd leave them to it, she turned her attention back to—

A loud yelp made her glance at the hounds. Four were circling a canine, protecting it from the others of the opposing side. It wasn't dead, but its chest was very weakly rising and falling. Her stomach rolled. She sure hoped it wasn't from Teague's pack.

Refocusing on the hellhorses, she saw that Ronin's beast and those flanking it had backpedaled even more. They weren't simply tired, they were beginning to panic. They knew they were being overpowered, and they had no way to escape the situation they'd put themselves in. Well, ha.

She sent another hail of hell-ice at the bastards. She did it again. And again. And again. Hurting them. Distracting them. Coming at them from the rear so they had no way of evading attack.

A hellhorse on Ronin's side went down, and its opponent immediately pounced—stomping on it, setting it alight with hellfire, delivering savage kicks to its head.

Another of Ronin's friends went down, followed quickly by another. One by one, the others in their group joined them on the ground ... until only Ronin's steed was left standing.

Though Teague's clan had killed their opponents, they didn't leap on the surviving foe to aid Teague's hellhorse. No, they stepped away. In a haze of smoke and ash, they shifted shape as the last two battling hellhorses went at it.

Observing the duel closely, Larkin quickly realized that the reason Ronin's steed hadn't yet been defeated wasn't that it was some tough motherfucker. No, it was still on its feet—well, hooves—because Teague's demon was choosing to drag the duel out. It wanted to have its fun and make its foe suffer.

Considering that Ronin had plenty to pay for, it wasn't a surprise.

She didn't aid Teague's steed, knowing it would want to finish this itself. Instead, she lowered herself to the ground near his clan, who were tugging on jeans even as they watched the duel.

As she and the six males circled the fighting demons, five bloodhounds gathered close. All were battered and bruised, and some were limping. The other hounds were either dead or dying, as were five ravens. The live birds had congregated on nearby branches, looking worse for wear but not fatally wounded or—

Ronin's hellhorse went down.

Her pulse leaped. Her demon clapped its hands with morbid glee.

The steed dragged itself upright, clearly in pain. She expected Teague's beast to lunge and deliver the killing blow. It didn't. Oh, it gave the fallen stallion a vicious kick all right. It simply made no attempt to kill it. Her hellhorse apparently wasn't done yet.

Pulling her wings tight to her body, she let them 'go' and kept a close eye on Teague's demon. She sure hoped he'd hurry this along, because her demon *really* wanted to join him, and Larkin just knew it would act like a weirdo if it did.

Time drifted from Teague's steed as it got lost in its private battle. Attacking. Punishing. Terrorizing. Prolonging the agony. Not in any rush whatsoever to stop.

The taste of blood sat on its tongue. The thrill of battle pumped through its veins. The craving of pain and triumph came from deep in its soul.

Every counterattack from Ronin's stallion was as weak as it was desperate. The demon was losing and knew it. Was *dying* and knew it.

Teague began pushing for supremacy. The demon ignored him, caught up in the duel. But Teague kept on pushing and pushing and pushing. Snarling at the persistence, the steed took its annoyance out on its opponent, bombarding it with more savage kicks.

Ronin's bucking demon went back to all fours in an awkward move that made a rear leg buckle. It struggled to get to its feet. Failed. Struggled again. Failed once more.

Satisfied, Teague's hellhorse snarled down at its prey and shot it a scathing look. It was during that one unguarded moment that Teague surged to the surface, forcing the demon to subside.

His teeth gritted, Teague breathed through the pain as his

demon's injuries became his own. Fire raced over several parts of his body. Aches seemed to have settled in his bones. Sweat trickled down his face, making the cuts there sting.

Ignoring the aches in his fatigued muscles, Teague honed in on his half-brother, whose own beast then retreated.

Ronin rolled onto his back, the move stiff and awkward. But he didn't even attempt to get up. He lay there, heaving in gulps of air, injured in too many places to count.

For so long Teague had imagined seeing this male so bloody, bruised, and broken. Ronin had given Teague's mother no peace. Had made life hell for her. Had taunted, insulted, and spat at her on a regular basis, blaming her for Soren's infidelity; for how his parents had from then-on slept in separate beds; for how their relationship had eventually deteriorated until there was nothing left of it.

Teague's mother had never blamed Ronin or defended herself to him, despite that Soren had lied to her; convinced her that he and his partner were separating. She'd been so ashamed of herself for her naivety that she'd taken Ronin's abuse almost willingly.

Though Teague had made a deal with Soren to keep her safe from Ronin's antics, Teague had always sworn to himself that he'd one day beat the asshole bloody. So he felt nothing but grim satisfaction as he stared down at the male who could have been a true brother to him if he wasn't instead determined to hate him.

"You shouldn't have come for me, Ronin," said Teague. "You should have just gotten on with your life and pretended I never existed."

Lines of pain carved into his pale face, Ronin swallowed. "How could I, when I was being constantly compared to you and always coming up short in other people's estimations?" he sniped.

"Considering you're dying right here from wounds I gave

you, I'd say that their estimations were bang on the mark. But you already knew that they were right. It's why you never wanted to duel with me, and it's why you brought chupacabras with you tonight." He gave the male a look that called him pathetic.

Ronin shook his head. "I didn't bring them here to weaken you. I just wanted to see you suffer awhile before I ended you."

Teague's beast snorted. "You had no confidence that you could end me."

An agonized cry burst out of Ronin, whose eyes went wide as his head snapped up. His gaze slammed on something behind Teague, darkening with anger.

Glancing over his shoulder, Teague saw that Larkin's demon had shoved a chupacabra spine through Ronin's leg.

It blinked at him, its brow knitting. "What?"

His beast nickered, amused. Teague supposed he should have expected that her crazy-ass entity would involve itself. He turned back to Ronin. "Was coming at me really worth it? Your friends are dead. Your hounds are dead. Your ravens are dead. Your hired help is dead. And soon, you will be as well."

Ronin's lips trembled, baring his grinding teeth. "If you hadn't had backup—"

"*Your* backup would have overrun us all," Teague finished. "Which, of course, was your plan. You should have known better than to think that I wouldn't be prepared for such a move."

Ronin slid a look at the Black Saints, who stood clustered together a few feet away. "What are they?"

"Don't you worry about them. They certainly aren't worrying about you."

Ronin went to speak again, but then another scream tore out of him.

Teague didn't need to look to know that his harpy's demon

had probably rammed a quill into Ronin's other leg. Still, Teague *did* look. And yeah, he was right.

His face red and scrunched up in pain, Ronin stuttered out a breath. "People will look for me, Teague. They won't ignore my disappearance. They will search. Especially my father. He will know to look at you for this."

Teague pursed his lips. "I don't see why he would, unless you told him you were coming here. Which I doubt. He would have put a stop to it, because he'd have known you wouldn't survive it."

Ronin looked as though he'd argue, but then he swallowed, a brief glint of vulnerability in his eyes. "He was ashamed."

"What?"

"When he heard from others that I'd lost my position, he was ashamed."

And that had no doubt been a contributing factor into why Ronin had been determined to see through his plan to execute Teague. "Does his pride really mean so much to you?"

"You say you never wanted it. But why else would you have joined the Wild Hunt, when you knew it was what he wanted *for me*?"

"My decision to be part of the Hunt was nothing to do with him or you. I didn't set out to steal your future and be better at it than you could, if that's what you think. I never thought about either of you when I accepted the position."

Ronin's lips compressed into a line. "I might have been fired, but the Dark Host will still seek to avenge my death."

"Maybe. But only if they know you're dead. They may even come here asking questions. They'll never learn what happened, though." Teague caught the jeans that Saxon threw to him. Pulling them on, he hid a wince as the denim chafed the fast-healing wounds on his legs. "We'll never be held responsible for the deaths of you and your unit. Did you forget that we're damn good at cleaning up after ourselves?"

"I think he did," said Larkin's demon, skirting around Teague, a spine in each hand. Pausing near Ronin's head, it smiled so very, very sweetly at him. Then it shoved a spine into his left shoulder.

He cried out, arching his back, almost choking on a scream.

Flexing its hand around the other spine, her demon held it directly above his head and then looked at Teague. "Can I burst his eyeball?" it asked, no emotion. "I'd like to feel and hear it pop."

Teague stifled a smile. "Maybe in a few minutes."

Appearing somewhat disappointed, it used the tip of the spine to peel back Ronin's upper lip. "I like his teeth."

Jesus.

Ronin stared at the entity, horrified. "What the fuck?"

It met his gaze and giggled.

Teague couldn't help but shudder, so he wasn't surprised when Ronin recoiled from the creepy sound. Eager to get this over and done with, he conjured a lethal orb of hellfire and raised a brow at Ronin. "Any last words?"

He snarled. "I have no regrets about coming for you. I may not have won this duel, but I have won the bigger battle."

Teague frowned. "What does that even mean?"

"It means you will not be able to stay in this realm," he replied, his eyes gleaming with delight. "I have exposed your presence here. There is a renege group of fallen angels in Vegas—one of whom might even be an archangel. You and I both know how much angels despise hell-born creatures, don't we? I left a message at their MC compound. I informed them that hell-born hellhorses have made a home for themselves here, and I gave them the location of your camp. They will come for you." Ronin lifted his chin, smug as a motherfucker.

Feeling his lips kick up, Teague looked around the clearing, glancing at each face. They all started to laugh.

Ronin scowled. "What could possibly be so amusing?"

Grinning, Viper rubbed at his jaw. "Fallen angels, huh?" He gestured at his brothers. "Yeah, that would be us." He glanced at Teague. "You didn't tell me he was funny."

Teague shrugged. "I haven't seen him in a while. Forgot about it." Orb still in hand, he took a few steps closer to the male sprawled on the ground in front of him.

Ronin looked like he'd try to scoot backwards, but the spines held him in place. He lifted a palm. "Wait—"

"No." Teague lit him up with hellfire. The flames whooshed up his body, covering every inch of him, burning and consuming.

Ronin screamed and screamed and screamed, his body bucking and writhing as much as the quills would allow.

No one spoke. No one moved. They all simply watched and waited.

Or that was the intention, anyway.

Larkin's demon rammed the chupacabra spine through Ronin's eye and into his brain. His screams became gurgles, and his struggles turned weak and awkward. Then his flaming body sagged, lifeless.

Her entity wrenched out the spine, pulling out a ruptured eyeball with it, causing blood to spatter across the ground. Then, seeming rather pleased with itself, the demon finally retreated.

Puffing out a breath, Larkin grimaced at the eyeball and tossed the spine aside. She turned to Teague, and her face darkened. "You look awful."

He hauled her close, ignoring the twinge of his wounds. "You give the best compliments." He dabbed a quick kiss on her mouth.

Viper eyed his injuries. "Want me to take care of those?"

Teague shook his head. "They'll heal quick enough."

She cocked her head at the MC president. "What is that ultraviolet shit you were tossing around earlier?"

"Nothing as cool as hell-ice," replied Viper. "Nice gift you got there."

Teague held his hand out toward the president. "Your aid was appreciated, though I think it would be safe to say it was more that you wanted an invite to the party than that you felt compelled to help us."

His mouth quirking, Viper shook his hand. "You didn't need our help. You only didn't argue about us being here because you knew we'd turn up either way."

"Why *did* you help tonight?" Larkin asked him. "Really?"

Viper arched a brow. "Why would we fight creatures that come crawling out of hell when they have no business doing so?" He shrugged. "Old habits die hard, I guess."

Her brow furrowed. "They tried invading the upper realm when you guys lived up there?"

"More often than you might think." Viper stuffed his hands in his pockets. "They probably always will, even though it never gets them very far."

"You and your brothers keep an eye on things here in this realm now," she guessed. "You watch out for signs that some might be around."

"Do we?" Viper asked, airy.

She flapped an unimpressed hand at his evasiveness. "Whatever. Just remember not all hell-born who come here do so with ill-will."

Viper held up his hands, his expression serious. "I'll only have an issue with those who do. You don't need to worry that I'll come for your hellhorse."

"If that changes and you target him, I'll come for you."

Viper smiled. "You know what, I like you."

"So you should. I'm fucking amazing."

He laughed and then turned to his brothers, who all stood around looking casual as you please even while injured and boasting streaks of blood on their skin and clothes. They looked not one bit unsettled by the evening's experience. More like amped up. As if they'd just left a concert or live sports' event or something.

Once the fallen angels had tended to the bloodhounds—like Maddox, they had the ability to heal wounds—they offered to help the ravens. The stubborn avians were having none of that, though. As such, the Black Saints then teleported out of the camp.

Teague swept his gaze over the clearing, taking in the bodies, ashes, and gore. "Let's clean up." As a thought occurred to him, he frowned at Larkin. "What took you so long to get here?"

She lightly scratched the corner of her mouth with one nail. "Huh. Funny story."

CHAPTER TWENTY-THREE

Leaning against the wagon's bedroom doorjamb an hour or so later, Larkin watched as a broody Teague roughly kicked off his shoes, his expression hard as granite. "Are you going to be like this all night?" she asked.

"Like what?" he bit out, sharply swiping out his foot to kick both shoes into the corner near the laundry bag.

"Snippy and gruff."

He shot her a petulant look. "I'm not snippy or gruff."

"Not usually, no. But your current mood is somewhat foul."

His lips tightening, he planted his hands on his hips and glared at her. "Of course it is. You were *kidnapped* earlier."

Larkin bit down on her lower lip. Unsurprisingly, he hadn't reacted too well on learning what had delayed her arrival. His face had flushed a deep red, and a string of harsh expletives had all but exploded out of his mouth. He'd then gone on something of a rant, fluidly pacing up and down like a caged animal.

Knowing she would have reacted in a similar fashion in his

shoes, Larkin had remained silent as he'd ranted, letting him get it all out of his system. His clan had done the same, sensing he needed it. Eventually, he'd cut himself off, sucked in a long breath, and announced that they all needed to focus on cleanup. So that was what they had done.

With the help of Slade, Archer, and Tucker, she and Teague had piled up every corpse—hell-animal, chupacabra, and hell-horse—and then eradicated them with hellfire. The smell of so much burning flesh and meat had been nauseatingly atrocious. Several hard flaps of Larkin's wings had thankfully cleared the air of the terrible scents and had also sent all the ashes scattering.

Meanwhile, Leo had dug out a hose and used it to rinse away blood spatter and other bits of gore from the wagons, trees, and ground. It hadn't been a fast or easy job, but the meticulous male had persevered until not a trace remained.

Saxon and Gideon had washed the dogs' blood-matted coats with shampoo. Most of them had liked it. But Reggie had made whines of complaint during the entire process, and Dutch had tried to run off a few times as if they were bathing him in acid. Hugo, on the other hand, had fallen asleep mid-wash.

Once the hounds were all clean, Saxon and Gideon had put their collars back on. The simple act had morphed them back into their typical-canine form. According to Archer, a mage down in hell had enchanted the collars so that they'd alter the bloodhounds' forms.

The ravens had washed themselves in the birdbaths in the wooded area. Baths that the guys had placed there, away from prying eyes, because the flock apparently didn't like to bathe with an audience ... like they stripped naked or something. It was weird, but Larkin didn't say as much.

Once the cleanup was over, Tucker and Slade had made

sandwiches for everyone. With the exception of Tucker, who'd made a point of washing his hands, the hellhorses had immediately gathered around the firepit to eat—evidently uncaring that their clothes and skin were still stained with blood.

They'd chatted between bites of their food, casual and relaxed. Like they hadn't just participated in a battle. Maybe she should have expected such nonchalance, but it had surprised her.

Unlike the others, Teague hadn't done much chatting. He'd mostly just sat there, surly and sullen, chewing a little too hard on his sandwich. As such, she'd known that he was still stewing over what went down with Holt.

Once they'd finished eating, he'd gruffly ushered her into his wagon ... and so now here they were. And he was still glaring at her.

She sighed. "I'm not suggesting you don't have a reason to be snippy—"

"I told you," he gritted out, "I'm not snippy."

Larkin rubbed at her temple. "Right. My mistake." Tired, she was tempted to perch her ass on his bed, but her clothes were in a gruesome state.

"And for the record, it wasn't a 'funny story' like you said it would be." He spoke like she'd cheated him out of a few laughs.

"I hadn't meant you'd find it amusing." Though with his non-sensical sense of humor, it wouldn't have been a complete shock for Larkin if he'd found something about the incident worth snickering about. "Now stop shooting me glares. I don't blame you for being pissed. I get that it couldn't have been nice for you to hear about it all after the fact—"

"Then why didn't you reach out to me earlier?"

"The net prevented it. You know that already." She'd explained everything. "Though it wasn't like I couldn't handle three dumbass cambions—something that's perfectly apparent, considering they're dead. And there wasn't anything you could have done anyway, considering you were smack bam in the middle of a battle. Or did you forget that part?"

"I didn't forget," he clipped, his hands slipping down to his sides. "I also didn't forget that you could have telepathed me once you'd escaped the net but you didn't."

"There was no sense in me being like *oh, by the way, I just survived a kidnapping attempt.* Especially when you needed to focus on fighting." She held up a hand when he would have spoken. "I won't apologize for making the call I made. It was the right one. *You'd* have made it in my shoes."

"No, I wouldn't have."

"Okay, that was a complete and utter lie. Don't even deny it." She pushed away from the doorjamb. "Instead of being upset with me, be pissed at Holt."

Teague's gaze glittered with fury. "Oh, I am." His eyes bled to black as his demon rose just long enough to rumble an enraged growl, and then it retreated.

Her own entity, totally over the Holt incident at this point, yawned and settled down. Most of its anger had drained away when it'd eradicated the asshole's existence, and the last of the emotion had dissipated after the demon delivered a little pain to Ronin.

Teague rolled his neck on his stiff shoulders. "I want to resurrect the little fucker so I can kill him myself."

"It would be satisfying to bring him back for exactly that purpose. He died *way* too quickly. But death by hell-ice at close range isn't by any means a painless experience, so there's that."

"He deserved worse." Teague ground his teeth. "I would have tortured him over and over until he begged for death."

Her entity smiled, finding that sweet. Yeah, *sweet.* "You really should be careful, Teague, or you'll make my demon fall for you." He didn't yet need to know that the entity was already gone for him.

His face softened slightly. "It doesn't seem to be riding you hard. I'm assuming it isn't bothered that you had to kill Holt."

Her demon snorted, finding it ridiculous that he might believe otherwise. "Not even a little. It despised him."

Teague slowly crossed to her. "Can't have been easy for you."

"What?"

"Killing your anchor."

"He was never my anchor. Not in any *real* sense of the word." Even at the end, he'd only wanted the bond for his own self-ish reasons.

"I know that." Teague slipped his arms around her waist. "But it has to go against the grain on a primal level to harm your psi-mate. Some elemental part of you must have struggled with it."

She pursed her lips. "Honestly? No, no part of me rose up in protest or pain. Probably because it was a matter of survival—that will trump anything else on a primitive level. He wanted to take my choices from me; force me to bond with him, leave with him. For me, it was either kill him or be his captive and forever be psychically stuck with him. Nothing in me hesitated at choosing the first option, and I will never regret or feel bad about it."

She grieved the bond that they *could* have had if things were different, but she didn't grieve Holt. And now that he was gone, a psychic weight had been lifted—she couldn't feel the call of the bond anymore; never would again. The relief of that warmed her very soul.

Stroking Teague's upper arms, she asked, "Was it hard erasing Ronin's existence? I mean, he was a total shitbag. But he was also your half-brother."

"He was never my family, just as Holt was never your

psi-mate. I would prefer that I hadn't been placed in a position where it was Ronin or me, but I can't say I found it difficult to end him."

"Yeah, I get that."

Teague pressed his forehead to hers, exhaling a long sigh. "I hate that I was deep in battle with no clue that you were in danger."

She slid a hand up his chest to splay it over his heart. "I hate that you were in battle at all. I can't lie, I'm absolutely ecstatic that Ronin's dead. So is my demon. I'm surprised it didn't do a happy dance around his ashes."

Feeling his mouth curve, Teague pulled back. "Your entity sure had some fun with him. I think it scares my clan."

"My demon scares most people. But not you," she mused, regarding him closely. "Never you."

"The entity's nice to me," he reminded her, still rather smug about it. He tilted his head. "Is it still sulking because it didn't get to pluck out any of Ronin's teeth and keep them as trophies?" Teague had vetoed that on the basis that it was not only plain weird but also a bad idea, since he needed every trace of Ronin to be gone from this realm.

"No. It was placated by your gift of a chupacabra fang."

He smiled. "I knew it would be. I almost took one for myself. Would have made a nice toothpick."

She stared at him for a long moment, a look of blank incomprehension on her face. "You're both nuts."

He shrugged one shoulder. "We can live with that."

"I've noticed."

As he recalled the question he'd meant to ask her earlier, he studied her closely. "How did you escape the net? You never said."

She merely gave him one of her enigmatic smiles.

"Ah, come on, tell me," he coaxed, squeezing her hips gently.

"Maybe later. I need a shower in a major way. So do you."

"We'll have one together. Then you can tell me what I want to know."

She made a noncommittal sound.

So he bit her. Right on the neck. Hard.

With a hiss, Larkin gave him a little shove that was more playful than annoyed. "Watch those teeth, Black Beauty."

"You like it when I bite you," he taunted before landing a hard kiss on her mouth, savoring her taste. Breaking the kiss, he gave her ass a soft pat. "Get naked. I'll grab some towels."

He stalked over to the wall near his bed and opened up one of the high cupboards that were built into the wagon's walls. Spotting something, he felt his brow knit. "What's this?" As he pulled out an unfamiliar book, he noticed Larkin awkwardly poke her tongue into the inside of her cheek.

She cleared her throat. "My demon stashed it there."

"Your demon?"

"It likes to hide its belongings in little hidey holes."

He felt his frown deepen. "In *other* people's homes?"

"It stores things wherever it feels like." She said it like it was no big deal, her voice overly casual.

He couldn't help squinting. "You know, *you're* no better than your demon when it comes to stuff like this. You leave your shit here all the time, you just don't secrete it away." He was starting to wonder if Gideon was right and this was her way of leaving a mark on his territory.

"I can pack it all up and take it home with me if you want," she offered without hesitation.

He should say yes. But he weirdly found that he didn't mind having some of her things spread around his wagon. He even kind of liked it, as did his beast.

Deciding not to question why, Teague flicked a hand. "No, it's fine." He glanced around, his mouth twisting. "Has your demon stashed other stuff around here?"

"No, just that."

He bit the inside of his cheek, not so sure he believed her. The look she gave him was just a little too innocent.

She glanced at the book he still held. "Do you want me to take it home? I mean, I can't guarantee that my demon won't just put it back in your cupboard at some point, but you never know."

He felt his lips hitch up. "The book can stay."

"All right, if you're sure."

"I'm sure."

Walking toward him, she said, "This is one of many reasons why you shouldn't be so smug that my demon likes you. Where you're concerned, it'll feel it's entitled to do all kinds of things that you won't be happy about."

"It's a law unto itself," he agreed with a nod. "I approve."

"You would," she mumbled.

"I don't know why you'd think I shouldn't."

"Of course you don't." Rocking back and forth on her heels, she eyed the book again. "You, uh, should really put that back in the hidey hole."

Sensing the issue, Teague felt his smile widen. "Your demon's getting antsy about me holding it, huh?"

"It doesn't like other people touching its things."

Affronted, he pointed at his chest. "I should be an exception to that." It liked him. A lot. And he gave it presents.

"You are to an extent. Which is why it hasn't surfaced to punch you in the throat. And yes, it has done that to others who'd dared put their hands on its possessions. The entity is pretty territorial."

"Hmm." Rather than put the book back in the cupboard, he briefly flicked through it.

She put a hand on her hip and cocked her head. "So, what, you *want* my demon to hurt you?"

"Not especially."

She blinked. "The answer should really be an absolute 'no'."

"Meh."

Lowering her arm to her side, she slowly shook her head and turned away. "Sometimes, when I consider that your sense of self-preservation is shaky at best, I have no clue how you're alive."

"It is a conundrum," he allowed as he replaced the book and dragged two towels out of the cupboard. "But no one will come at me when I'm fake-dating a badass harpy who'd kick their asses or let loose her nutcase of a demon on them." He closed the cupboard, frowning as her expression changed. "Why are you smiling at me like that?"

Her lips twitched, widening her smile a little. "Like what?"

"Like I'm clueless or something." It made his beast bristle.

She cradled his face with her hands. Cradled. His. Face. "You're just so cute," she said, squishing his cheeks as if he was five or something.

He drew his head back, making her hands slip away. "I don't think anyone has ever described me as cute before. Hot. Sexy. Big-dicked. Never cute." He wasn't certain how he felt about it.

"There's a first time for everything. Right?"

Narrowing his eyes again, he pointed an accusing finger at her. "You're just trying to distract me from my line of questioning." It made him so proud that she'd picked up that habit from him.

She gave a breezy shrug. "If you say so."

"I do say so, and I won't be sidetracked this time. No way."

"Good for you." She swiped a towel from him. "Now, are we taking a shower or what? I want to put that big dick of yours to good use, but I can't right here and now."

And he lost his grip on the question he'd meant to ask. "Wait, why can't we have sex here and now?"

"We're covered in blood." She didn't add *obviously*, but he heard it in her tone.

Teague felt his brow furrow. "So?"

"So I don't want to have sex while smears of blood are all over my skin and that of the person who's fucking me."

"Why not?"

She fired a disbelieving look at him. "Because it's icky."

"Icky?"

"Yes, icky."

He did a slow blink, struggling to follow her line of thinking. Finally, he shrugged. "All right, if it's really such a big deal for you . . ."

Her eyes flashed. "How could it *not* be a big deal? Like, for anyone?"

Teague opened his mouth to speak but then bit down on his bottom lip. "I get the feeling that I don't have a response that won't irritate you. Which would normally please me. But I want to fuck you, and I don't think you'll let me if you're mad at me. You didn't last time." Which was completely unreasonable.

Her eyelids lowered slightly. "Because last time, you tried sticking a mini marshmallow up my nose while you thought I was sleeping."

"It was an accident."

Her brows snapped together. "How does one do that by accident?"

Scratching his nape, he raised his shoulders. "Okay, so I wanted to wake you up," he admitted with an incline of his head.

"And you couldn't have just, you know, gently shook me or something?"

Well … he supposed he *could* have, now that he thought about it. It just really hadn't occurred to him at the time.

Closing her eyes, she slammed up a hand—something she did a lot around him in pure exasperation, which he really loved. "Just don't try stuffing things up my nose again," she said. "That's all I ask."

"What do you have against things being stuffed in holes? I still can't believe you're not open to figging. You can't be scared of a little ginger peel."

Her eyes flipped open. "I'm not scared of it. It just isn't going up my ass. Ever."

"But—"

"No."

"Just give it a chance."

"No."

"You'll like it."

"Uh, no, I won't. At all. Not in the slightest. Now can we end this pointless conversation and just. Go. Shower?" Her hand clenched around the towel. "What, why the fuck are you grinning like an idiot?"

"I can't help it, I plain love it when you snarl and—fuck, don't throw shit at me, Lark!"

CHAPTER TWENTY-FOUR

Two months later

Standing in one of the racing stadium's VIP boxes, Larkin watched through the glass wall as twenty hellhorses trotted onto the oval dirt track. Whistles and cheers split the air, loud and laced with anticipation. Their heads proudly held high, the steeds came to a smooth halt near the start line. Among them was Teague's beast.

Larkin cricked her neck, edgy with nerves. How could she not be, given how dangerous the sport was?

Even before she'd crossed platonic lines with Teague, she'd felt a little nervous when he raced. It was worse now that they were mates—something he wasn't yet aware of, but she didn't feel that his obliviousness was necessarily important.

Unlike her, Teague's hellhorse wasn't at all restless. It held itself tall and still, oozing self-assurance. Most of its competitors, on the other hand, nervously swished their tails or scraped a hoof at the earth.

Her own demon was very close to the surface, so eager for the race to begin that it practically bounced on the spot with anticipation. It wasn't worried for their mate. Nor was it bothered by how utterly inhumane the obstacles and ditches were. In the entity's opinion, the more sadistic they were, the better. And it had every confidence that Teague's demon would not only escape relatively unscathed but prevail.

Larkin slid the imp beside her a quick look. "Sometimes, I don't know why Teague's beast persists in putting itself through this again and again. Then I remember it probably wouldn't do it at all if it *wasn't* for the risky hurdles."

As edgy as Larkin, Khloë tipped back her glass to drink some of her champagne. "The demon is an official danger junkie. It likes to live life on the edge in just about every way possible."

Larkin blinked. "You say that with perfect understanding."

The imp gave a slight shrug. "Danger spices things up."

"Injuries don't. And his beast always walks away with plenty after these damn races."

Khloë grimaced. "Yeah, I don't like that part. It's why I get nervous."

Asher toddled over and planted his palms on the glass wall. "I wanna go down there." He looked up at Maddox expectantly . . . as if the male would obligingly teleport him to the track. The little boy thankfully couldn't pyroport that far away.

An arm draped around Raini's shoulders, Maddox peered down at Asher. "Why?"

"To ride a horsey," the boy told him.

Sighing from her spot on the chic leather seating, Harper cut in, "Kid, we've been over this—you can't ride a hellhorse. They don't let people ride them."

That wasn't strictly true. If they wholeheartedly trusted a

person, they'd allow it. Teague's beast had given Larkin a ride around his land multiple times.

Tossing an empty paper plate in the trash, Piper looked at Harper. "Have you not considered just buying him a pony or something?"

"I thought about it." Harper bit into a spring roll she'd nabbed from the buffet table. "But since he's going through a phase of setting his toys on fire when he's bored with them, I figured I'd better not."

Gently bouncing her daughter on her lap, Devon grinned and said, "That's a typical imp phase."

Raini nodded, sucking milkshake through a straw. "He's probably copying the other kids."

A crackle of static came over the intercom, and then a male voice announced that the race would now start.

Every cell of Larkin's body tensed. The hellhorses went motionless. All the spectators in the stadium fell silent.

Moments later, a horn loudly rang out.

The steeds pitched forward as one and rocketed along the track, their hooves kicking up dust and grass. They crossed the individual lanes and gathered into a tight herd. Teague's beast didn't bolt straight to first place, though Larkin would bet it could. Instead, it settled in the center of the herd and kept its pace steady.

Khloë blew out a breath. "That's it, go easy, you got nothing to prove."

Larkin heard hinges creak behind her. Heard soft footfalls—rhythms she recognized as those belonging to Knox and the male sentinels. She didn't look away from the racing steeds.

Hellhorses were mesmerizing when in motion. Their sleek muscles rippled, their powerful legs were a blur of movement, and their lush manes fluttered with the astonishing speed at which they ran.

The stadium echoed with the thunder of hooves, the rapid commentary coming over the loudspeaker, and the shouting of the spectators.

"Here comes the first hurdle," said Keenan, walking over to stand behind his mate. "And it's on fire."

Devon groaned. "I almost don't want to watch."

Feeling her stomach wind tighter and tighter as the steeds neared the obstacle, Larkin bit down on her lip. And then they were there.

Timing the jump just right, Teague's hellhorse leaped over the eight-foot wall, neatly avoiding contact with the flames, and cleared the ditch of lava.

A few others weren't so lucky—the fire grazed their under-belly, charring their coat and skin. Still, they didn't fall. They kept running hard and fast.

Levi hummed. "That went smoother than I thought it would."

"Not sure we'll be able to say the same for the next hurdle," said Piper, chewing on her thumb. "Look at it."

Oh, Larkin was looking. Snakes were writhing all over the wall. Big-ass snakes that appeared somewhat keyed-up.

Again, Teague's beast leaped high. A snake lurched toward him, snapping its jaw closed, missing the steed's leg by mere inches. The stallion easily cleared the wall and forged on ahead.

Another steed got bit right on its flank as it jumped. Larkin winced. Maybe it was the surprise, maybe it was the pain, but though the hellhorse avoided the lava ditch, it landed awk-wardly on the track. As its foreleg crumpled beneath it, it went ass over tit.

The steed behind it had no time or way to skirt around the

fallen beast. It went down hard, tripping another hellhorse in the process. That simply, all at once, three competitors were out of the race.

"And then there were seventeen," intoned Keenan.

Cricking her neck again, Larkin watched Teague's beast up his speed just enough to slide into eighth place. The demon beside it spared the steed a quick glance and then puffed out a billow of snort, attempting to distort its vision.

It worked, but her mate continued onward.

So the prick did it again moments later. Once more, it worked. Which was an issue, because they'd approached a mean-ass wall that was covered in moving, thorny vines that lashed out like whips.

She held her breath as Teague's beast made the jump. It seemed to spring off its powerful hindlegs as it smoothly soared over the hurdle. *Thank God.*

The puffing steed wasn't so fortunate. Its front hooves scuffed a vine hard enough to rock its balance and momentum. The demon landed right into the pit of blazing shrubs, letting out a high-pitched squeal of pain. The lashings of vines caused two other steeds to hit the ditch, their squeals just as piercing.

The remaining contestants kept on tearing across the track. As the minutes went on, they leaped over obstacles, raced through bubbling puddles of oil, and sprinted across patches of ice.

Some stayed on their feet. Others went down. Teague's beast not only didn't fall, it didn't slow.

When they surpassed the first half of the race, the cheating promptly began. They tried distracting one another—setting each other's tails alight, biting into necks or flanks, bashing their bodies into that of others.

Her gut tensed as the stallions either side of her mate

converged on it in a rush, trying to squash it between them and fuck with its steady pace.

Larkin hissed. "Those little"—she slid Asher a quick glance—"meanies."

"Big meanies," Asher declared.

Said meanies didn't succeed in making her mate fall. Teague's stallion put on a quick burst of speed, escaping them. They gave chase, the shitheads. One nipped its butt hard. Her mate's head jerked, and it swished its tail like a whip.

Khloë growled. "Oh, I could *murder* them . . . jerks."

One of the aforementioned jerks were taken out by the next hurdle—it scraped its belly *badly* on the shards of broken glass that littered the surface of the wall. Larkin's demon gave a haughty *that's karma for you* sniff.

Teague's beast thankfully made the jump without a problem. It also sailed into fourth place.

As the race went on, the hellhorse came up against yet more jumps and ditches. It also dealt with yet more tricksters trying to take it down. One even body-slammed it like a pro, almost knocking it into a fence. Though the beast's pace faltered, it didn't lose its footing. It recovered fast and raced on ahead of the little prick.

Rubbing at her nape, Larkin chewed on the inside of her cheek. At this point, her mate sported many burns and bites, as well as a fair few gashes from the more sadistic obstacles. She could see that it was not only in pain, it was beginning to tire. All the runners were, so fewer and fewer were clearing hurdles.

Keenan commented each time a steed fell, letting everyone know exactly how many were left in the run-in. She didn't need his input at this point. It took a single look to tell that five remained. Teague's beast was now in second place.

"Okay," began Devon, "we're at the last part of the track."

Which was why Larkin's nerves were having an absolute breakdown. This was where the obstacles became higher, wider, crueler, and closer together.

Joining her hands together as if in prayer, she placed them against her mouth. Her stomach twisted each time her mate approached a jump. Her breath snagged each time it made a leap. Air gusted out of her mouth every time it cleared a hurdle.

"One jump left," Raini muttered.

It was at that point that the cheating went *crazy*. There was lots of biting and bashing and puffing out noxious smoke to fog the air. One asshole set alight her mate's tail with goddamn hellfire, but a strong flap of that tail fortunately made the flames die down.

As it neared the overgrown prickly hedge around which a swarm of hornets were gathered, Larkin sank her teeth down into her lower lip.

The beast jumped. High. Fast. Skillfully.

Part of the hedge scraped its belly, and she sucked in a breath. The beast landed hard, but it didn't fall. Nope, it slid into first place as it then ran for the finish line.

Larkin shifted from foot to foot. "That's it, keep going, you're almost there."

The chants of the spectators became louder and more urgent. The commentator's speech became more rapid and intense. Khloë began spouting more encouragements, her words coming out fast.

Every last hellhorse dug deep for strength and sprinted on ahead, their hooves pounding the track, their metallic black coats shimmering with sweat. Each edged forward little by little, and some overtook others. But none caught up to Teague's stallion.

It darted across the finish line first.

Only then did Larkin's gut unknot.

Keenan slapped her back a little too hard, amusement gleaming in his eyes. "You weren't nervous for the demon, were you?"

Larkin twisted his ear.

He hissed. "Ow, that hurt."

Khloë snickered. "Don't be a baby."

He huffed at the imp. "You're supposed to be sympathetic."

"Sympathetic," Khloë echoed, tasting the word. She closed her eyes. "I know what it means, I do, I just can't remember right now."

He cast her a droll look. "I need a beer." With that, he walked off.

Smiling, Khloë turned to Larkin. "So ... are you still going through with your plan to tell Teague tonight that you guys are in a relationship?"

Larkin exhaled heavily. "Yup." Honestly, she'd thought he'd have worked it out for himself by now. She was starting to wonder if he was choosing the bliss of ignorance.

Khloë knocked back the last of her champagne. "Why did you delay it this long?"

"I just wanted to give him time to get used to having me around so much. It'll make it easier for him to adjust to the fact that I'm not going anywhere." Her demon wouldn't allow it even if Larkin was prepared to walk away.

The entity was so firmly attached to him that, little by little, it had gravitated all its belongings to Teague's wagon. He'd come across some of it, but not all. The demon hadn't left them in plain sight. The stuff was stashed here and there.

He never commented. Just curiously studied the object and then put it back.

"Personally, I think he'll react well to realizing he's been firmly snagged by you," said Khloë.

Larkin cocked her head. "You do?"

Nodding, the imp placed her empty glass on a nearby high table. "The way he looks at you . . . it's hard to describe. There's an electric possessiveness there that's mingled with pride and something seriously warm. He's utterly gone for you. Not sure if he's acknowledged it to himself yet, but he's got it bad. So has his demon."

"Hopefully you're right, because if Teague tries to chase me off, my demon will hurt him." She wasn't kidding.

"*I'll* hurt him. You're good for Teague; he'd be a fool to turn you away. I will tumble all over his shit if he messes this up."

It was only a few minutes later that he strolled into the VIP box. People hollered out their hellos and congratulations. He came straight to Larkin, his mouth curving into that grin he wore solely for her.

She felt her own lips hike up. "You won. Again. Congrats."

Splaying his hand on her back, he pulled her close. "Thank you, baby." He pressed a soft kiss to her mouth and then looked at Khloë. "Hey, gorgeous."

It no longer bothered Larkin when he used that term with Khloë. The same couldn't be said for Keenan, though. Hence why the approaching sentinel glared at him.

"Every time you do that, you insult Larkin," Keenan stated.

Teague frowned. "Do what?"

"Call another woman gorgeous," said Keenan, curling an arm around the imp's shoulders.

Teague double-blinked. "How does that insult Larkin?"

"Because *she's* the one you should be complimenting."

"I do compliment her. Just this morning, I told her she could wield a paddle like a pro."

Larkin let out a heavy breath and exchanged a look with a chuckling Piper.

Keenan's lips pressed into a tight line. "Just stop calling my mate—" He grunted as said mate dug her elbow into his ribs.

"Let it go, Keenan," Khloë groused.

The incubus sniffed. "I don't want to."

"Here," Devon interjected, holding out her daughter, "make yourself useful and hold Anaïs instead of bothering people."

Keenan threw up his arms and stepped back. "No. No way. I like to *breathe*. For some reason, she has an issue with that and wants to put an end to it."

Devon rolled her eyes. "Would you stop being dramatic? She's just a baby."

"She's an assassin in the making." He looked at Levi. "Back me up on this."

The reaper sighed. "You're overreacting."

"*You* hold her, then."

"Fuck, no."

Devon glared at both males. "You are terrible, terrible people."

Chuckling, Teague turned to Larkin. "Ready to go?"

"Couldn't be readier," said Larkin.

Since she'd arrived at the Underground in her car, she drove behind his bike as he headed to his camp. Aside from Tucker and Saxon, the clan was outside.

Slade was cleaning his own bike with a rag that, like most materials he owned, appeared to be bloodstained. Leo was wiping bird shit off his wagon while glaring at a raven that was circling overhead. He appeared to be cursing at the bird—it was hard to be sure, since it was impossible to hear him over the Bob Marley tune that was filtering out of Tucker's open window.

Sprawled in his porch chair with a bottle of brandy in hand, Gideon sang along to the music while waving a lighter in the air. Archer was doing the same from his own porch, a bag of mushrooms on his lap.

The dogs rushed to Teague as soon as he was off his bike. Larkin parked in her usual spot near where Saxon's truck tended to be parked. It was currently nowhere to be seen, so it seemed he was out and about—and likely going after yet another mark for a fee, but she wasn't judging.

None of the clan had mentioned the Ronin thing since the evening of the battle, totally over it ... right up until their old commander paid them another visit a week ago. He'd informed them of Ronin's disappearance and—apparently at the request of Soren, who believed his son had no enemies other than Teague—questioned her mate about it.

Of course, her hellhorse had played clueless. Vine had bought his act, since he himself didn't suspect Teague of any involvement. Mostly because it hadn't only been Ronin who'd gone missing; it was his entire unit. Vine couldn't see why Teague would wipe them all out—he seemingly had no motivation to do so.

As she exited her vehicle, Gideon raised his bottle to her while Archer gave her a lazy salute. Leo tipped his chin her way and went back to glaring at the raven. Slade probably would have said his hellos if Dutch hadn't chosen that moment to try to snatch the bloodstained rag from his hand.

Once she'd grabbed something from her trunk, Larkin crossed to Teague, who was stuffing his riding gear in his saddlebag. After exchanging a few words with his clan, he clambered up the steps to his wagon and unlocked the door. He gestured for her to precede him inside and then closed the door behind them.

Teague frowned. "What's that?" he asked, flicking a look at what she was carrying.

"My overnight bag," Larkin replied before walking to his bedroom.

Following her, he scratched at the branded side of his neck. "Looks like a suitcase to me."

Larkin dropped the luggage on the floor near the dresser and then kicked off her shoes. "Some might call it that." Because that was exactly what it was.

He hummed. "What have you brought that couldn't fit into a duffel?"

Most of her wardrobe. "Right, look, here's how it is. I don't intend to live in a separate place from my mate. Which is what you are. My mate. And not a fake one. Our relationship—yes, we have a relationship; we've been in one for months now—is nothing close to shallow. It's serious, and it's *permanent*. Deal with it."

He didn't react. Didn't tense. Didn't speak. Didn't blink. Nothing.

Her demon stirred, watching him very closely, trying and failing to read his expression. Likewise, Larkin couldn't determine what was going on in his head. But knowing Teague, it was nothing predictable.

"We're in a relationship?" he asked, no inflection in his tone.

She lifted her chin. "Yes."

"A real one?"

"Yes. Oh, and everyone knows." She figured it would be best to throw that out there.

"Everyone?"

She felt her nose wrinkle. "Well, I'm not sure about your clan, but the others in our circle know. I thought you'd cotton on to it eventually, but you just didn't."

"So this is why Khloë keeps laughing at me?"

"Probably. You never can tell with Khloë."

Seconds of excruciating silence ticked by. "How long, exactly, have we been in a relationship?"

"Officially? Since the night before we first babysat Asher together."

His brows flicked up. "That long?"

"Yes. It became real before then somehow; I just didn't really realize it until that night. I said nothing, because you would have run like a rabbit. I instead made the official decision that we'd be a true couple from then on, and I worked hard to sneak past your defenses so I'd be more easily able to make you accept it."

"Wait, *that's* what you were plotting when you were watching me all weird back then?"

"Uh-huh. At this point, I feel like it worked. If it hasn't . . ." Her demon would go apeshit, and Larkin would have to kick his ass.

He twisted his mouth, staring down at her, his expression still inscrutable.

Her nerves starting to play up, she arched a brow. "Well?"

"Well, what?"

"How do you feel about the situation?" She paused. "I should warn you that my demon has—despite its issues—formed a huge attachment to you. It plans to eat your spleen if you try wriggling out of the relationship."

"Why my spleen?"

"I don't know, don't care. Now answer my question."

His jaw beginning to tighten, he lifted his shoulders. "Honestly? I'm annoyed."

Her stomach clenching, Larkin felt her eyes narrow. "Expand."

"For weeks on end I've been wondering how best to bring up that me and my demon have decided to keep you. I wasn't sure if you'd put up a protest, and I kept obsessing over it. And now it turns out that I had no need to chew on it. So yeah. I'm annoyed."

The tension in her body slipped away. Her demon relaxed with a smirk, feeling rather self-satisfied. "Keep me, huh?"

Hooking his finger through a belt loop in her waistband, he

pulled her close, his expression softening. "My kind generally don't take mates, as you know. It's not in our nature. I never thought I'd want to claim someone for myself. It really just never appealed to me. Until you. I wouldn't have thought my demon would be on board but it is, like, *mega* attached to you."

Larkin swallowed, settling her hands on the twin columns of his back. She wasn't a person who spouted soft, fuzzy words, so all she said was . . . "Then you get to keep your spleen."

His lips twitched. "Your entity really would have eaten it, wouldn't it?"

"If you'd rejected it, yes. It had planned to cut out the organ with a rusty spoon."

His smile widened. "I totally dig your demon. It's ace."

A sigh escaped her. "There's no hope for either of you. There just isn't."

"You'll learn to live with it." He glanced down at the suitcase again. "You're truly good with moving here?"

"I like your wagon. And your camp. I even like your clan, though they're all certifiably nuts to some degree. But I won't leave my lair." She lifted a hand. "Before you ask, no, I'm not going to request that you leave your clan. Because then you wouldn't be happy. I don't want that. We don't need to be part of the same lair or clan to make this work."

"You've squared this with Knox?"

"Yes. I made him very aware that though I'll remain his sentinel, my loyalty will always be primarily to you. He's fine with that. He has his own mate, so he understands."

His chest tightening, Teague slid his hand up her back. This harpy got to him. Big time. Had burrowed so deep inside him that she touched him in ways he hadn't known anyone could.

He dropped his forehead to hers. "You have my loyalty in a way that no one else ever will. Not even my clan."

Warmth bled into her eyes. "Then we're even."

"We're even," he agreed, wrapping a hand around the back of her neck. To seal the deal, he brought his mouth down on hers. The kiss was soft and slow. For about six seconds. Then an electric intensity crackled between them that charged his body and demanded an outlet.

It found it.

Need took him in a burst of flames. Their kiss became wild and desperate and ragged. Each slide of her tongue and raspy little moan pecked at his control, until it was in tatters.

A vicious hunger fired through his veins, as basic as it was potent. It made his blood hot, his nerve-endings sing, and his body tighten painfully.

He gripped her nape hard in a proprietary hold, skimming his other hand down to cup her ass tight. His. She was his. Every fucking part of her, inside and out.

Teague tore his mouth free. "Strip," he ordered, his voice like gravel. He whipped off his tee and dumped it on the floor. "I want to fuck my mate."

"Your mate has something she wants to do first." Larkin dropped to her knees and snapped open the buttons of his fly.

A low curse of surprise flew out of him. He watched as she fisted his cock, her grip firm and possessive. Then she took him in her mouth—no hesitation, no teasing, no playfulness. She got right down to business.

He sank his hands into her hair, gritting his teeth as she slid her lips down his shaft again and again while keeping her hand curled around the base. "You're a little too good at this."

Her eyes flicked to his, hot and hazy with need. So hot her gaze seemed to burn deep into his own. The moment was so fucking intimate it made his balls ache and tighten.

He hissed out a breath as she began sucking harder . . . and before he knew it he was fucking her hot, wet mouth. Holding her head still with his grip on her hair, he pitched his hips forward over and over, sinking deep.

Her eyes glittered with a dare. A dare to lunge harder and deeper. So he did, and she took it—even urged him on with a prick of her nails to his thigh.

Only when he felt an orgasm begin to build did he pull back. Much as he loved it when she swallowed his come, he needed to be in her. He tugged on her hair. "Up."

The moment she stood, he reached straight for her fly. He tackled it fast, backing her into the wall, while she hauled off her tee. He crouched down and peeled away her jeans and panties.

Driving two fingers inside her, he groaned. She was already slick and ready for him. He suckled on her clit as he pumped his fingers in and out, wanting her wetter. Needier. So desperate to come she'd curse at and threaten him all while yanking at his hair so hard it hurt.

It didn't take long before it got to that point.

Only then did he stand and hoist her up, finding her now delightfully braless. He swiped the items off the surface of his dresser and planted her on it. As she looped her legs around him, he inched the head of his dick inside her.

"There's no going back after this," he warned, gripping the underneath of her thighs. He didn't merely mean to fuck her, he meant to claim her.

"*Obviously.*" She dug her fingers into his shoulders. "Now move."

He slammed his hips upwards, forcing his cock deep, making her head fall back with a sharp gasp. A snarl built in his throat as her scalding hot pussy spasmed around him. "Mine." The word was low. Deep. Pure steel.

She lifted her head to meet his gaze. "And you're mine." She fisted his hair with one hand, her eyes blazing, and curled her free arm around his shoulders. "You try to leave me and I'll kill you."

He felt his lips curl. "I really love it when you snarl."

He took her hard. Because he could. Because he needed it. Because his demon needed it. Because both he and his beast needed her to *feel* their claim to her; feel that it ran soul-deep and she'd never be free of them.

Her scent swirled around him, drugging his senses, making him more frantic to take and own and fuck. Her pupils all but gone, she didn't look away, letting him see everything she felt. A feverish hunger. A blinding pleasure. A dangerous possessiveness. A ferally desperate need to explode.

He kept pounding hard, growling when her nails pricked the skin of his shoulder hard enough to draw blood. His beast loved it when she did that. Loved that animalistic edge to her.

"Bed," she rasped. "Move to the bed. I want to ride you."

She asked that often, a fan of being in control. Sometimes he went along with it, sometimes he didn't. Tonight, he didn't want to. So he bit at those lips that were red and swollen from sucking him off and said, "No."

Her eyes flared. "*Yes.*"

"No."

She ragged at his hair. "Don't think you can—"

"You'll take what I fucking give you." Upping his pace, he angled his hips so that he rubbed her clit with every ram of his cock. The fight left her in a rush, her inner walls rippling and heating as her release crept closer.

"Come," she coaxed.

"You first." He bit into her throat, hearing her hiss at the sting of his venom. The pain threw her over, just as he'd known it would. She choked on a scream as she came, her pussy milking his own orgasm out of him as he drove his hips up harder and faster, slamming his dick as deep as it would go, wanting his come so deep she'd never get it out.

Their orgasms subsided, seeming to drain them of strength as they did so. They stood there, weak and panting and trembling.

After long moments, Teague carried her to the bathroom, helped her clean up, and then settled them both on the bed. Sprawled on their backs, they strived to catch their breath.

Her muscles deliciously loose and lazy and just the right amount of 'sore', Larkin swept her tongue over her dry lips. "Just so you know, I love you. And I should probably make you aware that you love me, too."

Teague looked at her, a line denting his brow. "I do?"

"Yeah."

His frown deepened. "You sure?"

"Yeah."

"Huh." His gaze turning pensive, he poked his tongue into the inside of his cheek. "I can't say if you're right on that."

She weakly flapped a hand. "I can, so don't worry about it."

"Hmm." Twisting his mouth, he rolled toward her. "Maybe we should review this at a later—"

"We both know I'm right, don't make me hurt you."

His mouth quirking, he palmed the side of her neck, his gaze flitting over her face. "Yeah, you're right. I love the fucking bones of you." He gave her a quick, hard kiss. "Soon as I can, I'm putting a black diamond on your finger."

Larkin's insides seized in pure shock. A *good* kind of shock, but still. Demons only gave a black diamond to those they were wholly committed to. Hence why her demon gave a joyous little clap. "How soon?"

"Like, tomorrow."

Her brows flew up. "That's not too fast for you?"

He gave her a look that called her slow. "I'm a hellbeast, baby. When we claim something, we claim it very thoroughly. We put our mark all over it. And we don't let it go."

That she had no issue with. "You'd better wear the ring I buy you, or we're gonna have problems."

"Why would you think I might be difficult about it?"

"Because you're you." Nothing could be simple or easy with him—she'd resigned herself to that.

"I'll wear it. Probably on my toe, though. I don't like wearing stuff on my fingers."

"You wear gloves almost every day when you ride your bike."

"Not seeing your point."

Larkin gave him a hard look. "You will wear a black diamond ring on your finger or pay the price."

His eyes lit up in interest. "What's the price?"

"I won't wear yours."

Just like that, the light in his gaze dulled. "That's not acceptable."

"Then stop being difficult."

"I don't know how."

"*Learn.*"

A corner of his lips winged up. "Your eyelid just twitched again. I'm telling you, it's gonna be a permanent thing before you know it, you'll—" He cut off when she growled, and his mouth curved even more. "I swear, that sound does shit to me." He shuddered in what seemed like delight. "I need to record it. I could use it as my ring tone."

"You don't have a cell phone."

His eyes slid to the wall. "Oh, yeah," he finally remembered . . . like that was something a person could forget. He shrugged. "I'll use it as my doorbell, then."

"You don't have a doorbell either."

"Hmm, I guess I could use it as my alarm."

"That would work. If you had an alarm clock. Which you don't."

He threw her a put-out look. "What is it with you and technicalities?"

More than ready to bring the pointless conversation to a halt, Larkin sighed long and loud. "Just kiss me."

"Why?"

"Because it will shut you up."

He gave her a mock frown. "That's not very nice. You should make it up to me. Preferably by letting me stick some ginger peel up—"

"Teague, if you don't quit with this, I swear . . ."

His forehead creased. "Ah, come on, the Romans were all over it."

"They used it as a form of torture, not pleasure."

"Don't be closed-minded. Where's your sense of adventure?"

"Nowhere up my ass. But I'm *all* for shoving some ginger peel up yours. Interested?" She wasn't surprised when he looked close to rearing back in horror. "Yeah, that's what I thought."

His eyes went wide. "I didn't say anything!"

"You didn't have to. But hey, tell me if I'm wrong." He didn't. She let out a *humph.* "Figured as much."

"I didn't say anything!"

Closing her eyes, Larkin planted her palm over her face. "Teague, just sleep. *Now.*"

"Do I have to?"

"Yes."

An unhappy grunt. "Fine. But I don't know why you persist in being a ginger bigot. It's not like you're—Dammit, Lark, nipples aren't for twisting!"

ACKNOWLEDGEMENTS

When I started the first Dark in You novel, *Burn*, I'd meant for it to be a standalone. But it ended in such a way that I thought, okay, I'll write a few more . . . and somehow here we are at book number nine. Which would not have happened without so many people. So thank you to the readers who stuck with the series, thank you to my publishing team for being THE BEST, thank you to my family for your support and encouragement, and thank you to my PA for all your hard work. All of you together helped make this happen, and I love you for it!

No one really knows what they are.

Only that they're the first civilization.

Aeons, they call themselves.

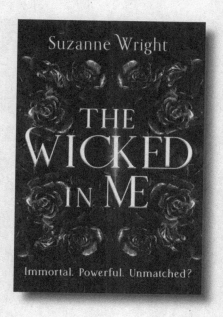

They're immortal. Powerful. Secretive.

Available now at

PIATKUS

Want more of the
Dark in You series?

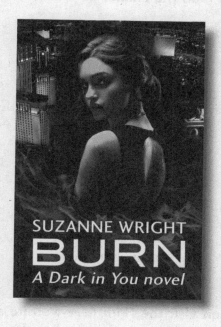

SUZANNE WRIGHT
BURN
A Dark in You novel

Go back to the beginning
and meet Harper and Knox.

Available now at

Do you love fiction with a supernatural twist?

Want the chance to hear news about your favourite authors (and the chance to win free books)?

Christine Feehan

J.R. Ward

Sherrilyn Kenyon

Charlaine Harris

Jayne Ann Krentz and Jayne Castle

P.C. Cast

Maria Lewis

Darynda Jones

Hayley Edwards

Kristen Callihan

Keri Arthur

Amanda Bouchet

Jacquelyn Frank

Larissa Ione

Then visit the *With Love* website and sign up to our romance newsletter: www.yourswithlove.co.uk

And follow us on Facebook for book giveaways, exclusive romance news and more: www.facebook.com/yourswithlovex

PIATKUS